AGE OF SECESSION : VINDIC/

SHADO

For Matthew Sut
sadly miss

AGE OF SECESSION : VINDICATOR TRILOGY PART III

SHADOW

Third Edition
Published in Great Britain by Roger Ruffles, February 2018

www.ageofsecession.com

Front cover artwork on license courtesy of stock exchange

First published by Roger Ruffles, December 2013

Printed by CreateSpace, An Amazon.com Company

All characters and events appearing in this work are fictitious. Any resemblance to real events or to persons, living or dead, is purely coincidental.

ISBN : 978-1494354732

Also By The Same Author

Age of Secession

Age of Secession: Vindicator Trilogy
#1 : Dissolution
#2 : Rosicrux
#3 Shadow
#4 Vindicator - Full Trilogy

Age of Secession: Blood Money Trilogy
#1: Crying Moon
#2 : Blood Feud
#3: Cost of the Hunt
#4: Blood Money - Full Trilogy

Age of Secession: Ascent of Mars Trilogy
#1 : Oncoming Storm
#2 : Darkness of Mars
#3: Rise of the Diadochi
#4: Ascent of Mars - Full Trilogy

Age of Secession: Standalone books:
The Unchained

Out Early 2018:
Pay Dirt: Dishonest Intentions

Coming 2018/2019:
Augmented Genocide
The Lost Kindred
Adare's Legacy: Kingdom of Blood
Collective Misdirection

www.ageofsecession.com

+++ Jacking Into Datasphere +++

+++ Datasphere Connection Confirmed +++

+++Incoming Transmission +++

JOINING THE AGE OF SECESSION

If you want

- early access to new eBooks months ahead of official releases
- Special offers and exclusive competitions
- Direct communication with the author and creator of the series

Then send an email requesting to join the age of secession to:
ageofsecession@gmail.com
or go to www.ageofsecession.com and register your details there.

Your details will NOT be passed to any third party,
and you have the right for deletion of those details at any time.

+++ Transmission Ends +++

Chapter I

The salvageship moved gently through the triple solar system of Khobar, on the far side of the planetary system orbiting the star of Khobar Tertiary. The weak sun did not cast much light on its multitude of planetary bodies and natural astral objects, Khobar Secondary and Khobar Primary being the main planetary systems which were inhabited.

The Khobar System was on the very extreme Frontier of the OutWorlds Alliance, literally one of the furthest inhabited solar systems to exist within the colonised galaxy. Even in the days of the Red Imperium of Mars, so very distant and far away in the very Core, this Frontier system had paid only a passing notice and lip-service to Imperial Law.

The salvageship was using its main drive engine on a very low propulsive power, driving slowly towards Khobar Tertius Two. It was of an odd construction, with not a graceful part to its design. It resembled a gigantic insect, with extendable arms and odd limbs jutting out at strange angles from its hull, the appendages designed to aid the collection of space salvage.

It had special laser cutters, its teeth, buried into its hull in numerous places, with four very heavy-duty versions at its head mounted on an arcing crown above the fore of the salvageship. They were already beginning to light up in preparation for firing, ready to break apart the larger pieces of the shipwreck that turned and revolved slowly in the depths of this area of space. The collection maw at the front began to open, a mouth distending obscenely wide to collect the scrap drifting in front of it, whilst larger collection bays like the overlarge and exaggerated suckers of an ancient sea-dwelling animal cycled upon on its belly.

Scrap metal from the destroyed ships in front of it began to fall into the collection bays and tanks, gathered by the open maw, whilst the heavy-duty cutting lasers began to fire into the nearest hulk of wrecked spaceship.

Captain Maria delos Reyes was concentrating incredibly hard on the displays in front of her, the holographic representation of a console all around her. Map displays plotted the exact position of the salvage she hunkered after in three-dimensions, her neural link to the datasphere of the salvageship *Jackaljaw* throwing the images directly into her cortex through her cybernetic implants. Her fingers danced like those of a musician on a keyboard, directed minute changes to course and the complex actions of the ship in both great and small detail.

She enjoyed this part of her illicit job immensely, not once in her long and often illegal career leaving it to anybody else. She loved plotting the course and actions of her ship, her crew following her orders as they played out across the datasphere they were all jacked into. It was better than a game of Universe, Blockers or even Chess, and often just as complicated to many people, but very simple to her.

She had absolutely no idea as she and her dedicated but rough-around-the-edges crew worked that her name was about to go down in the historical records.

<What do you think happened here?> asked her second-in-command, Chief Officer Cristof Gatdula.

<Beyond some sort of battle, it's impossible to tell,> Maria replied, like all augmented cyborgs able to concentrate on work but use some of her formidable processing power to engage in other tasks, such as conversation.

<The OutWorlds Alliance was hit hard,> commented Cristof. <It looks to me like three frigates, a destroyer, two cruisers, not to mention starfighters, all destroyed. This can't be the work of Black Jack, not even he could take on those odds.>

Black Jack was a corsair, a pirate who lived beyond the Frontier of the colonised galaxy somewhere, and preyed all across the Frontier and even into the Boundary of the Alegran Edge Segment. He was famous and romanticised in the vast stellar region of the Segment, even before the break-up of the Red Imperium had allowed it when the reporting restrictions were lifted. In fact, the embargo on his name and actions had probably added to the mythology.

<Well, just remember it's a lot of salvage for us,> said Captain delos Reyes.

<We're taking one Emperor-sized risk here, Maria,> said Cristof. <The OutWorlds Alliance isn't going to risk leaving this salvage here for long.>

<We're here for five hours then jumping out, no exceptions,> said Captain delos Reyes. One of her corrupt contacts in the OutWorlds Alliance military had informed her of the attack, for a share in profit when she sold the wreckage and scrap on. <Besides, it's safe enough. The OWA are far too busy trying to conquer House Villanueva.>

Maria then looked at him. <Sorry,> she said. Cristof was a House Villaneuva national, and was incredibly worried about his family back home. House Villaneuva was now all that stood between that and the House territory she herself was from, although her House was part of the Frontier Hegemony, eight large Frontier and Boundary Houses that had allied together to face the threat of First Lord Yassin Al-Zuhairi and his OutWorlds Alliance. Like everywhere in the colonised galaxy, the dissolution of the Red Imperium had led to war everywhere, as every one of the many hundreds of Imperial Houses jockeyed for power.

<It's okay,> he said quietly.

Out in the depths of space, one of the many planets that orbited the weak sun of Khobar Tertiary was mostly covered in darkness. Cold and frigid, Khobar Tertiary Two had no breathable atmosphere present. Unable to support any form of life, it was unremarkable except for its reasonably close proximity to the debris field the *Jackaljaw* was harvesting, at least in astronomical terms.

Suddenly the perfect roundness of its curve began to grow. The prow of some unimaginably large ship began to extend out, its three sharp points breaking the perfect curve with alarming suddenness.

<Captain!> the Second Mate who looked after the scanners and navigation console shouted across the datasphere. <I've got movement, looks like a ship. It's just moving out behind K-double-two!>

<Shit,> Captain Maria delos Reyes swore. <All hands, cease operations, we may have been discovered. Helm, get us out of the debris field, engineering, prepare for an emergency jump out-system.>

Chief Officer Cristof Gatdula was examining the sensors with interest. <Maria, it's emerging slowly, it obviously didn't expect us to be here. Starting to speed up now, think it's found us ..... but oh, sweet Emperor, it doesn't look like anything I know. It has to be the biggest ship I've ever seen. Look.>

As her crew panicked and red alert warning sounds echoed out around the entire ship, Maria accessed the long-range scanner information being fed through to them.

The ship was indeed immense. It was not designed like any other ship she had ever seen. Of a large size, it was obviously military, weapons battery ports opening up all along its hull. If this was the thing that had destroyed the OutWorlds Alliance ships, it certainly looked capable of being able to take on an entire squadron all by itself. No-one in the Human race had ever designed something this size. <It looks alien,> she whispered. Then, opened up to the entire crew across the datasphere, she roared, <Get us out of here!>

In full view the unidentified ship looked imposing and grand, as well as lethally capable of its duties as a warship. Like an animal it had turned around, weapons batteries opening, realising it had been observed and detected and now determined to eliminate its prey.

It was strange and alien in appearance, but not necessarily due to its design, although even in that it was unfamiliar. It was more to do with what could be called the hull, strange fields of energy covering it. More worryingly, parts of it seemed to be moving in and out focus, as if it were alive and its skin were rippling in wind. It was hard to look at, almost translucent at times, parts of the planet which was now behind it becoming visible through its very body.

It was immense, far bigger than anything any human had created, easily half again as big as a Praetorian dreadnought-class starship. It moved slowly but with dreadful accuracy. It looked martial despite its unearthly appearance, and sure enough, it obviously intended to prove its purpose as a war machine as it prepared to fire forward-mounted weaponry, the telltale signs of ports and guns going live becoming apparent. It was so broad at its three-pointed prow that it would be like receiving a broadside from a standard human-built ship.

<It's going to fire!> Chief Officer Gatdula cried.

<Jump initiation capacitors fully engaged ....> roared the helmsman, <warp accelerators firing, we are jumping in a few seconds!>

<It's fired!> Cristof Gatdula had sheer panic in his voice.

<Jumping!>

Captain Maria delos Reyes had her eyes shut, expecting at any moment for a heavy rumble and impact as whatever it was that was being fired at them struck. After a few seconds of sweaty anticipation, all she could feel was the familiar pull, that initial lurch as they first entered hyper-space.

<We're in the warp,> said Cristof, relief flooding his voice. <We're in the warp! Ah-hah, we're safe.>

Captain Maria delos Reyes opened her eyes. She inhaled deeply. <Cancel the red-alert,> she commanded. There was sweat pouring from her forehead. <We've not taken any damage at all?>

<We were lucky,> said her Chief Engineer, <we jumped before we took the hits. The amount of fire it threw at us was phenomenal, I've only ever seen anything like it on the holo-vids.>

<It was so huge,> said her helmsman.

<It was Emperor-forsaken alien,> replied her navigations crewman.

<It definitely wasn't made by any human,> Cristof agreed.

<Did we get a full sensor log and visual recording of it?> asked Maria delos Reyes. Her mind had been elsewhere whilst the datasphere had been hijacked by their conversation.

<Yeah, of course,> said Cristof, the puzzlement loud and clear.

<Good,> said Captain delos Reyes.

<Why, Maria?>

<Because,> she replied, <we may have just lost all that illegal salvage out there, but what we've got is something maybe better.> She stood and walked around the small civilian bridge of the salvageship. <We've got the

first ever recorded logs of that thing, and whatever it is, human, alien, whatever, the media companies all over the galaxy are going to pay a lot of money to get that footage and data-stream.>

*

First Lord Yassin Al-Zuhairi, leader of the OutWorlds Alliance and Head of House for House Al-Zuhairi, awoke at the insistent buzz of the personal droid hovering over the large, grand, and ancient and curtain-beshrouded four-poster bed he shared with his wife.

His wife, Lach Al-Zuhairi, began to stir in the bed next to him. He was already fully awake and swinging his legs out of the bed. "Hush, go back to sleep," he said gently.

"What is it?" she asked. He was already pulling on a light shirt over his muscled chest. It was of a light weave design, the gaps open and cooling. Even at night, the planet Zaharra retained the incredible heat of the day. Air-conditioning units and atmosphere controllers regulated the temperature in the bedroom, but still it was warm.

"Probably just yet another problem with my Sector Lords, or something, I do not know," Yassin Al-Zuhairi said. "Go back to sleep, I won't be long." The trousers he was pulling on were lightweight zaharran sandwyrm silk, made from the young wyrm in the first five days of it birth and thus extremely difficult to obtain.

He left the bedchamber, the guards outside in the luxurious and unbelievably large private upper floor lounge not surprised to see him emerging at this time of night. It was a regular occurrence, and had been ever since Yassin had formed the OutWorlds Alliance. Perhaps even before. Life on the Frontier was rough for many of his people, and despite his Imperial Academy of Mars schooling and ostentatious surroundings in the palace of the Great Citadel, First Lord Al-Zuhairi never forgot his youth and the hardship his people faced. He politely let the door close with a consideration for his wife many would not think the hard and ambitious man could show, before he began to speak.

"Droid, what is it now?" he demanded.

Before the droid could even answer, a very familiar voice called up from the lower lounge below. "Yassin, I'm down here. I didn't want you going too far, I knew you were asleep."

The personal assistance droid began to answer, and Yassin deactivated it with a wave of his hand, the droids sensors picking up the cancellation action. Yassin walked around the upper lounge, heading for the curving stairs at one end. As he walked, he shouted back, his voice echoing in the cavernous room. The upper lounge was half the size of the lower, and both were open to each other.

"Uncle," he said, addressing the unseen Amab Al-Zuhairi, Chief of his intelligence services, "Do you never sleep?"

He emerged onto the lower lounge, seeing that his uncle Amab was, as ever, fully dressed and grandiosely at that. The heavy rings around his eyes betrayed the fact he had not been asleep, and in fact, had probably been awake for days sustained on special drugs. The man worked far too hard, but would never listen.

"Time waits for no man, especially not one of my age," was the reply. "Besides, it's as well I was, there is something you absolutely have to see."

First Lord Al-Zuhairi stepped down into one of the recessed lounging pits, a suspensor-chair rising up to meet him as he lowered himself into a comfortable position opposite Chief Amab. "I know you wouldn't wake me without good reason, but I have had just about enough recently. If it is the Sector Lords of the Alliance again, I swear heads will roll." He had renamed the House territories into 'sectors', as another way of distancing his new and rapidly expanding nation from the old Red Imperium and the False Emperor.

"No, not them," Chief Amab shook his head.

"The invasion of Villaneuva? I thought that was all but a foregone conclusion, according to the briefing according to Chief Commander Al-Saadi this morn - yesterday." Omar Al-Saadi was from House Al-Saadi, itself a large Sector of the Alliance and very strongly associated with House Al-Zuhairi even in the days of the Red Imperium.

"It still proceeds according to plan - in fact, I have new intelligence suggesting that the House Lord of Villaneuva is closer to surrendering than we thought. We can go through that tomorrow though."

Yassin was tiring of this guessing. "So what is it then, uncle?"

"Perhaps it is better for you to see," said Chief Amab. He leaned forward and used a remote to activate the holo-viewer between them.

It came alive without a noise, as if it had never been interrupted. Yassin bristled somewhat as he saw that it was playing a recording of a live transmission by the StarCom News Media. Almost immediately following the Dissolution of the Red Empire, and the sudden formation of the StarCom Federation, he had banned StarCom's media from his territory and taken control of all their stargate assets and communications stations across the Alliance. His animosity had not been helped by the then-President of StarCom's attempt to have him murdered in retribution, and the numerous incidents since between the distant Federation and the Alliance. They were half the colonised galaxy away from each other, but still they fought both openly and clandestinely, in conflicts and espionage.

He paid attention to the broadcast as it downloaded in a constant stream from Chief Amab's restricted intelligence servers. Eventually the broadcast came to an end.

There was a long silence, and all that could be heard were the gossamer thin drapes on the open window balcony fluttering in the light night's breeze. It was still warm despite the hot desert planet of Zaharra now being at night. The lifting breeze at this time of year spoke of the approach of the terrible sandstorms that would wrack this entire planet as it neared the sun of Zaharrid.

Eventually Yassin said quietly, "I take it our own media have been restricted from broadcasting this in repeat?"

"Oh yes, nephew of mine. It was my first action to put a restricted notice on it."

"Good." Yassin paused as he assimilated what he had seen. "What by the Emperor's eyes was that? Surely it cannot be alien? We have found alien life-forms, many of them, but nothing of advanced intelligence, certainly nothing to create that .... thing."

"We don't know," said Chief Amab's answer. "But it destroyed an entire squadron in the Khobar System. If it had not been for those rogue salvagers, we would not have known about its existence. Why it was still lurking in the system we do not know."

"It looked huge."

"It was," said Chief Amab, "I have several teams working on identifying it, but the architectural design is nothing we have ever seen. It matches no known classification either - half again the size of a Praetorian dreadnought. There are some elements of Praetorian design there some of my analysts suggest, but nothing conclusive. The technology is certainly beyond anything we have seen. The way it appeared to be flitting in and out of existence is highly disconcerting."

"Could this be the StarCom Federation?" asked Yassin. "They may be distant, but they owe me dearly for the ISHM strikes."

"Possibly," said Amab, "but we cannot jump to conclusions. The colour scheme, when it materialised enough to become visible, was certainly StarCom Federation in nature, but that proves little again."

"Well, find out what it is," said First Lord Al-Zuhairi. "This new threat has just become our biggest priority. I want to know what it is, where it's from, and what it is capable of."

Chief Amab nodded and stood. "Yes, First Lord," he bowed, acknowledging the order.

*

StarCom Federation President Giovanna Pereyra sat in the Golden Room in the Palace of Communications, her ceremonial sceptre being carried by the special droid at her side. It was the same droid that had once carried it for President Nielsen.

Pereyra had been Vice-President of the Star Communications Network even in the days of the Red Imperium, for the insane False Emperor. Unfortunately, following her involvement in the Revolutionary Council under the inspired leadership of Rebeccah Nielsen, that insanity had continued. Pereyra had been instrumental in seeing to the end of Nielsen, conspiring with First Lord Yassin Al-Zuhairi to have the Imperial Faceless assassins remove her in spectacular fashion.

The possibility of ending the ongoing feud between the two aggressive nations, rising from the ashes of Dissolution, had been there. It was never seen through, and despite their long distance, the animosity, aggression and brutality continued between them.

Giovanna Pereyra had learnt much from watching the fall of someone she once admired and perhaps, even secretly looked up to. She was determined never to follow in Nielsen's footsteps, but she had inherited control of a new StarCom Federation, disliked by many all across the galaxy, maintained a stranglehold on others, and fresh from a large series of vicious invasions. Many of the new nations and old Houses hated the Federation - and feared their armies and navies, possibly the biggest and the best in the colonised galaxy.

The doors to the Golden Room entered, and her three advisors entered. The Commander-In-Chief of the StarCom Federation Army led the way, the rotund Jaiden Ryan. By his side walked the dark-skinned head of the Central Intelligence Department, Malika Chbihi. With them strode Vice-President Johann Schneider, blond haired, blue eyed, and possessed of a very dark if not unpleasant character. She regretted letting him into the position he now occupied. All of them appeared friendly enough, but the old politics of the Red Imperium died hard, and at this level it was knife-sharp.

All three stood before her. Ryan had brought back the Imperial Salute, and he now presented it, whilst both the other two merely bowed their heads in the way of the House Lords. They then took their seats around the small table before her. The throne Pereyra sat upon was Nielsen's invention, but the seats and chairs to make her advisors feel comfortable had been her addition. The huge circular table was regularly swapped out for smaller versions depending on the size of the gathering she wished to hold.

"So," said President Pereyra. "Director Chbihi, you wished to inform us of something?"

"Yes, President," said the Director, her face developing its usual furious frown. "As you know, we have many spies within the OutWorlds Alliance hierarchy –"

"And as fast as you put them in, the Alliance seems to find them," Vice-President Schneider interrupted with typical rudeness.

"- many spies," said Chbihi. "Overnight, Imperial Standard Time, there was a serious incident in the OutWorlds Alliance. Chief Amab is thought to have awoken First Lord Al-Zuhairi, and the orders coming back out from Amab suggest that they suspect our involvement."

"Wait," said Pereyra, holding up her hands, "what 'incident'?"

Jaiden Ryan cleared his throat and began to explain, confidently but evidently worried. He used holo-pics to describe the warship as it appeared, with early analysis of its capabilities, all of which was conjecture.

"It's painted in our colours," President Pereyra pointed out. "The white and regal blue, with our sky-blue trim and lining."

"A possible deliberate attempt to make it look like we are at fault for this," said Director Chbihi.

"Could this be an A-Zu Industries weapon, a new warship just for the OWA?" asked Pereyra.

"It is conceivable," said Commander-In-Chief Ryan, "if it were not for the technology, which is so advanced, and its undeniable alien appearance. It seems to shift in and out of reality and vision, in all spectrums."

"Well, there's no such thing as aliens," scoffed Vice-President Schneider, "not intelligent or advanced life-forms, anyway."

"Whatever their origins, the OutWorlds Alliance were not behind it," said Director Chbihi. "It took out an entire squadron of starships, and then was discovered by accident by this salvageship, the *Jackaljaw*. I have agents trying to track them down to confirm their story, be sure they are not part of some covert operation. However, my intelligence from within Chief Amab's office suggests that the OutWorlds Alliance is not deliberately stoking the fires of war. They are being open-minded as to who or where it came from, but they are looking at us."

"This could ignite another Tears Incident," said Vice-President Schneider.

"Never again," said President Pereyra firmly. "Well, if it wasn't us and it wasn't them, who in the name of the False Emperor's hell was it?"

"We don't know," said Director Chbihi after a long pause.

"Well, find out, and fast," President Pereyra ordered.

"We need to know who could design and make such a fearsome weapon," said Jaiden Ryan.

"We need to know who is trying to provoke war between us and the OutWorlds Alliance," Pereyra corrected firmly.

*

The Temple of Shadow was well named, the majority of its labyrinthine corridors, vast rooms the size of small cities and little box-rooms that could barely fit one person in, hideaways tucked out of sight, double-blind and fake walls, all that and more shrouded in shadow. It was sometimes absolutely dark, sometimes steeped in shadows so deep it leached the entire colour from anything, sometimes barely illuminated by fake torches of flickering fire, but it was almost never fully in the weak light of the place it was located in.

That was the thing about the Temple of Shadow. Over time many had come and then left, but of those that did, very few knew where to find it again. Those not in league with the Shadow never left once they arrived here.

The Master of the First Circle walked through the corridors, his elite guard escorting him on his approach. Many of the beings that resided in this part of the Temple were of the First Circle, his personal guard. He never left the Temple, but when the time came for him to do so, they would come with him.

As he approached the door that led to the circular holo-pit, the elite guard wearing their jet-black synth-skin suits and golden cloaks ignored the salutes that the similarly jet-black but white cloaked figures gave them. Elsewhere within the Temple all the colours of the nine Circles were represented in the cloaks of the blank, identical looking figures that wore them. Only the upper echelons of each Circle were actually anything anywhere near approaching human, and even then, many modifications and adjustments were to be found.

The Master strode through the doors, which were pulled and slammed shut behind him with a finality that spoke of the toll of a bell of death.

In his long black cloak, with no sign of his face visible behind the black face-mask, the Master walked directly across the floor at the centre of the holo-pit, crossing the beautifully designed but complex symbol woven into its cold metallic alloys. He took his throne at the biggest alcove of the nine, and as soon as he sat, every one of the other eight whispered the same thing.

"Hail the Master."

Some of the eight were actually there, although some were not. HyperPulse Communications Generators had opened up continuous holes in the fabric of reality, allowing messages to be transmitted across vast interstellar distances faster than any Human could think. With the holes ripped through real-space into hyper-space, it was possible for people on different planets to have long real-time conversations with one another, with fake holographic representations forming the bodies of the people involved. Sometimes there would be lag, but it was never something that had happened to the Shadow Council.

There were rumours of the Shadow Council throughout the colonised galaxy, almost entirely connected to the Faceless. The rumours were centuries old, dating back to the time of the True Emperor expanding the Red Imperium of Mars to all the edges of the colonised galaxy, as it had been back then. No-one ever knew of just how big and how diverse an operation the secretive Shadow Council truly was.

The Master looked at the eight Legates, one by one. He knew who all of them were, although identity was something very zealously guarded throughout the entirety of the Shadow, even more so with those members who took the title of Legate of the Shadow Council.

"Shadow Council," he said eventually, an image of him whipping into the centre of the holo-pit, to show that he was speaking. "There has been an error."

There was a palpable sense of tension suddenly, visible somehow even with those who were holographs only, despite the face-masks and the mostly form-concealing cloaks they wore. "Perhaps the Legate of the Second Circle would like to explain."

The image whirred away, that of the figure with the boxy and exaggerated silver lines on his face-mask replacing the Master. The First Circle represented these nine, the Second Circle represented the combined military of the Shadow Council. The Legate of the Second Circle spoke, her voice even. She knew of the Master's rages, and dreaded one appearing now, but nothing was more likely to provoke it than weakness.

"One of our juggernauts has been discovered, in the Khobar System," she said, and went on to explain what had happened. When she had finished, the Master remained uncharacteristically silent, merely looking at the Legate of the Fourth Circle pointedly, his eyes burning through the eye-slits in the face-mask.

The Legate of the Fourth Circle, which tended to look after secret investigations and intelligence gathering, took her place. He continued, "The salvageship which escaped then sold the information to the StarCom News Media, and numerous other media sources around the colonised galaxy." He stated how the news had spread, and also covered the reactions that he knew of, in the people and the politicians.

At this point the Legate of the Third Circle took over, his particular domain being that of politics. He expanded on the Fourth Legate's explanation, covering likely scenarios and particularly what they knew of the StarCom Federation and OutWorlds Alliance reactions. "Ironically," he said, "we have caused more disruption to our ultimate advantage, admittedly accidentally and in a way we did not wish to reveal."

His image whirled away, and for a long, pensive moment, all was quiet.

Finally, the Master's image took centre stage. "It is unforgiveable what has happened. The commander of that juggernaut warship must be disciplined," he said, in a worryingly calm voice. "But, it works to our advantage, as has been pointed out, so the disciplinary action must not cause lasting harm. I do not believe we have to take much action, although Legate of the Third Circle, take the opportunity to manipulate the political situation as much as we can. Use the Legate of the Sixth Circle's covert operations specialists if you must, or the Legate of the Fifth Circle's Faceless assassins. Whatever to make the situation go terminal."

"Yes, Master," came a number of replies.

There was another long pause, before the Master began to speak again.

"The Shadow Council has been called for a specific reason, and not to discuss the failure at Khobar," the Master said. "The time is fast approaching for us to move onto the next stage of the game. In fact, the time is here, and now.

"We have been manipulating situations, nations and Houses across the colonised galaxy, according to the master plan. I want all those efforts to be accelerated to their planned conclusions within two months. The fleet and the army must be ready and in place, the spies and covert operatives must be active, the assassins able to strike, our political manoeuvrings completed. When we begin, I want the colonised galaxy to tremble and then shatter before my coming.

"I will leave the Shadow Temple and bring my full wrath to bear upon the usurpers. I will re-unite the galaxy in my name again. The time has come for the Shadow Council to step out into the light. The time has come for a new order, and we shall usher it in with fire and with blood.

"We begin exactly two months from now. You have your orders, see it is done."

*

"High Justiciar Driscoll, the Supreme Court of the First Circuit is assembled and awaiting your presence," the young adjudicator said from the doorway, the entrance having just cycled open. He bowed his shaven head, the symbol of the Red Eagle clutching a pair of old-fashioned, ancient scales electronically tattooed onto his forehead below the close buzzcut's fringe.

"Thank you, inform the Supreme Court to expect my arrival," said the High Justiciar.

"Yes, Justiciar," the adjudicator said, bowing his head again, before retreating back into the circular corridor beyond.

High Justiciar Driscoll was the foremost of all Justiciars within the Levitican Union nation. She was responsible for not only the First Circuit, but for ensuring the laws decided upon by the Lord Minister for Justice were fully enacted within the environment of court and the street.

Driscoll was in some advanced years, middle-aged by modern standards at just over two centuries old. Her rejuvenation treatments had worked wonders on her, but the appearance of youth did nothing to alleviate her severe or imposing features.

"Good luck for today," said Lady Minister Monique Lapointe. "This will make history. It's probably one of the biggest cases since Dissolution. The colonised galaxy is watching you."

Her experience did not even allow High Justiciar Driscoll to feel nervous. She looked at herself in the holographic reflective display in front of her, examining her image. Although there were elements of light ceremonial gold-plated armour in the uniform she wore, it was a far cry from the militaristic armour the adjudicators wore for street justice.

"I know," Driscoll replied. "Silus Adare - who would have ever thought he would be captured." She turned in front of the untouchable mirror, seeing how her red-lined and red-furred heel-length golden robes rested on her bulky and imposing body. Like all Justiciars, she wore a plated kilt, and knee-length golden armoured boots. A high collar in Imperial fashion surrounded her head, which itself was encased in a ceremonial half-helmet half-mask, side flanges coming down to cover her cheeks and nose, ringed around her skull, her long brown hair cascading freely into special catching holes within the collar.

"We have Lord James Gavain and the Vindicatus Mercenary Corporation to thank for that," said Lady Minister Lapointe. "We all know there can only be one judgement here, don't we?"

"Procedure will be followed," said High Justiciar Driscoll, hearing the question. "But of his guilt, there is no doubt. I will be surprised if I hear anything to the contrary during the court sessions."

"Good. Let us not forget what he has done."

"Indeed not. Now, if you will excuse me Lady Minister, I must attend the First Circuit." With that, the High Justiciar bowed to the Lady Minister, now a House Lady of one of the seven Houses of the Union in her own right, and turned away, striding confidently towards the door.

Two adjudicators fell in behind her as she walked through the circular-formed tunnel-like corridor, heading through this section of the underwater city of Levitican Union Capital City. The corridor was close to the top of the massive underwater dome, and every so often there were vast sections where the water played dappled lights on the decking. The city had arisen to just below the ocean's water, not quite poking up into clear air. It allowed the sun to light the vast domed, floating city during planetary day times. As she walked, the High Justiciar was lost in thought, but not about the upcoming trial. She was thinking of how her life had changed with the end of the Red Imperium.

The history of the court structure in the colonised galaxy was an interesting one. In the days of the Red Imperium, each House was responsible for its own laws and maintaining its own justice and policing system. Those laws always took second place to Imperial Edicts which formed Imperial Law, and if a Justiciar - there being one for every court circuit - made a mistake or a bad judgement it could not only be overturned by the Imperial Justiciar of the Imperial Circuit, but would probably lead to that House Justiciar's own sentencing for incorrect judgement. The penalties were draconian.

There were a number of different Court Circuits, which dealt with a varying degree of crimes. It allowed the various Justiciars to specialise in certain criminological areas of expertise. Only severe crimes with potentially harsh penalties ever ended up before a Justiciar or in a Court Circuit. Many minor crimes were dealt with by the adjudicators, who when not on the streets dispensing justice, were serving in support functions at the various Court Circuits. The definition of 'major' and 'minor' crimes was one that varied significantly, of course, and was not always what the more liberal leaning of citizens necessarily agreed with. There was no such thing as an appeal in the Red Imperium, all sentences were final.

In the days since Dissolution, Imperial Law was still being followed in one fashion or another, its influence slow to disappear. Yet, more and more the various House Laws and the laws of the newly-forming nations, which were seceding chaotically from the dissolved Empire and from one another, were beginning to overrule Imperial Law. It was just another part of the end of the Red Imperium.

Interesting times, she thought to herself. The travellator-droid they stood upon came to a stop, having reached the grand, ornate doors which led into the rear entrance of the Court of the First Circuit. The adjudicators bowed, and the doors opened.

High Justiciar Driscoll walked into the vast and expansive auditorium that was known as the court room.

As she moved towards her seat she looked up and round, seeing the thousands of people, the public as well as the officials, the lords and ladies of all ranks within their noble houses, Administration servants, enforcers, and many adjudicators. Military personnel were present, those who had fought in the Levitican War, those who saw Admiral Silus Adare commit one of the greatest ever atrocities experienced since the Dissolution of the Imperium.

The First Circuit auditorium fell silent as she sat in her ostentatious throne, leaning forwards and tapping a metal ball upon a dais. Hovering droid microphones picked up the metallic bangs, and echoed them through the sound system all across the court, harsh ringing echoes dying away slowly. The silence after was truly imposing.

The court was in the pit of the auditorium, placed centrally, the stands centred all round it. There was a large, high bench and seat for the

Justiciar. Directly facing the bench was a podium, into which the mobile platform that transported the accused was capable of being locked securely. The accused stood surrounded by adjudicators, imprisoned by force-fields.

There were no prosecutors, no defenders, and no jury. It was just the judger and the one to be judged.

"Are you Silus Adare," High Justiciar Driscoll said imperiously and after a long pause, aware that this was being broadcast live all across the galaxy, "Former Rear-Admiral of the Red Imperium and supporter of the False Emperor, subsequently Rear-Admiral of the StarCom Federation's Third Fleet, and then Rear-Admiral of the organisation known as the Rosicrux?"

Silus Adare smiled, his black goatee beard widening around the corners of the mouth, and that smile was chilling to see. He did not seem in the least bit worried, just as confident as she was. The eyes spoke of the psychotic mind behind them. "I am," he said simply, voice strong, loud and confident.

"Admiral Silus Adare, you are accused of a war-crime committed during the Levitican War between the Levitican Union and the StarCom Federation. The charge is that during that war, you engaged and utilised a new Weapon of Planetary Destruction identified as the Tears of the Moon. This weapon is held responsible for the complete annihilation of the planet Alwathbah in the Blackheath System, and the deaths of over nine billion people. Do you wish to admit guilt?"

As she spoke, a holographic image was replaying the destruction of Alwathbah, showing the fiery red streaks as the warhead detonated in its atmosphere. The planet's air literally burned away, everything igniting and the once populous capital planet of House Towers becoming a burnt-out ball of rock in a hellish, nightmarish scene of pure flame and fire on an unimaginable, planetary-wide scale.

Adare stopped watching the image, turning his gaze slowly back to the High Justiciar. "No," he said, shaking his head. The crowd began to mutter, the muttering turning into a vast roar as he added, "No, I do not admit guilt. It was not wrong of me to do this. It was actually, quite enjoyable."

High Justiciar Driscoll angrily banged the metallic ball on its disc heavily, calling for a silence which did not come for a very long time.

Chapter II

The Dark Heart Artificial System was a solar system like few others, for a varied number of reasons. It was different because it had a total of five planets, two of which were artificial, all linked by space-lifts to ferry people up to platforms in orbit and then across by a complex series of interlinked space-corridors. It looked like they were joined by a colossal spider's web.

It was different because it had no moons or smaller planetoids attached to the rogue planets, beyond the two artificial ones. The entire structure was also held in place by vast planetary engines, which prevented further drift of the planets. There was no sun or star, hence the name 'rogue planet', to describe those that were thrown into deep space without having any home. They orbited slowly, and artificial light provided the fake sunlight. The technology in the artificial system was unlike much seen elsewhere, a complete mix of centuries old and forgotten, and so new it could only be considered advanced.

It was also different because it existed in the centre of a cluster of black holes, which vastly limited the possible paths into the system for interstellar craft and stargate corridors. It had a huge defensive capability, and many ships which even now were not yet fully staffed.

There was a stargate in the Dark Heart System, far out beyond close contact with the planets. The stargate itself was the very central point for a large number of others, over eighteen stargates spread out across the Gulf of Medusa, in an interstellar connected system colloquially known as 'The Web'.

The Dark Heart Stargate running lights began to flash, a visual sign that something was arriving. There was a flash of light, and a large object materialised extremely quickly in one of the terminus zones. The military craft reacted, shields up, weapons ready, but powered down as the three incoming civilian transporters began to broadcast the correct IFF identification signals.

The heavy defences of the system stood down.

The mass transporters lit their repulsors and then main propulsor drives, sliding forwards smoothly. They were all three of a very old design, so old they almost predated the centuries-spanning Red Imperium. Despite their age they were in very good condition, mainly due to centuries without use, and even without modified and updated engine powerplants and merely an overhaul and maintenance review, they still operated with efficiency.

They came in under the chameleonically-shielded watchful gaze of numerous droid weaponry systems, which were almost completely invisible to any form of detection. The transporters slowed down as they reached the commercial space station which had been moved away from the planetoid designated Delta, hauled by a great fleet of straining power-tugs to its new position two-thirds of the way to the stargate. The transporter liners followed a particular path, communicated only once they were in-system, to avoid the mine-fields that were also chameleonically-shielded from casual view. To the uninformed it would have been random, almost drunken.

The mass transporters had been jumping through the Web, having made a fast run to the Erdogan nation. All fifteen of the mass transporters were constantly moving along the Web and into Erdogan territory and near to the front-lines with the Compact. The number of refugees pouring out of the rapidly dwindling Erdogan nation, formerly House Erdogan, was increasing by the day. They were coming here to the Vindicatus nation, newly set up under the brand new House Gavain, by House Lord Gavain's invitation.

The transporters had originally been designed for long-range colonisation, and certainly no real comfort was provided for. Each mass transporter could carry eighty thousand people. There were refugees from everywhere, but by far the greatest number was coming from Erdogan region of space. The persecution the borgs were facing there at the hands of the extremist humanist Zhou-Zheng Compact was truly frightening, with deathcamps set up to commit genocide against any augmented cyborg life.

The starships came in to dock at the commercial space station, their terrified cargo now safe. Nearly another quarter of a million had escaped the deathcamps of the Zhou-Zheng Compact, where millions died every day. There would be another landing later in the Imperial Standard day.

Everyone knew the Lord Gavain did not think enough were being saved.

Lord Gavain stood near to the high railing of the observation lounge, hands clasped behind his back. He was staring down the open space of about seven large decks, within the spacious entrance hall inside the fourth docking sector of Commercial Spacestation Delta. As he did so, his usually impassive face betrayed no sign of the anger he felt. He was on view, after all, and the waiting people were staring alternatively up at him, or at the holographic representation of him standing above their heads.

"This is never going to end," he said, face not betraying his feelings.

"When you opened up our borders to all the refugees from the secession wars," said Admiral Harley Andersson, off-camera, "you guaranteed that this would happen. And that's not a criticism, Jamie, we all agree it was the right thing to do. No-one else in the galaxy is reaching their hand out like this, without wanting something in return." Andersson had not only obtained the rank of Admiral in the new Vindicatus nation Gavain had created, but he was also heading up the new civil service and was referred to as the Solar High Chancellor.

"There's suffering all over the galaxy since the Dissolution," said James Gavain, his ice blue eyes scanning the thousands of frightened people below, "but the genocide in the Zhou-Zheng Compact conquered worlds is amongst the worst we have seen yet."

The planet of Dark Heart Alpha had its own ecosystem, which supported forms of life not seen elsewhere. One of them was a huge but aggressive herbivore, already nicknamed a 'Red Devil' by the influx of new inhabitants, with a thick red-coloured skin similar to an expensive leather but with some unusual properties. The red skin made up a large part of Gavain's new clothing, especially tailored for him personally.

He was dressed grandiosely, the martial background that so influenced the emerging Vindicatus nation reflected in his clothing. There was an undeniable military cut to his noble clothing, which had the Imperial-style high collar and long cape, but was modelled equally on the Praetorian Guard red-and-black uniform. The cape was slanted over his right shoulder, blending seamlessly into the diagonal cut of the black across the padded and secretly armoured red jacket. He had point-blank refused a crown much to the amusement of his colleagues and friends, but had conceded to a large silver neck chain, bearing the new flag of the Vindicatus nation worked into it. Black palmed red backed gloves, black boots, black belt and red trousers with black and silver trim completed the appearance. There were many different shades of red within the material, going from crimson at the top to a lighter but still deep shade of red at the bottom. For those not serving solely in the military, this was how they dressed if they were a member of his still-forming government and noble House.

"It is taking far too fucking long to process the refugee immigrants," said Marine Field Marshal Andryukhin. He had refused to take any part in the government, so wore his Praetorian Guard Marine dress uniform. He was a soldier, he had said at length, and a politician's life was not for him.

"It's a necessary evil," said Vice-Admiral Jonathan O'Connor, who unlike Andryukhin also to the title of Chief of Intelligence within the government of House Gavain. "With such a high influx of people, we have to run security checks on all of them before letting them further in-system. We could have Faceless trying to get through, let alone spies and agents from the other Houses and nations, criminals, all sorts. This is the first chance we get to vet who has arrived here, in the docking sectors."

"We don't doubt the wisdom of the methodology," said Chancellor Andersson. "Or that security takes precedence. But we do need to find a way to complete immigration and processing more expediently."

Lord Gavain nodded once, in agreement. As he did he looked at Harley, not a clue to his thoughts running across his face. Harley still had strong feelings for him, something that James just did not return. He had not understood what was meant by a relationship, being genetically enhanced and even created artificially for the sole purpose of war, and despite Harley's obvious wishes, that connection and even understanding had never existed for him. Until he met Juan Ramirez. Lady Sophia had warned him to be careful, that when Harley discovered that James's affections lay elsewhere, it could create a major problem within his government. Like so much nowadays, it was so far out of James's realm of experience, he did not know how to deal with it.

He merely went with what felt right, and that was all he could do.

Suddenly Chief of Intelligence O'Connor stiffened, and he said across the datasphere to all of them, communicating at the speed of thought, <There's a problem down there, one of the special biomorphic sensors has activated.>

<Faceless!> said Andryukhin. The next was a transmission of what he saw, more than a coherent thought-out sentence, his super-fast eyesight trained by numerous battlefields spotting the disturbance in the mayhem and chaos below.

The entrance hall had hundreds of new security stations where the checks were being carried out, before allowing egress into the cleared zone of the docking terminal proper, and access to the rest of the commercial space station. At one of them, so far away that the people looked almost no bigger than half a hand in perspective, laser fire had broken out, the enforcers policing it going down quickly.

A figure was morphing into something new, its reality as a cybernetic biomorph becoming apparent as its left arm melted and moulded into a long-barrelled projectile weapon. James Gavain's cybernetic eye enhancements automatically zeroed in and magnified the area, showing the biomorph swinging the weapon up to point directly at him.

"For the Zhou-Zheng Compact!" the biomorph roared, its voice enhanced by special implants of its own. The crowd screaming and running away did not overshadow the loudness of the roar, many within the hall hearing it.

The weapon fired, a strong laser shot preceding the bullet projectile behind it. As energy shields sparked up all around Gavain and his comrades, the laser shot ploughed into it, the special energy designed to punch through most force-fields.

Gavain was already ducking, but looked up to see that the biomorph had predicted this and lowered its shot just a fraction. The personal force-field he had built into his belt was designed to withstand Faceless technology, itself unique throughout the galaxy. The laser shot failed to penetrate the field, and the bullet exploded violently against the shielding. The blast angrily roiled out all around his personal force-field, those of his comrade's activating automatically to prevent any damage or harm coming to them.

At the point when the blast had cleared, Gavain was standing up as the entire entrance hall had dissolved into panic. Some of it began to ease as the holo-camera, still centred on him, showed that he had escaped unscathed.

<The assassin has been terminated,> said Chief of Intelligence O'Connor, <Brigadier Vantanik's special enhanced Marines were in the entrance hall concourse, under cover. They have killed the target.>

<There may be more,> said Lord Gavain, <As for this being Zhou-Zheng Compact behind it, they don't have access to Faceless assassins.>

<Agreed,> said Ulrik, <this was an assassination attempt by the Rosicrux, or whoever controlled them. The fuckers have just painted it up to look like the Zhou-Zheng Compact as a cover.>

<Well, there's only one of them that we know of, but there may be more in the vast majority that are unprocessed down there,> said O'Connor. <The biggest danger now comes from the panic of the immigrants.>

<Harley, appeal for calm, get this situation under control,> Gavain ordered.

Andersson just looked at him. <Jamie, you're on camera still. It will be better coming from you.>

There was a long pause, before Gavain said, <Yes, you are right. Get me vocals and I will address them.>

Gavain sat at the head of the circular table, in the Heart Palace on Dark Heart Alpha, capital of his new nation of Vindicatus. The Cabinet Office was a large room, one of many military briefing rooms converted to a multifunctional governmental and military operations centre. It was accordingly very large, with numerous seats for viewers or audience always left unfilled. Gavain still had to decide how he wanted the minutiae of his government to function. The Vindicatus nation was still forming, and there was much to do.

Around him sat his closest advisors, those who he had absolute trust and faith in. He found it a little disappointing that more had not chosen to form part of his government, but he understood; they were all bred for war, and it was his conscience and desire for a better galaxy that had led him to form this new nation from the ruins of his invasion into the Dark

Heart System. It left him in the unenviable position of needing new support to run this ambitious venture of his, and not knowing where to find it.

Harley, Ulrik and Jonathan were all present, having come from the commercial spacestation with him. Next to Ulrik Andryukhin, who as Field Marshal commanded all his Marines, was Lucas De Graaf, who now held the rank of Admiral-of-the-Fleets. Both of them stayed purely within the Vindicatus Mercenary Corporation, which consisted of his military-for-hire, the mercenary army of every military ship and asset in the Vindicatus nation. They all had their roots in the mercenary organisation, which he himself had set up following Dissolution. Gavain was the Commander-in-Chief of the VMC, amongst his many other titles.

Brigadier Vantanik was present, the biomorph super-soldier and spy created from the stolen technology they had obtained from the Faceless assassins. Admiral Danae Markos, who commanded Second Fleet, was also present, having refused a political post just like Viktor Vantanik. Doctor Erin Presson was the Chief Medical Officer for the VMC, as well as taking the political role of Chief Medica, setting up the infrastructure of their medical facilities.

All of them were his closest advisors and friends, and for the last few months since setting up the Vindicatus nation, he would have been lost without their support and encouragement.

"Despite his death," O'Connor was saying, "using the secrets we learnt from the previous Faceless assassin we captured, we have been more successful in analysing his brain and mind posthumously. Much of the detail had faded of course, the Faceless biomorphs not being built to give away secrets, but it did confirm he was not in the employ of the Zhou-Zheng Compact. Its orders were to infiltrate Dark Heart Alpha and the Heart Palace, and then make it appear it was the Primarch Zhou and Primarchess Zheng paying for your assassination, James."

"No clue as to who was paying for it?" asked Lord Gavain.

"No, it's not apparent from the mind-probe."

"Well, at least it wasn't successful, thanks to Viktor's men closing it down," said Admiral Markos.

"There were another three trying to come through, eliminated quickly and quietly," said O'Connor. "I am surprised it has taken our unknown enemy this long to make the attempt."

"Speaking of them," said Ulrik, "Do we have any frikkin' idea who they are yet?"

"No," said O'Connor, "the secret masters of the Rosicrux operation are still unknown to us."

"For a fucking Chief of Intelligence, you're a bit low on the informative intelligence front, Jonny boy. Every fucking answer's 'don't know.'" Ulrik

Andryukhin laughed his deep, dirty bellow, and the rest of the table joined in the light humour.

"What *do* we know about them?" asked Lord Gavain.

"We have a lot more information," said O'Connor, "but my data-tac sections are still going through the recovered data from when we took the Dark Heart System. We are getting better at verifying what is false and what is not. Unfortunately, whilst much of it is interesting, it does not give us that golden nugget of who was controlling the Rosicrux beyond the woman known as the 'Solar Administrator' and some other unidentifiable figures. We know much about their procedures, what the Rosicrux did, who and how they manipulated the political scenes and situations in the Eastern Segment, and some possible indications of other plots in other segments.

"She remains largely unbroken, her powers at resisting our interrogative methods never seen before. We do have some clues, particularly that she was a member of something called the 'Third Circle'. We have had a number of references to 'The Shadows' as well, but no real information on them.

"We do have a new, solid lead, however," said O'Connor, grinning in a way he had not done for a long time when having to report on progress, leaning back and folding his arms.

"At fucking last," commented Ulrik, with mock severity.

O'Connor explained about the sighting in the Khobar System and the background to it, also stating that his early intelligence penetrations into the StarCom Federation proved that they had nothing to do with it, despite a strong suspicion otherwise from the OutWorlds Alliance. Al-Zuhairi was reported to be keeping an open mind, but there was a lot of bad history between the two distant nations. The intelligence on Al-Zuhairi was also third hand, obtained from StarCom's penetration of his intelligence agencies.

"The situation between them is worsening again," said Harley Andersson quietly.

"Definitely," said O'Connor. "The interesting thing about all this though, is that whilst the colonised galaxy has never seen this type of so-called 'alien' ship before, we have." He grinned again, a holographic image snapping into place over the table. It showed an image some of them had seen before, of a set of ships above the planet. It had been taken from the minds of various captives. "These 'white-ships' are the same as that seen in the Khobar System, or the same design structure anyway."

"So," said Lord Gavain, "whoever controlled the Rosicrux, or interacted with them, commands these ships and is also active out in the Frontier."

"That is the only conclusion," Chief of Intelligence O'Connor nodded. "I'm giving this a priority, I'm sending some of our biomorphic soldiers out towards the Frontier, with Viktor Vantanik's kind assistance."

"Good news," said Gavain with typical shortness. "Anything else?"

"Not as of yet," said O'Connor.

"Picking up then on the politics, galaxy-wide as well as our immediate concerns," Lord Gavain took over, "There are some truly major problems. The growing antagonism between the OutWorlds Alliance and StarCom is just one aspect of it. The StarCom Federation has rebuilt its naval, marine, and standard military assets, and has moved into full production. They are growing again, in terms of territory as well as offensive power. We know they had begun limited invasions again, but there is a heightening of tension here."

The holographic display before them switched to a starmap of the entire galaxy, and then focused in on the Core, the white and regal-blue colouring denoting StarCom. It switched further to the galactic west and south.

"There is an excessively large build-up on their borders with the south-westerly League of Suularitsaar. There is much rhetoric between them, but it looks as if the Suularitsaar intend to provoke war. We know from the Rosicrux information this situation is most likely caused by the secret forces behind the deliberate destabilisation of the colonised galaxy, with historical reasons, not least of which was the complete seizure of all StarCom assets and the initial wars started by the former StarCom President Nielsen."

The map shifted rapidly, heading up to the galactic north-east-east. "They have also rebuilt and have forces massing in secret on their borders here. The target is doubtful, as they could strike in any direction if that is their intention. The possibilities are that they intend to take advantage of the worsening situation between Amiens and the Republic of Varrental, who are maybe only weeks away from open war, or the re-ignited triple-way war between Korhonen, Cervantia and Hausenhof. The build-ups in both cases are too large to be coincidental."

"The Rosicrucean masters were involved in all those areas," said Admiral Markos. "Do you suspect that the StarCom Federation had something to do with it? They seem best placed to take advantage."

"It's possible, but in my gut and my instinct it does not feel right," Lord Gavain answered. "Then of course we have the political situation with our mutual defence pact allies, the Levitican Union. House Towers has been betrayed by House Zupanic, and Zupanic and Marchenko still plot to invade House Jorgensson as a result of Rosicrux manipulations. The situation there cannot be allowed to develop, if only because the Levitican Union is still within reach of the StarCom Federation, and it cannot be allowed to fall. I have no intentions of being sucked into a deadly war in the Union."

"What can you do?" asked Doctor Presson.

"Firstly, I will shortly be leaving for Leviticus, to try and argue the case peacefully for a proper alliance with House Jorgensson, maybe even them joining the Levitican Union," said Lord Gavain. "Secondly, I have given Brigadier Vantanik special orders. House Marchenko is the key; it is them with the largest military in the Union, and according to the disruptive Rosicrux, 'Shadow' or 'Third Circle' plans their betrayal that will split it apart following the invasion by House Jorgensson. If war is unavoidable, it will trigger a special event."

"That it will," said Viktor Vantanik, smiling evilly. The man was not a man at all, being a cybernetic biomorph capable of taking any form at will. He assumed a certain appearance to make normal humans and cyborgs feel more relaxed and at ease, but despite that there was something very dark about the specialist commando. "Marchenko will be broken overnight."

"It will," said Gavain shortly, preventing any further questions. "Coming back to it, the war between the Alliance of Aalborg and the Helvanna Dominion proceeds badly for the Alliance. Here, the borgite Dominion is ripping the humanist Alliance of Aalborg apart. Lastly, the Erdogan nation is probably only a month away from utter surrender to the genocidal Zhou-Zheng Compact.

"To our galactic east and beyond the Gulf of Medusa, well into the Mid-Sectors proper, the vast humanist nation of the Benedict Democracy continues its successful defence against the equally large Calamarite Confederacy, having now turned it into an invasion of Confederate territory. The Mitsubasha nation continues to provide weaponry to both, profiting massively from the conflict and openly supporting its continuation.

"The OutWorlds Alliance accepted the surrender of House Villaneuva, and now moves aggressively in its continuing expansion towards the alliance of houses known as the Frontier Hegemony." Lord Gavain continued in this vein for some time, ending with, "in short, the Dissolution of the Red Imperium continues with the never-ending wars of secession as the old Imperial Houses tear themselves apart."

"No wonder our immigration intake is so high, following your announcement to the galaxy," said Dr Presson, referring to Gavain's broadcast where he openly invited refugees to head for the Blackheath System or to various locations where they could be picked up by the transporters at his Deepspace Stations.

"What is the immigration and refugee situation?" Lord Gavain asked, already fully aware but wanting it to be played out in the conference.

Andersson fielded the question. As Solar High Chancellor, at the moment it fell to him. "We are struggling significantly," he said, "the intake is too high. We have new ships with people appearing at our Deepspace Stations all the time, jumping in from the drop-off locations you specified. We have by far the largest number coming in from the collapsing Erdogan nation, with the second highest being from the humanist Aalborg Alliance. But we also have House Van Der Meer nationals coming in now they have lost their war against Amiens, and numbers are growing from the Calamarite Confederacy. We have Korhonens, Cervantians and Hausenhofs, even some StarCom rebels. We have them coming in from everywhere.

"On the one hand, we have a vast talent pool arriving. Our cities are filling, Jamie, and we are setting up new structures even as new businesses are being set up. There is a real sense of adventure out there, which is good. All of these people had something to run from, if you exclude the chancers and the drifters. Our military is growing rapidly, as we are attracting vast numbers of Praetorian Guard.

"But we are creaking under the pressure. We really do need to set up a proper system of government, sooner rather than later. It is taking too long, Jamie."

Lord Gavain nodded. "We have spoken of this often," he said at length, "Harley, you and I do have a proposed structure, if you would."

"Of course," Harley nodded. The holographic display changed, to show an illustration, a graphic with Lord Gavain's representation at the top.

"The top of the structure is obvious, with James in control of the new House," Harley said. "Military-wise, we have filled all the posts within the command structure." As he spoke, the miniature holographic figures appeared in the senior roles. "On the political governance side, I take command where Ulrik and Lucas do for the military. Where we are most advanced in terms of structure and organisation is in medical support, and in intelligence operations and analysis, both of which have heads in the form of Erin and Jonathan. Whilst I do the best I can, I think we need more people to deal with some of the other major challenges we face. Therefore, I'm proposing and Jamie has agreed with six more posts."

Blank shapes of figures appeared underneath Andersson's representation.

"We need an Administrator for Migration Control, to control immigration, refugees and even emigration should we ever face it. We need an Administrator for Justice, Law and Security, as before long we will begin to face some real problems with criminality. We need an Administrator for the Treasury and Trade, to promote our nation and control our finances. We need an Administrator for Communications and Transport, to control our civilian shipping and communications within and without our territory. There could be an Administrator for Colonisation and Expansion, because of our plans to expand rapidly using the five colonyships that were abandoned here centuries ago. We could also do with an Administrator for Ambassadorial Service, to control our relations with other nations. We not only need to spy on them, we need to talk to them. That will be the toughest, recruiting people like that from our new influx of refugees."

"I like it," said Lucas De Graaf, nodding. "Just a thought - has anyone thought of Jason Bramhall for the Colonisation and Expansion post? He could do a dual-role just like the rest of us, and he has proven himself to be an excellent scout. Our new Captain Bramhall would enjoy it."

"That is an outstanding suggestion," said Lord Gavain, nodding. Jason Bramhall was instantly likeable, and his courageous actions in the Dark Heart invasion as well as in numerous actions previously were very encouraging. It was almost a natural fit for the exceptionally young man.

"He's certainly capable," said Andersson, "In fact, he reminds me of a young James Gavain in many ways, and he shows so much promise. Competition for you, Jamie."

People began to laugh, but Gavain cut it off with a sharp wave of the hand. He had been contacted first, but nano-seconds later Admiral De Graaf received the same notification, both of them pulled into jacking in to the battlenet datasphere.

"A squadron of military warships just appeared at Deepspace Eight," Lucas De Graaf said to the rest of the assembled people, by way of explanation.

All of a sudden Gavain said, "the ships have been identified. We are not under attack."

"No?" asked Andersson. "Who is it?"

"An Erdogan fleet of ships," said Lord Gavain. "Carrying Feldmarshall Horatio Grant of the Erdogan military, and the Lord and Lady Erdogan themselves. They are asking for asylum."

*

The Dark Heart Stargate opened up, allowing the House warships to jump into the Dark Heart System proper. There were seven warships, and in the centre, a noble barge and some smaller civilian ships accompanying them.

The Praetorian Guard T-class dreadnought *Thor's Hammer* glided forwards to meet them. One of the largest ships in the colonised galaxy, possibly excluding the unknown make discovered at the Khobar System, it was formidable. It was more than capable of engaging the entire squadron entirely on its own, partly due to its immense size but also because of its incredibly advanced Praetorian technology.

The necessary politenesses were exchanged, and then smaller shuttlecraft began to make their way from the Erdogan ships to the *Thor's Hammer* dreadnought.

Lord Gavain stood in the civilian docking bay for the *Thor's Hammer*. Like all military Praetorian ships, it had one bay that was designed to allow civilian craft to dock. The landers the Praetorians used were capable of fast disengagements from their mothership, and equally quick returns, so were not suitable for this politer and gentler docking bay.

The shuttles opened, and their people disembarked. <Attention!> Field Marshal Andryukhin ground out, and the entire company of Marines arranged before snapped to full parade stance, imposing and gigantic in their power-armour. Their guests formed up before the corridor the two lines of Marines had created, and escorted by their own House Guard, walked along it and the red carpet laid out for them to come to stand before the grandly-attired Lord Gavain.

Lord Gavain stepped forward out of the rank of his senior officers, and met the gaze of the Lord and Lady Erdogan before him. He did not bow or offer his hand, because with his new title of Lord it was not the correct protocol. He met them as an equal, and that felt somewhat unusual still. Virtually the entire House Erdogan family stood behind them, the three daughters and two sons, uncles, aunts, and cousins, Gavain accessing their data-files quickly through his link to the datasphere.

"Queen Ebru Erdogan," he said, addressing the ruler of the Erdogan nation by her new post-Dissolution, secessionist title.

"Lord Gavain, may I introduce my consort, Lord Kemal Erdogan," she said. He exchanged the pleasantries required.

He looked directly at Feldmarshall Horatio Grant. The impressive man looked unusually gaunt, the signs of stress and concern easily visible in his drastically altered appearance. "Feldmarshall Grant," Gavain acknowledged. "Can I ask what brings you all here?"

The Queen of the Erdogan nation lowered her eyes, and then when she looked back up, there was a fierce determination there. "We have come to ask for asylum," she said quietly. "The Erdogan nation is about to fall."

"This was the warship used by the infamous Silus Adare," said Feldmarshall Grant, looking around the private ready room that Gavain had occupied as his own. "I last remember seeing this ship firing upon your battlecruiser, the *Vindicator*. A right mess he was making of your forces."

"It was all part of the plan," said Lord Gavain. He had remained sat as a crewman served their drinks. He found it annoying, being used to doing it himself. He resolved suddenly that despite his newfound position, he would not follow all the trappings and procedures most House Lords of the Red Imperium had once observed. He would serve his guests his own drinks. Somewhat more aggressively than he intended, he said, "So why are you here asking for asylum?" he asked "There must be many nations or Houses you can go to. Why mine?"

"Many of our people, fleeing the terrors of the Zhou-Zheng Compact, come here," said the Queen Lady Ebru. "Your actions in the Kyiv System showed us you cared. This is seen as a safe place for my people. The Primarch and Primarchess of the Zhou-Zheng Compact are killing us because we are borg."

"Why do you particularly chose to come here?" Gavain repeated the question.

"We know that you accept all refugees," said Feldmarshall Grant quickly, interrupting. "And the noble family needs somewhere safe. We also know you are setting up a new nation. We can bring much to you, in terms of equipment to assist, but also knowledge in how to run such an undertaking. A nation is not an easy thing to administer and govern."

Gavain thought of his conversations with Harley Andersson, and his own difficulties. "That is certainly true," he agreed.

"Our military will mostly be destroyed holding the enemy Compact ships back, but whatever survives, we shall bring with us," Grant said. "We will hold out until the last, to ensure as many of our people escape as they can."

"We do of course intend to conduct a resistance, a rebellion to try and save as many of our people from the genocide of the Compact," said the Consort Lord Kemal, "but that is something we can discuss in detail later. For now, we need to abandon our home systems. Sadly." He reached out for the Queens hand, but she did not take it. Gavain saw the incredible, burning, aching sorrow within the woman.

"But until then we would help you build yours, whilst we try to rescue the remnants of ours," said Feldmarshall Grant. "The least we can offer is to do that."

Lord Gavain thought hard on the matter. "We would be pulling ourselves even more into the possibility of direct conflict with the Compact," he stated. "Especially if I offer asylum to those who seek to actively rebel against them, however evil and wrong I may see the Zhou and Zheng families."

"You have told me before that it was their deathcamps in the Kyiv System that convinced you to turn against them," said Feldmarshall Grant quietly, "and that indirectly led to you setting up your own House and nation."

"That is true," Gavain nodded. He had kept in contact with the Feldmarshall, and it was a shortened but accurate version of events, as far as it went.

"Then may we have asylum?" the Queen Ebru asked, obviously unaccustomed to begging.

He took pity on her then. In the space of a few seconds, he decided that if he was going to upset the Zhou-Zheng Compact, he may as well go for it with all his power. "I will offer asylum," he said, "if you three take a position in my government." He saw the shocked looks on their faces. "I need to set up my own nation, and need the help," he said, "that is my price, what I ask of you for the risk I am about to take on your behalf."

Some hours later, they had agreed all the details.

Chapter III

Lady Principal Sophia Towers, elected by her peers to be the leader of the Levitican Union and also head of House Towers, sat in the conservatory that was annexed onto her large and spacious personal quarters.

The planet Leviticus, capital of the Levitican Union, was mostly a water planet, with what land that was available being uninhabitable. Following the destruction of Leviticus and its cities by the StarCom Federation, the capital city had been rebuilt, and work was already starting on a secondary city. It was a matter of pride to re-populate the system.

She leaned back in her long chaise lounge, enjoying the day of recess in-between scheduled Council meetings, which were every other day. She had the morning free, with no appointments, and so had invited her brother and their special advisor, the spy chief known as The Spider, to join her.

She rested a hand on her belly. It could no longer be hidden that she was pregnant, and the baby boy was due in two months or less. She tried not to think about the conception and the father as she stared up at the deep waters of the planet-wide ocean above her, but it was impossible not to.

In the depths of the ocean a large predator, long and sinuous, swam in search of its prey. The usually bountiful ocean, filled with all sorts of marine life, was now empty as all the morning sea-life had realised it was present. The dome of the capital city was rising towards the surface, and shortly it would be just below the water level, it was that early in the morning. During the day it rested just below water level and at night it sank down to the depths of the ocean, trying as hard as possible to keep to Imperial Standard time for the benefit of its inhabitants, bearing in mind the planet Leviticus' own particular rotation.

"The Lord Gavain is due today," said Lord Luke Towers, her brother. "He's coming in by stargate. He must be spending money like there is no tomorrow."

"The Vindicatus nation needs to watch its financials carefully," said The Spider Elaine Carrington, the closest advisor either of them had ever known. She had advised their father when he was alive, and had been in service to House Towers before even Sophia or Luke had been born. "They are going to have problems if they do not generate more income soon, despite all the money he conned out of us all for destroying the Rosicrux."

Lady Principal Sophia looked forward to seeing her friend come back to Leviticus, although the purpose of his visit was not clear. "He did not con us," she said lightly, "he merely used the mercenary and mercantile skill one taught him to its best advantage."

"He charged a lot of houses and nations to go and carry out the same contract," said Lord Luke.

"One taught him well," Lady Principal Sophia laughed gently.

"He's being called 'the Mercenary Lord' by both his fans and detractors, you know," said Lord Luke, reclining on his own chaise lounge.

"Children," The Spider Carrington said, the only one who would dare address the two very adult nobles in such a way, "We do have serious business to discuss."

"It is always serious," said Lord Luke wistfully. "There is never any respite nowadays, not in this Age of Secession and since the Red Imperium dissolved."

"You want to go back to the days of the Red Imperium?" teased Lady Sophia.

"Absolutely not," Lord Luke replied. "Although if we did, our brother Jared would still be alive."

Lady Sophia noticed that Elaine Carrington reacted very strongly to the mention of their dead elder brother's name. Jared Towers had been a dynamo, a formidable political operator, and first in line to inherit the Senatorship and command of House Towers. The False Emperor had taken him as a political prisoner to ensure House Towers' continuing service, and he had died like so many others. Sophia herself had then been taken hostage, but had survived her luxurious prison in Mars where her brother Jared did not.

"Lady Sophia, Lord Luke," said Elaine, "House Zupanic?"

Lady Principal Sophia's face fell. The beautiful day was undoubtedly spoilt. "One's husband Lord Micalek has been revealed to be a liar," she said, "the information Lord Gavain pulled from the Dark Heart System when he invaded has proven that. House Zupanic, which includes Micalek, and Ramicek and Wyn when they were alive, were working with the Rosicrux."

"And the plan was for House Zupanic to get House Marchenko into the Union, which they were successful in doing," Lord Luke continued. "Marchenkan ships now make up a vast majority of the Levitican Union army, and cover a vast swathe of our territory. When the war is ignited with House Jorgensson, there will be a betrayal, and Marchenko and Zupanic will turn on the rest of the Union, either before or after the war with Jorgensson is completed. It is a gross betrayal."

"What one does not understand," Lady Principal Sophia continued, "is if they were in this plan altogether, why did Lord Micalek conspire with me to have so much of his family murdered, including his father and mother?"

"He wanted power, is the logical assumption," said The Spider. "With his parents removed he is head of House Zupanic, and also the Lord Minister for Military Defence. He obtains absolute power whilst ending up in the best Union Council position to ensure the plan succeeds."

"One can still not believe that after all the doubts and heartbreak," said Lady Sophia quietly, "that Micalek after all has proven to be so ruthless."

"Well, believe it," said The Spider Elaine Carrington sharply. "He is. He knows of your pregnancy by now, I assume? Have you told him?"

"No," said Lady Sophia, "and the holographic disguises you gave one are hiding the bump. But they may have the tech to see through it. There are rumours out there in the Union already. It is time to admit it, Elaine, we can hide it no longer. The baby is due in two months."

"That would be very dangerous," said Lord Luke.

"No," said Elaine Carrington, "we cannot hide it any longer. You must go to him and explain you are pregnant. They will already know or suspect from the rumours in the media and social blogs. Reveal it to him before you reveal it to the galaxy. We must try to keep him on-side, whilst we fight against him."

"And how are we going to stop his plan to rip the Union - and us - apart?" asked Luke Towers.

"I don't know yet," said Elaine.

"Well, James Gavain is on his way here to Leviticus, as I said," said Lady Sophia slowly. "His message said he has a suggestion for me on the matter, and he will discuss in person. Once more, James comes to our rescue."

"He does," said The Spider, "just a word of warning. He is trustworthy at the moment, but he is new to politics at this level. He learns very quickly though. We can rely on him for now, but should our interests and that of his new nation ever diverge, we all know what will happen. There are no friends at this level of politics, Sophia and Luke. And sometimes as Micalek has shown, no such thing as family either."

*

Lucas De Graaf wore the title of Admiral-of-the-Fleets with some unease. It was going to take him a long time to get used to, he knew, as he strode onto the bridge of the *Thor's Hammer*. Although Gavain had borrowed it to receive the visit from House Erdogan, it was officially his ship and his to use, the flagship of the entire First Fleet of the Vindicatus nation.

<Admiral on the bridge,> announced his second-in-command.

<You have the bridge,> he said, continuing along it. <I will be in the war-room.> He had designated one of the many side rooms as a permanent war-room, a strategic centre given over to his management of

all six fleets of the Vindicatus nation. Every time he thought of that it made him go white with fear.

What was Jamie thinking of, he thought to himself, giving me this to command. I should never have accepted. I am just not ready. He knew that many others thought that too, despite his successful commands of several ships and a destroyer squadron. Even then, it was a large jump from a small squadron to six fleets, even small ones like theirs!

He crossed the bridge of the *VSS Thor's Hammer*, observing as he did so that everyone watched him, some more openly than others. He had seen the same reactions to Gavain aboard the *VSS Vindicator*, as his prowess became more and more recognised. The bridge was designed like all Praetorian bridges, with the main command posts on the dais at the back, a floor with the second consoles, and then a walkway bridge with two pits either side for the tertiary stations. The number of bridge crew on the dreadnought, the most powerful ship of its type, was the highest also found in any Praetorian Guard designed ship, and most of them watched him.

It was with some relief that he felt the doors cycle shut behind him as he entered the strategic war-room.

It was quiet, no-one else being present. There was no war to fight, after all. He made his way to the centre of the room, taking the command seat. He would sit out in the main bridge, but he was not on duty and did not want to crowd his new second-in-command, Captain Layton. He was a Praetorian who had served with the VMC in the battle for Dark Heart, newly promoted to the post from being a Commander in charge of the strikecruiser *Snake-Eyes*.

Lucas De Graaf was already jacked in, but he took his access to another level. There were command-specific layers of the datasphere that only certain people could access, and he had the full run of the battle-net. It was a safety precaution, a tiered approach to data that protected them as well as reinforced the chain of command.

All around him, holographic images appeared, and even more materialised inside his minds-eye, his cerebrum fooling itself into thinking it was 'seeing' the data-streams as images, to allow the human side of his borg-enhanced brain to process the vast amounts of data being flung at it.

Leaving the normal House Army to one side, which in itself consisted of a curious mixture of droid, human and borg elements, and the borg Praetorian Marines, and the cybernetic biomorphic super-soldiers, Lucas De Graaf had complete control of all the military warships. The fleets were split themselves into the House Navy, and the Praetorian Navy, a hybrid of droid, human and borgs.

There had been some debate about activating the broader droid defences and elements, but Gavain had given it his affirmative on the basis that all of them were thoroughly checked for any latent signs of the Droid Intelligentia, the command code that had led the artificial intelligence to see itself as individual and declare war on the human race. Unrestricted and unlimited artificial intelligence not linked to a human mind was outlawed by Imperial Edict, and no-one would be mad enough to let something like the Droid Intelligentia rise again. The human race had fought for its very survival against their maddened creations.

He looked at all the data before him. Although he had overall command of all military naval warships and battlecraft, he also had personal command of the First Battle Fleet. Like Admiral Danae's Second Battle Fleet, it consisted entirely and only of Praetorian Guard ships-of-the-line, the finest of the True and False Emperor's ships. Between them, that was no less than fifty-four ships-of-the-line.

The Third Support Fleet consisted of a mix of Praetorian and old droidships, and for old-time's sake the erroneous inclusion of a Cervantian cargo-freighter called the *Featherlight,* modified heavily to Praetorian specification. The Praetorian cargo-freighters were in the Third Support, themselves heavily armed for their classification, and then there were the three droid controlships, the droid transporters, and the massive droid mine-layers.

The Fourth Support Fleet was much bigger, containing all the Praetorian Guard frigates, all their corvettes, the vast number of G-class fusion tankers they had inherited, three I-class medical frigates, and four F-class Repair-Ships.

Fifth Marine Fleet was more of a squadron, but it carried the super-transporters and the military transporter for their Marines. It was purely Praetorian Guard only, and it was Gavain's insistence on that division. He wanted the droidships separated from the elite Praetorian Guard Marines.

Finally the Sixth Home Fleet consisted of the ancient and old Imperial House Guard ships-of-the-line and frigates. Whilst the other fleets could split and re-arrange function according to their mission, the Sixth Home Fleet would not do so. The job of the Sixth was to protect the Dark Heart System at all costs.

It was an impressive armada, and did not even include all the civilian ships they had. The ships that had been damaged in the invasion of the Dark Heart Artificial System - some of them nearly to the point of destruction, there being literally less than a minute's worth of survival time for some of them - had now been largely repaired. Lord Gavain was pushing Lucas to confirm when the two main battle fleets would be ready for action, and on looking at the data, he knew that the answer was they were ready now, at least in terms of ship-readiness.

Crewing them was another matter, and that was something that applied not only to the Praetorian Guard ships but the Home Fleet and old

Imperial House ships too. The droidships had largely been released for combat, and would be fully operational in another two weeks, all checks completed. The intake of Praetorian Guard was useful, appearing in their thousands every week. They were even more thoroughly checked than the civilians coming in-system.

Some ordinary borg had been selected for Praetorian Guard-style implants, the bioartificers under Doctor Presson working extremely hard to upgrade them. They still had to go through a month's worth of intensive training, but Lucas knew there were already signs of friction between the 'real' Praetorian Guard from Imperial times, and even the new ones they had created in the biovats themselves post-Dissolution, so these newcomers had no chance. They had vast capabilities in the Dark Heart System to create their own Praetorian cyborg replacements, with thirty thousand Praetorian grade cyborgs due to be ready in one month's time.

Lucas smiled. When that happened, his problem of staffing the ships was nearly over and they would be fully operational. The naval crew were getting priority over Field Marshal Andryukhin's marines, much to his disgust.

Outside the Dark Heart Artificial System, they had Tahrir Base in the House Towers system of Blackheath, with the Kavanagh Shipyards in orbit around it, and they still maintained 'Location X', a secret hidden cache of technology and equipment which they maintained for emergencies in a system they once used for training and exercises. In Tahrir Base, they were pumping out two and a half thousand cybernetic biomorphs every three months. In one more months time the forces of Brigadier Vantanik, who reported into Andryukhin, would number five thousand five hundred and fifty. Lucas faced the problem of transporting them.

To that extent, the Kavanagh Shipyard and the much larger and monstrously enormous Dark Heart Shipyard were already working on building new Praetorian Guard design ships. Most were established designs, but there was a new top-secret project ship, a special type of stealthship capable of planetary landings and interstellar travel, designed to insert the biomorphs in utter secrecy on their target worlds. Lucas read the reports with interest. It was just one of many new weapons Gavain had signed off on, with all the new technology they had found in Dark Heart.

In terms of static military assets, Lucas was also responsible for the eighteen Deepspace Stations spread out in the Web. He had the two military starbases in Dark Heart, twenty-five droid Battery-Barges, thirty droid Stellar Gun Platforms, ninety-six droid Orbital Gun Platforms, over three and half thousand drone mines, a hundred and twenty-four Orbital Gun Batteries on the surface of the five planets, and the InterStellar HyperSpace Missile Facility which even now was producing its own

Weapons of Planetary Destruction. The technology had been stolen and copied from the Rosicrux and Admiral Adare.

Lucas De Graaf leaned back, a big happy smile on his face. It was all going well. He had a flair for organisation that made him more than suitable for this role. A recovered alcoholic, he had almost faced severe disciplinary action from James Gavain, but the man had supported him and earned Lucas' undying loyalty by doing so.

The smile faded slightly. The temptation to drink was growing stronger every day, he knew, but he would resist. It was not the command or the responsibilities he now carried that worried him, at least not in terms of preparation. It was more whether he would be able to manage such a large collection of fleets. Surely Danae Markos would have been better for this position than him? The responsibility in that regard scared him thoroughly.

He was terrified, knowing he could never live up to the reputation of Lord James Gavain.

*

Lord Gavain sat aboard the heavily armoured military Freiderich-class shuttle lander, launched from the *Vindicator* high in orbit above the planet Leviticus. They had arrived in the Newchrist System less than half an hour before, the designated jump-point for expected military and political ships being quite close to the planet, almost as close as it could safely be without being interfered with by the gravity distortions the water-world placed on real-space.

He was jacked in, watching through the sensors of the lander as it rapidly flew at almost assault insertion speed dangerously close to the waves of the ocean. The water was ploughing up into the air behind the powerful Praetorian designed lander craft. Freiderich-class landers were typically used to insert land forces on hostile planets, not for carrying political dignitaries, but as with everything James saw no reason to forget his military background. He had not entirely relinquished it, and never would.

<Approaching the Leviticus Capital City, Lord Gavain,> said his pilot.

<Go ahead and dive then,> Gavain replied.

The lander used powerful repulsors to tilt at a nearly impossible angle, rear drives ploughing it down into the water. It inserted quickly, diving deep down into the ocean. The vast dome of the capital city could be seen clearly ahead of them, distant lights beckoning them into the underwater docking bay. It looked grand and majestic, like an impossibly large Earth-based jellyfish, complete with tentacles and fronds hanging down below, a man-made creation capable of holding well over a hundred million people comfortably.

"Lord Gavain," said Lady Principal Sophia welcomingly, serene and displaying her celebrated grace and poise.

"Lady Principal," said Gavain, stepping off the lander with his honour guard pulling back. "You used to call me Jamie."

"One wondered if one was still allowed," said Lady Principal Sophia teasingly.

"Of course," said James Gavain, his severe public face breaking into an unusual smile. They began walking side by side, their honour guards following them as they headed for their droidcar, clearly marked amongst a waiting convoy of protective military vehicles.

"It is good to see you," said Lady Principal Sophia with feeling.

"How are you finding overall command of the Levitican Union?" he asked.

"One finds it difficult," she said, "the politics is of another dimension entirely. Much of it you already know of course, but it seems there is an angle to everything, something to look for with every conversation. One copes, but the ..... personal worries at the moment do not make it easy."

They had reached their droidcar and were settling in, the doors closing. With a final snap-hiss, they sealed shut. They were alone in a secure environment. The engine of the droidcar hummed as it powered up.

"You talk of Lord Minister Micalek," he said quietly.

"Yes. He has played me for a fool. My unborn son is in danger, we are all in danger. We helped him to command of House Zupanic, to murder his own family. We also helped him to the exact position where he is perfectly placed to ensure this Jorgensson and Marchenko plan succeeds. Attack Jorgensson, and whether we win or lose the House War, the Levitican Union is finished as Zupanic and Marchenko will tear us apart. No wonder he said he never wanted official title to my House when we married; he never intended to need it. He wants to take our territory by force, openly."

"My best analysts have viewed all recordings of your private and public interactions," said Gavain quietly. "I am informed that the feelings for you are genuine. But of course, you cannot take the risk. And apparently he loved his wife on Balthazar too, but it did not stop him putting the entire planet to the sword, her included."

"He must be stopped," said Lady Principal Sophia quietly, "and in such a way it does not damage the Levitican Union."

They were passing into some of the underwater tunnels, reinforced pathways outside the dome that allowed them to progress with speed across the city. Lady Sophia was staring out the non-reflective window, a look of anger on her face. Lord Gavain was watching her closely.

"It is that I wanted to see you about, and why I am here," he said. "I do have a plan for dealing with this, and a back-up plan it case it fails. After all it is in my own interests that this Zupanic and Marchenko plot never comes to fruition, not just because it is what the Rosicrux wanted and their masters probably still want, but because my own nation has signed a mutual defence pact with the Union. I do not want my forces pulled into another conflict on that scale, I need them free to go out and earn money. Mercenary work is still going to be our biggest export for some time to come, at least until Dark Heart functions properly."

Lady Principal Sophia looked at him with hope in her eyes. "What is your plan?" she asked. "And the back-up if it fails. House Towers always seem to rely on you, Jamie."

He ignored the compliment, apart from a small smile of acknowledgement. "Well, my first suggestion is that we attempt a peaceful solution. Propose in the Council that we approach House Jorgensson and ask for a diplomatic, peaceful end to the growing conflict."

"We have and are already trying that," said Lady Principal Sophia. "It is not working."

"By 'we', I meant the Levitican Union and the Vindicatus nation together. Once Jorgensson realise they would be facing all of us, particularly two full fleets of Praetorian Guard starships, they should back down. I would lead the negotiation," said Gavain. "I would suggest your brother attends as well, and Lord Minister Brin Claes as he now heads the Ministry of Foreign Relations. We offer to go into Jorgensson territory. My ships will make up the bulk of the escort."

Lady Principal Sophia hesitated, and then said, "It is impossible to tell if it would work, but it has to be worth a try. At this point, a peaceful solution is more desirable than not. But there will be attempts to derail it," she said, "the Council meetings are getting very heated on the debate at the moment."

"I am sure," said Lord Gavain neutrally. "But it is worth the attempt. If nothing else, it will create the one month's space I need to get my fleets to full operational capacity."

"Already?"

"Yes."

"It's only been two months! And you'll be ready in a month?"

"Praetorians work fast," said Lord Gavain. "I do also have a back-up plan beyond destroying House Jorgensson, if the attempts at peace fail. It is a bit of a gamble, but Marchenko and Zupanic cannot be allowed to rip the Union apart with treachery, taking it from within." He explained what he planned.

"And you can do this?" she asked.

"Yes," he said confidently. "It is not without risk, but it can be done. You would have to be ready to move fast, as it would throw much into chaos. Discuss it with your brother and Elaine Carrington."

"I will," said Lady Principal Sophia.

"So, tomorrow shall I present my plan to the Levitican Union Council?"

"Without a shadow of a doubt," said Lady Sophia. "James? Thank you."

"I do this not just for you and the Union, but Vindicatus and perhaps the Eastern Segment, if not the whole colonised galaxy," he said, "whoever controlled the Rosicrux is planning something big, Sophia. We cannot afford to have a distraction in our own backyard when whatever it is happens."

Lord Gavain stood in the 'balcony' of his luxury quarters, feeling somewhat uncomfortable. As a Lord, even if most of the galaxy called him a pretender and did not recognise him as one, there was no way he could refuse the penthouse. It was at the top of a very tall inner rib within the underwater dome, almost two-thirds towards the apex, with an unrestricted view on one side of the inner city and on the other, a perfect enhanced view of the ocean outside.

He found such luxury uncomfortable. Even residing in the Heart Palace back in Dark Heart he found that he looked for as many excuses as possible not to sleep in the rooms he had taken as his own. He did not even feel comfortable on planets. He was born to be in the stars, to be a military man aboard a warship, living in Spartan quarters without any form of luxury at all.

<Incoming call for Lord Gavain,> the apartment's computer told him, connecting to his internal modem to deliver the message. <Source : Harley Andersson and Jason Bramhall, Dark Heart Artificial System, Vindicatus. This is a live transmission via pulse-channel. Do you accept?>

<Accept,> he said.

He turned away from the astounding and beautiful underwater cityscape, and walked back into the penthouse apartment. His own technicians had broken into the computer systems within the apartment, and ensured with Praetorian tech that he would be able to have unrestricted communications, coded beyond the ability of anyone in the Levitican Union or anybody else's spies to break.

The life-size holographic representations of Harley Andersson and then the newly promoted Captain Jason Bramhall appeared before him. They were in what looked like Andersson's office. "Gentlemen," said Lord Gavain, "This is unexpected. What is the problem?"

Harley Andersson laughed. "No problem, Jamie," he said, "We'll keep it quick. I and our new Administrator for Colonisation and Expansion here have a suggestion for you. Captain Jason Bramhall's work, this."

"Go on," said Lord Gavain. Even via pulse-channel, Jason Bramhall looked nervous talking to him. Despite his exemplary actions and the high praise and standing even the senior staff thought of him, he appeared not to be aware of it. Talking to James Gavain was an honour for him. He was going to have to deal with it, thought Gavain, as he would be doing so a lot more often in his new governmental role.

Part of the reason for creating a large governmental office such as Colonisation and Expansion was that amongst the many starships and civilian craft left abandoned for centuries within the Dark Heart System were no less than five early Imperial colonyships. Each one was capable of starting its own colony on a planet, with all that was needed to get an entire mega-city into operation in little under a day. Gavain intended to use them to settle other systems in the Gulf of Medusa, to spread his risk. The Dark Heart System was now famous throughout the galaxy, and the process of expansion would reduce the chance of him losing everyone and everything should the centre of his nation come under attack and be conquered.

"I think - we think we've found a potential system for colonisation, out here in the Gulf of Medusa," said Jason Bramhall. "Here, my Lord - I'll send -"

"James," Gavain insisted, "Call me James or Jamie, Jason. You've earnt the right."

"Ah, yes, sir ... James ... Anyway, I'm sending the details across to you now."

Gavain received the data-feed, and began examining it straight away. There were numerous ships out trawling the Gulf of Medusa at the moment, using the G-class fusion-tankers, looking for systems they could colonise and populate. It was probably one of the first attempts at new colonisation for decades, if not a century.

"This looks promising," Lord Gavain said, his interest piqued.

"Yes," said Jason nodding, at a prompt from Andersson. "It is a binary solar system, outside the black hole cluster surrounding Dark Heart. One of the stars has collapsed into a black hole, but the other is a powerful sun. It lies on a path where we could set up a stargate and have a connection from Deepspace Six or direct from Dark Heart.

"It has twelve major planets, of which seven are gas, three classified as giants. The others are rock and largely uninhabitable, with the exception of one which would only require minimal terraforming that could be carried out even whilst the colony was being seeded. Interestingly the Droid Intelligentia used one of the other planets, and there are ruins from several cities and possibly even more technology we could utilise. There are numerous planetoids and intra-stellar objects, including several asteroid fields. It would be easily defensible, as well as potentially very profitable and a great contributor because of its natural resources. There is numerous evidence that the Droid Intelligentia have left equipment scattered all over the system."

"Why did the Intelligentia abandon it?" Gavain asked, and then found the data even as Jason answered.

"Our scouts found that they pulled out and back to Dark Heart as the Droid Wars began to take their toll, and they were being pursued across the Gulf," Jason answered.

"I like it," said Gavain. "Well done on finding one so close to Dark Heart, astronomically speaking. Why does it not show up on most commonly held starmaps, Imperial Charts and scans from long-range astronomical arrays?"

"The True Emperor's father insisted on their destruction in the purge of all information on the Intelligentia," Harley Andersson answered. "The black hole and then the cluster surrounding Dark Heart prevents most astronomical arrays from detecting it."

"And of course," said Captain Jason Bramhall, "the greatest advantage to the system is that it is rich in the constituent chemicals and ingredients that make up raw Amerimax moleculisation blocks."

"Amerimax molecular blocks," said Gavain neutrally, although he suddenly saw the biggest advantage yet to the new colony.

Amerimax was the name of an ancient Earth corporation, which in the very early days of solar travel was the first in the race to successfully design, create and manufacture the raw chemical blocks and fluid that allowed organic food to be made, or synthesised, by food simulators. Amerimax had become the name applied to both the fluid or the blocks, that could now synthesise not just food but any form of organic or vegetative life, and quite beyond food could also create replica simulants - literally people's bodies built in much the same was as buildings, machinery and equipment were manuprinted from raw materials.

Most of Amerimax was made from commonly available materials and chemicals, the ingenuity being in the process, but also some elements were very rare indeed. If this system was abundant in the materials to make Amerimax, it not only created a brilliant export to be carried across to other nations by gigantic tankerships, but it answered a growing problem with the immigrants. They had plenty of food simulators to synthesise food, but were in danger of running short of the raw materials to make Amerimax to drive the food simulators. Buying it was exceptionally expensive, and if they could make their own it would virtually solve their impending food shortage problem.

"Then the decision is made," said Lord Gavain, nodding. "You have my permission. I'll think of a name. Start the colonisation."

Chapter IV

Lady Principal Sophia Towers banged the metal ball on its disc, a few sparks flying up as she said, "Then it is decided, the Council of the Levitican Union has spoken. On votes of five to two, we will follow Lord Gavain's plan and try this last piece of diplomacy with House Jorgensson, and invite them into the Union. The Council session is finished for today."

She slammed the ball one more time, to signify the end of the day's session. She looked at Lord Gavain, who occupied the guest seat used for visitors to address the Union Council.

The vote had been interesting, she thought. Her own vote had been in favour. Micalek Zupanic had voted in favour, following her direction, and Brin Claes as the puppet of House Zupanic had similarly followed. Monique Lapointe voted with Sophia, House Lapointe anxious to settle a score for the murder of her mother at the hands of the Rosicrux. Moafa Obamu had voted against, as had Eranisch Marchenko, both Houses having more to gain from open war on House Jorgensson.

Lady Principal Sophia got to her feet, crossing down towards the floor and approaching Lord Gavain. "So," she said, "we got the result we wanted, and it is started."

Lord Minister Moafa Obamu stared hard at the two of them, his face thunderous, and stalked noticeably from the Union. Sophia watched him go. House Obamu only ever seemed to get what it wanted on minor votes in the Council, not any of the major ones. Lord Moafa's temper and dissatisfaction was becoming more obvious. She would have to approach him and look after his interests more; the incumbent previous to her, Ramicek Zupanic, had not been too concerned about Lord Moafa.

"I will be contacting the House Lord of Jorgensson immediately," said Lord Gavain. "I have already had preliminary discussions with him, all we need now is to set up the location. He does not want war, but he is weak and it is more his sons and daughters pushing for it. It is some of them who were part of the Rosicrux operation."

Lady Minister Aria Galetti walked past, saying to Lady Principal Sophia, "Hopefully this may be the end of the increasing aggression," as she walked on. "We cannot afford more conflict. The Union is fragile enough as it is."

Lady Principal Sophia did not have a chance to reply. Lady Monique Lapointe nodded a respectful goodbye as she left the room. Lord Brin Claes walked out slowly, not making eye-contact with anybody. The man looked defeated. Sophia would have to speak to him too. There was something odd about the stranglehold House Zupanic had on him, her brother Luke had told her of it when he had been Lord Minister within the Council, but she could see it for herself now more than ever.

"And how many ships will you be taking with you to the rendezvous, assuming House Jorgensson agree?" said a deep, mechanical, unearthly voice.

There truly was nothing feminine about Lady Minister Eranisch Marchenko. All the hive-consciousness Marchenko borgs were connected to each other, and their borg implants, even for the noble House hold, were dirty and functional and obvious, rather than hidden discretely. It was like they revelled in being different.

Eranisch was immense in size, a gorgon of a nightmare. Her face was half metal, with whirring servos and sensors all over her body. She had six legs, all of which were required to support her gargantuan bulk. Her lower half was insectoid, and she had an additional pair of arms which ended in a laser-scribe and a heavy manipulator claw. All the borgs of House Marchenko looked different, their modifications being obvious, crude and frightening in equal measure.

It was not just their alienness which marked them out as different. To be a member of House Marchenko was to be part of the hive-mind, a collective consciousness based on the datasphere technology, but with no room for individuality or opting out. Slavery was uncommon in the inner segments of the Red Imperium, but an exception had been made for House Marchenko as they did not even realise themselves it was nothing more than enforced slavery.

The hive-mind, with every member of their population slaved into the nobles of House Marchenko, had the problem of interstellar distance to deal with. That was why any significant group of Marchenko citizenry was always accompanied by a member of the noble family, who would control and direct their actions away from the main up back on the Marchenko homeworld. That individual noble would periodically connect back to the main hive-mind, which in itself was embodied by House Lord Gregori Marchenko.

"That is classified and for me to know," said Lord Gavain firmly.

"Not even one herself knows that," said Lady Principal Sophia smoothly, easing over the abrupt reply.

"Where will your ships stage for launch into the rendezvous with House Jorgensson? Where will the rendezvous be held?" asked Lady Minister Eranisch Marchenko.

"Again, that is classified," said Lord Gavain.

"Truly?" asked Lord Minister Micalek Zupanic, coming up and placing a hand around the shoulders of Lady Sophia. She was able not to react negatively, now being long-accustomed to playing the role of believing

Micalek Zupanic was hers. "As the Lord Minister for Military Defence, I appreciate the need for secrecy, but I should really know."

"I will give you the co-ordinates to send Levitican Union Armed Forces to," said Lord James Gavain, "beyond that, operational security demands secrecy. This is too delicate."

"You will have Lord Luke Towers, Lord Minister Brin Claes and I with you," said Lord Micalek. There had been an amendment to Gavain's proposed line-up of initial politicians, and whilst far from pleased about it, politics was politics and he could not refuse the vote of the Council of the Levitican Union. "I could really do with knowing."

"I appreciate that," said Lord Gavain, "but operational security is my concern really. Remember I am leading the negotiations, seen by House Jorgensson as an intermediary."

"Will they really think that considering your close allegiance to the Levitican Union and House Towers in particular?" said Lady Eranisch.

"They appreciate I have my own self-interest involved in it," said Gavain, "but they trust me. Or the House Lord does, and that is all that matters."

"Well, if it fails," said Lord Minister Micalek, "we have our forces in place and ready all along the borders, and more. If this plan fails, we invade and put an end to the question of House Jorgensson once and for all."

"So make sure it works," said Lady Principal Sophia lightly, but with more meaning behind it than would ever appear in her voice.

*

"Enough!"

The roar, especially from someone that everyone else in the holo-pit held in so high regard he was almost a god, was enough to silence those present both in real-life and via a HPCG pulse-channel. After the exclamation, the heated argument that had been raging was abruptly deafened and killed.

The Master stood, and actually walked into the centre of the room. The holographic representation of him followed, whirring into place around him, a slightly larger-than-life version of him with the real figure stood in the middle. "I have had heard enough of your disagreements and conflicting information," he said.

He turned, pointing down at the complicated symbol woven into the centre of the holopit. It was directly beneath his feet. "I am the Master of the First Circle, which is everybody in this room, and all the people you command in my name. This symbol will become a reality, and those of you that do not do as I command will not live to see it happen. That applies to everyone in this room, no matter how powerful or strong you may think you are. No-one is irreplaceable, except from me."

He looked around at all of them. "Now, listen to me closely. Legate of the Second Circle, you will have all our military forces ready and in place at their staging positions. There will be no talk of supply problems, training issues, problems with the minutiae detail of the masterplan we have designed together. Make the problems go away. If you do not, you will be executed. Do you hear me?"

"Yes, Master," said the Legate of the Second Circle, bowing her head, the silver lines on her face-mask catching the dimmed light of her alcove as she did.

"Legate of the Third Circle," the Master addressed the Shadow Council member robed all in black like he was, but with the white lines on his mask, "You will have all our support and administrative staff in place to deal with the conquered territories, as well as ensuring that those Houses ready to declare for me do so at their appointed time. Do you hear me?"

"I hear you, Master."

"Legates of the Fourth, Fifth, and Sixth Circles," said the Master, "You will ensure that all, and I do mean all, of the plans to disrupt the colonised galaxy are fully active and in fruition. There will be no more mistakes or failures such as the Rosicrux operation. In particular, Legate of the Fourth, you will instruct the Frontier Hegemony agents to declare war on the OutWorlds Alliance now, you will ensure the StarCom Federation and the OutWorlds Alliance are firing InterStellar missiles are each other, you will ensure the League of Suularitsaar is tying up StarCom Federation resources, you will ensure that the Calamarite Confederacy and Benedict Democracy are tearing themselves apart, and you will most definitely make sure that this Lord Gavain's attempt to bring peace to House Jorgensson and the Levitican Union fails and a war is ignited. On that subject, Legate of the Fifth, your Faceless will kill James Gavain and not fail on their second attempt. Is that clear, both of you?"

"Yes, Master, it is clear," said the Legate of the Fourth Circle, the blue lines on his face-mask shaking as he replied.

"It is clear, Master, we will not fail again," said the Legate of the Fifth Circle, her voice calm and strong.

The Master turned rapidly between the last three. "Legate of the Seventh Circle, you will ensure we have enough money coming into our coffers to support ongoing operations and the new empire I am building. Legate of the Eighth Circle, you will ensure that all my ships are working, all my armies are fully equipped, that the stargates are ready for deployment, that all the support equipment and assets are capable of being put in their assigned places as we advance. Legate of the Ninth Circle, you will ensure that the various support elements, regardless of their race or designation, are there to replace losses in the other circles as required. You will be ready, you will not fail me."

"We will be ready, Master," said the Legate of the Seventh, yellow-lines on his face-mask.

"We will not fail, Master," said the Legate of the Eighth Circle, green-lines on her face-mask.

"I am ready and shall not fail you, Master," said the Legate of the Ninth Circle, orange-lines on his face-mask.

"And," said the Master, creating a long pause as he turned slowly, staring at each in turn again, "No more calling me Master! The time has come!"

He reached up and removed his face-mask, opening the long black robes he wore and allowing them to fall to the floor. Underneath he was dressed in finery that seemed very familiar to everyone in the room, with them having seen it before either in real life or in holo-images.

There was no denying the family line, it was obvious in the face as well as the bearing. In many ways, the figure once known as the Master could easily have been one of the two figures he so looked like.

"My grand-father was the First Emperor, known to many as the True Emperor. My father was the Second Emperor, known to many as the False Emperor. I am the Third Emperor, and I shall be known as the Shadow Emperor! Long have I waited here, with you the Shadow Council, in the shadows awaiting the day this would have to happen. And that day is almost here!"

In the rage and the rant that he cried, the Third Emperor saw that his Shadow Council had given the Imperial Salute, and then fallen to one knee, heads bowed deeply.

"This symbol!" he shouted, pointing at the symbol in the floor below him, "this symbol is of the colonised galaxy as it will be! The Red Eagle will return!" Set on the starscape depicting the colonised galaxy in the symbol was the Red Eagle of the Imperium, but with three black slashes through its chest and wings.

"All of you," said the Third Emperor, "the time to hide in the shadows is no more. Remove your masks."

They all looked shocked. Even in the time of the False Emperor and before, they had never removed their masks. "Do it!" screamed the Third Emperor insanely.

They removed their masks, some quicker than others. Some pulled back their hoods, others removed their robes. Some of the faces had never been seen before, but others were very familiar indeed. It was with some shock they looked at each other. None of them had ever known who the other was, only that the Master was truly the Third Emperor. Some of the faces were famous and deeply unexpected, others belonged to people who were supposed to be dead, and others were unknowns on the interstellar stage.

Of the famous faces, the Deputy Head of the Interstellar Merchants Guild was one of the surprising ones, although his position as the Legate of the Seventh Circle in charge of money made a lot of sense and was understandable.

The Legate of the Ninth Circle was a monstrous hybrid of technology, human, and something else, a kind of alien life-form almost. The head and the body did not look right at all.

The Legate of the Third Circle, which looked after the political administration waiting to run the Third Empire and manipulated many of the politicians of the colonised galaxy was someone supposed to be very dead. The man who stood there had been executed by none other than the False Emperor, or the Second Emperor depending on your political leaning.

His name was Lord Jared Towers, of House Towers.

*

Juan Ramirez hit one wall, clasping hold of the hand-bars, bringing his feet round to kick off again in the opposite direction. The zero-gravity room in the one of the rest and relaxation gym areas was large, and there were a number of other people utilising their off-duty time to train. Through the clear windows, ranks and ranks of machinery designed to allow crew to train and exercise were also in heavy use.

He reached the far end of the spacious zero-gravity room, and the panel in his lane turned green. He had completed his set circuits for the day. He hauled himself down to the ground to avoid the other 'swimmers', and then aimed for the special exit, not too dissimilar to an air-lock, designed to allow people to acclimatise back to normal ship-wide gravity.

After leading the Vindicator Mercenary Corporation, as it was then known, to Dark Heart, Juan had joined the *Vindicatus* crew under James Gavain. He had taken the rank of Midshipman, the lowest possible officer rank in the old Praetorian Guard navy, training as a third shift navigator. His training was now complete, and he had progressed to second shift and was now aiming for his Sub-Lieutenant rank.

He exited the gravity acclimatisation chamber as it cycled open, normal gravity restored. He had a short five minute break before beginning the next phase of his training regimen. All crew followed a physical training regimen set by the ship doctors, to keep their genetically enhanced bodies at the peak of perfection.

Juan was still undergoing surgery and genetic enhancement, with implantations of Praetorian-grade cyborg technology to bring him up to the same technological level as if he had been born in a Praetorian accelerated growth biovat. The bioartificers were also upgrading his genetics, turning him into a super-human. Although he was one of the first, there were thousands from the influx of refugees now undergoing exactly the same process back on Dark Heart, to fill the ranks of the Vindicatus Mercenary Corporation army and navy.

On one of the benches outside, Lord Commander-In-Chief James Gavain looked up at him. The man's usually impassive face broke into a smile, and Juan's heart leapt. He sat down opposite the Commander-In-Chief, trying not to stare, and failing miserably.

"You need to make it less obvious, Juan," said Lieutenant Ellen Forrest, a first-shift communications officer. She was technically on her sleep-time, but the rules about resting were relaxed in that regard. Many Praetorians did not use the proportion of their Standard day allotted to sleep to actually go and sleep. They were in the same dormitory, and despite her rank they had become friends.

"What do you mean?" he asked suddenly, worried.

She leaned in closer. "Everybody knows your psych-profile indicates an almost equal gender-attraction to both male and female, yes?"

Juan laughed, and out of the corner of his eye he saw Jamie Gavain react to the forced laugh, curiosity obvious. They were lovers, but they were ignoring each other in front of the crew. It was too difficult, and the difference in rank was just one issue. "I've never hidden that," he said.

"No, you haven't," Ellen Forrest agreed. "However, it is becoming more and more obvious that you and our Commander-In-Chief are ... engaging, with one another."

His instinctive response was denial, but somehow he could not bring himself to do it. "Is that what rumour is?" he asked, trying to feign anger. He was certainly scared.

"That's the scuttlebutt, yes," said Ellen, "and also I know you now, so I can see it for myself, and I have served with Lord Gavain for years going back into before Dissolution. Just be careful, Juan. The Lord Gavain is supposed to be in some form of relationship with Admiral Andersson, and you do not want to get involved in that."

Juan could not reply, as his stomach had just turned. He was due to see James tomorrow once they were back in hyper-space. He would wait until then, and tell him that the crew of the *Vindicator* battlecruiser were beginning to suspect. Their affair could obviously not be kept quiet much longer.

Silus Adare stood quietly within his shielded prison block, staring up through the podium's force field at High Justiciar Driscoll. Although his eyes were locked on to her, his expression told of his amused contempt at the entire proceedings. He thought he unsettled the High Justiciar. He knew that the media were baying for his blood. The only way this was going was his execution.

He looked to his left, and then to his right as High Justiciar Driscoll spoke. Commander Zehra Sahin and Lieutenant-Colonel Iyan Lamans stood either side of him, in their own shielded podiums. They were his senior officers, and they had been included in his trial.

His trial of judgement had been expanded by the High Justiciar. She had already let it be known that her verdict was guilty, particularly as Adare offered no defence beyond the fact that he was following orders. High Justiciar Driscoll had ruled that insufficient, and had decreed that all staff on the *Thor's Hammer* who had participated in the war-crime directly, from those who received the Tears of the Moon warhead when it was first delivered, to those who oversaw its storage, those who loaded it onto the torpedo, any who knew of it, right up to those who pressed the button to fire it, had to be included in this trial. There would be well over a hundred people in this court-room at the end of it.

Every single one would face the same sentence, Driscoll had said. There was only one possible sentence, and Adare knew that it was execution.

"Before we conclude for the day, does the primary defendant have any remark? Do you wish to address your plea?"

Silus brought his attention back to the court circuit. The smile he gave was not pleasant. "No," he said, "I still object to the farce that this is. Why you don't just have me executed I do not know."

"Because Imperial Law will be observed!" snapped High Justiciar Driscoll.

"The Imperium is dead, and so is your law - as dead the nine billion I killed on Alwathbah," Adare smirked as the entire court burst into a roar. The people sat observing proceedings were on their feet, and the enforcers monitoring them had suddenly charged their weaponry and had shields up to prevent a riot starting.

Adare was still laughing aloud when quiet finally returned to the theatre-sized courtroom, and eventually stopped when the High Justiciar slammed her metal ball on its dais.

"Court of the First Circuit is adjourned until tomorrow," the High Justiciar Driscoll said, shooting one last venomous look at Adare. "Remove the accused."

Adjudicators came forwards and unlocked the magnetic clasps linking his moveable prison block into the podium. It floated up into the air slightly on its anti-gravity repulsors, the droid mind within it automatically setting it off on its pre-programmed journey out of the court. Adare could not sit down or relax within the thin rectangular block, so he contented himself with watching the progress of the blocks containing Zehra Sahin and Iyan Lamans.

A heavy squad of adjudicators walked all around each prison block as they floated into the access tunnels. Adare squinted as they entered the darkness, shielding his eyes as the motion sensors activated the lights. Enforcers appeared from recessed offices all along the tunnel, heavily armed and watching their progress.

Adare stood perfectly still, legs apart and hands clasped behind his back, not looking at their helmeted visors as they moved to track his progress. He knew how hated he was, and he did not care.

The tunnel was designed to take them out of the Court Circuit Building, and directly into the reinforced garage with the waiting prison droidlorry. Military, enforcer, and adjudicator vehicles made up the protective convoy, which would transport them back to the high-security prison facility at the bottom of the Leviticus Capital City. It was a routine that Adare found as boring as it was predictable.

They emerged into the reinforced garage, the prison droidlorry's sides opening up. It was capable of transporting up to twenty prisoners at any one time, with holding bays for twenty prison blocks. Just like with the podium, the prison blocks were designed to lock into the droidlorry. Reinforced armour would then shut down over the bays, sealing them back up again. It was like being in a tomb, all dark and unlit.

"Sahin, Lamans!" Adare suddenly called out, "See you on the other side."

"*Prisoners to be quiet*!" roared a senior adjudicator, and Adare just laughed as his prison block rotated and then reversed into the droidlorry.

As soon as the armoured doors shut on his bay, he was plunged into darkness. Adare merely used his implants to switch to night-vision, despite the fact there was not much to see. He was in a small metal box, he could not even raise his arms to their full extent.

He was still smiling, knowing what was coming.

Eventually the prison droidlorry engines gunned, and it rocked as it began to move. They were not built for comfort or ease of travel. He timed the movements in his head, keeping track of where they were in the labyrinthine building.

He began to tense as they reached the final exit, passing through the multitude of security barriers. Even through the heavy reinforced doors sealing him in the bay of the transport lorry, he could hear the sirens of the enforcer and adjudicator cars. The droidlorry was floating up in the air, and as it emerged into the underwater dome of the Capital City proper, military vehicles would be falling in all around the convoy. The media and crowds would be outside, baying for blood.

The convoy passed out into the open air of the underwater dome.

He laughed to himself as the droidlorry shook with a massive impact, and knew that the media outside would be recording his escape.

There was the sound of multiple explosions, and screams of panic from the crowd outside on the footwalks down below. A trio of starfighters jetted by overhead, and there were more explosions, vehicles blowing up. There was the distinctive sound of multiple shoulder-mounted rocket launchers firing, and more destruction being dealt out on the convoy.

Adare did raise his arms to brace as he felt the droidlorry falling, and he was ready for the impact as it crashed into the crowd below. The screaming was intense, people crying out in pain and terror. It sounded like it had fallen right onto the amassed crowd.

He shrugged. More people dead in his name, no doubt.

The decking of the underwater city was shaking as some large vehicle approached. All of a sudden light burst into his bay, and he looked out to see the massive form of a constructowalker ripping the bay armour away with one giant manipulator claw.

His internal modem received the link-up call dialling in at him, and he joined the battlenet. The people seeing to his escape had set up a datasphere in secret. The constructowalker continued on, quickly ripping open the prison blocks contained Zehra Sahin and Iyan Lamans.

<Commander Sahin, Lieutenant-Colonel Lamans,> said Adare quickly, <There will be a car waiting for us, make your way to it now! We do not have long to escape from this city.>

<Silus, what is happening?> asked Sahin, absolutely confused. <We're escaping?>

<Yes, we're about to blast out right through the underwater city dome, and cause a lot of damage in the process,> said Silus Adare, stepping over the corpses of the crowd as he headed towards their escape vehicle.

Lord Gavain was walking through one of the *Vindicator*'s ship corridors, returning to his quarters from the gym area, when the red alert signal was sounded throughout the entire ship. He immediately jacked into the datasphere fully.

<Report,> he demanded.

<Commander-In-Chief,> said Captain Erica Georgia, his second-in-command, <There is a situation in the Levitican Capital City. Silus Adare is escaping, with some of his crew.>

<I'm on my way to the bridge,> said Gavain.

He jogged for the turbolift, other crew passing him as they scrambled to battle stations. Through his neural link he knew that within seconds, the battlecruiser was going from its sedate normal status up to full battle readiness.

During the short time it took him to travel up to the bridge, he was monitoring the situation the entire way. Military Command down on the surface of the planet of Leviticus was asking them to be alert, to provide space-based support if required. It appeared that heavily armed force had struck the prison convoy as it was transferring Adare away from court.

Gavain analysed the information itself. Whoever was breaking Adare out from the prison system had somehow accessed Levitican Union Armed Forces assets and equipment, even stealing three starfighters to assist in the ongoing escape attempt. Instantly he realised there must be biomorphs down there, and that only pointed in one direction. Whoever controlled the former Rosicrux organisation was masterminding this escape attempt.

Gavain walked onto the bridge, Captain Georgia simply stating, <Commander-In-Chief on the bridge. You have command of the bridge, sir.>

<Command accepted, Captain,> said Gavain formerly and according to protocol. He did not always take command of the ship, usually having a strategic role controlling a squadron or fleet, but in this instance with only the *Vindicator* present in-system there was no reason for him not to assume direct control.

Particularly with Adare escaping, he wanted that control.

<Levitican Military Command is reporting that they have broken through the underwater dome using ground-based surface-to-air strikepods, sir,> said the data-tac officer, Lieutenant Woolfe.

<The same tactic we employed in Isdalsto, to rescue Juan Ramirez,> said Captain Georgia, on a private channel direct to Gavain.

<The city is flooding, but emergency force-fields are already activating to contain the rupture,> said the scanners officer, Lieutenant Agrawal. <Estimate six seconds until the strikepods break atmosphere into space.>

Observing the holographic tactical map, Gavain ordered, <Move us into range of their projected pathway. Prepare forward weaponry batteries to fire, we will need long-range weaponry.>

<Aye, sir, moving now,> said helmsman Lieutenant Vries. <It will take us two minutes and ten seconds to reach their location, accelerating to full speed now.>

<It will be too long,> Captain Georgia said privately to Gavain. <There must be a chameleonically shielded ship there, running silent.>

<I agree, it will be out there somewhere,> said Gavain. He opened up to the main bridge, <Prepare to fire torpedoes on my mark, as soon as we identify a potential target. The strikepods are not our primary target, there will be a ship out there to pick them up.>

Inside the strikepod they were sharing, Admiral Adare looked directly at Commander Zehra Sahin. "Zehra, welcome to freedom," he grinned.

"Are we being met by something?" she asked.

"There is a ship waiting for us," he said confidently. "Something new. The Leviticans will not know what has hit them."

Lieutenant-Colonel Lamans was looking out of one of the observation windows. "I can see the *Vindicator* in the distance," he said, "it's cresting around the planetary horizon now. Gavain is here."

"Ah, my old friend," said Adare. "Let's see if he catches us." He leaned forwards with an evil glint in his eye. "He won't of course - he has no idea what's waiting for him."

The strikepods sped through space. There were Levitican Union Armed Forces ships all around the capital planet of the young nation, and some of them began firing. The whole design of the strikepods was aimed at speed and weaponry evasion, and none of them struck any one of the five targets speeding away from the planet.

All of a sudden, space began to ripple, and an enormous starship appeared as it dropped its chameleonic fields. It was advancing rapidly, speeding up to full propulsion, but it was massive, half again as big as a dreadnought. It was all white and regal blue, and bore the symbol of the StarCom Federation on its flanks and fore.

It began firing, and its weaponry was terrible to behold. It released full broadsides in all four directions, engaging two Union battlecruisers, a strikecruiser and a dreadnought simultaneously. They fired back in panic, but the unknown starship shimmered, its hull becoming translucent, and the projectile and projection weaponry simply passed through the ship. It was as if it were made of something insubstantial, a ghost that was not really there.

<Firing torpedoes,> said Gavain's weaponry officer. The Praetorian battlecruiser was still distant from the fight, but within long-range fire.

<Unbelievable,> said Gavain to Captain Georgia on their private channel, <It's exactly the same design as seen at the Frontier, and in Dark Heart.>

<How can you destroy something you can't hit,> said Captain Georgia. <It's swallowed the strikepods. They've found something material to land in.>

<He's going to get away,> said Gavain, <It can't be helped. Make sure we get full sensor recordings. We need to analyse all data on this. We have a new weapon out there to face.>

He watched as the battle unfolded, the behemoth of a warship already turning, ready to head out-system. It was slow, but with its weaponry and armour and unbelievable immaterial defence it did not exactly need to be fast. It was already accelerating, and would doubtless be jumping out-system shortly.

Gavain watched as the Levitican Union ships, and his own, pursued quickly. It was useless however. He wondered if it truly was StarCom Federation as the symbology implied, or if that was misleading, a deliberate ruse.

The pursuing Union ships only managed to strike hits as the gargantuan starship prepared to jump into hyper-space, it actually seeming to solidify for some moments before it jumped in a blinding white flash, elongating and disappearing in the blink of an eye.

Chapter V

"All stand to attention for First Lord Yassin Al-Zuhairi!" the House marine guard shouted. He was wearing A-Zu Industries power-armour, one of the best types of House armour available.

Everybody on the bridge of the noble barge *OWSS Pairika* stood immediately, saluting in the House Al-Zuhairi way, palm out and back of the right hand to the forehead. "At ease," said First Lord Al-Zuhairi, striding confidently through the large bridge towards the central command section. The rest of the crew relaxed their salute, returning to their stations and tasks.

The bridge was circular in design, with the command section in the centre. The ship had been built by the interstellar commercial success that was A-Zu Industries, owned entirely by the Al-Zuhairi family and providing military equipment and designs all over the former Red Imperium of Mars.

The *Pairika* was a Persian-class noble barge, itself a design bought by many Houses throughout the former Imperium. It was built for luxury, but also had significant hidden weaponry systems that made it one of the best noble barges available. Yassin owned the first one ever produced, passed down to him from his father.

"We are nearing the translation into the terminus point, First Lord," said the Captain of his barge. "We will translate back into real-space in less than two minutes."

"Carry on, Captain," said First Lord Al-Zuhairi, sitting in the throne situated in the very centre of the bridge.

There was a flash of white light, and then an eye-wateringly elongated and distorted hull of a series of starships appeared out of the nothingness. Their forms snapped back into their proper shapes as the translation out of hyper-space into real-space was completed, drifting forwards at the same slow rate of propulsion as they had been using before they jumped into warp.

The noble barge *OWSS Pairika* was in the centre, two Type-II Marauder-class A-Zu Industries battlecruisers behind, and a Type-I Behemoth-class dreadnought in front. The four ships increased their forward propulsion, automatically raising shields as soon as they had full power back and the warp fields had dissipated enough to allow it. Weaponry batteries were open in a display of power. The ships had jumped into a dangerous target-zone, after all.

The Bukhara System was in complete disarray. There were signs of heavy fighting, with warships of all sizes and descriptions listing, dead in the water or heavily damaged and barely functioning. Space-based defences were destroyed, and a gigantic military starbase where most of the ruins and wreckage were focused still had crackles of energy around it as it died. Even as the OutWorlds Alliance noble squadron approached, a half-squadron consisting of a dreadnought and two battlecruisers were busy firing on it, completely taking the starbase apart.

A ring of destroyers surrounded the largest planet, Bukhara VI, firing down onto its surface. Military transporters were in orbit, and fleets of small landing craft bearing the sunburst orange and brown OutWorlds Alliance symbol were still shuttling invasion forces down to the ground.

There were more destroyers around Bukhara V and Bukhara III, assisting the forces taking the other two populated planets in-system. Smaller Alliance frigates were actually docked to the two mining stations around the gas giant Bukhara IX, marines having captured and subdued the facilities. The Bukhara Stargate had been conquered early on in the fight.

The majority of the starships that were either captured, damaged or destroyed were Frontier Hegemony, and it was clear to anyone that the OutWorlds Alliance now had the system.

Chief Commander Al-Saadi stood and saluted as the holographic image of First Lord Yassin Al-Zuhairi appeared in front of him. Omar Al-Saadi was still aboard his dreadnought, the *SS Persepolis*, having led the invasion of the Bukhara System.

"At ease," said First Lord Yassin Al-Zuhairi. "You have virtually conquered this system within ten hours, Chief Commander. The congratulations of House Al-Zuhairi are owed once again to House Al-Saadi."

"Thank you, First Lord," said Chief Commander Al-Saadi. "The fighting was heavy, but we were victorious. The Frontier Hegemony forces in-system were prepared, but we took them unawares. The land invasions of the Bukhara planets should be completed within another two hours, and then the system is owned by the OutWorlds Alliance."

"How is it gone in the other theatres?" asked First Lord Al-Zuhairi.

"I'm transmitting a full report for you to read at leisure," said Chief Commander Al-Saadi, nodding at the communications officer nearby. "We struck in five systems simultaneously, without warning. The Frontier Hegemony defensive forces have folded in all but one system. I have had to authorise a reserve fleet to jump in, as our intelligence was off – there were more ships and more defensive gun platforms and droid mines than expected."

Al-Zuhairi gave a wry smile. "Chief Amab will not be impressed at the intel failure. I will enjoy telling him."

Chief Commander Al-Saadi actually laughed. His eyes were alight with the joy of the fight, it had made the normally reserved man come alive. "The invasion of the Frontier Hegemony has begun very well, my Lord."

*

Lord Commander-In-Chief James Gavain sat on the bridge of the *Vindicator,* not displaying any sign of nervousness. In truth, he was not anxious at all. He had jumped into major war-zones and battles of an unimaginable scale, and despite the possibility for things to go wrong, he had been in much more dangerous situations than this.

<Exactly twenty minutes to the jump, Jamie,> said Captain Erica Georgia on their private channel.

<Lieutenant Forrest,> he said over the datasphere, <set up the comms conference connection for me now, please.>

<By your command, sir.>

As he waited the few seconds for the four-way conference call to be set up and the holographic projectors to engage, Gavain reviewed the sensors and scanners feed one more time.

His own *Vindicator* battlecruiser had been met in another system by the Vanguard Squadron of the Vindicatus First Fleet, so he had no less than six ex-Praetorian Guard ships-of-the-line leading the jump to the rendezvous within House Jorgensson territory. The Vanguard Squadron was led by the promoted Vice-Admiral Kenzie Viederhaun aboard the battlecruiser *Revenging Angel,* and also consisted of the *Carnivorous* C-class battlecruiser under Captain Zane McDonnagh, the *Ubermacht* destroyer under the promoted Captain Huyton, and the two strikecruisers *Snake-Eyes* and *Slaughter.*

The Levitican Union Armed Forces ships were also present, protecting the noble barges *LSS Divine Right* and *LSS Crown of Claes,* the ships used by Lord Minister Micalek Zupanic and Lord Minister Brin Claes. Leading those was the personal warship used by Lord Luke Towers, the dreadnought *LSS Knightsword.* House dreadnoughts were far inferior to the version produced by Praetorian technology, but they were still among the most powerful warships available to the Houses.

The Levitican Union Armed Forces had sent a mixed force consisting of no less than twelve warships, which themselves were carefully chosen to represent the seven Houses that made up the Union itself. Amongst them were three House Marchenko ships, with the two hundred and first son of Lord Gregori Marchenko aboard. No Marchenko ship could travel without a House Marchenko noble family member on hand to provide a focal point for the collective consciousness of the Marchenkan people.

The presence of the three House Marchenko ships, and the two House Zupanic warships, worried Gavain greatly but there was nothing he could do about it. It was Marchenko and Zupanic who were conspiring secretly together to begin the war against House Jorgensson, and their involvement in this attempt to forge a peace was a potential real conflict of interest. There was no way to avoid it however, as not only was Lord Minister Micalek the person in charge of the Levitican Union Armed Forces, but the entire structure of the LUAF was for a combined mixture of ships-of-the-line from all the Houses that formed the Union.

The holographic images of Lord Luke Towers, Lord Micalek Zupanic, and Lord Brin Claes appeared before Lord Gavain. How much his life had moved on, he thought; even in the run-up to the Battle of Mars and the death of the False Emperor, he had never imagined he would be in a position or situation such as this, the ruler of his own nation and meeting with the heads of state of others.

"Gentlemen," he said, treating them as equals and not his superiors, "We are all assembled here in the JC-3403 System, within the House Towers region of the Union, and I assume all of you are ready to jump? We have twenty minutes until it is time for us to leave, according to schedule."

"We are ready," said Lord Micalek, who was in charge of the Armed Forces with the exception of Gavain's ships. "It would be helpful if you told us where we were jumping to, Lord Gavain."

Lord Gavain nodded. "I am sure all here understand the need for secrecy. The nature of this negotiation is far too delicate to allow it to be derailed. We are jumping into House Jorgensson territory, taking the direct one-jump route to the Alesund System."

"The Alesund System?" said Lord Luke, frowning. "That is heavily defended, one of the more important star systems in House Jorgensson's landholding."

"We are formed up in half a major fleet, Lord Luke," said Lord Micalek pointedly. "I am sure Lord Gavain knows what he is doing."

"I do," said Gavain shortly. "I have up to date intelligence on what is in that system, obtained by my own Chief of Intelligence. Transmitting the data now."

"So who are we negotiating with?" asked Lord Minister Brin Claes, "I know you are leading the preliminary discussion, but afterwards I need to take control."

Gavain kept his expression neutral, as he said, "We are not meeting the House Lord Oren Jorgensson himself, but two of his sons. We will be rendezvousing with Lord Jorrik Jorgensson and Lord Sven Jorgensson. After the preliminary discussions, Lord Oren Jorgensson will meet with

Lady Sophia Towers in House Towers territory to conclude the agreement, if any."

Gavain was not happy about the choice of people they were meeting. Lord Jorrik Jorgensson was the eldest, and due to inherit the throne when his ailing father passed away. He had a fearsome reputation, almost as bad as Lord Micalek Zupanic's, but he was not the concern. The major worry was the younger Lord Sven Jorgensson, who was named in the data-files they had obtained from the Rosicrux conspiracy as being an active supporter and funder of the plot to tear the Union apart. He was supposed to take control of whatever remained of House Jorgensson following the war, as Marchenko and Zupanic divided the Union between them. He was just as much implicated and guilty of the shadowy manoeuvrings as Houses Zupanic and Marchenko.

"What exactly have you said to House Jorgensson?" Lord Brin Claes asked.

"That we wished to meet," said Lord Gavain, "that we were aware that war was brewing between our nations, and that I personally had no wish to see my nation dragged into it through the defence pact we have with the Levitican Union. Lord Oren believes me, and sees the truth in my words. He also realises I think that House Jorgensson could not hope to win against our militaries, and that it would spell the end of Jorgensson. I have suggested to him that the first objective of our discussions is to avoid war and a reduction in the military build-ups on Jorgensson-Union borders, the second is to create a formal treaty of non-aggression, and the third possibility is the joining of House Jorgensson to the Levitican Union."

"It sounds good," said Lord Brin Claes, "but they refused joining initially because of House Towers being one of the founding members of the Union. What has changed there?"

"Apparently they view House Towers differently," said Lord Gavain, "Among other things, it was based partly on a dislike of Lord Erik Towers, but also the humanist leanings of the House under Erik. With Lady Sophia as head of house, they see a change, particularly with Sophia's strong alliance and friendship with me, a borg. The borgite House Jorgensson believe things have changed and the Union is different, and that's why Lord Luke is here, to help convince them of that."

"Well, let us all hope it works out," said Lord Micalek, with a sincerity that Gavain just did not believe. "Otherwise, we are at war."

*

"It is intolerable, Admiral Harley Andersson," said Solar High Chancellor Zhou Mao. Mao was a member of the House of Zhou, one of the two ruling mega-Houses of the Zhou-Zheng Compact. "The continuing support of this upstart Vindicatus nation of yours is destabilising the entire situation here."

Harley Andersson had disliked the man from the instant the conversation had started. He was a part of the leadership that had led to the deathcamps in Compact territory, where borgs were being killed in the millions simply because they were augmented. This was a conversation via pulse-channel using a streaming Hyper-Pulse Communications Generator, and for that Andersson was glad. He would have utterly detested meeting this untrustworthy man in real life.

"We have a right to ally ourselves with who we wish," said Admiral Harley Andersson. "House Lord Gavain has publicly stated that Vindicatus is not borgite or humanist in its leanings, but free-thinking. We support people from all backgrounds and all walks of life, be it augmented or unaugmented or something else entirely. And whilst I am an Admiral, in the political life of the Vindicatus government, my title is the same as yours, Solar High Chancellor."

Chancellor Zhou Mao sneered. "I earnt my title during the years of the Red Imperium of Mars," he hissed, "My title is real, yours is not. Like everything else in your upstart nation, it is a parody of the Imperial House structure and a mockery of the glory that was the Red Imperium."

"As you say," Andersson said non-committedly.

"I do say. I also say that you must cease your support of the Erdogan nation and House Erdogan. The nation is about to fall to Compact forces, you cannot deny that, we all can see it. Erdogan will surrender in full to the Primarch and the Primarchess of Zhou and Zheng. If at that point the Vindicatus nation continues to support Erdogan cyborgs, particularly accepting them in such high numbers into your territory, we shall see it as an act of sedition aimed at ourselves, and respond accordingly."

"It will be no act of sedition," said Chancellor Andersson, "It is an act of mercy, and protection against genocidal persecution."

"You have already hidden Lord and Lady Erdogan in your territory, and are accepting large numbers of Erdogan military into your borders. That in itself is enough to provoke an attack by the Zhou-Zheng Compact."

"You are simply not strong enough to succeed," said Chancellor Andersson. "We are in strong possession of Praetorian Guard technology, remember that. Many of us are ex-Praetorian Guard."

Zhou Mao laughed, and then said furiously, "Hand over the Lord and Lady Erdogan, and Feldmarshall Grant, and extradite all Erdogan nationals to our custody. Reject those military assets that have transferred into your land. Refuse the entry of any more. Otherwise we will see continued support to be an act of aggression. So says the Zhou-Zheng Compact. *Solar High Chancellor* Zhou Mao so speaks." With that, the communication ended.

Chancellor Andersson let a strong exhale of frustrated breath flow out, rubbing his eyes tiredly. Handling the politics in Gavain's absence was nerve-wracking, especially when receiving threats or dealing with situations like that.

The thought of Jamie Gavain made him frown, but he dismissed it. He was getting an inkling that all was not right between them, but he was not sure what the issue was. There was no denying it though, Jamie was changing rapidly. He had always been a great man, but now he was exceeding all expectations in terms of what he could achieve.

Andersson jacked fully into the datasphere, reviewing the latest reports from all sections of the Vindicatus nation. He paid first attention to those of Lord and Lady Erdogan.

The Lady Queen Ebru Erdogan was now their Administrator for Treasury and Trade. She was by all accounts doing a very good job. It was part of the Erdogan mindset to be industrious, and when it came to money both in terms of controlling it and making it they were naturals at it. She was well with Andersson in terms of setting up the industry of the Dark Heart System, expanding the mining operations in ways he had not thought of, creating surplus material and releasing it onto the trading markets of the Interstellar Merchants Guild. They had ships coming in from numerous Houses now to collect raw material stocks they had mined.

Quite beyond that she was excellent at managing the books, having introduced a very low tax system. She had even suggested a form of welfare support for the immigrants, but Andersson was holding back on that until they were more established in terms of a stable economy. The signs they were heading for one was there though, probably because of the immigrants rather than despite them. The immigrants were a main driving force behind the burgeoning trade and industry the Dark Heart System was already generating.

The Lord Consort Kemal Erdogan was acting as their Administrator for Communications and Transport. He had set up their own national media service, taken excellent control of the stargate service and the HyperPulse Communications Generators, and had their civilian ships chartered out to many new start-up businesses. The income being generated from his department of responsibility was growing rapidly, and many had commented on the improved service.

Feldmarshall Horatio Grant was acting as the Administrator for Law, Justice and Security. He had implemented Imperial Law and new versions of House Law, set up their own Justiciars and their enforcers. The crime rate was still low, but he was dealing with what existed in exemplary fashion.

Of course, all three also had other duties. Grant was maintaining a regular presence in the Erdogan territory as it collapsed, ensuring as many people as possible could escape from the genocide of the Zhou-Zheng Compact, in the process angering them and prompting Andersson's conversation today. Lord Gavain fully agreed however, and was ready to risk war with the Compact to prevent or even curtail the horrific genocide taking place in their deathcamps.

Andersson turned his thoughts away from the Erdogan nobles. Immigration into the Dark Heart System was still heavy, with every transport coming in through the Web being full to capacity, and even more civilian and personal starships arriving. Inevitably a new culture and world was being created within the Dark Heart System, a hybrid of Praetorian military, Erdogan, Van Der Meer and more.

Andersson had been resisting the implementation of a class system, but it could not be avoided. In the Praetorian Guard there was no such thing, but the burgeoning populace had virtually formed it themselves. People liked to know where they stood, he realised, and would put themselves in these artificial boxes whether he wanted them to or not. Earlier this week he had formalised it, but as yet all it affected was the universal tax contribution charged directly to each individual, with those in the higher classes paying more.

The Imperial class structure therefore survived. The alpha-class were the highest and the richest, with following beta-class, gamma-class, and then the lowly delta-class. The epsilon-class, the 'undesirables', made up their prison population and criminal fraternity, which still consisted mostly of Rosicrux prisoners-of-war. In many Houses and throughout the old Red Imperium, the class someone was placed in affected much more than just tax, being an indicator of quality of life and all sorts of additional benefits from advantages in law, to birthing options, to education and even health-care. The richest paid the most towards the state, and accordingly got the most benefits back, but in the Vindicatus nation that was not true. They paid more because it was their duty to. He and Gavain both agreed on this philosophy, and so it would be.

They were still looking for an Administrator of Migration Control, and an Administrator of the Ambassadorial Service. Andersson was not sure on how to approach this. Advertising for the positions seemed wrong somehow.

He came across the latest report from Captain Jason Bramhall, and read it with interest. The man was preparing in his role as the Administrator of Colonisation and Expansion to colonise and populate the new binary system. One of the colonyships would be used to start the colonisation, and some of the Mass Transporters would be used to take those migrants who had volunteered out of Dark Heart. Constructoships were being transferred across by an interstellar ferry-ship. It looked like the colony would be seeded with close to four hundred thousand people initially, with another three hundred thousand planned to come in afterwards. Captain Jason Bramhall was doing a brilliant job, and the colonisation was set for only three days away.

Field Marshal Andryukhin was working hard to build up his Marine forces and the droid army, but had still found time to swear violently over the escape of Silus Adare from Leviticus. O'Connor had stepped in, calming the aggressive man down, and was taking personal charge of the search for Adare. There was a direct link to the Rosicrux and whoever had controlled them, so O'Connor was already working on it in one respect. He had penetrated more of the StarCom Federation, and he was shortly due to have agents active in the OutWorlds Alliance and the Frontier Hegemony, where war had just broken out. That was in addition to his other big operation, the one in the direct control of Brigadier Vantanik, to deal with House Marchenko should all go wrong in the Levitican Union.

Andersson looked again briefly at the defences of the Dark Heart System, although that was more Lucas De Graaf's job than his. Harley had noticed that Lucas seemed to be handling the role as Admiral-of-the-Fleets well, although both he and Ulrik Andryukhin had shared concerns about the man's capability for the position.

Of course, Admiral De Graaf and First Fleet were no longer in the Dark Heart Artificial System, having left over two weeks ago. Andersson knew what the mission was, but their absence was top secret, and Chief of Intelligence Vice-Admiral O'Connor was carefully monitoring for any signs of their exit from the system being reported externally. So far, there was no indication First Fleet's quiet disappearance had been overtly reported by external or foreign intelligence agencies. Admiral Danae Markos was still present with Second Fleet, and Andersson knew he would have to inform her of the heightened threat from the Zhou-Zheng Compact.

All in all, things were progressing very nicely in the Vindicatus Nation.

*

Lady Wyn Zupanic walked through the secret corridors of Zupanic Palace quietly, without guards, still resenting the necessity which was causing her to hide her existence even in her own palace. She was supposed to be dead, and indeed that was why everyone thought her son Micalek was now the head of House Zupanic. It was a necessary blind, however, and she firmly had her sights on the future.

Zupanic Palace was on the planet Zupanica, in the centre of the city of Savrecik, within the Dalcice System. It was the capital of capitals for House Zupanic. She still had absolute control of the intelligence agency of House Zupanic, although she ruled from the shadows. She provided the same service to her eldest son as she had to his father, just not openly. The Rosicrux operation continued without the Rosicrux, she had her son as head of the House, and all was proceeding as she had always planned it.

She emerged from the secret corridor into the private quarters of another of her sons. The medic and the servants moving around his reclining suspensor-seat took one look at her robed figure, and quietly left the room without word. They did not know who she was, but they all knew Xavier received this mysterious visitor and that when he did, they had to leave.

Her heart almost broke as she looked at the destroyed face of her son, still under reconstruction. Half his head had been removed by what she strongly suspected to be agents of Lord Gavain, and the brain damage was still ongoing. Although Xavier had always been considered insane, so the nastier rumour-mongers suggested there was little difference. There was certainly no love lost between the two brothers, Micalek and Xavier.

"Mother," said Xavier, drooling slightly as she pulled back the hood on her robe.

"Xav," said Lady Wyn. "You look well," she lied.

He giggled with child-like amusement, the sheer madness obvious in his eyes. "As well as I can be," he gurgled. "I can't wait to get back to playing with my experiments," he added. Lady Wyn carefully did not reply, finding his medical experiments something more akin to brutal torture, although it did have its uses, sometimes.

"You should be moving around normally and back in full operation in another week or two, I am being told," said Lady Wyn, taking a seat opposite her beloved son.

"Yes, I should," he said, clapping his hands excitedly. "I'm just so sorry that you can't be the same, mummy," he added, "How long do you have to hide? I can't stand Micci being the House Lord."

"He won't be for long," said Lady Wyn. "He plays his part well, but he is not his father, and I do not trust him."

"Where is he now?"

"He is with the party going into the House Jorgensson system. Lord Sven Jorgensson and Micalek have their orders from me, they know how to play their part to disrupt this pathetic attempt at peace."

"Another betrayal," said Xavier excitedly, opening his eyes melodramatically.

"Yes," said Lady Wyn, "Lord Sven Jorgensson will attack the peace party as they arrive, and start the war. There will be no warning. With luck they might even dispose of James Gavain for us."

"And then we split the Union between us three? Jorgensson, Marchenko and Zupanic?"

"Just Marchenko and Zupanic," Lady Wyn replied. "Sven Jorgensson thinks he will replace his father and elder brother, and maybe he will for a short time. But we will prosecute the war against Jorgensson to its fullest extent, not curtail it as Sven expects. He will lose his territory. And then, we will divide the Levitican Union between us, Marchenko and Zupanic splitting the war-weary Armed Forces apart and taking full control. Micalek is in the best place to do that, as the Minister for Military Defence."

"And after that all happens?" asked Xavier.

"House Marchenko is fully in my thrall," said Lady Wyn, "Lord Gregori Marchenko will not betray me, both of us have connections to the Shadow Council, we both know the truth of what is coming."

"The Shadow Council? They who run the Faceless assassins?"

"Them and much more," said Lady Wyn. "It was them behind the Rosicrux. There is a big change about to happen in the galaxy, and we shall be a part of it. Of course I trust no-one, not even the Shadow Council, so we will be ready for betrayal by House Marchenko. The plots run by the Shadow Council are incredibly convoluted, plans within plans, and I trust them as much as I trust our own House."

"How interesting, mother. What is to come?"

"That I cannot speak of, my son, in truth partly because even I do not know the full details. I trust that the Shadow Council will doubtless spring some form of surprise on me. The data from Vindicatus shows they were involved in far, far much more than I suspected."

"What will happen to Lady Principal Sophia and Micalek, then? Will they die?"

"Well, Lady Principal Sophia is about to have her baby," said Lady Wyn. "She has finally come out publicly about it, although of course even she doesn't know that Micalek inseminated her in her sleep, using a deep-ranging dermal hypojector. Micalek's inclusion in my plans was on the basis that nothing happened to her, but of course, once the war is concluded and his part is done, I will not keep that promise. She will be killed, and her brother Luke. We will have House Towers territory by both conquest and correctly in name, something that should pacify the populace."

"Micci will not like that," Xavier said.

"He will not live to dislike it," said Lady Wyn, an evil glint in her eye. "My son has fallen for Lady Sophia. He is no longer loyal to me. I have no doubt he plots to do away with me himself. All Zupanics are the same, even you, Xavier."

"No, mummy, not me, I am ever loyal to you."

"Well, maybe you are in that, and that is why I love you," you absolute insanely mad psychotic man, she thought to herself disparagingly with anything but love, "but Micalek can no longer be trusted. He is tainted. He has signed the document with Lady Sophia saying he will never have any claim on her territory. It matters not. Micalek will be assassinated, Sophia and Luke Towers will be assassinated, and I will emerge from the shadows again. I will take my rightful place as the Head of House, and Micalek and Sophia's son will inherit the thrones of both Houses joined together. It will be glorious. It is the future."

Xavier giggled again madly, clapping his hands as he did so. "Yes, mother," he said, "oh yes."

*

The Alesund System was heavily populated, with many planets terraformed and colonised. There were several space stations and starbases, its own stargate, a massive astronomical array capable of long-distance observation on an unimaginable scale, and more besides. It had a significant military presence, with an entire planetoid devoted to being a House Jorgensson military base and complex.

There was usually a heavy influx and egress of interstellar commercial shipping, but it had all been denied entry. No-one in the system knew why. All noted however that the naval starships had lined up near one of the designated jump points roughly half-way into the system, facing in towards the jump point. There was a media blackout. Even intrastellar shipping was restricted to the fringes of the system. The entire system was locked down, at the cost of a fantastic amount of money.

The reason become apparent as multiple sensors and scanners detected the jump-signature of a vast fleet of incoming ships. The disturbances created in real-space by the approaching warp-capable ships caused a major spike in heat signatures on infra-red, magnetic disturbances, and a gravity distortion. The incoming signs of the imminent arrival of a large number of ships did not allow the precise number to be identified by the civilian watchers, but the military awaiting them knew all about who it was, and how many there were.

The flash of white light was so blinding as the fleet arrived in-system that it could be detected even beyond the boundaries of the solar system. As it cleared, the mass visual distortion of the arriving ships was as fearsome as it was unusual, the fleet solidifying in seconds.

The Jorgensson naval ships did not have their shields raised, although weapon ports were open. The incoming ships had their weapon ports open too, but that was not in itself unusual and was permitted according to the protocol they had agreed.

The Jorgensson naval fleet came in to meet the Levitican Union and Vindicatus nation naval ships as they remained where they were, also again according to protocol. The civilians who watched from afar were nervous, this being completely unexpected, not knowing where it was going to lead.

<All the expected ships are present, Lord Jorrik,> said his second-in-command aboard the House dreadnought ship *JSS Heartrender.*

<It appears as if they have kept to their end of the bargain,> said Lord Jorrik Jorgensson, <My father was right. This Lord Gavain can be trusted. What do their Praetorian ships look like?>

<Here, sir,> said his Captain, calling up a holographic image for him.

<Amazing ships,> commented Lord Jorrik.

<That battlecruiser, the *Vindicator,* is now famous throughout the galaxy,> said his Captain, <Just one Praetorian battlecruiser can quite comfortably engage up to five House cruisers, and it could eat us for breakfast, Lord.>

<Just as well they are here in peace, and we do not intend to start a war,> said Lord Jorrik. <As much as my brother would like one.>

<The *Vindicator* is hailing us, identity is the callsign of Lord James Gavain,> said the communications officer.

<Signal the fleet. Cancel the red alert, stand down to yellow,> Lord Jorrik said, relaxing somewhat. Hopefully this was all going to go according to plan, and there might yet be hope for peace. <Accept the comms.>

As Lord Gavain spoke in his private, secured channel with the holographic image of Lord Jorrik, Captain Erica Georgia busied herself with checking the disposition of their ships against those of the House Jorgensson military welcoming committee.

In their case, the Praetorian Guard ships of the Vindicatus nation were at the forefront, arranged in a vertically one-up, one-down tooth line. Behind came two rows of six LUAF warships each, sandwiched between them the two noble barges.

The twenty-two House Jorgensson ships awaiting them were grouped into four squadrons, in a rough quarter circle all around the designated jump-point. It was obvious from reading the data intelligence they were already stealing secretly through their advanced technology that two of the squadrons were directly under the control of Lord Jorrik, and two under Lord Sven, although nominally Jorrik was in effective command of all of them. They had two dreadnoughts there, House built but still formidable, as well as two star-carriers, a number of heavy battlecruisers and a mix of strikecruisers and old-fashioned light cruisers. They were light on destroyers and frigates, with virtually none present. It was quite a heavy show of force, but the Praetorian Guard ships of the Vindicatus Mercenary Corporation more than evened the odds.

Then it all began to happen very fast.

<Captain, are you seeing this?> said the data-tac officer, Lieutenant Woolfe.

<Yes,> she said, frowning, <There is an increase in comms signals from the dreadnought *Heartbreaker*, identified as the flagship of Lord Sven. He is the one who we know was affiliated to the Rosicrux.>

<Warning, warning, the two squadrons under Lord Sven are raising their shields!>

<Red alert,> said Captain Georgia, triggering the automatic procedure to raise their own. As it was happening, she broke into Lord Gavain's mind through the datasphere to tell him what was happening.

<Lord Gavain,> said Lord Jorrik, frowning, <It appears that your Praetorian ships are raising their shields. What is the meaning of this?>

<Lord Sven is raising the shields on his two squadrons,> said Gavain, <We did not agree this. Are you about to attack us?>

<No, I swear to you, I have given no such order.>

Gavain believed the reply. He checked again, and then said, <Lord Sven's ships are preparing to fire, Lord Jorrik. Stop your brother now.> Gavain thought fast. <Look,> he said, <I'll transmit to you secret data we have on Sven, do not trust him, he's working against you! Sending the data now!>

<Lord Sven,> said his Captain aboard the *Heartbreaker*, <Your brother Lord Jorrik is attempting to contact us, demanding to know why we are raising shields.>

<Tell him my reply is that we will never have peace with the Levitican Union, and I am doing what he should have done months ago, starting the beginning of the end,> Lord Sven Jorgensson said.

Then he stood, leaned forwards, eyes alight, and said aloud, "Fire!"

Lord Micalek Zupanic watched as it all began to unravel exactly according to plan. Lord Sven had turned traitor to his brother, and had begun to fire on the Levitican Union Armed Forces. The Praetorian Guard ships of Gavain were taking the brunt of the attack.

"Signal the entire fleet," Lord Micalek said, pretending to be surprised, "We must protect the noble barges. All ships, raise shields and return fire, move into attack vectors now."

"Aye sir, the order is given," replied his Captain.

<How can I believe this data, Lord Gavain, it says my brother is a traitor. That he plans for war, and to betray me and my father,> said Lord Jorrik.

<Believe it because he is starting a war,> said Lord Gavain urgently. <He is firing on us, I have not given the order to return fire. But I will if you do not stop him.>

Lord Jorrik read the return message from his brother's ship. It was inconceivable, but it seemed that Lord Sven had indeed intended to start a war here today. It did not mean he intended to kill Jorrik though, or their father. That could just be all part of a trap, and besides which, his tactical map was telling him that the Levitican Union ships were now firing

<I am sorry, Lord Gavain,> said Lord Jorrik, <Whatever the truth, it has gone too far. We must resolve this battle, and then maybe one of us can talk to the other as a prisoner afterwards.>

He signed off, cursing his brother Sven privately as he did so.

<All ships, return fire on the Levitican Union ships-of-the-line,> Lord Jorrik ordered.

"I have failed," said Lord Gavain aloud, shaking his head. He too was now standing on the bridge of his own ship, in sheer disbelief. He shook himself though, mentally if not physically. The war was beginning and heavy weaponry fire was splitting space apart with multi-coloured, beautiful traces and trails of pure death.

<We have an incoming hyper-pulse message from the Blackheath System, as scheduled,> said Captain Erica Georgia.

<Tell Admiral Lucas we have failed, and he is to jump to the Alesund System immediately,> said Gavain. Even though he had wanted this to work, he had to allow a back-up plan in case it failed. <He is to bring First Fleet here immediately, we take the Alesund System in its entirety.>

<Aye sir,> said Captain Georgia.

<And inform Brigadier Vantanik that the Black Ops plan to deal with House Marchenko is now active,> said Gavain. There was no chance he was going to let House Marchenko and House Zupanic turn this further to their advantage. The Union might be about to enter a war with House Jorgensson thanks to the treachery of House nobles on both sides, but Gavain would see to it that it ended the way he wanted it to still.

Chapter VI

Admiral-of-the-Fleets Lucas De Graaf was nervous. They had been waiting, disguised within the Blackheath System, fully chameleonically fielded so no-one knew they were there. At the appropriate time they had dropped their 'stealth' fields, and whilst dealing with the surprised Union military, he had accessed the Hyper-Pulse Communications Generators and sent the planned message direct to the *Vindicator* in the Alesund System.

The message back from James Gavain was not good. They had been ordered to jump directly to the Alesund System, using the stargate to travel there quickly and across the distance, which was much in excess of what even a Praetorian warship was capable of travelling without recharging.

He placed a Code Red on the Blackheath Stargate, ordering its Chief of Station to target the Alesund Stargate, and gave the order for the twenty-three ships in the four remaining squadrons of First Fleet to jump through. Within minutes, they were on their way.

The actual journey took weeks in transit time, but in real-time they were due to translate through the Alesund Stargate only five or six minutes after the battle had started.

<We are translating in less than ten seconds, Admiral De Graaf,> said his Captain.

Fully jacked in to the datasphere of the Praetorian T-class dreadnought *Thor's Hammer*, Admiral De Graaf acknowledged the report.

The translation was smooth, as stargate jumps always were. Being fully jacked in, it took barely seconds for full scanners and sensors to operate, and he realised that his full fleet had successfully translated through.

The battle had just turned for the Levitican Union. Under his command and included the five ships of the Vanguard Squadron that had accompanied James Gavain, besides his dreadnought Admiral De Graaf had five battlecruisers, four destroyers, three interdictors, three star-carriers, and seven strikecruisers.

<All ships,> he said, reading the data transmitting in from Gavain already on the House Jorgensson ships and their identities, <Break squadron formation in attack plan alpha. Strikecruisers to advance ahead of the main fleet, use your speed to engage the enemy. Star-carriers to launch all starfighters and starbombers for a second wave. We attack in waves, destroyers and interdictors last. Interdictors to activate your interdiction fields as soon as the translation disruption dies away, we are not allowing any of the enemy to jump out-system.

<Our primary targets are the *Heartrender* and *Heartbreaker* house dreadnoughts, to be boarded and captured with the detention of the two Jorgensson Lords a priority. All other ships can be destroyed. Those are our rules of engagement. Good luck, people. De Graaf out.>

He found it somewhat reassuring that his first naval action at his new rank was one in which Gavain was also present, just in case he did do something wrong. It was nice to know his friend and colleague was there for support, and that he was also leaving command up to him.

*

Lady Principal Sophia was sipping her early morning coffee, the eating wand on the cleared breakfast plate before her, when The Spider Elaine Carrington suddenly called her.

"What is it, Elaine?" she said into the holoretta controlled projection of Elaine Carrington. The holographic image of her personal spy chief was being sent directly onto her retina.

"I thought I ought to give you advance warning," said Elaine Carrington, "you're probably about to be told officially."

"This does not sound good," said Lady Principal Sophia.

"It's not. War has just broken out in the Alesund System. There is a heavy engagement underway."

"By the Emperor's eyes," Lady Principal Sophia swore. "Lord Gavain's plan has failed."

"He had more plans, I think," said Elaine Carrington.

"Really? Such as what?"

"A large portion of one of his fleets has just left the Blackheath System. They're jumping to Alesund, they must be there by now."

"At least we will win," said Lady Sophia, sipping her coffee. She was frowning, sharp pain affecting her stomach. She did not really think about it. It was common during the pregnancy. "I will have to convene a special meeting of the Council. We are now officially at war. One did not want –"

Elaine Carrington's image frowned. "Sophia, what is it?" she asked. "Is it the baby?"

It all hit her suddenly, like a slap across the face. "I'm giving birth," she said quietly, in a shocked voice. "I think this is it .... I'm giving birth!"

*

Brigadier Vantanik was in the Levitican Union, on the planet Leviticus. He was a cybernetic biomorph, one of the many thousands created by the accelerated growth biovats of Dr Erin Presson and formed from Faceless technology. He was not currently hidden in a secret operation, and nor was he displaying the usual image he wore to make the normal humans and cyborgs feel relaxed. He appeared as a blank, featureless, jet black-skinned creature, his natural state.

The incoming message from Lord Gavain was received. He had been aware of what was at stake in the Alesund System, and he was not surprised that it had all gone bad and they were now engaging in the first battle of a new war. Gavain had ordered him to activate the Black Operation.

He sent a message via his implant to the Hyper-Pulse Communications Generator on Leviticus. <This is Brigadier Vantanik of the Vindicatus Mercenary Corporation,> he said.

<Receiving you loud and clear, Brigadier. You are speaking to the Chief of Station.>

<Lord Gavain has prepaid for a Code Red priority usage of the HPCG, I believe.>

<He has indeed. I must say, never have I been paid up-front for so many Code Red signals. There are well over a hundred.>

<There are,> said Brigadier Vantanik, <I have transmitted you the coded communications as we have spoken. Send them now, Chief of Station, identical messages to all destinations.>

<Of course, as you command, Brigadier.>

<In the events that are to follow, remember the confidentiality agreement you signed with Lord Gavain and Lady Principal Sophia. You will soon work out from where they have been sent and the news media what we have done. Ever speak, and you will be exterminated, Chief of Station.>

Vantanik broke the connection before the poor Chief of Station could answer, and then sent a message to the units he had in position on the Planet Leviticus. <Team, we are go. Commence attack.>

Lady Minister Eranisch Marchenko was relaxing in her quarters in the Levitican Capital City, in as much as any slaved mind to the Marchenko cyborg consciousness could ever relax. She was connected into the Hyper-Pulse Communications Generator, uploading and downloading data directly to Lord Gregori Marchenko on the capital planet of House Marchenko, Tal'chyn.

Lady Minister Eranisch Marchenko did not see or feel the servant behind her disconnect from the hive consciousness she broadcast, partly because such a thing so rarely happened. When it did, it was usually a temporary glitch, a failure which could lead to insanity in the borg unit that had disconnected.

She did feel the deaths of the servants around her, and despite the constantly streaming data roaming through her enlarged cranial cavity, she turned to look. The blade of the biomorphic soldier went straight between her eyes, a second blade severing her neck and spinal cord with a viscous spray of arterial blood.

Lord Gregori Marchenko and his wife, Lady Banuska Marchenko, were in the Marchenkan Tower Palace on Tal'chyn, many jumps away from the death of Lady Minister Eranisch. He only knew of it instantly as she saw the creature killing her, and he stared in shock at the download he had just received via pulse-channel. With unbelievable volumes of data flowing through him and his wife, it had taken a short few seconds to identify what had happened.

There were some other House Marchenko sons and daughters currently directly connected via continuous HPCG, and suddenly more of them began to die. In some cases he saw images of biomorphic soldiers attacking, their identities unknown. He had only ever seen the Faceless assassins of the True and False Emperors behave in such a brutal and direct way.

<We are under att -> he began to say to Lady Banuska.

He never finished the sentence, as the biomorph standing behind him had plunged a blade through the back of his head and out of his mouth. As his brain short-circuited and died due to the energy crackling along the blade, he saw the head of his wife toppling into her lap, another biomorph still twirling around where he had decapitated her, severing her spinal cord.

The Lady of House Marchenko was in charge of the civilian convoy, awaiting a jump from the House Lapointe solar system. All ships had to recharge, and the Lady who ruled the small convoy and provided the central intelligence consciousness for the Marchenkan hivers was paying attention to the mechanical running of her convoy of cargo-freighters and transporters.

She looked up as one of the crew disconnected, about to call for a medic, but halting when she saw the figure morphing physically into something else. She sent out a localised warning, a bare second before the biomorphic figure blew her brains out with a well-aimed and precise laser shot. The blade through her neck was just to make doubly sure of the kill.

"All of you must pay attention to the creed of House Marchenko," said the Lord of the Marchenko House, addressing the potential converts before him. He was part of the Ministry for Transformation and Integration, but was preaching at the packed crowd in front of him in this busy city square of the Claes world. They would take as many converts to the hive mind consciousness as he could possibly convince.

The crowd in front of him began screaming, and he wondered why. Then he looked down, at the long, bloody blade poking out of his chest. He realised he was dead when his brains drooled down his shirt front, parting either side of the sword blade, and then the data-stream that was him in the pool of localised consciousness vanished and he was gone forever.

The battlewalker was storming along the ground, engaged in precise manoeuvres with the rest of the Levitican Union military. The Lord of House Marchenko was also a General in the Levitican Union Armed Forces, and he loved his job as much as someone slaved to the hive mind could. He was a focal point for the Marchenkan military on this planet, someone they linked to, so he had more individuality than the rest but he was still a slave.

At least he was, until the pilot suddenly stopped the battlewalker. The General and Lord of House Marchenko was still demanding of the pilot to know what had happened, even as the pilot was jumping out of the emergency hatch.

A moment later, the battlewalker control cabin exploded, and the Lord was killed outright, atomised into nothingness.

The Lady of House Marchenko walked through the gardens on the Marchenko world, using what was left of her individuality to take enjoyment from the surroundings. She stopped, kneeling to smell a flower before her.

The orange petals went pure red as the blade swished through the air.

The young Lord of House Marchenko was no older than eight, but he had already taken full command of the consciousness. Over four hundred thousand Marchenkan mind-slaves depended on him, despite his weakened physical state. He lay in his bed, awaiting more surgery to attach another hideous implant to his body. He was asleep, but his mind burned with data.

He therefore never saw nor felt the blade that decapitated him, staining the pure white bedclothes a strong vibrant colour as he died.

*

The Vindicatus cybernetic biomorph was disguised as a House Marchenko marine guard. He had a half-squad of four other cybernetic biomorphs with him. The technology they were using to pretend they were members of the Marchenko hive consciousness was very advanced, in itself a special implant placed into his head to ape the behaviour and actions of a Marchenko hive-mind linked drone cyborg.

The starship he was assigned to was currently fighting in the Alesund System, one of three fighting against the House Jorgensson fleet that had ambushed them. Regardless of the situation, he had his orders, a pulse-channel message directed to his personal communications implant. Disconnecting the special implant from the hive-mind, he used his internal modem to signal the other four.

He leapt forward, morphing as he did so, both hands and arms changing into blades. He was stood directly behind the Lady of House Marchenko in charge of the hive-mind linked three Marchenko starships. He crossed the blades over her neck from behind, his right blade on her left shoulder, his left blade on her right.

In one smoothly violent motion and before anyone could react, he uncrossed his arms, and decapitated the Lady. The other three members of his squad were already firing as the Marchenko individuals began to lose their minds, no longer connected to the hive mind consciousness that had been their life. Escape from the ship would be easy.

<The Marchenko starships have ceased firing,> said the tactical officer aboard the *Vindicator*. <They are losing all power.>

<Brigadier Vantanik's agents have done their work then,> said Gavain, pleased at the quick response.

<The biomorphs on board will be exiting via life-pod, heading for insertion back to one of the Jorgensson planets,> said Captain Erica Georgia. The biomorphs would change appearances several times before catching a civilian transporter off-planet, and eventually returning to the Vindicatus nation.

Gavain was monitoring the situation in the battle closely, pleased to see how well Lucas De Graaf was handling his fleet. <What is the situation on the two primary targets?>

De Graaf had brought his *Thor's Hammer* dreadnought forwards at the forefront of the First Fleet attack, and the Praetorian Guard ships were making mincemeat of the inferior House Jorgensson warships. He had launched marine strikepods from his dreadnought on the *Heartrender*, and Gavain's Captain Georgia had launched marines at the *Heartbreaker,* even as both Vindicatus dreadnought and battlecruiser battered the target ships with heavy fire.

De Graaf answered him quickly, <In both cases, the Marine commanding officers are about to hit the bridges of both dreadnoughts.>

<Good,> Gavain replied, returning his attention to the slaughter of the House Jorgensson defensive fleet. They were cutting through them in a very short period of time, and it was inevitable who the victor was going to be in the Alesund System.

Lord Jorrik Jorgensson was watching the situation unfold with quiet horror. Not only had his brother started this insane war against his wishes, but now they were losing in the face of a massive assault and invasion by the Praetorian ships-of-the-line of the Vindicatus nation.

His own ship, the *JSS Heartrender,* was itself under heavy attack. The Praetorian Guard dreadnought *Thor's Hammer,* once the flagship of the infamous Silus Adare, was battering several of his House warships, but had also launched strikepods at his own warship. The highly efficient Praetorian Guard Marines had struck his dreadnought in their many hundreds, and were quickly shutting it down.

<They are about to break through!> shouted his own House Marine commanding officer, and Jorrik was just getting to his feet and drawing his personal hand-laser as the floor of the bridge exploded upwards, surprising them all.

Marines in Praetorian Guard power-armour rose through the hole, wearing anti-gravity repulsorpacks, firing in all directions as they came. The bridge became an interconnected web of laserfire as crew and Marines died quickly under the assault. Explosions sounded out as more of the Vindicatus marines came through the walls, their attempts to break through the doors nothing more than a clever diversion.

Jorgensson was firing, and never saw the Marine that slammed into him from behind. He lost consciousness with the impact for a few seconds, knocked out.

He came round very quickly, looking up into the barrel of a rotary cannon, pointed down at his head. Another Vindicatus marine was applying restraints to his wrists. "Wha –" he began, noticing that the sounds of gunfire had completely ceased on the bridge of his ship.

"I am Lieutenant-General Petra Raimes, of the Vindicatus Mercenary Corporation," said the Marine, her helmet clicking back into the collar around her suit. "We have control of this House dreadnought. And you, Lord Jorrik Jorgensson, are my prisoner."

Lord Sven Jorgensson was down on one knee, with a protective circle of House Marines stood all around him. He had a sub-laserchine carbine in his hands, strap around his shoulder, ready to fire at any one who managed to get past his protective circle of Marines.

There were multiple explosions, and suddenly the Vindicatus Mercenary Corporation marines were storming his bridge. There was the roar of several chemo-flamers and the screams of the *Heartbreaker* bridge crew, the deep throaty grumbling of rotary cannons, the buzz of power-swords and weaponry, the thrum of plasmacannon and the whine of laser cannon. Most of it was not from his own protective soldiers, unfortunately.

His squad were ripped apart, blood spraying in all directions and particularly drenching him as the Praetorian Guard power-armoured Marines ripped through his would-be defenders. He fired his sub-laserchine carbine, only for a power-claw to grip the weapon and rip the barrel in two. The muzzle of a much stronger laspulser fired into the last marine defending him, before the red hot barrel slapped Lord Sven to the floor.

The firing had virtually stopped, and the helmet of the figure retracted into its collar. "I'm Major Adeoye of the Vindicatus Mercenary Corporation," said the dark-skinned figure, "and you are my prisoner, Lord Sven Jorgensson."

Lord Luke Towers looked at the devastation the Vindicatus Praetorian Guard starships were causing, shaking his head in disbelief. His own dreadnought was participating, engaging two small frigates simultaneously, but they were outmatched. The Levitican Union Armed Forces had been helping to even the odds, but the arrival of the Vindicatus First Fleet had swung the battle heavily in their favour.

Everywhere he looked, the Praetorian Guard ships were ripping the House starships apart. Some of the House ships had been boarded, but the squadrons were working perfectly well in unison. Battle formation had fallen apart as they pursued their targets, the Praetorians ceasing to operate even as a squadron and merely punishing the House Jorgensson ships. It was a slaughter.

The sudden loss of the three Marchenko ships was interesting, each of them floating dead in the water. Luke presumed that it had to do with Lord Gavain's so-called 'back-up' plan in case the peace did not occur, and war began. Lord Micalek would doubtless be fuming. Luke was already receiving reports from across Levitican Union territory that Marchenko ships were falling apart.

He looked at the noble barge where Lord Micalek resided, and felt nothing but hatred. The man wanted to do incredible harm to his family, and tear the Levitican Union apart. Luke had no respect for him. He had never fully trusted him, not even when his sister had believed Micalek's double-blind actions. He knew how hurt and wounded his sister was, and he vowed that Micalek would pay for this. The failure of the peace action today and its descent into war was only the start, a failure in the skirmish more than made up for by the apparent destruction of House Marchenko's noble family.

This was all far from over.

*

The Spider Elaine Carrington stood outside the maternity ward of the infirmary, keeping perfectly still and for once not having to fake the look of worry. She was in her 'Sarah' disguise, as an aide to the Lady Sophia, one of the many disguises she maintained so that no-one would guess her identity. In this instance it allowed her to remain close to the Lady Sophia.

There were guards on the door, Towers House Guard. A small contingent remained to the House, as all but a few in comparison had transferred into the Levitican Union Armed Forces. The Spider had her own agents all over the hospital, and the doctor was cleared and vetted at the highest level.

No risk was being taken, The Spider had prepared for this months ago.

She looked at the clock again. She had experienced childbirth herself, as once she had been a member of a noble family. Only the Alpha-class and the Beta-class within many Houses of the old Imperium had reproduced legally by the traditional reproductive methods nature had given them.

The doors cycled open, and a nurse appeared. As the sound-proofed doors opened, Elaine Carrington could see over the shoulder of the nurse. "Sarah?" the nurse said, looking behind him, "The Lady Principal is asking for you to come in."

Elaine had already walked past, into the wardroom properly. The doctor was standing back, the nurses were watching with big smiles on their faces, and the medical droids had retreated into their docking units.

Lady Principal Sophia sat upright in the bed, looking exhausted and tired, but cradling a small bundle in her arms protectively. The bundle was so small, it was hard to believe it was actually human or real.

"Look," said Sophia, the tiredness fading. She appeared to be completely on another planet, perhaps because of the drugs to numb the pain completely and make the childbirth as easy as possible. "This is Benjamin, Benjamin Towers."

Elaine placed one hand on the shoulder of Lady Sophia. "May I?" she asked.

"Of course, but be gentle." It was a tender moment, as Elaine very carefully took the child. The baby boy had big brown eyes, and looked upon the world with an innocence that only a newborn could possibly have. With all the evil they experienced, the plots, the deaths, the destruction and the sheer pain of existence, to look upon an angelic thing of such beauty and health, promise of the future and above all hope was truly humbling.

"My first grandson," Elaine Carrington whispered to herself, not even realising she had been about to say it, the words slipping out unbidden. It was not like her to let herself fall that way, but the moment was too special.

"What?" asked Lady Sophia, frowning suddenly in confusion. "Your grandson?"

"Forget it," said Elaine Carrington quickly, "I – I am pleased for you, Lady Sophia."

Elaine passed the newborn Benjamin Towers back to Lady Sophia, and hoped beyond hope that her little faux pas would be forgotten in the heat of the moment.

*

Captain Jason Bramhall sat in the command seat of the O-class *VSS Occupier*, the frigate which his crew referred to as his own personal flagship. He had relinquished command of the corvettes, particularly his last one the *VSS Adventurous* after its damage in the invasion of the Dark Heart System. He was just as lethal in his new command however, and the bigger ship just gave him more potential.

<Reporting that all ships are now in position, Captain,> said his second-in-command.

Jason Bramhall stood up, facing the holographic image before him displaying the positions of all the ships he had in-system.

There were five Mass Transporters out there, carrying the four hundred thousand volunteers who would settle here and form the first population of the new system. Their absence from the immigration and refugee effort was going to hurt the relief efforts, but there was no avoiding it. A Ferry-Ship was also present, carrying numerous intrastellar craft, from small shuttles and mining barges right the way up to constructoships.

There were four Type-I Cargo Freighters, two Type-II Cargo Freighters, and a Tanker, which would be dedicated to the system for the early days of its settlement and carry supplies and more from Dark Heart. An interstellar Miningship and a Salvageship were also in the formation, the miningship to take advantage of the natural resource, the salvageship to collect the remains of the Droid Intelligentia presence that still floated throughout the system. There were a number of old Pre-Imperial and early House starships present from the Sixth Home Fleet, three lightcruisers and two frigates, in addition to the Praetorian Guard frigates from the Fourth Support Fleet, the *VSS Brotherhood, VSS Neptune,* and the *VSS Overseer,* which would also remain in-system to protect the colonists whilst the defences were built. To build them there were two Droid Mine-Layers.

The jewel in the crown was the Colonyship. It had been renamed the *VSS Praetor,* in honour of the Praetorian Guard who had founded Vindicatus, and this would become the name of the planet it colonised in this binary system. The Colonyship was large, at the head of the formation, and its design was as ingenious as it was breathtaking.

Gavain had decided on a name for their new system. It was to be called the Praetor System, another hark back to the roots of the founders of Vindicatus. Its existence would be kept as secret as possible, the security operation to keep the volunteers from communicating an unbelievable undertaking in itself.

Feeling the moment, Captain Bramhall jacked in to the taskforce-wide datasphere, addressing them all. He kept it simple, in emulation of his hero. <All ships,> he said, <Today we make history once again, not just for Vindicatus but to colonise the first solar system in many, many decades. Welcome to the birth of the Praetor Solar System. *VSS Praetor*, begin the colonisation.>

The *VSS Praetor* began to drift forwards, accelerating towards the large planet awaiting it. It took some time, particularly as it began to slow as it neared the atmospheric envelope of the planet. Before it began to make entry, it fired numerous missiles from its fore, the missiles spreading out and detonating in the atmosphere.

They carried terraformation warheads, which had been painstakingly and carefully coded into ensuring that the minimal changes required to the atmosphere and the climate would occur. It might take years for the full effect, but there was no hurry. The planet was still inhabitable, but to avoid long-term adverse effects the terraforming had to take place. It was minor from a scientific point of view, as they were not trying to drastically affect the way the planet operated in terms of ecosystem, or make any changes at all to how it looked from a geological and geographical point of view. Planetfall was not always required immediately by a colonyship, as it could terraform for years if necessary before it landed, but in this instance the terraformation could continue whilst it was in-situ.

The *VSS Praetor* burned as it entered the planetary atmosphere, glowing red as it aggressively pounded into entry. It was large, of such a size that once it was committed to a landing it would never leave a planetary surface again, but then it was never meant to.

The *VSS Praetor* began to change as it drifted towards the landing target zone, sections of its hull opening and changing. Landing gear extended, and it slowed more and more as it neared its designated landing point. It was out on a plain, with a large river which would be shored up against flooding, near to an ocean. Alien forests lay further inland, with metal rich mountains rising up in the distance. The air was cool and temperate, but at the height of summer it would burn.

It fired burning lasers before it landed, extending massive holes for the landing gear to punch down within. The ship would be secured forever into the tough bedrock. The ship was itself half the size of a space station in width and length, and easily in terms of height.

Once it had settled, the clouds of soil and dirt settling, the ship began to open like a flower's petals pushing themselves open. Hull became new flooring, decks became rising spires and blocks for people. As the day wore on and the ship fully transformed and opened in a complicated genius of engineering that it had been designed for many centuries ago, it became obvious that it was becoming the basis of a new city.

In the sky above, the Mass Transporters could be seen beyond the atmospheric envelope, the first landers bringing the colonists down. The Ferry-Ship had begun to release its cargo, and numerous shuttle landers were bring thousands of vehicles to the surface to enlarge on the construction of the new capital city of the Praetor System, Praetus City.

As easily as that, a new colony was born.

*

Lord Gavain stood in one of the supporting operations rooms set off from the bridge of the *VSS Vindicator*, his back to the conference table which had been brought in to re-configure the room for the meeting today. He stared out of the wide observation windows of the battlecruiser, the blast shutters peeled back.

Out there in the Alesund System, he could see the remains of the devastation they had wrought. Besides Lucas De Graaf's First Fleet, there had also been a number of ships waiting in Blackheath in support, ready for the jump to Alesund if all went wrong but they won the battle with their superior numbers.

He had a number of his own ugly and unattractively designed salvageships from the Dark Heart System here, ripping through and eating the wreckage of House Guard ships like bottom-feeders feasting on corpses. He also had a Ferry-Ship, which had brought some constructoships with it. The constructoships did not just build things, they pulled them apart, and at this precise moment they were taking the large astronomical array apart. He wanted it in the new Praetor System, where it could be used to spy rather than for astronomical reasons. They and a number of tugs were loading it into numerous cargo-tanks, the cargo-freighters awaiting the all clear to pick them up and begin the transport. If there was time they would take the Alesund Stargate apart as well, but he did not intend to be here that long and besides which, he did not want to rob House Jorgensson of too much. They would be annoyed enough about the array.

He had still not given up hope. He had destroyed House Marchenko, severely weakening the Levitican Union in the process, but ultimately protecting it from a greater threat. The only way he could see forwards was peace with Jorgensson, and them joining the Union. Otherwise the battle that had occurred here today would lead to a full war, if it was not one already.

The door behind opened, and Major Adeoye entered with a group of Marines, still fully helmed and attired in their power-armour. Some of it was still battle-scarred. Admiral Lucas De Graaf walked in front of them. In the midst of the group of Marines were two figures, now released of their restraints but no less the prisoners for it. The Lords Sven and Jorrik Jorgensson both looked the nobles they were, but there was no hiding their nervousness despite their Imperial Academy training.

"To the seats, Lords," said Gavain, pointing at the two seats at the table. "We await the Lords of the Levitican Union."

"This is intolerable –" began Lord Sven.

"Be quiet, brother," Jorrik ordered. "I am the heir-designate, remember that. Traitor."

Gavain took the division between the brothers as a sign of hope. Perhaps his communication of Sven's treachery and involvement with this mysterious Rosicrux organisation had convinced Jorrik that he should listed to Gavain.

<James,> said Admiral Lucas De Graaf, approaching Gavain on his side of the table.

<Lucas,> Jamie replied through their private communication channel on the datasphere.

<It is good to see you again.>

Gavain felt the relief pouring through the mental connection. Private communications were always harder to hide emotions from. It was the technological data equivalent of reading someone's body language in an oral conversation. <You did well in the command of First Fleet.>

He felt the pride emanating off De Graaf. <Thank you. The fact I was in command with you in the operational theatre was noted by all.>

<It will ensure they follow your leadership,> said Gavain warmly. He admired how much Lucas had developed, and very much wanted to see him succeed in this role. Although he rarely showed it, James Gavain was excellent at reading people and empathising with them. In all ways but his personal, romantic life, he thought, that was too far out of his sphere of experience.

<Have you seen the reports from Brigadier Vantanik?> said Lucas.

<Yes,> said Gavain simply. <An impressive interstellar mission, virtually unparalleled since the Night of Knives orchestrated by the False Emperor.>

<I agree,> said Lucas, <Over two hundred Marchenko nobles killed in the first real-time hour, most of them simultaneously. The rest killed afterwards as soon as their ships reached systems with HPCG Stations. All for the confirmed loss of just four biomorphs, as we suspect the ones we

have not heard of will shortly be returning to our safety points. The Marchenkan's just fell apart as predicted, allowing the escapes. Not a single hit missed.>

<It is the advantage of being based on Faceless technology,> said Gavain simply.

<It was brutal and ruthless,> said Lucas, and for a moment there was a look in his eyes. Before Gavain could enquire further, the doors opened and Major Adeoye returned, this time with the Levitican Union guests brought aboard from their ships. Lord Brin Claes, Lord Luke Towers, and Lord Micalek Zupanic entered. They went through the acknowledgements and greetings, and then sat opposite the Jorgenssons. Gavain and De Graaf took the head of the table.

Before he began, Gavain looked at both sides he was mediating for. There were divisions on both sides of the table, he realised. No wonder the Red Imperium of Mars had fallen apart.

Chapter VII

The Third Emperor was dressed in the flowing red robes of the Imperium, and sat upon his throne aboard the behemoth-sized starship he was using as his personal conveyance. It was unique and individual, there being nothing like it. The Imperial-class noble barge was heavily armed and armoured, bigger than some warships.

After spending so long in the shadows, plotting and planning and preparing for the day that was now fast approaching, he felt exhilarated. He had spent much of his life in the Temple of Shadows, the latest Master of the Shadow Council, and now he was nearing personal freedom.

As well as personal vengeance.

The herald droid floated up near to him, and announced, "Legate of the Third Circle and Legate of the Fourth Circle requesting audience."

"Enter," replied the Third Emperor.

The guards opened the doors at the end of the long throne room, and the figures entered. The Third Emperor diverted his attention away from reviewing once again the Legate of the Second Circle's plans, mentally minimising the images and graphics so they remained in his vision and accessible while he participated in the discussion. With full cybernetic implants of an unbelievably advanced nature, there was virtually no limit to his multi-tasking capabilities.

The two legates were both wearing their new robes of office, the black synth-skin suits now removed and replaced with a new Imperial fashion. The high collars were there, but long heel-length capes were added, chains of office and small crowns to denote their position in place. The colours that lined their face-masks were also present in their primarily crimson-red robes. The Legate of the Third Circle, the once-dead Jared Towers, wore the white highlights of the political branch, whilst the moving holographic representation of the Legate of the Fourth Circle, a very recognisable person within the galaxy, wore the blue highlights of the secret investigations or intelligence operatives in his.

Both Legates saluted and then knelt before him, before he said, "Rise." He waited a heart-beat, before saying, "This is unexpected."

"We come bearing particular news, Third Emperor," the Fourth Legate said, "News which we are sure you will wish to be appraised of immediately."

"Stop ingratiating yourself and explain," said the Third Emperor curtly.

Third Legate Jared Towers began to explain, "There has been a major setback in the Eastern Segment, in the Core and Mid-Sectors region, in the

Levitican Union and Jorgensson operational theatre. There have been a number of developments."

He went on to explain that the Vindicatus nation under Lord James Gavain had led a peace party into Jorgensson territory, and they had planned to counter it with treachery from Lord Sven Jorgensson, who would fire unprovoked upon the ambassadorial fleet. "Unfortunately, Lord Gavain had prepared for this. He had another full fleet of ex-Praetorian Guard ships ready to jump in-system, which as the battle broke out, they certainly did."

"Apart from that last, it sounds according to plan," the Third Emperor drawled, paying more attention.

"Lord Gavain destroyed the Jorgensson House forces, not unsurprisingly, and then began plundering the system in typical mercenary fashion, true to his first calling," said Third Legate Jared. "However, he also revealed the truth of our plot to Lord Jorrik using details obtained from the Dark Heart System victory. After the battle was over he called House Jorgensson together and the Levitican Union ambassadors, in an attempt to prevent the battle sparking the war we hoped it would."

"And he has been successful?" the Third Emperor asked.

"Very successful," said Jared regretfully. "Lord Jorrik has turned against his brother and my pawn, Lord Sven. They are returning to their father, and House Lord Oren Jorgensson has already stated that Sven will be imprisoned and punished. House Jorgensson believes the data they have been given, and have agreed to rendezvous in Towers territory to discuss the terms of their joining the Levitican Union. Lord Gavain has averted a war."

"This is a disaster," said the Third Emperor coldly. "The region is becoming stronger, not weaker. What of the Marchenko and Zupanic gambit?"

"I still have Zupanic in our control - in the terms of being allied to us, not being our puppets as elsewhere - but they are greatly weakened. House Marchenko is another story." Jared explained about the destruction of House Marchenko's noble family.

"How in my name has this happened!" the Third Emperor roared suddenly.

The Fourth Legate was nervous as he replied. "I have received certain intelligence on the subject, Emperor. The Vindicatus nation used their cybernetic biomorphs to have kill-teams in place around every Marchenko noble. At the given signal they all activated, a precaution as they knew of the plan to betray the Union. They crippled the House that led Marchenko military might, and removed our allies in the collective consciousness. I have this information from a spy located near Lady Sophia Towers, with enough secondary evidence from a variety of sources to give it a high probability rating of truth. The entire Marchenkan people flounder, but already new leaders are emerging."

"And they are not in our favour, the race of House Marchenko citizenry remembering their alliance with us," Jared Towers added. "It may only be a matter of time before they reveal House Marchenko's part in the conspiracy and their allegiance to us."

"To us?" The Emperor's voice had a rough, harsh edge to it. "They know of the Shadow?"

"No," said Jared Towers hastily, "by us I meant the proxy Rosicrux organisation we used, like so many others, to protect ourselves and our identity. But too many know of it now and are not in our favour or control - this upstart House Gavain, House Marchenko, House Towers, House Jorgensson; it is only a matter of time until it explodes. House Zupanic may suffer, but Micalek has been weakened severely by this. He was never really allied to us, it was always his father and mother - and of Lady Wyn I strongly suspect she was only ever truly using us to her own ends, if we turned out to be unsuitable she would have switched loyalties quickly just like Ramicek Zupanic did during the Levitican War."

"This is not acceptable," said the Shadow Emperor, suddenly standing up. He walked down the steps of the throne's dais, a thunderous look upon his face. "Do either of you - does any of the Shadow Council, have any plans or suggestions on what to do about this disastrous failure? Every nation along the path is vital to the plan, failure is not an option."

He was now stood in front of them, and they physically balked in his presence.

"Do you mean what to do about Gavain and his Vindicatus nation, or what to do about the Levitican Union, Emperor?" Jared asked.

The Third Emperor turned a burning gaze upon Jared. "You fool," he hissed, "I meant both! And don't suggest killing Gavain, the Faceless of the Fifth Legate have tried and failed, although I shall certainly order her to keep trying!"

"We have rescued Silus Adare," said the Fourth Legate quickly, "the Sixth Legate saw to that. We could utilise Adare against Gavain, they have a long history against each other. Adare is bound to unsettle Gavain more than any other."

"Do it," said the Third Emperor. "But I need more. Third Legate?"

Jared replied quickly, "Vindicatus is only on the path because of Gavain's involvement with the Union, but they are a credible threat because of their military size. We could turn this situation to our advantage yet, in a very old fashioned way. We could use the truth and bend it against him. In fact, there may even be a blacker side to the truth that we are missing."

"Explain, quickly," the Third Emperor was frowning, puzzled.

"Gavain trades on his post-Dissolution reputation as much as his military size," said Jared. "We could hurt him with a 'dirt campaign'. If we release full details to StarCom Central Intelligence, and simultaneously a juicy story to the StarCom News Media, we could rubbish Gavain and cause dissent in the Union as well as getting StarCom to look in yet another wrong direction. We reveal that Gavain had the Marchenko nobles killed in a mass assassination. It makes him look dishonourable, and would cause ructions because of the involvement of House Zupanic. We use his strong alliance with House Towers more than any other nation, to make it look like he is secretly manipulating the Union. He has a base and a spacestation in their territory, my sister Sophia funded them as mercenaries immediately after Dissolution, it will be believable.

"We would also drive a wedge between House Zupanic and House Towers, opening up publicly what they both know in private. Micalek and Sophia's duplicity towards each other would ruin the news of the birth of her child, my nephew. The truth could work to our favour exceptionally well, turning the StarCom Federation against him and possibly split the Union apart still. At the very least we could drive a wedge into the Union that breaks it apart more than it already is."

There was a long pause, and then the Third Emperor smiled. "It is devious, Machiavellian, and I like it. You saved yourself there, Third Legate. Do it," the Third Emperor said.

"By your word, it will be done," said Jared, his words repeated a moment later by the Fourth Legate.

*

Lord James Gavain sat in his own private ready room, just off the bridge of the *Vindicator* battlecruiser he had built his name with. How many other nobles had an ex-Praetorian Guard starship as their personal noble barge, Ulrik Andryukhin had joked.

He was sipping from a cup of real coffee, enjoying the taste. It was one of his few admitted luxuries, and something he would not do without. He would never go back to the synthesised rubbish again.

He was staring out of the window of his battlecruiser, lost in thought. The *Vindicator* was orbiting the planet Leviticus in the Newchrist System. It had not taken long in terms of real-time to return here. Once the House Jorgensson deal was reach with Lord Jorrik and then his father House Lord Oren by pulse-channel, they had jumped from Alesund directly back to Blackheath in House Towers territory by using the stargate. The stargate at Blackheath had then sent Admiral-of-the-Fleets Lucas De Graaf and the rest of First Fleet back to the Dark Heart System and Vindicatus territory, whilst Gavain had carried on with the rest of the Levitican Union ships to the capital solar system of Newchrist.

He did not intend to be here long, but he wanted one last discussion before he went to visit the newly seeded colony of Praetor. He had to return to the business of his nation, even though he trusted Andersson to do a very good job as Solar High Administrator.

Finally the message came from Captain Erica Georgia, <Jamie?>

<Yes,> he replied.

<The council session has ended, and Lady Sophia is ready to speak to you, comms channel is open.>

<Patch it through,> he ordered, turning around to face the holoprojected image as it materialised in front of him. Lady Principal Sophia sat before him, in what looked like her own quarters, a child in her arms.

"Jamie," she said smiling. She was still one of his closest friends, ranked equally with Harley Andersson, Ulrik Andryukhin, and Lucas De Graaf. There were others very close, but they were the ones he trusted the most. The thought of his betrayal of Harley with Juan was leading to a feeling he had never felt before; guilt. Had he felt more for Harley than he realised?

"Sophia," said James Gavain. "You have had no time to recover since childbirth?"

"The wonders of modern medicine," said Lady Sophia.

"How is ... it?" he asked. Childbirth to him, like many borg and even many humans, was something alien nowadays, a reserve and predilection of the rich and higher-classed. He was a Praetorian, vat-born, so the social niceties surrounding children and natural birth events were completely beyond him.

"You mean Benjamin?" she laughed in that pleasing way she had, "he's fine, thank you, Jamie. But we did not start this call to discuss that did we?"

"No," Jamie confirmed, back on safer ground. "What happened in the Council session?"

Lady Principal Sophia, elected leader of the Council and the Union, kept her face neutral as she reported matter-of-factly. "Lord Micalek was very aggressive, no doubt feeling the utter devastation at the loss of his plans to tear this Union apart and increase Zupanic territory at our expense. He has demanded successfully for a full, urgent investigation into the killing of House Marchenko nobles. Are there any traces back to you one should be aware of?"

"None," said James Gavain, shaking his head. "It has all been covered, all my biomorphs escaped, and those four that didn't self-combusted with no evidence retrievable. Even if their bodies had been left, there is nothing to lead back to me or the Vindicatus nation."

"Good," Lady Principal Sophia nodded her head. "House Marchenko is developing a new leader, a brother to Lord Gregori Marchenko, a Lord Vladmir Marchenko. It will take time for him to become the new leader, and for the hive consciousness to fully reassert itself, but probably not as long as we think. He has already sent one a message apologising for Lord Gregori's treachery. He has promised to support the Union. The Union Council today voted to recognise Lord Vladmir as the successor, not that we have any choice in the matter. The hive-mind consciousness is a world and law unto its own."

"He definitely had no part in the plot," Lord Gavain confirmed, "it was only Lord Gregori, his wife, and their children who had full unfettered knowledge. Well, the rest of the Marchenkan race knew of the basics of the plot as well through their hive mind connection, but Gregori and his 'immediate' family of several hundred children were the only ones who had the individuality and control to decide on their participation and duplicity fully."

"Lord Claes reported back to the Council on the negotiations you held, and that the Battle of Alesund will not lead to a new war with House Jorgensson. Sven Jorgensson is imprisoned by his own House, and House Lord Oren Jorgensson has already contacted me to ask if we can hold discussions in Blackheath very shortly on Jorgensson joining the Union. One has floated this idea of Jorgensson joining the Union in the Council, and we took a vote - it was unanimous that they should join if the negotiations head in that way, no dissent. Even Lord Moafa Obamu agreed."

"It puts you in a powerful position," said Lord Gavain thoughtfully, "you can go into the negotiations knowing you can offer membership of the Union to Lord Oren there and then."

"Listen to the mercenary commander become a politician," Lady Principal Sophia teased. "But you are right, of course. You have done it again, Jamie - we have hope for the future, and maybe peace, at last."

"Providing Jorgensson stick to their word," said Lord Gavain darkly, "but if they do not, my fleets will be ready should there be an issue."

"Lord Oren has asked for the astronomical array you 'liberated' from Alesund back," said Lady Principal Sophia.

"I will ask him to undamage my ships, then," said Lord Gavain, straight-faced. "That is the cost of war. I was a mercenary, as you pointed out - and still am."

"Many call you the Mercenary Lord, you know, Jamie," said Sophia.

"I know," he nodded, not rising to the bait. "And what of Lord Micalek and you?" he asked.

"He looks at me with new fear," said Lady Sophia, her happiness fading for the first time. "He must know from the destruction of Lord

Gregori's branch of the Marchenko family that the Zupanic plot was discovered. One has her House Guards on full alert. One fears that Lord Micalek's only hope now to grab control of House Towers is to try and do so through our son, Benjamin Towers. He certainly won't gain all the territory he thought he would with the destruction of the Union."

Lord Gavain read the message there. "You are considering having him removed?" he asked.

"This is not something we can talk about, Jamie," said Lady Sophia, but he saw the answer there. "Even with your superior technology and on a closed and encrypted channel, we must not talk of such things. But one suspects that he will try to do away with me and Luke. Lord Micalek looks pushed to the brink, fraying at the edges. He knows House Jorgensson know of the plot, he knows Lord Vladmir Marchenko does. It is only a matter of time perhaps until he is outed and he knows it."

"At least you can plan to deal with it," said Lord James Gavain. "If you need my help, let me know."

"One will, Jamie," said Lady Principal Sophia, "One knows she can always come to you. But this is something one must deal with on one's own. He is my husband, even if he plotted to take my land and was complicit in the killing of my father. Thank you, all the same."

*

"So, even now Lady Principal Sophia is heading to the Blackheath System from Leviticus in Newchrist, to meet Lord Oren Jorgensson to discuss the terms of House Jorgenssons admission into the Levitican Union," Vice-President Johann Schneider finished, with a grim look upon his stern face.

"An incredible story," commented President Giovanna Pereyra.

They were sat in the Golden Room of the Palace of Communications on Earth, the emergency meeting of her closest advisors being called on short notice. The most powerful people in the StarCom Federation were briefing their President on the outbreak of war between Jorgensson and the Union, and its equally quick ending.

Commander-In-Chief Jaiden Ryan leaned forwards awkwardly, his round bulk causing a problem as he tried to rest on the table. "What concerns me more is the size of the military Lord Gavain now possesses, and how quickly he was able to turn the situation to his advantage. What do you make of this information you have received on Gavain, Director Chbihi? Where did it come from?"

"The sources are trustworthy," she said, "agents I have had in the Levitican Union for some time, and in some cases in some of the Houses going back decades into the Red Imperial years. There is no doubting it. Lord Gavain had over two hundred members of the Marchenko noble family assassinated in a co-ordinated multi-site attack at the same time as the Battle of Alesund was taking place."

"He used biomorphs, of a technological state we have only ever seen the Faceless use before," said President Pereyra thoughtfully.

"That is what is so worrying," Ryan agreed. "With that technology, he becomes very dangerous indeed, above and beyond the fleet of Praetorian ships he has. His reach is obviously further than we thought. How did he get it?"

"We don't know," said Director Chbihi, "but there is an indication he was also involved through his links with the Towers family in the assassinations of the Zupanics."

"The question is why," said the deep, aggressive voice of Vice-President Schneider. "It looks like the intelligence suggests, that he is the secret power behind the Levitican Union. He is manipulating and controlling them for his own ends."

"Well, the secret is out," said President Pereyra, "the StarCom News Media is playing some of the lighter details of the story to the entire galaxy. How in the name of the Emperor did they manage to release this information without our control, Director?"

Malika Chbihi looked uncharacteristically uncomfortable. "The censor system we have is based on certain codewords, there is too much information flowing through. This did not trigger any of them, so the SCNM went live with the story."

"You need a greater control of the News Media service," Schneider growled.

"We are not going back to the dark days of President Nielsen," said Pereyra sharply. "State control of the media is a necessity to protect ourselves, but similarly if we wish to maintain a presence throughout the galaxy, the SCNM must be free to report certain things. In this case it is our restrictions that were wrong, not the organisation itself."

Schneider paused, then bowed his head. "As you say, Madam President."

"We watch the Levitican Union from a military point of view," said Commander-In-Chief Ryan, "although Suularitsaar is my biggest worry, and the OutWorlds Alliance because of their capability to strike us with Weapons of Planetary Destruction, and our previous history to date. I have to upgrade the threat rating of the Levitican Union in light of this information, Gavain was the primary reason we lost the Levitican War. If he is now manipulating the Union to gain control of the entire region, as this intel suggests, we may shortly have a major problem there. He shows signs of expansionism policies with his own Vindicatus nation."

Pereyra remembered some of the old briefings on Gavain, and of course knew of him from some of his exploits, but there were many people in the galaxy causing headlines. "There is something about this that just does not sit right with his image," she said, "although of course, I know an honourable and pleasant image is something that can hide many a dangerous, poisonous character underneath. What do we know of him, Director? What does the intelligence file say?"

Director Chbihi accessed the datasphere, pulled the files, and sent them to the rest of the group of advisors. "We have a lot of information on Gavain, both from our own observations post-Dissolution and from Imperial records. He was vat-born in the Deimos Praetorian Genesis Facility here in the Sol System, now thirty-six Imperial Standard years of age in real-time. After his accelerated growth cycle was completed, psychologically he was assessed as suitable for entry into the officer class of the naval division of the Praetorian Guard, and became a Midshipman before he was one year old.

"His psych-profiling up until Dissolution suggests a ninety-two percent homosexual inclination which increased to ninety-seven percent as he matured and environment and experience affected him. A controlled and balanced emotional state even under pressure seen in three percent of the Guard, behavioural boundaries acceptable, advanced strategic capabilities and above normal cognitive abilities. An intelligence quotient of above normal. He was classified as most likely to proceed to high rank, with reviews and notations suggesting he was expected to qualify for Admiral rank and capability at a comparatively early age."

"He has certainly proven that," said Jaiden Ryan sourly.

"During the civil war which led to the destruction of the Red Imperium of Mars," Chbihi continued, "he played a role in the Battle of Mars. His objection to the False Emperor and sympathy to the rebels was never detected or predicted until he openly joined the revolution, only his free-thinking classification made him a possibility and a risk. For that reason he was kept as a Commander under a borgite Captain Evanleigh aboard the *Vindicator* battlecruiser, his career stymied without his knowledge in the last five years leading up to Dissolution. When Evanleigh turned it was more of a surprise to the False Emperors Imperial Intelligence agents."

"He definitely made up for that career block," said Vice-President Schneider.

"When the Praetorian Guard received the Dissolution Order, the one that applied to the Guard only and not the Dissolution of the Red Empire, some facts we are not aware of, up until he went off-course unexpectedly and disappeared. He then re-appears and creates the Vindicator Mercenary Corporation with Lady Sophia Towers, who at the time was more interested in her businesses than politics and had the money to support him."

"Already there is a link," said Pereyra, "but who influenced who? Was Gavain already playing a long-term game at this point?"

"We do not know," said Chbihi, "but their alliance is close-knit, and obviously not sexually based considering his inclinations. Money and power would be the most obvious conclusion. How far reaching that plan was, we have no evidence. Through strong tactical and strategic expertise, good negotiating, and some luck, he built up the Vindicator Mercenary Corporation relatively quickly. The Levitican War was what brought him openly onto the political stage, when he appeared in the Levitican Union and led their defence against our invasion. He masterminded the whole defensive strategy."

"Displaying a capability his profile suggested he had," said President Pereyra, "but had been prevented from realising in the days of the Imperium."

"Yes," the Director nodded. "From there, thanks to previous Federal aggression, he was seen as a hero throughout the Core and Mid-Sectors, and even beyond. We were at the time expanding aggressively ourselves, under Nielsen as we all remember."

"Are there any other indications that he has been manipulating the Levitican Union for power?" asked Schneider.

"Many," said Chbihi, going through them all briefly. "His taking of Dark Heart was the seal on it all. He has links all throughout the Eastern Segment because of his mercenary activities. His own nation grows apace. He obviously has always had an ambition for personal power his psych-profile did not suggest, with the rapidity in which his own national powers in the Gulf of Medusa increases."

"He is becoming a serious threat," said President Pereyra, "or we could try making him into a very dangerous ally."

"He would never be likely to," said Director Chbihi, "he is very anti-StarCom. He will never be someone we could trust."

"And now he is very obviously deeply embroiled in the Levitican Union politics, potentially facing off against us, and antagonising the Zhou-Zheng Compact with his support of the Erdogans. He is pulling the strings of a vast number of systems out there," said Vice-President Schneider.

"What do you project his ultimate goals to be?" asked Pereyra.

"In light of this information, obviously far greater than we thought," said Director Chbihi. "Ultimate control of the Levitican Union, either through Lady Sophia or without her is one. He is deeply embroiled in the Compact theatre, the Erdogans making up much of his nation's population. Aalborg national immigration is increasing as the Helvanna Dominion continues to invade and smash the three houses that make up the Aalborg Alliance. He has fingers everywhere across the Eastern

Segment. He is building rapidly, and expanding his military power, and has access to technology we were not aware of."

"Is he trying to be the next Emperor?" said Ryan bitterly.

"Don't even joke about it," said Malika Chbihi. "That is the last thing we need."

"We need to watch him so carefully," said Pereyra. "Take time to think, and then give me recommendations on how to deal with him."

*

Lord James Gavain was furious, but only the way his eye colour had changed from their steely grey to a dangerous ice-cold blue gave away the boiling emotion underneath his calm demeanour. The advisors around him knew how much of a sign that was.

"I don't understand why the StarCom Federation has allowed their News Media to put this out into the galaxy," said Dr Erin Presson shaking her head, "it's just not true."

"Well," said Ulrik, unable to resist, "there may be some element of truth to it. You are becoming a stronger and stronger power within the Levitican Union, Jamie."

"That is not helpful, Rik," said James Gavain, neutrally. Then he paused, and said, "Well, you may have a point. But I am not doing it for my own sake."

"None of us think that Jamie," said Harley Andersson, "but this is politics. This is what will be said, and how some people could perceive you. This is just a fact of life. The fact it does the Vindicatus nation damage is to StarCom's benefit."

"If indeed it is them," said Lucas De Graaf.

"What do you mean?" asked Ulrik Andryukhin.

"The Rosicrux, and these Shadows behind them," said Lucas, "they pull the strings of much of the colonised galaxy. They could have fed this to the Federation."

"Actually," said Jonathan O'Connor, "there is some evidence for that. The story was leaked to their StarCom News Media, with more detail going into their Central Intelligence Department. They know that we were involved in the Marchenko deaths. My own agents are well embedded, and have confirmed it. The information came from sources they trust, but not part of their own organisation."

"Track it back," Gavain ordered curtly. "We need to know. There is a security leak somewhere."

"What is the Levitican Union making of this?" asked Andersson.

"I do not know yet," said Gavain, "but I imagine I shortly will. This could cause severe problems, right at the point when Lady Sophia is not physically there in the Council to contain them. Emperor alone knows what it will do to the negotiations with Jorgensson."

"This is bad," said Andersson, "but, undeniably, based on the truth in terms of facts. It is just your motivations they call into question, but reputational damage is enough. We need to answer this."

"I will prepare something," said O'Connor.

"Good," Gavain nodded.

Chapter VIII

The Third Emperor, the Shadow Emperor, was exhilarated. He sat in his second throne, at the very rear of the bridge of the dreadnought-sized Imperial-class noble barge *ISS Emperor of Shadows*. The blast shutters and protective armour plating had been pulled back, and he could see out into the starscape beyond the gigantic ship where just one of his fantastically advanced new fleets were lined up. They were in an uninhabited star system, just beyond the Frontier.

<Connect me to the local datasphere, and through the pulse-channels to all the dataspheres of my fleets and my armies,> the Third Emperor commanded.

<Access being granted, connecting ... It is as you command,> came the reply.

"My people, my loyal people," said the Third Emperor, "the time has come for the day of judgement to commence. This Judgement Day will be known throughout the colonised galaxy as the day when the Third Red Empire arose from the shadows.

"Never forget what my ultimate target is. My many enemies will doubtless realise at some point what the final aim is, but by then it will be too late. Strike hard, take and hold the territory along the battleplan. Do your duty, give your life for me, your Emperor. Be victorious, in my name.

"We will strike hard, and we will strike fast. Speed is as much a key to reaching our final target, as holding the territory we take is vital to building the Third Empire. The Dissolution of the Red Imperium was a travesty, which we will rectify.

"This is a war that will take place on many fronts, and in fact has been running since before the Red Imperium fell. We were already in place, in the Houses, amongst the people. We will fight militarily, with intelligence, with propaganda and technology.

"Those in the fleets performing the first strikes in this blitzkrieg, ensure that your first disguise as StarCom Federation starships is activated and in place. I hereby give the order to jump to your designated targets, from the depths of uncolonised space and across the Frontier and into the Boundary. Make the Frontier Hegemony disappear today before our might, and hurt the OutWorlds Alliance.

"To all of you, good luck in my name. I am the Third Emperor, the Shadow Emperor, and I will be watching you as you build my new Imperium." With that the Third Emperor stood, and gave the Imperial Salute, something that never happened. All across the uncolonised parts of the galaxy where the ships were waiting, the naval crewmen and the marines stood, saluting back.

"The order is given, by my command," the Third Emperor said, sitting back down upon his throne. "Go and conquer in my name."

*

The Catanauan System was right on the Border of the colonised galaxy, the thin strip of colonised worlds and systems that circled the outer shell of the expansion of the human race into the stars. Part of the newly formed Frontier Hegemony, and despite its position on the Border, it was heavily defended, being one of the strongest hardpoints in the defensive shield of the Hegemony.

The reasons were two-fold. Firstly, a heavily armed station was needed to protect against the bandits and pirates that roamed out in uncolonised space, although they had fallen strangely quiet recently. The second reason was that Catanauan was the last inhabited system before the Frontier Hegemony touched borders with the OutWorlds Alliance.

With the fall of House Villaneuva, the landholding of the aggressively expansionist OutWorlds Alliance almost completely buffered up against the territory of the Frontier Hegemony, all the smaller House territories being eaten up. The Hegemony owed its existence to the principle of defending against House Al-Zuhairi, and the Catanauan System was a key part of that defence.

The majority of the single-star system was arranged around a small number of planets out to the edge of the super hot star at the centre, those few that were closer burning red hot. There were not many natural jump points into the system, due to the Catanauan sun's sheer size. It dwarfed the military bases and defences around the small, sparsely populated planets. Only the valuable resources and the military purpose had kept the system populated.

The Frontier Hegemony had many starships here, and no traffic was expected. Only military traffic ever really came here. Any attempt by the OutWorlds Alliance to cross their borders would meet with a swift counter-strike from this system, and any attempt by Al-Zuhairi to take the system directly would prove very costly.

When the jump-signatures of the incoming starships were detected in heavy numbers, there was only one possible conclusion to reach. The Admiral in charge of the system sent an emergency distress call out back towards the rest of the Hegemony, and they all began to raise shields, moving towards the jump signatures. The enemy, presumed to be the OutWorlds Alliance, were coming in so close to the Fleet they would actually be within long-range distance.

It was suicide. It would be a slaughter.

Real-space opened up and the ships appeared, and that was when all hell was let loose.

The ships did not wear the brown and orange of the OutWorlds Alliance, or deep black camouflage, or neutral metal grey colouring. They wore the white and blue of the StarCom Federation, and bore the StarCom symbol upon their hulls.

And the ships at the front were massive, unlike anything that had ever been seen before. Some of the fleet crewmen recognised them as the same type of ship that had been detected in the OutWorlds Alliance, but already the order to fire was being given. At this range, only torpedoes could reach.

The sheer volume of torpedoes striking out towards the large enemy fleet of behemoth-sized warships was truly terrifying. The Frontier Hegemony House ships were moving in, desperate to cause damage.

But in the time it took for the torpedoes to close in, everything changed. The enemy warships in the StarCom Federation colours began to flicker and shimmer, their very forms becoming immaterial and ghostly. The torpedoes simply passed straight through, even as the enemy ships began to fire back with an equally frightening volume of fire.

The Admiral in charge of the system realised he was fighting an enemy larger than he had ever fought before, with weaponry systems equal or stronger to his own, that could not be fired upon as the weapons he did shoot simply passed straight through them, and that he did not know how to fight.

It was going to be the slaughter he expected, but the winners would not be the Frontier Hegemony.

The capital seat of the Frontier Hegemony was a world just outside the Frontier, but not far into the Boundary. The eight nations which made up the Hegemony were in theory equal, although seven were in thrall to the dominating military power of just one House. House Cruz had its capital here, in the binary solar system of Teodoro. The other House Lords now resided here, separated from their own territory, in thrall to the overwhelming political power of House Cruz.

Noble barges were in orbit, surrounded by the various unified hegemonic military. There was a vast number of civilian starships, or at least considerable for the position of the system out near the fringes of colonised space. Amongst them was the *SS Jackaljaw*, the salvageship which first saw the strange 'alien' starship.

The *Jackaljaw* floated out at the edges of the solar system, not allowed to approach too closely because of its dubious trading history and the high number of political and military starships present. However, the Frontier

Hegemony had forbidden them from jumping, and they were awaiting clarification on what the Prime of the Hegemony wanted them to do. They had been waiting for weeks, pounced upon by Frontier Hegemony warships out near the border as House Villaneuva collapsed against the OutWorlds Alliance.

<Maria,> Chief Officer Gatdula suddenly said, <the military networks are going haywire, there's something going on.>

<Show me,> said Captain Maria delos Reyes, suddenly worried despite herself. Ever since their unfortunate encounter in the Khobar System with whatever the ship had been, she had been unable to relax fully. Their status as guests in her home nation's capital system was not helped by the presence of the House frigate constantly circled their stationary position.

They had hacked the pathetically poor Hegemony comms network and datasphere with ease. It worried Maria, as she thought that the OutWorlds Alliance would rip through her home nation with equal ease. The military traffic was indeed spiking, and she read the message traffic at the same time as Gatdula did.

<How many incoming jump signatures?> she said.

<Shit,> was the comment from Gatdula simultaneously.

She watched with mounting terror as the House ships in system began to form up rapidly, and the various static defences floating in space visibly went into full readiness. The enemy were coming in all over the system, with numerous jump-signatures visible. More and more began to appear, it becoming clear that there was a large number of incoming starships.

<This is an invasion,> said Maria.

<Our friend the frigate is pulling away, rushing back in-system,> Gatdula pointed out.

<Helm, we're taking our chance, lets jump out of here, anywhere further corewards,> Captain delos Reyes ordered.

The *Jackaljaw* was still gearing up, firing its jump initiation capacitors and awaiting the warp accelerators to ignite the warp field, when the first of the many strange warships appeared. There was no denying it, they were mainly identical to the one she had recorded in the Khobar System, although there were variants.

The tremendous and one-sided battle was just beginning in the capital system when the *Jackaljaw* jumped, and they escaped.

Admiral Jana Ahmadi could not believe what she was seeing, or that she was giving the order she was.

"All ships, repeat all ships, withdraw and jump," she demanded, "I am ordering a full retreat." She then stepped forward, and spoke quietly to the communications console. She may well answer for this next quietly spoken order with her head, if she escaped. "Order the remainder of the rearguard, the sixth the fifth squadron to sacrifice themselves to allow the rest of us to escape."

She walked away from the communications console, losing her famous grace as the entire ship shook. "Multiple torpedo hits, severe damage sustained."

"Do we still have warp capability?" she asked, sitting down in her flag chair.

"Yes, sir," her captain answered.

"Then we jump, all power to the main drive engines and rear shields. I have signalled the retreat."

She watched as it dissolved into chaos. Her entire fleet had been assembled in the House Villaneuva system of Tacurong, looking towards the nearby border with the Frontier Hegemony. They were part of the complicated build-up, ready for what they all thought was coming; the invasion of the Hegemony.

The enemy StarCom Federation warships had appeared without warning. That they wore StarCom Federation colours was obvious to see, and she recognised them from intelligence briefings as being the type of ship discovered by accident at the Khobar System by that salvage pirate. There were less than half the number of her own ships, but it was impossible to damage them, they appeared to be un-hittable, and they were ripping through her defences.

There were different types, some much bigger than anything she had ever seen. The large warships moved slowly but were deadly, and differently modelled but similarly designed star-carrier like ships were also in attendance, spitting out smaller starfighter vehicles of an equally unknown design. There were much smaller jump-capable ships like frigates that moved with dazzling speed, and were severely harassing her retreating ships. Even the smaller frigate-like ships were dangerous, as they could fire upon her fleet but could not be shot.

As her fleet retreated, she saw yet another class of ship coming in, moving slowly into position over one of the captured planets. As those few of her own ships that were left began to jump out-system, she saw the extraordinarily large starship begin to fire down towards the planet, and she shuddered. It was a full-scale invasion, she realised, not just a naval affair.

Finally her own ship jumped, and the awful taste of defeat hit her in her belly like a sour punch.

*

First Lord Yassin Al-Zuhairi stroked his carefully cut and maintained thin beard, shaped into particular circles around his cheeks and mouth. It just added to his widely-observed cruel look, and certainly today the evil fury in his eyes was enough to terrify the servants. His wife had ushered them all out as his briefing began, and she returned to the table, sitting next to him serenely, more than familiar with his incredible rages.

She placed a gentle hand on his arm, and the anger faded in his face, although there was a tightness there that would not disappear for some time to come. Their meal rested where it was at their dining table, hovering in the warm Zaharran night air. Despite the cloying closeness of the almost moistureless climate, he did not feel the heat as he turned his chair back around, focussing fully on the three people before him.

"So," he said, "explain to me again our losses?"

Chief Amab Al-Zuhairi, his uncle, was the only one actually there physically in real life. The other two were holographic representations, one being the Chief Commander of his Army and Fleet Omar Al-Saadi, and the other an exceptionally nervous Admiral Ahmadi. Their images were being projected live by a continuously streaming hyper-pulse communication.

"These ships hit almost in a straight line down from the Frontier into the Boundary, taking nine inhabited systems in one day," said Chief Commander Al-Saadi, a map appearing behind his left shoulder to graphically illustrate his commentary. "This includes three OutWorlds Alliance systems and six newly conquered from the House Villaneuva invasion. Unfortunately we were building up for the forthcoming invasion of the Frontier Hegemony, so we have lost four full fleets of ships-of-the-line and two support fleets. Our entire galactic eastern flank is open, with only the reserve fleets in position and more ships moving up so far untouched. Another couple of days and our losses would have been much heavier."

First Lord Al-Zuhairi was holding a data-pad before him, holographic data appearing in the air above the pad. "Where did these images come from?"

"The Villaneuva theatre, First Lord," said Admiral Ahmadi. Al-Zuhairi looked up, detecting the faltering tone in her voice.

"Without Admiral Ahmadi escaping, we would not have military-grade intelligence on the enemy warships," said Chief Amab Al-Zuhairi quietly.

"And I would have lost thirteen warships to the enemy. Admiral Ahmadi was the only officer to rescue a portion of her crew and command," said Chief Commander Al-Saadi supportively.

There was a long pause as First Lord Yassin looked at the Admiral. His wife placed her hand on his arm yet again. "Well done," he commented with a minute nod of his head. He noted that Ahmadi looked incredibly relieved. "What does this intelligence show us?" he asked.

"It shows four different types of starships," said Chief Amab, "all of a design we do not recognise." He ran through the images they had received, and the data-scans retrieved by Ahmadi and some of the civilian starships that had escaped from the other systems.

"Have we positively identified them as StarCom Federation ships-of-the-line?" asked Yassin.

"They have the colours of the Commies openly displayed," said Chief Commander Al-Saadi. "We could not break their Identity-Friend-or-Foe signatures, their technology and firewalls are too strong."

"We cannot jump the conclusion that they are StarCom, although it seems most likely," said Chief Amab. "The timing is too perfect, they hit us at precisely when we were weakest with their new weaponry. Who knows what these ships are fully capable of? The StarCom Federation still hates us for seizing their assets after Dissolution, our part in the murder of President Nielsen - admittedly with their current President's knowledge - the Tears Incident. They have probably been planning this for some time, although I must stress we have no evidence. These are brand new warships, but you can see some small resemblances to Praetorian Guard designs. This looks like the next generation, and of course StarCom have the Uranian Shipyards in the Sol System and all of the Imperium's secrets and technology from before the Dissolution."

"It looks as if the discovery of that StarCom Federation ship in the Khobar System was an accident," said Yassin thoughtfully. "It may have forced an early reveal. They have been building here on the Frontier for some time."

"If indeed it is StarCom Federation," said Chief Commander Al-Saadi.

"Well, we have no other possible culprits," said Chief Amab.

"Could it not be the Frontier Hegemony?" asked Al-Saadi.

"That is impossible to tell," replied Chief Amab. "We have no contact with the Frontier Hegemony, no data as yet. I do have some limited reports of issues in Hegemony lands, but nothing to rely on. Information from my spy network there has been virtually cut-off completely."

"Enough," said First Lord Al-Zuhairi. He had straightened in his chair, his broad shoulders set back. "We only have one likely culprit at the moment, and that is the StarCom Federation. For the moment, we prepare to resist the enemy, somehow. We work constantly on discovering their weaknesses, arrange scouting sorties, and try everything and anything. Admiral Ahmadi will command the military scouting actions for us, whilst Chief Commander Al-Saadi will personally arrange our defences. Get me a recording session prepared as well, I want to send a very strong message to President Pereyra of the Federation."

"Yes, sire," said Chief Commander Al-Saadi, Chief Amab, and Admiral Ahmadi together.

"And prepare the InterStellar Hyper-space Missiles for launching," said First Lord Al-Zuhairi, "All of them. If I end up losing the OutWorlds Alliance to the StarCom Federation, if it is in fact President Pereyra and her Federation military, I will give the command to launch. We will destroy the Federation from afar with our Weapons of Planetary Destruction, and leave nothing remaining."

*

The holographic image of First Lord Yassin Al-Zuhairi froze momentarily, and then was replaced with the symbol of the OutWorlds Alliance before Vice-President Schneider ended the message with a vicious swipe of his hand.

"Who does that -" he began.

"Johann," said President Pereyra quietly, silencing him. "The First Lord is scared, as we would be if we had faced something like this."

"He is a scared man with enough InterStellar Hyper-space Missiles to wipe out much of our territory, Madam President," said Vice-President Schneider, "assuming his version of events can be believed."

"Director Chbihi, Commander-In-Chief Ryan?" asked President Pereyra. "What is the situation out there on the Frontier?" Once again, President Pereyra found it surreal that the actions and dire situation of a nation literally half the colonised galaxy away could be causing them so much concern. Such was equalising and unbalancing power of technology.

"Is what he says true, about losing so many systems?" Vice-President Schneider added quickly.

"Yes, as far as we can tell it is true," said Director Chbihi, "my intelligence agents report that they lost nine systems in one real-time day."

"To put it into context," said Commander-In-Chief Jaiden Ryan, "many Houses of the former Red Imperium were less than four or five systems in total territory. The Zhou-Zheng Compact has finished conquering Erdogan territory, it taking close to six months for them to occupy a total of twelve systems formerly owned by the Erdogan nation. Although they were using House technology, and this is some technology far in advance of the Praetorian tech we use. We conquered in waves when we were expanding under your predecessor, President Pereyra, but even then we limited the number of systems to a far greater extent."

"It's worth pointing out that First Lord Al-Zuhairi only has part of the picture," added Director Chbihi. "The Frontier Hegemony has been virtually swallowed. We provide the HPCG stations in the Hegemony, and they have lost eighteen systems. And that is confirmed and definite. In one day, the Hegemony has virtually disappeared. It no longer exists."

"It is astounding, and unprecedented even since the days of the First True Emperor when he was fighting to build the Imperium," said Jaiden Ryan. "It is unparalleled."

"These people took thirty systems in one real-time day?" asked Vice-President Schneider, paling.

"Admittedly some of those systems were small and comparatively undefended, we're not talking the defences of Core or even Mid-Sectors systems here, but they have carved a very neat block out of the Frontier and into the Boundary," said Director Chbihi. "Although with the OutWorlds Alliance they were facing some of the best House tech."

"Their intelligence on the dispositions of the Hegemony and Alliance defences must have not only been excellent, but extremely up to date," Ryan commented.

"This has been a long time in planning, obviously," said Chbihi.

"More to the point, why pretend to be us?" asked President Pereyra. "Assuming no-one in this room knows more about this than they are letting on?" She suddenly displayed the hardness that had got her through the dark days of President Nielsen and into this position. She was watching everyone's reactions.

The sudden shocked silence was broken by Jaiden Ryan. "Of course not, Giovanna," he said quietly. "Are you suggesting that someone here knew this was about to happen? That someone here is trying to provoke war with the OutWorlds Alliance? Why bother using the StarCom Federation if they can take thirty systems in one day."

"I know no-one in this room trusts me," said Schneider, "but to know about something like this would be a step too far, even for me."

"There were no signs this was about to happen, no reason to suspect," said Director Chbihi, her furious face glaring at President Pereyra. "We can all take conspiracy theories too far."

"Very well," said President Pereyra, "In that case, what do we think these people pretending to be StarCom Federation will do next?"

"It is impossible to say," said Director Chbihi, shaking her head.

"They have unknown capability, unknown resources, advanced technology, excellent intelligence, and superior strategic ability," said Jaiden Ryan. "The sheer size of their first foray suggests further expansion, although in what direction and for what aim remains to be seen."

"They want to cause a war between us and the OutWorlds Alliance," said Vice-President Schneider, "otherwise why use our colours?"

"They seem to be succeeding," said Director Chbihi. "For all we know, the OutWorlds Alliance could actually be in league with the enemy - we only have limited reports of the effect these invaders have had upon them, and the message from the First Lord. There is no denying that the Frontier

Hegemony, the OutWorld Alliance's next target, has been wiped out by this invasion."

"It would not be the first time in history a fake invasion, assault or terrorist attack was used as an excuse to start a war," said Vice-President Schneider.

"Regardless," said President Pereyra, "whoever these enemies are, they are distant from us. It is the OutWorlds Alliance who have threatened to use ISHMs against us, and to wipe us out if 'we' do not stop these invasions. We have no way of stopping the invasions, we are not behind them. First Lord Al-Zuhairi may be bluffing, but I think he is serious. We could be heading for multiple launches of the ISHMs equipped with Tears of the Moon warheads."

"We cannot allow that to happen," said Ryan, "we do have some defences against the Tears of the Moon, but not enough. We would be facing annihilation if the OWA launched at us."

"They know we can destroy them," said Vice-President Schneider.

"The only issue with a policy of threatening Mutually Assured Destruction," said Director Chbihi, "is when the political situation deteriorates so much that Mutually Assured Destruction actually happens."

"We have no alternative," said President Pereyra. "We must try to find out who is behind this invasion, Director Chbihi. Commander-In-Chief Ryan, prepare our own ISHMs and Tears of the Moon warheads, along with the secret Supernova warheads. Vice-President Schneider, prepare for me to record a new message to the First Lord."

"What will you say?" asked Schneider.

"I will protest our innocence, and beg for calmer heads to prevail," said President Pereyra, "but he will not believe me, I fear. So I will threaten to retaliate if he launches at us."

Chapter IX

"So, we are now in day three of the unexpected invasion," said Lord Gavain to his assembled officers and governmental officials, "explain what has happened, Admiral De Graaf."

The handsome Admiral Lucas De Graaf got to his feet. All the senior officers of all the VMC fleets were present in the Cabinet Office, as well as the many senior Erdogan and non-Praetorian officers who were largely in command of the Home Fleet. The government ministers were present, the Lord and Lady Erdogan, and Horatio Grant in his role as Administrator for Justice, Law and Security. The new Solar Administration Chancellor for the Praetor System was present, an illegitimate bastard of one of the Lords of House Van Der Meer, who took the name Mathis Van Der Meer.

Gavain reflected that it was a sign of how fast the Vindicatus nation was changing and growing that the Praetorian dominance, although still in a majority, was fading as the populace became more and more diluted. He did not see it as a threat, he saw it as a natural evolution of his nation. He wanted a diverse territory, a safe refuge for all those damaged by the Dissolution of the Red Imperium.

"The unknown enemy, who for now we are referring to as the Shadows," said Lucas, "took thirty solar systems in day one as we were briefed. Day two saw no action, the very few systems of the Frontier Hegemony that were left, and the OutWorlds Alliance, both desperately consolidating their positions. It is a reasonable assumption that the days delay was as the Shadows re-arranged and repositioned themselves, perhaps, as earlier this morning Imperial Standard time they jumped again and appeared in new systems."

A graphical map in the centre of the room flashed to show the sudden advance of the enemy. There was a series of gasps and mutterings as the assembled people saw the advance. "This time they took seventeen solar systems, expanding further into the Boundary. The Frontier Hegemony was almost destroyed immediately, there being only three systems in the Frontier left now, which remain ignored by the Shadows. Instead they swallowed a number of House territories whole, those who had declared independence following Dissolution but were not aligned to any larger alliance or nation. Those they did not swallow whole, their advance was carefully planned to cut through their military might or governmental seats, so the Houses are as good as destroyed."

"The advance is interesting," said Field Marshal Ulrik Andryukhin, "they ignored the might of the OutWorlds Alliance, and instead pushed into the Boundary further, going for weaker targets. It makes little strategic sense."

"It depends on what their ultimate aims are," said Lord Gavain darkly, with unusual feeling.

"True," Field Marshal Andryukhin nodded.

"The OutWorlds Alliance did not ignore them," said Admiral-of-the-Fleets Lucas De Graaf. "Approximately five hours after the sudden expansion of the Shadows, First Lord Al-Zuhairi ordered his military to jump into territory they had lost. He was obviously taking a gamble that the enemy might be overstretched. It was a mistake - more of the Shadows had jumped into the systems they had already taken, and his military forces suffered more damage. OutWorlds Alliance losses were severe, and they failed to take any system back from the Shadows. The Shadows did not pursue, they merely defended."

"There is a much deeper plan at work here," said Lord Gavain. "They have a bigger objective in mind, but without knowing what that is we are operating blind."

"We are always operating blind where the Shadows are concerned," grunted Admiral Harley Andersson.

"Why do you call them Shadows?" asked Lady Erdogan.

"Jonathan?" Gavain said.

O'Connor answered the Lady, but spoke to everybody. "We are releasing previously classified files to all of you. The Rosicrux conspiracy or organisation is a name some here will recognise, others will only know the lightest of details on. We have been able to discern that the Rosicrux, from whom we took this Dark Heart System, were working for another deeper group. We only ever heard them referred to as the ''Shadow', with some references to another group called the 'Third Circle'. We have since found references to a 'Second Circle' and a 'Fourth Circle', so we think that the Circles are actually different levels or organisations within this greater organisation known as the 'Shadow'. The details are in the files being released to you now."

"It is plans within plans," said Gavain, as various people were avidly reading their advanced intelligence. "The Rosicrux were a regional organisation, and we believe the Shadows were over all of the various regional organisations in different segments. We have no true idea of their exact reach. All we know is their military warships appeared to be exactly the same in design as the one that was revealed in the Khobar System, and all of these ships-of-the-line that are suddenly invading the Alegran Edge Segment out on the Frontier and Boundary."

Lord Erdogan, who looked after governmental Communications and Transport, said, "Galaxy-wide, some networks are referring to these Shadows as aliens. Is there any truth to that?"

O'Connor laughed. "No, we know they are human. We have one in custody, the former Solar Administrator of Dark Heart. They are human in origin. They are just very advanced."

"Still," said Andersson, "tell me what is human any more. We have simulant clones, advanced cyborgs, cyborgs born in vats and artificially matured, humans that are genetically engineered biologically, hive minds, biomedical genetically altered mutations where we terraformed the person rather than the planet."

"This is just another variant," Vice-Admiral O'Connor agreed. "We just don't know what, yet."

"What intelligence do we have on the actions of the other nations?" Lord Gavain said, bringing the discussion back on-topic.

"The Frontier Hegemony none at all," said O'Connor, "but then they don't really exist anymore. The OutWorlds Alliance and the StarCom Federation are probably just days away from launching InterStellar Hyperspace Missiles at each other, equipped with Tears of the Moon warheads, on a scale of devastation we have never seen before. Many systems on both sides would be completely destroyed, billions and billions killed. It would be worse than the Droid Wars all over again, the deaths played out in the space of hours real-time."

"The Shadows are deliberately pretending to be StarCom Federation aligned," said Admiral Andersson.

"They want to provoke the destruction," agreed Ulrik Andryukhin. "But, for fuck's sake, why?"

"We don't know," said Lord Gavain, "but we can prove it. Vice-Admiral O'Connor, Lord Kemal, get all the classified files we have on the Shadows to both the OutWorlds Alliance and the StarCom Federation. They need the intelligence, and I want to stop them from launching weapons at each other. We can prove these Shadows are not StarCom, and I will record a personal message asking them to cease and climb-down. The Shadows are their real enemy, not each other."

"Aye, sir," said Vice-Admiral O'Connor.

"Yes, Jamie," said Admiral Andersson quietly.

"What do we know of the Shadows, their warships, what's happening in their territory?" asked Gavain.

"Not enough, and very little, sums it up," said O'Connor.

"They are the greatest threat we have seen since the False Emperor," said Lord Gavain, "and we all thought the StarCom Federation's ambitions were bad enough. I need that information, Jonathan. What can you do about it."

Brigadier Viktor Vantanik looked up, having apparently been bored through most of the conversation. The man was a biomorph, and not geared up like most humans, augmented or not. "There are biomorphs approaching the area," he said, "aboard three frigates and some corvettes seconded to Vice-Admiral O'Connor's intelligence division. The mission was to find out what was behind the alien sighting, but current events have revealed that to us. They are currently out there, almost in range."

"Then use them," Lord Gavain ordered. "I am not operating blind any more. I need hard intelligence on the enemy capability, and what is happening behind their lines and in the territory they have taken. I need to know what their objectives are."

"All of this is very distant to us," said Dr Erin Presson, "and whilst it is highly alarming ....."

"It may be distant for now," said Lord Gavain darkly, "but the Shadows were behind the Rosicrux, attempting to orchestrate events here in the Eastern Segment. They are trying to influence the destruction of StarCom. We do not know their ultimate aim, but they have their sights set well beyond the Frontier and the Boundary. They are the biggest threat we face."

Admiral Jonathan O'Connor, the Chief of Intelligence for the Vindicatus nation, ignored the Imperial Salutes as he entered the operations room within Heart Palace. This was just one of many that made up his personal fiefdom of the Vindicatus Intelligence Agency, a number of floors and an entire wing devoted to the gathering of intelligence and covert non-military - and sometimes even military - operations.

He crossed the operations room as the various agents returned to their duties, approaching the central podium where the director of the room's activities stood like a conductor in charge of an ancient classical band. He stepped up onto the podium, saying, "Commander, you called for me?"

"Yes, Vice Admiral," the Commander replied, "we have received some disturbing information. You were aware that the party from the Interstellar Merchants Guild arrived in-system earlier today?"

"Yes," said O'Connor. "Go on." The Interstellar Merchants Guild had no official presence in the Dark Heart Artificial System, and their Deputy Head had been personally pressuring Lord Gavain to allow them to establish a proper base of operations in the capital city of Primaris Megapolis on Dark Heart Alpha. Their starship had arrived this morning, it had been covered as a brief annotation in the days briefing earlier.

"The Interstellar Merchants Guild is granted special status by all Houses, and we agreed to the same as part of their conditions for allowing them in-system. Part of that was that they are excused normal security checks."

"Yes," nodded O'Connor. He had been unhappy about it, but no House or nation conducted the security checks on the Interstellar Merchants Guild personnel or equipment. They had remained completely neutral since the Dissolution of the Red Imperium, never once showing favouritism or joining in the separatist politics that had wracked the colonised galaxy. Their entire position and strength of mercantile control was founded on trust, so they would never jeopardise that. The Star Communications Network, once also granted the special status, had lost that the moment President Nielsen had formed the Federation and revealed the size of their secret army. They were two Imperial institutions, one still forming the backbone of the colonised galaxy in controlling and moderating interstellar trade impartially, the other losing control and position through their attempt to grab territorial power in the vacuum left by the False Emperor's forced removal.

"As you directed, we allowed them through the commercial Spacestation Delta without security checks. They were escorted through to Starport Primaris, on the fringes of the capital city, and again allowed through the terminal checks. As we transported them in their convoy of honour aboard our air-cars, we scanned them all secretly using the biomorphic scanners we developed to check for the body-chameleons. We are confident we were not detected by them, it was our only chance to perform the scans. Here are the results."

Jacked into the datasphere, Vice-Admiral O'Connor could not help a reaction as he accessed the data. Of the seventy-nine people the Interstellar Merchants Guild had sent, twenty-two were biomorphs. The IMG did not have such technology, not to the level which the scans were showing. Only the Vindicatus nation, the Faceless Imperial assassins, and the Shadows had such technology.

"We have just let twenty-two biomorphs into the system," O'Connor repeated, feeling his anger growing. "The IMG probably did not know, they have probably been infiltrated, but this is a disaster."

"I have already informed Brigadier Vantanik," said the Commander, "he has scrambled his own biomorphic soldiers. We were not expecting this. We have all the IMG personnel under observation, as once they enter their purpose-built complex we have no visibility. We will track everyone who leaves or enters that compound."

"Good work, Commander."

"But of course, they are due to meet Lord Gavain later today. There is a significant security risk there. What if these are Faceless?"

"There are too many for this to be assassination, but then again, we have seen them operate in these numbers to take back our captured Faceless," said O'Connor thoughtfully. "I will discuss it with the Lord. We will just have to monitor them and try to control them. We will cancel the meeting today, with apologies, and tell the IMG just to proceed with establishing their headquarters. We may be able to turn this to our advantage, and track them back to the Shadows."

O'Connor connected directly to Lord Gavain, and appraised him of the situation. A couple of moments later he said, "Lord Gavain concurs, and the meeting is cancelled. We have an opportunity here. We need to discover how they penetrated the IMG, what they are doing here, and whether we can track them back to the Shadows. At last, we have another lead."

*

Admiral Adare was wearing his new uniform. He was exceptionally proud of it, the symbols of the new Third Empire displayed proudly on the chest and flash-patches. For the first time since the fall of the False Emperor, he felt he had found a new purpose, something he really, truly could believe in. He was helping the Shadow Emperor, and that renewed sense of meaning was not only surprising to someone who had his psychopathic profile but very overdue and welcome. It was leading to a superiority of feeling towards those ex-Praetorians who had not had the same opportunity to join the new Empire.

His uniform was red, but with the silver colourings and trim that denoted his membership of the military. He was officially a member of the Second Circle, and had been granted the rank of full Admiral. The Shadow Empire wanted him, and he had joined willingly.

Even more joyously, he had been told in no uncertain terms that the reason why the Shadow Emperor wanted him was to finally put an end to James Gavain should the upstart Lord interfere further with His Imperial plans.

Iyan Lamans and Zehra Sahin walked behind him respectfully, as they entered the turbolift heading to the bridge. <This is it, my friends,> he said across the datasphere, <now we see our new home.>

The turbolift doors opened, and they strode onto the bridge of the ship that had rescued them from the Levitican Union. The Captain of the ship wore the Second Circle naval uniform, and stood up to salute as Adare entered.

<Admiral on the bridge,> the Captain said.

<At ease, you have the bridge,> Admiral Adare said, striding across to his flag chair. <How long until we translate?>

<Two minutes, Admiral.>

<Carry on, Captain.>

Iyan Lamans, now wearing a Colonel's rank insignia, and Zehra Sahin, now ranked a Captain, stood by the side of Adare as he sat. They were to be his new senior command crew on the ship he was about to receive, courtesy of the Third Emperor.

The Shadow Empire's ships were based on next-generation Praetorian technology. Adare had been presented with full access to the military classifications and data of the Shadow Empire's forces. The Shadow military had some of the more recent standard Praetorian classes of ships-of-the-line in its fleets, which consisted of S-class strikecruisers, T-class dreadnoughts, U-class destroyers and V-class battlecruisers, none of which had been revealed yet in the blitzkrieg invasions so as not to expose the Shadow Empire's links to the previous Red Imperium of Mars. All had been upgraded with the new Shadow-grade technology of the Eighth Circle.

It was the next generation of advanced technology, the next generation of Praetorian technology that had never seen the light of day in the previous Imperium that astounded Adare. Not only was some of it truly ingenious, but it had been hidden even from the Praetorian Guard of the False Emperor themselves.

They had new classes of ships-of-the-line. The W-class was a star-carrier packed with new starfighter and starbomber designs, and with an amazingly large capacity. The new Y-class frigate was a compact demon, perfect for multiple roles and operating individually. The X-class destroyer-transporters combined the power of a destroyer, typically used for long-range and planetary bombardment, with the carrying capacity of a transporter, with large marine contingents. One or two could lead a planetary invasion. And finally, there was the jewel in the crown. A new type and classification of warship, the Z-class juggernaut, one and half times the size of a dreadnought and the largest military ship-of-the-line ever built in all of history.

<Translation in three .... two .... one ...... we have translation,> the helmsman said matter-of-factly.

Adare paid special interest to the data that suddenly flooded the datasphere as they jumped back into real-space. They were within an uninhabited solar system within the Helvanna Dominion, hidden away from casual eyesight. The solar system was deserted, with few planets and nothing of interest. Apart from a rapidly moving super-comet, there was nothing else in the system apart from them.

<Broadcast the IFF and ciphered clearance codes,> the Captain of the Y-class frigate ordered.

<Broadcasting, aye, sir.>

Moments later space began to ripple as Adare watched through the frigates sensors, the three small squadrons of ships hidden here suddenly revealing themselves in all their glory. Two squadrons consisted of the Praetorian ships known throughout the galaxy, but one squadron had the new ultra-modern advanced Shadow vessels. Largest of all were the two juggernauts, and of them, Adare's eyes were drawn to the one that was to be his new ship.

The name was clearly inscribed across its hull. The *ISS Zero Tolerance*.

Adare could not help but smile, his eyes shining with greed and mad delight.

"Isn't she beautiful?" he whispered to himself.

*

The hovering droids announced her arrival, as Lady Principal Sophia Towers walked back into the Council Chamber. The Lords and Ladies of the Houses of the Union remained seated, but the various aides and servants all stood and gave the Imperial Salute. She gracefully continued on to her seat, and after a moment or two, she lifted the metal ball and hit the disc it rested upon once with a heavy metallic clang.

"The session break is concluded, the Council is back in session," she announced calmly and clearly.

There were two new faces in the room. One was the new House Lord Vladmir Marchenko, who had elected to take the dead Lady Eranisch's position as the Lord Minister for Transformation and Integration. His skull was malformed by the heavy-duty and archaic borg alterations, the massively elongated cranium supported on his right shoulder by a clunky armature. He had an extra two legs for the vast weight he carried, and when he moved it was very slowly. His chest was open to the air, lights flickering around his heart cage. Like all Marchenkans, he looked like a mad doctor's mental image of a nightmare.

The other new face was that of Lord Jorrik Jorgensson. He looked confident and reassured. Despite the history of bad blood between her house and his, Lady Principal Sophia found herself quite warming to the man; it had certainly made their negotiations easier. His brother Sven was incarcerated by his father, House Lord Oren Jorgensson, who was too ill to attend himself. Jorrik was now permanently granted a special seat in the Council, Minister without Portfolio, and a new position.

"To recap," Lady Principal Sophia said, "As of this morning, House Jorgensson officially joined the Levitican Union. They have done so under special terms, taking one seat in the Council without a Ministry. They will pay tax and contribute to the welfare of the Union, but their military will not unify with ours and remain independent, although we may call on it at any point. They will remain in control of their own law, and retain their own monetary independence. Their infrastructure will remain under their control, although they will divorce themselves from StarCom control of their stargates and HPCGs. Such are the terms of their joining the Union. Today we are one House bigger, Lords and Ladies.

"The vote before the Council session break was on the re-organisation of the Council itself, and amendment to the Levitican Union Charter. From this point on, we have a two-tier Council and two-tier Union membership. Full members have a Ministry, and accordingly greater control of the Union's political direction. In Council votes Lord Ministers of active Ministries have two votes each, whilst House Jorgensson has one vote as a second-tier member. Lord Brin Claes will approach other Houses on our borders and ask if they wish to join the Union as second-tier members; in such a way, we hope the Union will continue to grow. Congratulations are due to all concerned for this restructure and peace."

A series of polite applause broke out amongst the assembled Lords and Ladies, their aides joining in. Eventually Lady Principal Sophia hit her gavel once again to appeal for silence. "We now move on to a very serious matter. I must ask all aides to leave the Council Chamber, only Ministers may remain. The record of this next debate will be classified top-secret, and either destroyed after conclusion or classified restricted for three hundred years."

There was respectful silence as the aides and servants left the room. There was now only the eight of them in the room.

Once the doors had closed, Lady Principal Sophia leaned forwards. She was nervous despite herself, but the look she focused on Lord Micalek Zupanic hardened and he looked down at the table. "Our next vote is to discuss what we do about the revelations on the Rosicrux organisation and the involvement and treachery of House Zupanic, as revealed to us by Lord Gavain of the Vindicatus nation, Lord Vladmir Marchenko and Lord Jorrik Jorgensson. Does anyone wish to take the floor?"

A number of people signalled for the right to speak, but Lady Sophia gave the floor to Lord Minister Vladmir Marchenko.

"House Marchenko is disgusted by the leadership of Gregori Marchenko and his line, in leading us to betray the Levitican Union. Let us reassure you that House Marchenko under my family-branch leadership will take no part in such plots to harm the Union. The damage to our nation and reputation is considerable. The elements of Marchenko that conspired with the Rosicrux against the Union are now dead. The elements of House Jorgensson that conspired with the Rosicrux are also now removed. All that remains from the attempt at betrayal and destruction of the Union now lives within House Zupanic, the same House that once led the Union. We move that they, and Lord Micalek, must be punished, but in such a way that the Union is not further damaged. We are open to suggestions on what form that censure takes."

Lord Jorrik Jorgensson took the floor next. "House Jorgensson also formally apologises, although our situation was somewhat different. It has indirectly led to our joining the Union, which is perhaps something we should all be thankful for. The Rosicrux plan almost brought us to war, but because of its failure, we have peace. From our point of view, we were never in league with House Zupanic or the old leadership of House Marchenko. Our own traitors were allied to the Rosicrux. On the subject of House Zupanic, we appeal for a measured response, but agree that some form of punishment is required. Zupanic must pay reparations, but the Union cannot gain one member and lose another."

Lady Monique Lapointe had her turn next. "House Lapointe does not appeal for such calm, or such a measured response. I have revealed to you all how my mother Elouise was deliberately targeted and murdered by the Rosicrux, and how I was threatened by House Zupanic. It is not known how much House Zupanic had to do with the murder, but their knowledge and use of it and their alliance with the Rosicrux has severely harmed my House, as well as the Levitican Union. We move for the removal of Lord Micalek Zupanic as the head of house, and whilst we do not want Zupanic to leave the Union, their territory should be divided and reduced as a punishment, and their remaining territory policed very carefully by every other House. House Lapointe also demands Lord Micalek is formally charged, and answers for his crimes under Levitican Union Law."

Lord Brin Claes stood. "Many here noticed that House Claes was voting with and very strongly allied to House Zupanic. It came as a surprise to many. The truth was that the former Lord Ramicek Zupanic was blackmailing us, on a deep, dark subject I have revealed to you all in confidence. Whilst it shames my House personally, I thank you all for your understanding. But we were being blackmailed. House Claes moves for heavy censure of House Zupanic, but also appeals that the reparations are moderate, to prevent significant damage to the Union."

"Thank you, Lord Brin," said Lady Sophia, "we all understand the difficult position you were in. Lady Aria Galetti?"

Lady Galetti said, "House Galetti was not touched by the treachery of Zupanic so much, but ultimately House Zupanic planned to conquer us through betrayal of the Union. I remind you that House Marchenko and House Jorgensson were not without some blame in this. I move for moderation in our punishment, but their actions must be recognised."

Lord Moafa Obamu actually stood, his tattooed muscle on open, bare display. "House Obamu is grievously injured by the plans of the Zupanic, but ultimately the damage to us was minimal as the plot was uncovered in time. We cannot ever trust House Zupanic again for the plot to conquer us by betrayal. We move for the division of their territory, with some small amount remaining to House Zupanic. We also move that they are removed from the Ministry of Military Defence and put in charge of a different Ministry. They cannot be trusted."

Lady Sophia Towers was the last to speak. "House Towers was greatly harmed by House Zupanic. My father was killed. I was married to Micalek, and he has betrayed me personally. We conspired with Zupanic to assassinate much of House Zupanic, partly to protect ourselves I admit, but also to protect the Union. The thing we feared, that this all came into the open, has unfortunately happened. We believe also House Zupanic must be punished. On a personal note, although such things are rare, we also ask for annulment of the marriage between our Houses. Benjamin Towers must be brought up as a Towers, without Zupanic influence. House Zupanic must be punished for their betrayal."

She cleared her throat. "Lord Minister Micalek, do you have anything to say in your defence?"

He too stood, and looked at her directly. "No," he said, "not really. I personally was aware of some of the plots, but not all, and sometimes only at later dates than you may imagine. But I appreciate no-one here will trust me anymore. I am complicit in the murder of some of my family and my father and mother, but remind you all that I did do it with the assistance of our Lady Principal. House Zupanic does not wish to leave the Union, and will of course accept any punishment delivered to us. But I also appeal for understanding. On the marriage issue, I will accept annulment and not challenge, but on a personal level, I will openly say that I do genuinely love you, Lady Sophia Towers. I beg you to reconsider."

He sat back down, looking absolutely destroyed.

Lady Sophia Towers stood in the second bedroom attached to her quarters, looking at the blissfully sleeping form of her child. It had been a long and emotionally stressful day, and she was more than glad it was over.

The Council had voted and decided upon what to do. They would not reveal the treachery of House Zupanic, and would concoct a cover story to tell their citizens and the galaxy at large. They would claim ill-health of Lord Micalek Zupanic, and that he himself had requested for assistance from the Union in managing his House.

The punishment was something much worse. All money in the Union, with the exception of House Jorgensson, was pooled, so the reparations could not be monetary. All House Zupanic truly had was its landholding.

House Towers, House Obamu, House Claes, House Lapointe, and House Marchenko would all take a number of systems from House Zupanic, drastically reducing their territory. Lord Micalek was being moved from the Ministry of Military Defence, instead taking the Ministry of Integration and Transformation. Lord Vladmir would become the Minister for Military Defence.

The amount of money reserved for House Zupanic from the Levitican Union treasury would be vastly reduced, the people suffering for the actions of their House. Although all the military was unified, no more recruits would ever come from House Zupanic. The Houses internal affairs would be closely monitored by Lady Aria Galetti, including their intelligence activities. Lord Micalek would be carefully monitored and kept on Leviticus, not allowed to leave, but he would not be formally charged with treachery under Levitican Union Law. It would be kept quiet.

On a personal note, the marriage between their Houses was formally annulled that evening. House Zupanic truly had no claim on House Towers territory.

As Lady Sophia looked at her son, she felt relieved that she had protected him from Micalek. Yet, she also had a niggling feeling of self-doubt. She had loved Lord Micalek, and in her heart of hearts, she knew he had loved her too.

But sometimes love was not enough to stop someone doing wrong to you, if the stakes were high enough and the benefits to them were great enough.

Chapter X

Captain Jason Bramhall removed the orange-flavoured revitalisation drink from the food simulator, drawing deeply from it as he returned to his desk. Even whilst he was physically focusing on the task of sustenance, his mind was jacked in to the datasphere through the borg modem implant, his computer processing centres rapidly filtering and working through the data he was analysing.

<Incoming pulse channel call from Solar High Chancellor Andersson,> said his communications officer, breaking in on his reflection.

<Patch it through,> he ordered. Within moments a holographic image of Andersson had appeared in front of him, the graphic so perfect it was almost as if he was stood in the *VSS Occupier*'s ready room.

"Admiral Andersson," he said.

"Captain Bramhall," Andersson said, "Just a quick call about Praetor. But before that - have you seen the latest on the advance of the Shadows?"

"I saw the intel briefing from Vice-Admiral O'Connor. They have expanded their captured territory again," Captain Bramhall nodded, "moving further into the Boundary. After repelling the OutWorlds Alliance counter-attack, they are eating through more Houses. This is a phenomenal assault, Admiral."

"I find it exceptionally worrying," Andersson nodded. "Some of the ships from the Fourth Support Fleet are leading our attempt to get into the area, to get intel. I assume you've not heard anything yet?"

"I and Brigadier Vantanik are not due to hear for some while," said Jason Bramhall, sipping from his drink again. "At the rate of the Shadow advance, it won't be long until our ships are within the territory caught in the invasion. They're almost advancing faster than we can jump there. It's just the distance from here and the span of stars our scouting parties have to cover that is causing a delay now, the colonised galaxy is huge."

"We know," Andersson nodded. "We need to know what the Shadows are doing with the territory they control. All we know at the moment is that all communications end, no intelligence comes out of it, no shipping, it just all goes quiet. But anyway, I wanted to talk to you about the colonisation efforts. How are they proceeding?"

"There's good news there at least, sir," said Captain Bramhall. "The colonisation efforts here in the Praetor System continue at a fast pace. The population is now two million, we're taking in lots of immigrants."

"Our immigration expands every day with the refugees," said Admiral Andersson. "The Aalborg Alliance is collapsing, and many of the Aalborg Alliance citizens are now flooding into our territory, as if we did not have enough from the Erdogans and all the rest. The Helvanna Dominion will have ended the war in a week or two. And we have more Praetorian Guard than ever coming in, in addition to our new batch from the biovats about to be 'born'."

"Have you considered allowing them direct access to the Praetor System?" asked Bramhall.

"Jamie says not," said Andersson. "The security risks are too high, and we need to ensure every person coming in as a refugee is scanned for biomorphic technology. We're keeping the existence of the Praetor System secret for as long as possible. And also, we have indications that the Zhou-Zheng Compact is building up to try and exact revenge us - if they attack Dark Heart it is one thing, but the Praetor System has nowhere near the defences."

"That's not quite true," said Bramhall, "the colonists here are working exceptionally hard. There is a good atmosphere of motivation. The fabricators and manuprinters are churning out new constructs, and that applies to the military defences as well as the colony infrastructure. We'll never be as heavily protected as Dark Heart, obviously, but the Praetor System has improved defence-wise ahead of schedule."

"And is the long-range astronomical array we liberated from the House Jorgensson Alesund System under construction?"

"Yes," Bramhall nodded, "I think five more days and we will have it re-constructed here. Then we can use it for astronomical observations, as well as spying."

"Send me the reports," said Andersson, "but well done. Any other news?"

Bramhall spent some time going through the latest developments in the Praetor System, and overall they were ahead of schedule in virtually every respect. There was an intra-system political structure, an enforcer, adjudicator and justiciar circuit established, local home guard defences, charity and assistance organisations, industry and commercial associations already in place. Cloning facilities, insemination surgeries and artificial growth biovats were already in full production, and the population would shortly explode with home-grown simulant clones of existing colonists and brand new genetically bioartificed people. The solar system was already self-sufficient, capable of providing its own food and sustenance, and the mining for the Amerimax moleculisation constituents had already begun. In another two weeks, they would be in full production, and the approaching food crisis in the Vindicatus nation would forever be averted. They would actually have a surplus.

"Jamie is very proud of you," said Admiral Andersson, "as am I. This is an outstanding achievement, Jason."

"Thank you, Admiral," Jason glowed under the praise, unable to conceal his pride over the compliment. "But as you know, I still have my nine exploratorships out there in the Gulf Of Medusa, searching the abandoned solar systems. I think we may have found another one we could colonise."

"Really?" asked Andersson. "I'll set up a call with Jamie, if you're sure. What are the benefits? Where is the system?"

"We're focusing on systems heading towards the Levitican Union, as directed," said Bramhall, "although we're still looking in every direction around the black hole cluster of Dark Heart. This one is further out than Praetor, two full jumps from Praetor towards the Union. It's a triple solar system, rich and abundant in more constituent parts for Amerimax around one of the suns. Metals and natural resources are high. It has a number of super-planets suitable for colonisation, all of which have advanced eco-systems. Minimal terraformation required. Some droid technology is present - and in addition, we have found an entire ISHM facility, a second one, in the second of the three solar systems."

"Is it fully loaded?" asked Andersson.

"Some of the missiles have been fired, but the majority are present," Bramhall confirmed. "The third planetary system has an ancient HPCG system, and there is even a dilapidated and broken stargate there which we can fix. It would link nicely into the Web of Deepspace Stations. Some of the planets are truly beautiful, long-term we could even use them as tourist attractions. The natural wildlife on some of the planets is highly unique. The third planetary system of the three is heavily shielded by asteroid fields, and another cluster of black holes another jump or so on towards the Union and the Aalborg Alliance and Helvanna Dominion prevents its easy detection. The other two planetary systems are not so easily defended, so there is risk attached there, although again there are old droid defences there. Some of the defences almost destroyed one of my exploratorships actually, it was a close run thing, so we would have to be careful as we approach and deactivate the defences."

"It sounds good," said Andersson. "We'll speak to Gavain, Jason. You're doing well."

"Thanks, Harley," said Jason, smiling broadly. All may not be going well in the galaxy, but at least he was carrying out his job exceptionally well.

*

The atmosphere in the Golden Room of the Palace of Communications on Earth was exceptionally tense. President Pereyra, Vice-President Schneider, Director Chbihi and Commander-In-Chief Ryan were all quiet as they read through the intelligence briefing and reports before them. Pereyra had demanded the full detail, not just a summary, and they had been here for two hours going through it all. Even with the datasphere and their cybernetic implants, there was a lot of information to digest.

Pereyra was aware that the other three were waiting for her to finish, but she was re-reading the information again. Eventually, she looked up, leaving the reports and minimising them within her mind. "And all this information came from the Vindicatus nation, and Lord Gavain?"

"All of it," Director Chbihi confirmed.

"How much of it can we believe?"

"It is all there in the reports, Madam President," Vice-President Schneider said.

"Humour me, Director," Pereyra directed, ignoring her Vice-President.

"We can verify some of it, and other elements match secondary and tertiary information we had gathered. My analysts think it fits some information we were becoming aware of, but that is not proof of course. The holographic imaging and holo-pics all seem to be real and untampered with. Analysis of Lord Gavain's foreword and introductory cover-note to the information suggests that he is telling the truth or what he believes to be the truth, according to the psych-profile we have on him."

"So we can trust this?" asked Commander-In-Chief Ryan. "He is getting painted as a skilful political manipulator at the moment."

"You sound like you don't believe it," said Vice-President Schneider, "the release of this information proves he is."

"Maybe," said Ryan, "but in showing us all this about the Shadow's he is trying to prevent a war between us and the OWA, one which would see us firing missiles with planetary destroying warheads across half the galaxy at one another."

"He states it is stop the Shadows from progressing with their plans, whatever they may be," said Chbihi. "He says he doesn't know what those plans are, and that may well be the truth, but we can't deny that with Suularitsaar on our doorstep a war with the OWA is the last thing we need. Especially as these Shadows seem to want to provoke that war for some reason."

"It is unfortunate Lord Gavain does not know why," said President Pereyra.

"It is to weaken us, or them, or both," said Ryan, "it is the only reason. But the Shadows are so distant, why would we be seen as a threat to them?"

"Look at how fast they are moving," said Director Malika Chbihi, "they are eating worlds and systems at a phenomenal rate."

"Their expansion is not sustainable, their supply lines will become untenable," said Ryan.

"By normal standards, but these Shadows are not normal," said Chbihi. "They have evidenced technology we do not have. Who knows what they are capable of in terms of supply and logistics."

"Lord Gavain says he will try to find out and pass us the information," said President Pereyra. "But he also appeals to us to end our antagonism with the OutWorlds Alliance. He has sent all this information to First Lord Al-Zuhairi too, the cover note was addressed to both me and him."

"Can we determine what First Lord Al-Zuhairi's reaction will be?" asked Vice-President Schneider.

It was then that Giovanna Pereyra showed the decisiveness which made her so suitable for her role. "There is only one way to find out. Request a live transmission pulse-channel with First Lord Al-Zuhairi, right now."

First Lord Al-Zuhairi felt the warm, hot air of the midday sun burning his skin on the balcony, as the holographic image of President Giovanna Pereyra appeared before him. His own advisors were stood in the main quarters of his private chambers, watching the broadcast, and he had no doubt that Pereyra's own advisors were just off-camera in the Golden Room of the Presidential Palace of Communications.

Where he was dressed in traditional Frontier and Boundary clothing, further marked by the hot, arid worlds of his own House with its light, cooling design, President Pereyra was dressed in the full white and regal blue regalia of the StarCom Federation. Where he looked like a sophisticated but also barbarian savage chief, she looked like an advanced political supremo, a master of all she surveyed and fit to rule an Empire herself. She was good looking, he noticed, and he saw the small smile as she looked at him. Maybe in another world, and another circumstance.

"President Giovanna Pereyra," said First Lord Al-Zuhairi, "Well met, in the name of the one True Emperor."

"Well met, First Lord Al-Zuhairi," the President of the StarCom Federation replied.

"I will not waste time with you, but I appreciate your calling me by continuous hyper-pulse. I was about to request the same of you." The language was courteous and polite, but the hardness in his eyes belied the pleasant words.

"Good," said President Pereyra. "As my approach said, I wanted to discuss the information from Lord Gavain, on the Rosicrux and these mysterious Shadows. Have you had a chance to review it all?"

"Oh yes," said First Lord Al-Zuhairi. "It is very interesting indeed. Although the ships all carry StarCom Federation colours and IFF markings, apparently you are innocent. According to Lord Gavain. It all seems highly unbelievable, considering our recent past."

"Without getting side-tracked from the discussion of the Shadows," said President Pereyra, "you and me, and some others, realised the damage President Nielsen was doing to the Federation and the core, and wanted to fix her growing insanity. You and I took the co-operation we showed during the Revolutionary Council and the rebellion against the False Emperor, and worked together to get rid of yet another tyrant in the form of Nielsen. Is it not time to show that level of co-operation again?"

"It was not co-operation, it was expediency," said First Lord Al-Zuhairi. "She wanted to build another Red Imperium, and her insanity was threatening all of us. She tried to have me killed. It was self-defence as much as altruism towards humanity."

"Either way, we worked together once. We now face a similar threat."

"Do we, though?" asked First Lord Al-Zuhairi. "In Lord Gavain's opinion we do. I am not so sure. Whilst you have probably analysed this information from the Mercenary Lord, and it appears to be genuine, you know as well as I he has access to advanced Praetorian technology."

"So do we," said President Pereyra, "the Praetorians were born here in the Sol System, and you benefitted greatly from the Dissolution of the Praetorian Guard."

"True, but he has found more from somewhere," said Al-Zuhairi. "And these Shadows, if that is what they are, seem to have greater and more advanced technology than all of us. How do I not know that the Mercenary Lord is not working with you, President Pereyra, and you are both trying to lead me astray."

"We have no intention –"

"Look at the Tears Incident," Al-Zuhairi interrupted. "StarCom betrayal led to my punishment. We are both arming again, ready to fire, we both know it."

"I have today ordered my ISHMs with Tears of the Moon warheads to stand down," said President Pereyra. "Your own spies will doubtless confirm this."

"Regardless, what guarantees do I have that this is not some trap? The politics of the old Red Imperium were Machiavellian and complicated enough to make this plausible."

"It is paranoia, with the greatest respect, First Lord," said Pereyra. "And I know despite your posturing you believe me and my nation may be innocent or we would not be having this conversation. The StarCom Federation, Vindicatus or the OutWorlds Alliance does not have the technology that these Shadows are displaying. That is fact, without doubt. Nor do we have their drive. They are working towards some unknown aim – but be honest, on your own your nation would be dead. Look at how they ripped through your territory, and batted aside your counter-attack like it was an inconvenience."

"Maybe," said Al-Zuhairi, unwilling to show any weakness, "but it is also true that they are continuing on, further into the boundary, ignoring me and on some plan or quest of their own. They may come back for my territory, they may not. Why are you so concerned?"

"Because Lord Gavain saw fit to warn me," said Pereyra, "and no-one knows what their ultimate aims are. They have been manipulating politics all over the galaxy before they suddenly appeared out on the Frontier, so they are preparing for something big. End our growing tension and join with me, First Lord. Look to Lord Gavain. At least let's co-operate, and end this growing aggression between us. We cannot afford it with these Shadows, whoever they are, pulling everyone's strings. There are deeper things at play here. And First Lord Al-Zuhairi?"

"Yes?"

"I ask you this in all genuine honesty, and I respectfully request for you to agree to my humble request."

He kept his face straight, and then laughed, surprising his advisors. "You know my culture and my people well, President Pereyra," he said, his entire demeanour changed.

"It is what I said to you when we plotted against Nielsen, and before, in the Revolutionary Council when we worked with her," she said.

"And in your time as a Solar Administration Chancellor a century ago, here on the Frontier, you learnt the significance of those words," said Al-Zuhairi, "you are remembered and you know, Giovanna. Very well. We have a truce, for now. Let us work together. Let us see what else our brave Mercenary Lord can find for us. We have a new enemy, a new common goal. We work together, until this threat has passed. My blood on it."

"My blood on it," replied Pereyra.

"I will direct Chief Amab to contact your Director Chbihi. Let the co-operation start there. First Lord Al-Zuhairi out."

He then leaned back in his suspensor chair as the holographic image faded, and he laughed his dark laugh again. "Game well played there, Giovanna, well done," he said to himself.

"Can we trust her version?" Chief Amab asked.

"Without doubt," said First Lord Al-Zuhairi confidently. "For what it was."

*

<Lord Gavain?>

James Gavain awoke. In a nano-second he had jumped to full wakefulness, remembering where he was and who he was with. He was in the Heart Palace aboard the planet Dark Heart Alpha, and he had been asleep, with Harley Andersson in bed with him. His mind instantly went to Juan Ramirez, and he found his heart lurched. He had great respect for Harley, but it was Juan he wanted to be with.

<Gavain speaking.>

<An advance warning from the Deepspace Stations. The Web is tingling, Lord. We have many incoming ships, from the galactic east-east-east."

<Aalborg Alliance and Helvanna Dominion?>

<Yes, sir. They are all identified as either House Lindholm, House Rantanen, or House Haugen-Berg, of the Aalborg Alliance. It has collapsed, and they are fleeing the incoming Helvanna Dominion. There is a massive influx of ships on their way. Their House Lords and Ladies are in the fore-front, requesting our assistance.>

<The waves of refugees from those systems has just turned into a flood, then?> Gavain asked.

<Yes. We're about to be swamped.>

<Call a major meeting of the government. When do the lead ships get here?>

<Ten real-time minutes.>

<Hold all refugees at the space station. I will meet the advance representatives on board the *Vindicatus*. Prepare the battlecruiser,> he ordered.

<Aye, sir.>

Lord Gavain entered his ready room, Field Marshal Ulrik Andryukhin, Admiral Harley Andersson, and Admiral Lucas De Graaf following him. Between them all walked another man, wearing the uniform of another House military. He still bore the rank insignia of Admiral-of-the-Fleets, even though he really did not have any more fleets to command.

"Would you like a drink, Jakub?" Lord Gavain asked.

"A whiskey, just on ice," said the Admiral Jakub Halvorssen, of House Lindholm and what had once been the Aalborg Alliance. In the early hours of the morning, the Helvanna Dominion had declared the war over. The Aalborg Alliance had collapsed quicker than the Erdogan nation, General Helvanna and her Dominion taking complete control. Many civilian ships had escaped and were en route here to Dark Heart or elsewhere, and what few military ships had survived were fighting a desperate rear-guard action as the Dominion ruthlessly pursued them.

The Vindicatus nation had sent its Second Fleet out on the Web, with the First Fleet ready to jump in support. The Helvanna Dominion would not be allowed to proceed into the Gulf of Medusa and attack his assets. Gavain had told the Lords and Ladies of the collapsed Aalborg Alliance that in no uncertain terms.

"It is synthesised alcohol," James Gavain warned.

"I really do not care," said Jakub Halvorssen. He looked tired, and miserable.

"I'll do it," said Lucas, moving to get the drink. "You sit down."

Gavain and Halvorssen sat around his desk, as Ulrik laughed. There was a devilish look in his eyes. "A recovering alcoholic getting a synthesised drink? Wonders never cease."

"Rik," Harley Andersson chided.

"It's okay," said Lucas, shrugging it off. As he walked past Ulrik, he stage-whispered, "bastard." Ulrik and Lucas had once hated each other, but they had grown to have a friendship that pleased Jamie no end. He liked his staff to gel, and his immediate circle of friends to like each other. His eyes fell on Harley, and his heart fired with guilt once again.

It was nice to hear laughter, but Gavain realised that Jakub could not relax. The man had been going through his own form of hell recently.

"Look, Jakub," said Gavain, "we cannot offer you any words to make you feel 'better'. All I can encourage you to do is look towards the future."

"I am trying," said Admiral Halvorssen. "My own House has all but died, and the Aalborg Alliance is gone. Some of the House Lords and Ladies have survived, but not all. The assassinations began just after you finished smashing the Rosicrux. We suffered badly, it seemed like the Faceless assassins were everywhere. General Helvanna must have paid the fortune of a small solar system for them."

Gavain carefully did not respond. He was beginning to suspect the Faceless were more than just assassins for hire. He had no evidence though. Just a gut feeling; but then, his gut feelings were often very right.

"We will take all your refugees, give you all new homes, and protect you from the Helvanna Dominion," said Admiral Andersson. "Jamie gave that word to your nobles, and his word is unbreakable."

"Yes," said Admiral Halvorssen. He paused a long time, sipping hard from the generous whiskey. "Thank you," he said slowly.

"You are welcome," said James Gavain, with an awareness of the pleasantries he would not even have come near demonstrating three years ago when he had been a Commander in the Praetorian Guard. "I do have another suggestion for you though, Jakub."

"What is that?" he asked.

"Something for you to focus on in the future. I have offered some of your house Lords and Ladies positions in my government Administration service, perhaps even Solar Chancellorships as we expand. I have something much better in mind for you."

The others began to smile. He had communicated the thought to them across the datasphere whilst the discussions were going on with the delegation from the now defunct Aalborg Alliance.

"What would this be?" Halvorssen asked.

"The situation for you of the Aalborg Alliance is not the same as my new allies in the Erdogans. You cannot resist, the Helvanna Dominion has moved too quickly and too strongly. Your national identity was just not there to ensure survival." Gavain paused as he thought on that and his own nation. "You are not going to try and fight against the Helvanna Dominion as the Erdogans attempt to resist the conquering of the Zhou-Zheng Compact."

"No, we are not," Halvorssen shook his head. "There is no point."

"But you have a new home here. Let me offer you, Jakub Halvorssen, a seat in my government. I need a new Administrator for Migration Control. It gives you a chance to help your people, and you will be helping me as well. I need it. Do you want the position?"

Ten minutes later, the former Admiral Jakub Halvorssen had said yes, and he had become the Solar Administrator for Migration Control for Vindicatus.

*

The holomap revolved in front of them all, the images from the holo-retinal vision beaming the perspective of the map directly into each one of their eyes. It ensured that they all saw the same image, wherever they sat in the room. The Third Emperor sat on his throne, his nine Legates around him in a semi-circle and on a lower tier.

The holomap showed the entire colonised galaxy. Sections of it were burning in the orangey-red colour of the Third Empire, hazed where they knew they would have some form of support. The solid blocks of colour showed their advance so far, into the Frontier and the Boundary, and a blister like extension on the former boundaries of colonised space showed the additional space beyond the Frontier that the agents of the Shadow Empire had claimed as their own, in absolute secret. They had ripped through the pirates there quietly, removing them as they silently and quietly approached the Frontier, before they exploded into colonised space.

"We are advancing according to plan," said the Third Emperor. "All is going as I envisaged it."

"It is, Emperor," said the Second Legate, in charge of the army and the navy. She was there as a holographic image, once again back on the front lines in her cover position. "The progression of the fleets and the army is all according to plan. On the next advance, we pass out of the Alegran Edge Segment altogether and progress into the Diamond March."

"Is the infrastructure to support our advance being maintained and established to plan?" asked the Third Emperor.

"Yes it is, Emperor," said the Legate of the Eighth Circle, "the new railway is being constructed behind our advance. The defensive forces are there, and utmost secrecy is being maintained."

"No word has passed beyond our new borders," the Legate of the Fourth Circle said.

"And we are pacifying and subjugating the populaces as directed," said the Legate of the Ninth Circle.

"Then all is good. We are approaching the second phase," said the Emperor. "How are the political, covert operations and assassinations proceeding?"

The Third Emperor did not miss the sudden delay, but listened patiently to the telling of the various situations he and his Legates had carefully manipulated around the colonised galaxy. Eventually he said, "and what has not gone right? What are you not telling me?"

The long pause again, and then finally the Third Legate, Jared Towers, said, "We have an issue with the plans to cause war between the OutWorlds Alliance and the StarCom Federation."

"The plan where our entire advance was designed to trigger it, that war, you mean?" said the Third Emperor with a dangerous tone to his voice.

"Yes, Emperor," said Jared Towers. "It appears that despite my attempts at manipulation, and those of the other Legates, First Lord Al-Zuhairi and President Pereyra have reached a state of non-aggression. They are both standing down."

"Why? How has this happened? They should be blowing each other apart?"

The Legate of the Fourth Circle said, "It appears that they have been informed in great detail of our activities and a fair part of our real nature by ..... Lord James Gavain."

"How?" the Emperor said coldly.

He was updated quickly, even bombarded with the same information that Gavain had provided to Pereyra and Al-Zuhairi. "This is intolerable," he said, anger rising quickly, "inexcusable. I thought I ordered this man dead!"

"We finally have Faceless, Fox and Phantom agents in the Dark Heart Artificial System now -" began the Legate of the Fifth, commander of the Faceless assassination branch.

"But he lives! And does this! The weakening of the StarCom Federation was key, the distraction of the OutWorlds Alliance designed to tear them apart. At least Suularitsaar is still threatening them, I assume?"

"Yes, Emperor," said Jared Towers, "the Suularitsaar gambit is still in play."

"This is a disaster," the Third Emperor stood. "Once again this 'Lord' Gavain has caused me an issue. I want him dead."

"It will be done," they all whispered.

"I will wait no more," the Third Emperor said. "On the subject of Lord Gavain, or that of the second phase. We progress to it now, today."

"Some of the nations out there will declare for you straight away, as we have planned, to provide the support," said the Third Legate Jared Towers doubtfully.

"But it is too early –" the Second Legate began.

"It is not!" the Emperor roared. "There was flex in the plan, and it is my plan, so I will decide if I wish to bring it forwards! Set up my announcement address – *now*!"

All across the colonised galaxy, the speech went viral. It worked its way through small localised bulletin boards, into social gossiping sites, and across local and personal dataspheres. It was reported on all major news networks. The encryption on the datapackages transmitting the inaugural speech was so strong, it burned through even the sophisticated StarCom Federation networks and hyper-pulse communications generators, and it leapt from system to system. It hit every major news media network, taking over the broadcast. It burned its way even into the nationwide House media networks.

In the space of minutes in real-time terms, everyone across the galaxy stopped what they were doing. The galaxy fell silent and quiet, work stopping, traffic halting whether it was an aircar above a city or a starliner above a planet or sun. The people of the human race, varied and mixed as they were, augmented, un-augmented, hiver or biomorph, traditionalist human or genetically altered to suit their environment, stopped and as one the vast and varied human race listened to the man who appeared before them, in the skies above them or in the mind's eye.

He spoke for a long time, and the people listened.

"I am the Third Emperor, the Shadow Emperor," he said. "I am the son of the Second or the False Emperor, the grand-son of the First of the Third Emperor. I call on you all, renounce your heretic Lords and Ladies if they do not declare for me. Rise in rebellion if they deny the truth of the Third Red Imperium of Mars and Man. I call on you all to join me in my name.

"Join the Third Red Imperium, for your Emperor is here, and he wants you."

Chapter XI

Lord Gavain entered the Cabinet Office, robes billowing out behind him as he smartly marched down the raised main entrance towards the centre of the amphitheatre like briefing and conference room in Heart Palace. Apart from those members of Second Fleet and First Fleet on standby for Dominion response to his acceptance of the Aalborg escapees, and those on special missions, all available and free officers of whatever rank had been given permission to enter the Cabinet Office if they were off-shift. It was packed, and as his arrival was noted, a tidal wave of recognition followed him on his way down to the central conference table at the bottom of the spacious room.

He had ordered that no secret should be held from his people in this, but that if anything confidential was to be discussed, then the secrecy screens would be raised and his senior military and governmental advisors would have their privacy.

The Third Emperor's sudden announcement had rocked the galaxy to its core.

He approached the conference table, moving to take his head. As people began to fall silent, he mentally encouraged them through the datasphere to continue. He did not want the presence of his name and position to stop the conversation and revelations so far.

"Ladies and gentlemen, we have just reached twenty real-time hours since the announcement by this Shadow Emperor, and the birth of what he is calling the Third Imperium," Admiral Andersson was saying. "He appealed for nations and Houses all across the colonised galaxy to respond to his call, and declare themselves part of his Third Red Empire. To date, we have the following analysis of the situation galaxy-wide."

Gavain analysed the holographic map that flicked up in great detail, the map itself swamping the gigantic auditorium with its sheer size. The light it cast was like that of a sun on the darkened room.

It was approaching three years since the collapse of the Red Imperium of the False Emperor, and many of the fractious Houses had divided amongst their own lines. In many ways, the Empire had been dead long before it had truly known it. Not all Houses had agreed with the end of the Red Imperium and the beginning of the Age of Secession, as the houses splintered apart and re-formed into their own nations. It was a process that was still on-going.

Into this maelstrom had stepped this Third Emperor, the Shadow Emperor.

The holographic map showed that some Houses had already declared for him. They were scattered all across the galaxy, the orangey-red colour denoting the Red Imperium making the map look diseased and infectious. None of the major nations or Houses had declared either way. The first thing Gavain noticed was that of those smaller houses that had declared themselves part of the Red Imperium, the overlay on the map showed that some were of old True Emperor loyalty, and others of old False Emperor loyalty.

<He is re-writing history, this Third Emperor,> said Gavain to Lucas De Graaf, on a private channel. <There was only ever one Red Imperium, not a first and a second one. Two Emperors, one Empire in contest.>

<The victor writes the history books, Jamie,> said Lucas De Graaf.

"We have now seen the immediate result closer to the incursion of the Shadow Empire, or Third Red Empire's, forces. At the time of the announcement, they jumped out of the Alegran Edge Segment and into the Diamond March, extending their land. Simultaneously, following the announcement, a number of houses in the immediate territory declared themselves for the Emperor. All contact has been lost, there is no information coming out of the systems that have declared for the Shadow Emperor," Andersson was continuing.

<Jamie,> Vice-Admiral O'Connor said, <our own spies were caught in this new advance from the Third Imperium. We now have people behind their lines. It took us time to get them there, but hopefully, we should soon find out what is happening behind the veil of secrecy they are pulling down behind them.>

<Good work,> said Gavain, but he was paying attention to something else. It was hard to discern properly, but a suspicion was growing upon him as he looked at the map and compared it to the enemy actions so far. <As soon as you have the information from behind the Shadow lines, I need to know.>

"Wait -" said Andersson, "- yes, we have more information coming in now. Lord Kemal Erdogan, Administrator for Communications and Transport?"

Lord Kemal took the podium. "We have just received word through our access to the StarCom News Media, although it is unconfirmed as yet. The SCNM is not allowed to broadcast within Vindicatus territory, but if the government instructs we shall permit this story onto our own networks. It appears that General Helvanna of the Helvanna Dominion has declared herself strongly in support of this Third Red Imperium and the Third Emperor, and has named her territory part of the nation."

"Display the broadcast," Gavain ordered.

They all watched, hundreds of them at first in silence and then with a growing muttering as the story progressing. The relatively young but vicious and accomplished General Helvanna, who had overthrown her own house and then led a vicious campaign of war against neighbouring houses and nations, including the crushing of the houses of some of the people in this room, had just declared her autocratic and un-nobled nation to be not only allied but fully in the name of this Shadow Emperor.

<I cannot fucking believe this,> said Ulrik Andryukhin.

<I can,> said Gavain, <Maybe not the Helvanna Dominion particularly, but I thought there would be a big announcement going on somewhere here in the Eastern Segment.>

<Are you fucking surprised by anything, Jamie?> said Ulrik.

<No, Rik, nothing in this crazy galaxy would surprise me anymore.>

"We shall add this to the reports we already have of potential demonstrations or even rebellions starting elsewhere in the galaxy, both in favour and against declaring for the Third Emperor," said Andersson. "By far, this is the largest nation yet to declare for the Shadow Empire."

"What is happening in the Zhou-Zheng Compact?" Admiral Horatio Grant asked. "Do we have any intelligence? Which way are they swinging?"

"Vice-Admiral O'Connor?" Andersson said.

O'Connor took the speaking podium. "We have very good intel coming out of the Compact; Primarch Zhou and Primarchess Zheng are strongly putting down any form of protest or rebellion in favour of the Third Emperor. They are not declaring in favour whilst the House of Zhou and Zheng is still alive."

Andersson re-took the speaking podium, his voice blasting out across the auditorium as he continued to recount what was now happening across the galaxy. Gavain listened for some time more.

Up until now the biggest nation to declare for the Third Empire was that of Solomon, formerly House Solomon. It had been engaged in a long-running intermittent war with House Krzarzjic, and on looking at it that declaration had puzzled Gavain somewhat. It did not fit the pattern of what he had expected to see.

Cervantia, Hausenhof and Korhonen were not declaring for the Third Emperor at all, although only Cervantia had so far denounced him. The other two were suspiciously silent, and that was worrying. Gavain had been watching Suularitsaar with some interest, particularly as they threatened the StarCom Federation, but they too were not declaring either way. The OutWorlds Alliance under First Lord Al-Zuhairi had declared the Third Emperor an imposter despite his likeness to the Imperial lineage. Many nations were quiet and uncommitted yet, completely silent on the matter.

Gavain was asked at one point if he knew what the Levitican Union intended to do. He replied that he had discussed it with Lady Principal

Sophia, but the Council of the Union was still in session, and did not know how to react to the announcement.

"And that is rather the point," he said, "the announcement petrifies the galaxy. Now, excuse me, but we will have to raise the secrecy screen for a moment. I must have an urgent discussion with my government and my senior military."

He left his throne, walking around the table as the secrecy screen went up. All of his government figures and military advisors were present, the holograph of Lucas De Graaf flickering slightly as it was allowed through the blocking barrier of the screen, De Graaf currently being with First Fleet out on the edges of the Gulf of Medusa waiting for a Helvanna Dominion strike in retribution for accepting the Aalborg refugee ships.

No images, broadcast or sound would be emitted from their immediate area while this discussion occurred.

"This is worrying, people," said Gavain, using spoken word for the benefit of his non-augmented government officials. "Our immediate strategic concern for the protection of Vindicatus is the possibility of the Helvanna Dominion being directed by the Third Emperor to cross into our territory. I want scouts out in the Gulf now, on the secret approaches, searching for ships with fusion rechargers coming in."

"Yes, sir," said Admiral Lucas De Graaf. "It will be done."

"Of more import is the timing. I think we are seeing a large part of the Shadows plan revealed here. Look at the nations that have openly declared - they are all over the galaxy, but a number of them lead in a very direct path. If we combine that with the direction the Third Empire forces are roughly moving in, you can see a clear path. Add it to the plots we know of, their spheres of influence, and it all points to this."

Gavain activated a smaller holographic map, within the secrecy screen, showing the colonised galaxy again. He controlled it, using his mind to draw a new route within its three dimensional picture. The large line he drew ran straight from the Frontier and the Third Empire, through a number of segments, sectors and systems, straight to one overall target.

"This all points to one target," he said. "The evidence is tenuous, and more proof is needed. But I believe we have a likely overall aim for this Shadow Emperor now." He pointed with his finger unnecessarily.

"Mars," Harley Andersson breathed.

"The fucker is after Mars!" Ulrik Andryukhin roared. "Of course."

"Mars can be the only target," said Lord Gavain. "Longer term, he wants to rebuild the Imperium of course. But first he will cut a swathe down through the colonised galaxy, coming from where he was hiding on the frontier, bursting through to take the Sol System and Mars. That is why he wanted the StarCom Federation so weakened by a war with Al-Zuhairi, they have the strongest collection of Praetorian Guard ships and the manufacturing capability to be his biggest threat."

"That and there is the symbology of it all," said Admiral Andersson. "Hold Mars, and his claim to the throne of the Emperor is sealed."

"A shame for the Commies that they stand in his way then," Ulrik Andryukhin chortled.

"But so do we," pointed out Vice-Admiral O'Connor.

"Not quite," said Andryukhin. "Look, roughly, the line passes through the edge of the Gulf of Medusa but it does not even enter the voided, uninhabited space. It is more nations like Helvanna - who are already for the Third Emperor - or the Levitican Union which get chopped up."

"And Cervantia, and Korhonen, and Hausenhof, Amiens, maybe the Republic of Varrental, and many, many more," said Lord Gavain. "And those are just the ones here in the Eastern Segment, the March of Hope and the Inner Core Segment. Look at it."

"All this is if you are right, Lord Gavain," said Lady Ebru Erdogan.

"He usually frikking is," said Ulrik.

"This is serious, Rik," said Lord Gavain. "This is the most serious threat we have faced since the False Emperor, worse than President Nielsen. Look at what the Shadow Emperor intends to do. He has manipulated the galaxy, he has power we cannot imagine. We may or may not be ignored as he passes us on his journey to Mars, but eventually he will return for all of us. He wants to rebuild the Imperium."

"So what do we do?" asked Admiral Andersson.

"We fight," said Lord Gavain, "we prepare in the months we have before he reaches us, we make our mark. We fight here and now, before he passes us, and we have no allies to turn to because they are all dead and conquered."

*

Lady Principal Sophia emerged from her particle shower, cleansed and refreshed but still somewhat tense. The Council session had been gruelling. The Third Emperor's announcement had surprised them all.

Baby Benjamin gurgled in his droid-cot, and she smiled as the personal assistance droids remade her hair for her and brought her new gown. It was slipped onto her with the expert slender touch of a restricted intelligence robot. The one-way holograph in front of her was dialled up to a fully reflective surface, to act as a mirror.

There had been a vote. Do they declare for the Third Red Empire, and the Third Emperor. The Shadow Emperor did not have any fans within the Levitican Union, they had suffered too much at the hands of his Rosicrux and Shadow organisation, now revealed. The vote had been unanimous to reject the call, and shortly Lady Principal Sophia would appear on state broadcast networks to make that announcement.

A droid buzzed into her personal quarters. "Lady Principal Sophia, we have a Priority Alpha Message from the Leviticus HPCG for you. A live pulse-channel call."

She sighed, but at least she was fully dressed. "Who is it?" she said. Her brother and Elaine Carrington were on-planet, so unless it was someone like Lord James Gavain, they would be ignored. She had to make the announcement of their rejection in recognition of the Third Empire in less than an hour.

"He calls himself only 'Jarhead'. The message is heavily encrypted, but bears encoding in the header that matches old House Towers greeting protocols."

Jarhead, mused Lady Sophia for a long moment, before her eyes widened in shock. It could not be, she thought.

"Yes," she said, turning and instantly composing herself. She was fully dressed, she could receive the call. "I want the call played through, complete security." All the droids began to leave her quarters, and there was a long wait as the entire room was locked down in response to her commands.

'Jarhead' was what she had called her elder brother, Jared, when she had been a child, unable to say his name properly. He had died though, executed by the False Emperor in retribution for her father's suspected allegiance to the Revolutionary Council. This call could not possibly be from him.

She gasped as the holographic figure of Jared Towers appeared before her, relayed from far away across the stars.

Luke Towers and Elaine Carrington entered the private quarters of Lady Principal Sophia Towers carefully, Luke graciously allowing Elaine to enter first. He was much happier without his role in the Levitican Union Council, concentrating purely on maintaining the landholding of House Towers. He still kept abreast of what was happening, and helped his sister where he could, but he knew there was little advice he could give her. He was never more than a sounding board, but in truth, he was happier with his simpler role. He would leave the machinations of politics to her, it was like second nature to her.

Which is why he was so surprised to see her in such a state. He assumed it might be the chemical and biological after-effects of the birth, which despite modern medicine would still be having its toll on her he was sure. It was more than a little disconcerting to see her like this. She was hugging herself, unable to stand still, clearly distressed.

"Sophia," said The Spider Elaine Carrington, head of House Towers intelligence services, "what in the name of the Emperor is wrong?"

"Don't use that name to me," said Lady Sophia emotionally.

"Calm yourself," said Elaine Carrington harshly. "You are the Lady Principal of the great Levitican Union and the head of House. You have a broadcast to make in less than forty minutes. Explain, what is wrong and we shall help you." She took her by the hand, and bid her to sit, doing the same herself. Luke remained standing, unsure.

"Jared Towers is still alive," she said simply.

"What?" Luke demanded.

"How can this be? How do you know?" Elaine Carrington asked softly.

"He has contacted me," said Lady Sophia simply, and wordlessly waved her hand to begin the replay of the holoprojector. It sprang into life, the form of Jared Towers appearing.

Luke listened with disbelief as the conversation continued, the replay capturing Lady Sophia's part of the conversation. He was struggling with it, looking at a man he thought was dead. Jared was wearing the uniform of what he claimed was the Third Emperor, saying he had the rank of Legate, leading a certain section of the Shadow Emperor's newly forming land.

Eventually the recording finished.

Into the silence, Elaine Carrington said, "we will have it tested for accuracy and truth, and quickly. My own people can do it, but perhaps we should pass it onto your friend, Lord Gavain. His technology is far in advance of our own."

"Do it," said Lady Sophia, "but I know it is true."

"He knows too much about us, the family," said Luke, "he speaks like he used to - it is him. I can feel it. Do you not think, Elaine?"

There was a long pause, and then The Spider who had served House Towers for over two centuries said quietly, "Yes, it is him. It is Jared."

"He wants us to bring the Union into the Third Empire," said Lady Principal Sophia. "I cannot, even if I wanted to. We have just voted unanimously against it."

"And we are not letting him build Third Empire forces in House Towers territory in secret," said Luke, "not a chance."

"No," said Elaine, "it would be a mistake to do anything he asks. We cannot co-operate. The Third Empire of this Shadow Emperor is far too dangerous."

"I asked why he had remained hidden," said Lady Sophia quietly, "why he had not spoken to us. 'It was necessary'. My life was put in danger because of him! He was never executed he said, he was taken away, hidden from the False Emperor by those who were already preparing for his downfall. He let us think he was dead."

"We ignore this for now, before we decide on a response. Speak to Lord Gavain, see what he says," said Elaine, "By now I am sure he was working out a way both to deal with the Empire and to make money from it."

"Jared Towers, my half-brother and your full brother, is alive," said Luke speaking to Lady Sophia, shaking his head, "and with the enemy."

"Nothing in this family would surprise one anymore," said Lady Principal Sophia. Her voice had regained its Imperial accent, and the look she gave to Elaine Carrington was harsh, enough to pin a lesser person in place. "Elaine Carrington, explain to one the truth. No more lies, no more secrets."

"What do you me –"

"One does not wish for any more half-truths, deceptions or lies. One's brother Luke deserves to know too. Tell us the truth, about our family. One knows you called Benjamin your grandson. What is the truth? Who are we, who are you, who is he?" she pointed at the stilled holographic image of Jared Towers.

Elaine hesitated, and Luke saw all he needed to in that hesitation. With the voice of the former military leader of House Towers and all of the Levitican Union, he rounded quickly and snapped, "Spider! The truth! Do as your Lady Principal and head of house commands."

Elaine Carrington was silent for some period of time, and when she looked up, a very different, old woman stared at them.

"My real name was Elaine Carrington," she said, "although I married again. When Lord Erik Towers, your father, was first married he had Jared and you, Sophia, and the galaxy thought it was to the Lady Towers of the time. She was barren, I stood in her place. But I was of low birth, low class, chosen to bear Erik his children and no more. He was so humanist he did not believe even in vats and insemination faculties. We had known each other for decades before I volunteered. We fell in love in the process, I think. Jared and then Sophia were born, to me and Lord Erik Towers."

"In the name of the Emperor," Luke swore, his mind reeling.

"But his wife as well as being barren turned out to be a Zupanic proxy. Erik was told, by me, and he ordered me to dispose of her. I did. For a while, Erik was unmarried, but he selected a new wife to cement the future of the Towers landholding. In the run-up to the marriage, we were still 'with' each other, and I fell pregnant with you, Luke."

"What?" said Lady Sophia.

"So none of you three children are actually half-siblings or born to the mother you thought you were. You were all born to me. Erik married his second wife, and the marriage lasted until all political expediency had failed. The marriage ended in divorce, ratified by the True Emperor at the time. Lord Erik vowed never to remarry again, and we kept our relationship a secret forever more. It was to protect all three of you, as much as the people of Towers territory and the landholding."

"You truly are the Spider," said Luke in disgust. "Why never tell us this?"

"We debated telling you, but there was never a right time, and you were all accustomed to what you thought was the truth. Then the rebellion against the False Emperor came, and Jared was taken hostage. Then Sophia. We saw no need to make the hardship greater. Then Lord Erik was killed, and as much as I wanted to tell you, I could not."

Elaine Carrington looked up. "My children," she said, "you have found your lost brother, even if he is on the wrong side of the line, and your mother. Please forgive me and your father for the deception at least, and hope one day we can bring Jared back to us."

*

Commander Joanne Lancaster, captain of the Vindicatus *VSS Odyssey* frigate, was observing the silence orders she had placed on her own crew. They were deep into running silent, with virtually no power throughout the ship. They were even on reduced oxygen. They did have extremely passive sensors, but even those were mostly visual only. The greatest amount of power they were emitting was through their chameleonic fields, to hide their very presence here in the Pathonis System.

The datasphere was down to all, and so they communicated using the spoken word, but even then it was as a whisper. They had grown so accustomed to the reduced light, and the atmosphere of hiding, that they did not even speak.

Roughly three days ago they had arrived in the Pathonis System, out here in the Diamond March. They were just at the very edge of the Shadow advance, approaching rapidly. They had travelled hard, jumping through stargates where possible, and expending vast amounts of money. They had finally approached the target system under their own power, Vice-Admiral O'Connor changing that target system numerous times as they crossed the great expanse of colonised space, mainly because the Shadow advance was so quick and unexpected.

The Pathonis System was populated, and already civilian ships had jumped away as fast as possible, but there were still billions trapped in-system unable to leave. The exodus was still underway as the *Odyssey* had arrived at its very edge, slipping into running silent and approaching the capital planet of Pathonica V completely undetected by the local house systems.

They had inserted the biomorphs of Brigadier Vantanik stealthily and secretly onto the planet, using just two strikepods, one full of a squad of the biomorphs and another with supplies. The strikepods had not been detected thanks to the advanced Praetorian technology and the careful timing of the insertion. One of the strikepods contained equipment for the two biomorphic engineers to set up their escape pod back into the sky. The *Odyssey* took up its position a fair distance away to wait, knowing it could be days or weeks, or even longer. They would wait as long as it took for the spies to jump back up with their information.

The whole point of the mission was to gather intelligence about the activities of the Shadows behind their own lines. Commander Lancaster knew that Lord Gavain still intended to operate a mercenary outfit using the Vindicatus military, but she wondered if he was gathering the information just to sell it on to the highest bidders.

Then a day ago the next phase of the mission had begun.

The Shadow ships had jumped in, but now they did not wear StarCom Federation colours. They wore their own orange-red hulls, with Imperial Red Eagles emblazoned upon them, three black scores across the symbols. It had been tough for Commander Lancaster to watch as the Shadows destroyed the military defences in the system, ripping through them easily with their gigantic, alien-like warships.

She watched as the transporter-like but heavily armed and armoured warships dropped pods and landers down onto the surface of all the planets in Pathonis, including Pathonis V where her own biomorphic spies were. The invasion was quick and well-practiced.

They monitored what traffic they could, limited as they were, but eventually Commander Lancaster could listen no more. The planet Pathonis V was being torn apart. There were strange reports from the defending forces and the planetary media, but they were quickly shut down. Just like elsewhere, everywhere the veil of the Shadows was cast, the planet fell silent.

It was as they were waiting that eventually more ships jumped in, and this was where Commander Lancaster could not believe her eyes.

"Look," she said to her second-in-command, "recognise those?"

The shapes were unmistakable. "Yes, sir," he replied. "They are, aren't they."

"These Shadows are using Praetorian ships," she said in wonder. In this second wave of ships, there were V-class battlecruisers, U-class destroyers, S-class strikecruisers. There was even a T-class dreadnought. There were other support ships of even more humble House construction, including some new models of fabricator and constructoship vessels she had never seen before and they could not determine.

The first conquering wave of super-advanced warships jumped out, and whether it was on to another staging area or another target Commander Lancaster did not know. They could not break the enemy communications, and dared not reveal their presence in an attempt on their electronic firewalls. She had done some things in her life, but this was the furthest and most isolated she had ever travelled, to hide right under the nose of the enemy.

The fabricatorships and constructoships began to build something in the depths of space, and Lancaster watched in interest as it formed, even as they waited for the cybernetic biomorphic soldiers they had down on the surface to signal that the time was ready to escape by blasting up out from the surface.

*

Admiral Silus Adare walked onto amazingly large bridge of his juggernaut, the *ISS Zero Tolerance*. It even bore the name designation of 'Imperial StarShip', a designation which had not been seen since he served in the fleets of the False Emperor.

He walked proudly in his uniform, the dark orange-red and silver-trim of the Third Empire uniform refreshingly new but also styled in the old Imperial way. The peaked cap was on his head, with his rank on the brim, his collar and his chest.

<Admiral on the bridge,> the newly promoted Captain Zehra Sahin said, and the entire bridge crew gave the Imperial Salute.

<You have the bridge, Captain,> Adare replied formally, relishing the old phrases as he took his flag seat in the expansive command dais. The juggernaut had come out of hiding, leading a squadron of ships as they rolled over system after system in the Helvanna Dominion.

The Helvanna Dominion had declared itself for the Third Emperor, but then General Helvanna had always known of the existence of the Shadow Emperor and had always planned to declare for him. She had built her nation after disposing herself of the former House Lords and Ladies, increasing its size aggressively expressly for the purpose of handing it over to the Third Emperor when he revealed Himself.

The time had come, and that time was now.

The Helvanna Dominion still had to be subjugated, and the ships the Shadows had nestled in hiding within Helvanna Dominion borders had emerged. Already under a blanket of restricted communication, with her own military in harsh control, the Emperor's ships rolled out and widened His grasp. Adare was leading the fleet that was spreading the Emperor's Word.

"Are you ready, Admiral Adare?" asked the acolyte in the Imperial red and dark purple of the covert operations branch. Besides him was a senior Centurion in the Imperial red and orange of the training and subjugation branch of what was referred to as the Ninth Circle.

The Ninth Circle handled more than just the training of new recruits and their indoctrination into the Empire, as well as the internal propaganda, they were also responsible for the heavier types of subjugation of the populaces that fell under the hand of the Emperor. Adare knew what they did, having the clearance now to know, but he cared not, no matter how abhorrent some would find it.

Despite that he ignored the Senior Centurion, focused more on the covert operations Tribune. "Tribune, are we ready?"

"Yes," replied the Tribune. "You know the text, stick to it roughly but put it in your own way. You know the purpose of this. The Shadow Emperor is determined to see an end to 'Lord' Gavain, and you are seen as the best way to tempt him into the open."

"We have a long, old friendship me and Jamie Gavain," said Silus Adare with an evil and completely dishonest smile.

"I have heard of this Lord Gavain," said General Helvanna, "though I have never met him. By all means, bring him into what used to be the Dominion territory, but let us crush him before he can do too much damage. He seems far too capable."

Adare looked at the General Helvanna. Ruthless and determined, she had the bearing and attitude of someone very much like him, he thought. Hard-faced, facially beautiful perhaps in some ways, but with a steel and iron to the gaze that could burn through starship hulls. Her hairstyle was still kept military buzz-cut, and although she did not have a Praetorian Marine's physique, it was still far above average in terms of unaugmented humans. She still wore military uniform, but it had already been adjusted to show the colours of the Third Empire within its Helvanna Dominion style.

"He is," said Admiral Adare, "he should never be underestimated. But neither is he infallible. I am ready when you are, Tribune."

Adare settled back into his flag chair, ready to send his message to Gavain. It was designed to taunt him, to invite him into a foolhardy strike into the Dominion territory. Personally Adare thought it unlikely to work, Gavain was far too wise and cunning a strategist to fall for such a blatant ploy, but Adare had learnt never to underestimate people's emotions. Ultimately his existence within the Third Empire fleets was down to the Emperor's perception that Adare was a taunt to Gavain, and the Emperor wanted Gavain dead, so Adare would do this regardless just to protect his own position.

The holographic equipment began to record, and Adare gave his challenge to Gavain, taunting him to pursue Adare in to the Third Empire-allied territory of the Helvanna Dominion.

*

Lord Micalek was walking through the political section of the underwater city, within the area given to House Zupanic. His head was down, and he was utterly miserable. He felt uncomfortable in the Council sessions, seeing the eyes of everyone upon him. Even worse, he could not talk to Lady Principal Sophia. He had not seen his child for weeks.

He loved her, genuinely loved her, and she despised him for what he had done. He could not disagree with that hate. He felt himself unworthy to be alive.

Even as he walked through the section of the political quarters given to Zupanic, he could feel the looks of the lower-ranking Zupanic nobles and servants upon him. He tried to ignore them, but word had spread of his duplicity. He felt incredibly low, and wanted to give everything up, run away to a different life. Yet there was to be no escape for him.

He entered the building that was given purely to him, all the servants dismissed, the private quarters empty as it had been for days. He cycled through the security measures without paying them much thought, not even looking back at the beautiful gardens and entering the residence. He crossed the grand hallway, heading into the primary living room.

Instantly he knew he was not alone as he thought. He looked up, his warriors training warning him.

"Xavier?" he said, seeing his brother. The insane madman was lounging on an elongated suspensor seat, completely relaxed. He felt his anger rise. "What are you doing here on Leviticus? How did you get in?"

"I arrived earlier today," said the madman Xavier, clapping his hands in excitement. He appeared simple, and in many ways he was. "I came to see you, but asked them all to keep my arrival quiet."

"Why?" Lord Micalek walked forwards, stepping down into the recessed floor where the lounge seats were currently resting. There was a table between them, and he put his hands on his hips. "Explain yourself, now."

"It is you who needs to explain," said Xavier. "You have been a very naughty boy, Micci. Mummy is very cross with you." He uncrossed his legs and stood up, a look of mock sadness upon his face.

"Where is mother?" Micalek asked.

"Here," said a voice behind him.

Startled he turned round and looked. He began to open his mouth to speak to Lady Wyn, but a stabbing pain had suddenly spiked through the back of his neck and his throat. He could not speak, and he put a hand up to his throat.

He looked down, and his hand was awash with blood. He felt it bubbling up and out through his mouth, and he lost strength in his legs, collapsing to the floor. He looked up, his vision beginning to fade, to see his brother Xavier stood over him.

"I've waited a long time for this, Micci," said Xavier, the blade of the bloody knife he held humming with energy. "I'm enjoying this, brother."

Micalek could not even scream as Xavier methodically began to dismember and hack him apart. His last clear thought was of Lady Sophia and his son, and part of him thought that at least he would no longer be alive to cause them more pain. He loved Lady Sophia, with all his heart, the one that even now his bloodied brother Xavier was ripping out of his ribcage.

He lost consciousness, and was never going to wake up again.

"Enough now, Xav," said Lady Wyn, watching one of her younger sons killing her eldest son.

"But mummy –"

"Enough," said Lady Wyn. "He is dead. We need to get you cleaned up. I already have a fall guy to take the blame for his murder, a man who wishes to keep his family safe from me."

"Okay, mother," said Xavier, pouting in disappointment. "Are you taking the head of House now?"

"I am going to present myself to the Levitican Union Council, yes," said Lady Wyn, "and reveal that I am still alive, and take Micalek's position as Minister. They will know of course that I have killed my son, but I suspect they will not question my version of events. He was an embarrassment to them. I have been in hiding too long."

"It's good to have you back, mummy," said Xavier, grinning with sheer happiness. His brother's blood stained virtually every inch of him.

Chapter XII

Lady Principal Sophia was sitting in her own quarters, with her brother Luke. He was running through his own viewpoint on the state of the galaxy, with the ever-expanding Third Empire and the sudden announcement that the Helvanna Dominion had declared itself part of the Third Empire.

"They are saying they are no longer an independent nation," said Luke, focusing on the holographic map in front of them both. "They are calling themselves the Helvanna Province of the Third Empire. Their House military is strong, but we are seeing evidence of some of the Third Empire warships, including these massive ships they call juggernauts."

"Lord Gavain has contacted one," said Lady Principal Sophia, "he has received a message from Silus Adare. He is in the Helvanna territory. He wants the Union to pay him to jump into Helvanna territory and assault them, trying to capture one of the ships for intelligence and analysis."

"Are we going to?" asked Luke Towers.

"Pay him?" asked Lady Principal Sophia, "We vote on it later, but one is recommending that we do. The StarCom Federation and the OutWorlds Alliance have also put him on retainer, willing to pay for whatever information he can get."

"The Helvanna territory is not that far from us," said Lord Luke Towers, "It is exceptionally worrying. Lord Micalek needs to move as much of our military up to the borders. There is a lot of empty space and some smaller Houses between us and Helvanna, but in truth their systems are only what ..... eleven or twelve jumps away? We are in clear and present danger, right now."

"Which is why our Mercenary Lord is going to get paid to hijack one of their ships," said Lady Principal Sophia. Even as she finished the sentence she was looking up and away as the door was opening. Their mother, Elaine Carrington, was entering.

"Elaine," said Sophia. "Have you thought about our offer?"

Elaine Carrington smiled faintly. "It is very kind of you," she said, "and yes, I would like to accept. All I would say is let's not make it too public - I am your spy chief, after all."

"Excellent," said Lady Sophia smiling. "We shall have you officially named Towers in recognition of your secret marriage to Lord Erik. The news will love it. You are our mother, you deserve the name and the title."

"It is time for The Spider to become the Lady Elaine Towers, I could not agree more," said Lord Luke.

"It is not that I am here about, though," said the soon-to-be Lady Elaine. "I have some news for you, Lady Principal Sophia, and I am not sure what your reaction will be."

Lady Principal Sophia saw the serious look on Elaine's face as the smile faded. "What is it, Elaine?" she asked.

"Lord Micalek Zupanic is dead, he has been murdered," said Elaine simply.

Lady Principal Sophia was shocked as soon as she heard the words.

Lady Principal Sophia looked out across the city, staring out of the window, her baby Benjamin Towers in her arms. The false night had fallen, and the Council session had been completed earlier. They had voted to contract Lord Gavain to launch a secret mission into the Helvanna Dominion, to obtain the intelligence. It was money his nation sorely needed.

Lady Wyn had put in a surprise appearance. Elaine and Luke had wanted to discuss it all after the session, but Sophia needed some time to herself. They would talk about it tomorrow, but the revelation that Lady Wyn was not only alive but taking her sons place as Head of House had shocked everyone in the Council. They had agreed to her becoming the Minister, of course, as it solved an immediate problem for them.

Lady Sophia did not need to talk about the day's events with Elaine and Luke. She could piece it together herself. The man accused of Lord Micalek's murder was undoubtedly set up, but he had confessed to the adjudicators. He would be seen in the circuit court of High Justiciar Driscoll tomorrow morning. Lady Wyn and her mad son Xavier, who was also on-planet, were most likely behind his killing.

Murders among House nobles were frequent in the days of the Red Imperium, and in these days of post-Dissolution and the Age of Secession, were just as commonplace. High Justiciar Driscoll was not a fool, and may clear the man of the charges, but the evidence was there.

Regardless, Lady Sophia knew that Lady Wyn had killed her son. He had failed in House Zupanic's complicated treacherous plans, and this was her retribution. Lady Wyn had emerged, and was perhaps even more dangerous than Micalek.

She thought of her husband as she looked at her baby. The mix of emotions she felt about him were clearing, and she felt only one thing now. Her heart was a chasm, a hole, full of loss and hurt. She had loved him, despite everything, she was sure of that.

As her baby looked up at her, she thought of her murdered husband, and began to weep.

The tears did not stop for a long, long time.

*

The delegation from the Interstellar Merchants Guild had their own quarters and head office in one building given directly to them by the Vindicatus nation, in a thriving commercial district of the capital city on Dark Heart Alpha.

Brigadier Viktor Vantanik had his orders from Lord Gavain, and was in one of the buildings opposite with the secret observation team. He was a highly advanced cybernetic biomorph, but at the moment he had let his usual guise slip and was presented as his amorphous, asexual form. He looked like an alien, and in many ways, he was.

<We have movement,> he said on the datasphere, <all teams, the target is leaving the IMG building. Prepare for strike.>

One of the secret biomorphs who had been inserted into the delegation from the Interstellar Merchants Guild was leaving the front entrance, heading towards an aircar. The repulsors on the aircar began to lift it at the biomorphs approach. The enemy spy was disguised as a woman, and she got into the aircar.

<Target vehicle is leaving the grounds,> said Vantanik. <All units, we are go.>

The aircar carrying the biomorph spy was autonomous, and had its destination pre-programmed. The droid in charge of the car rose up into the air, joining a busy air traffic lane. It sped up to the maximum cruising speed, jetting across the city.

The biomorph agent was under cover in the IMG, a member of the Sixth Circle covert operations branch. She was completely calm and serene, on her way ostensibly to meet with a new business being set up by one of the immigrants to Dark Heart, but in truth to obtain more intelligence for the Third Empire and the Shadow Emperor.

She was sure that her presence, and the presence of the other agents within the IMG delegation, was completely undetected by the Vindicatus security services. That was why it was a complete surprise when suddenly she felt a jolt as a dermal hypojector was pressed against her arm.

She looked down, her implants going into overdrive as the powerful chemicals raced through her system. Her body was automatically trying to fight off the toxins, but it was impossible - the drugs were overpowering her system completely. Even as she began to lose consciousness, she tried to signal for help, but a powerful jammer signal had cut her off and isolated her from the other agents back in the IMG complex.

She lost consciousness as the enemy biomorph pulled itself out of the boot, through a hole in the collapsed seat at her side. The droid in charge of the aircar did not stop, continuing to drive through the fast lane as if nothing was wrong.

The Vindicatus biomorphic sergeant said, <I have the target subdued. Ready for drop.>

It opened the secret hatchway in the floor of the droidcar. Wind whistled into the aircar as it looked down.

<We are in position,> said Brigadier Vantanik, as a hovertruck moved into view some ten metres down. It was speeding, going faster than allowed in the slower lane. Vehicles were moving out of the way, horns blaring angrily. <Make it quick.>

The sergeant draped the body over its shoulder, and pressed the timer switch on the bomb it had left on the seat of the car. It was not a powerful explosive, but it was strong enough to wreck the car.

With a personal chameleonic stealth field activated, the sergeant dropped through the hole in the floor. He used a personal repulsorpack to slightly adjust his fall, dropping through the open roof of the hovertruck. As soon as he landed, the hovertruck slowed down, falling away as it hit the correct driving speed.

<Well done,> said Brigadier Vantanik.

The droidcar continued on in the fast lane, but after five minutes it began to display warning lights. It slowed down and dropped, heading for the ground. The other vehicles all around it were moving away, recognising that there had been either a mechanical or software failure in the aircar.

It began to speed as it dropped, falling out of control. Emergency services were automatically warned by the onboard droid computer system.

It smashed into the ground, at the precise point the bomb detonated, blowing the aircar apart.

Some hours later, the IMG biomorphic sleeper agent woke up.

As she regained consciousness, she realised her disguise had completely fallen away. She was naked, her jet-black skin exposing her origin as a biomorph. She was even more surprised to see that she was in a holding cell, and five biomorphs wearing the uniform of the Vindicatus military were before her.

"What is –" she began.

"Do not speak unless spoken to!" the man in front of her snapped. "I am Brigadier Vantanik, and you are an enemy spy. Your comrades inserted in the Interstellar Merchants Guild delegation think you are dead, killed in an accident. You are completely at my mercy, and have no hope of rescue. We know what you are, and we want you to give us information."

"I do not know –"

"Do not speak unless spoken to!" Brigadier Vantanik snapped again. He leaned over her, resting his hands on her restraints. "You are going to tell me everything I want to know, whether you want to or not."

"Torture is –"

"Do not speak unless I give you permission!" Vantanik struck her, hard. "Torture is just one of my methods. You have no rights, you have no existence. No-one knows you are here."

The interrogation began, and she resisted for a while, at least until the torture really started.

*

Pathonis V was well and truly under the command of the Third Imperium. The Vindicatus Mercenary Corporation cybernetic biomorph, ranked as a Captain and named Alicia Alansen, was under no illusions in that regard. She was co-ordinating the information that her team of inserted, undercover spies was gathering about what was happening behind the enemy lines once their communications blackout dropped on their conquered territory.

They had landed in their two strikepods, two of her team of ten dismantling one of the strikepods and setting the other up to blast them back into space as part of their escape to Commander Lancaster's frigate. The O-class frigate *Odyssey* would remain in space, holding a geosynchronous orbit in complete secrecy, until Captain Alansen's team was ready to be extracted.

Captain Alansen thought that time was fast approaching. The scenes 'she' was seeing on Pathonis V were truly unparalleled. Even her training had not prepared her for what her team was uncovering.

They had hidden inside the main city on Pathonis V, Pathonica. The Third Imperials had dropped directly onto the city, not caring what they destroyed as their strikepods hit with tremendous impacts. Something very different than Praetorian Guard Marines, or even some of the more obscure House Marines, had emerged from those first strikepods.

Stood within their temporary base in one of the quarantined zones of the city, a small family apartment residence in a spire that stretched high up into the clear blue sky, Captain Alansen looked down at the dead body of one of those hybrid soldiers that they had captured and ultimately killed in that first phase of the invasion.

The hybrid had some elements of human deep within it, but it had been genetically engineered, spliced together with some form of alien life-form.

With a human brain inserted into the cranial cavity, the hybrid had an alien's body, with naturally occurring body armour at least as hard as a House Marines power suit. Coupled with some form of upgrading Praetorian Guard armour, the hybrid was stronger and more powerful than even a bioartificed Praetorian Guard.

It had four arms, and powerful back-canted legs that allowed it to run and jump incredible distances. The maw was a weapon in itself, a special helmet designed to allow the teeth and a form of naturally occurring acidic bile to be used as a projectile weapon.

Medical analysis had shown the hybrid to contain some traces of human DNA and chromosomal traces. The brain was also human, although noticeably simulant in origin. The colonised galaxy of the human race had created many travesties, but one thing that had always been against Imperial Law by Imperial Decree, even laws predating the Red Imperium of Mars, stated that combining human and alien DNA was illegal and immoral. The thing was not human, it was an alien life-form, given human intelligence to raise it up the evolutionary chain. Intelligent alien life had never been found, at least anything beyond base primitive intelligence, and it was viewed as completely wrong to insert human intelligence into such an alien, even though such technology had existed for centuries.

The initial reports of aliens spotted when that juggernaut had been discovered by the salvageship on the Frontier were not inaccurate after all.

The spies had nicknamed this type of hybrid a 'Cataphract', after an ancient heavy type of horse soldier due to its speed and position in the forefront of the Third Imperium invasion force. There were others though, hybrids three times the size of a human nicknamed 'Carnosaurs', smaller and almost human 'Lizards', flying 'Locusts' and stealthy, dangerous 'Lethals'. They were the worst of all, capable of moving even in full light completely invisible through natural abilities, and they ripped through the populace without a thought.

After the wave of human-alien hybrids came more familiar soldiers, humanoid cybernetic biomorphs in heavy upgraded Praetorian Guard Marine armour. They even wore Praetorian Guard symbology and ranking. There were many cybernetic biomorphic support staff and typically officers, in the latter in overall command. After the initial, brutal, bloody subjugation of the city, these officers were the ones who appeared, directing the hybrids and the Upgraded Praetorians into herding the populace together.

Captain Alansen had a vast number of holo-picts and recordings of the buildings the biomorphic technicians fabricated in hours, in the rubble created by the strikepods and the landers. The city was divided into quarantined zones, the populace held in check by the hybrids who appeared to be the cannon fodder, the base troops of the Third Imperials.

The populace of the quarantined zones were taken one zone at a time into these new buildings. What emerged was still human, but Alansen, seeing initially no difference, had ordered some of the 'converts' to be captured. The people were being converted, forcibly augmented with biomorphic implants whether they were humanist or borgite. The converts were slaved into a hive mind, similar to that of the House Marchenko populace of the Levitican Union. Where the Marchenkans accepted it and even volunteered, these people had no such choice. They were being forced against their will, turned into mindless slaves.

Captain Alansen found it to be pure, sheer evil. No wonder no word was escaping from any of the captured planets, the invading forces held the populace under lock and key in quarantined zones until they were completely slaved into a local hive mind. There was no freedom, no attempt to escape. It was just as horrific as the use of the human-alien hybrids.

Yesterday Alansen had attempted to obtain intelligence on the location of the hive mind, but they were being hunted. She had lost four members of her team, and the city was completely locked down. The hive mind knew they were here, because of their taking of the slaves. Alansen had called it off, and decided the time had come to escape. They had to get their intelligence out of the city and off the planet.

<Are we all ready?> she asked.

She received a number of replies from the surviving members of her squad. <We make our move now,> she said, <We move under cover, in comms silence, disguised as Upgraded Praetorians. I will assume the disguise of a biomorph officer. We take an enemy HAPC vehicle and some of their hoverjeeps, and head out-city. At some point we will be discovered, at the least when we reach the city limits. We continue, no matter what. The vehicles then split on my codeword 'Discovery', and head for the strikepod location. Do we all understand our orders?>

<Yes, Captain Alansen,> was the unified response.

<Explain why you are leaving the city?> said the biomorph over the city-wide datasphere, directing the communication directly to Captain Alansen.

She rode within the HAPC, which actually had a faster top-speed than the three hoverjeeps they had also stolen. They were all Praetorian tech, upgraded as all these Third Imperium vehicles were, different versions of the *Rattlesnake* HAPC and *Leopard* hoverjeeps. They had stolen some Praetorian Upgrade armour, and Alansen wanted to steal at least one of the vehicles, getting it aboard the strikepod waiting for them.

That is if they survived the escape attempt.

<We are following orders to conduct external sweeps beyond the city limits.>

<What orders are those?>

<We have been given the orders.> Their vehicles moved outside the city limits. They were not yet being pursued, but it was only a matter of time. Alansen was playing for seconds now, delaying her responses.

<Given the orders by who? Upload the order confirmations to me, now, and identify yourself, Major.>

Alansen scrambled the signal as she communicated back. Problems within dataspheres were rare, but they did happen.

<Repeat uplink again, information not received.>

Alansen kept the reply scrambled.

<Cease and desist your forward motion. Pull up and confirm orders and identity!>

Alansen sent another scrambled signal across the datasphere.

<Major, this is your final chance. I will scramble interception units if you do not cease forward motion. Are you reading me?>

They were some fifteen seconds out beyond the city limits, and the closest enemy units were some thirty-odd seconds behind them. The fighters the enemy had would be more of an issue, but at top speed it would only take three minutes to cover the hundreds of kilometres to the hidden strikepod and their escape. They could load into the strikepod within seconds, and blast off this planet.

<Major, I am calling a pursuit and interception mission on you. Communicate with me!>

Alansen disengaged from the enemy datasphere. They had stolen much data from that datasphere too, taking the risk of jacking in. It appeared only the populace were to join a collective hive mind consciousness, not the soldiers, marines and troops of the Third Imperium.

<Discovery, repeat, discovery!> Alansen warned her team. The captured *Rattlesnake* HAPC she was riding in kicked as it rapidly accelerated.

<Commander Lancaster, we are detecting enemy movement in Pathonica, we've not seen something on this scale for at least three days. Early communications hacks suggest they have an incident occurring,> said her second-in-command.

<Acknowledged,> said Commander Joanne Lancaster, <Prepare to receive strikepod, hopefully.>

<Catchment fields are ready to be activated, Commander.>

<How long when the strikepod launches until it reaches us?>

<Nine point two seconds, Commander,> said her tactical officer.

<Prepare to fire main drive engines as soon as the strikepod is captured and aboard,> said Commander Lancaster, keeping her voice and thoughts level. <How long after propulsors are engaged before we can jump?>

<One minute twenty-two point four seconds, Commander,> came her helmsman's reply.

<Jump course is already locked in as pre-determined,> said her navigator.

<Sound red alert when strikepod launch is detected,> said Commander Lancaster. <What is the position of enemy capital ships?>

<We have a number of capital ships in area,> said her second-in-command. A tactical holo-map appeared, <but we are fully chameleonically shielded. Only the firing of the propulsors on full will give away our position. We are already pointed on the exact heading for the jump, we will fire sensor flares a couple of seconds before jump and adjust heading quickly to throw them off our jump co-ordinates to prevent tracking.>

<And we jump again immediately in the next system, and then again,> said Commander Lancaster. <An evasion course to get us away from them attempting to track us. And they will attempt to ->

<Strikepod launch detected!>

<Red alert, all hands, red alert!>

<Enemy ships-of-the-line reacting, Red One, Red Three and Red Four changing heading. They cannot intercept strikepod, they are in the wrong positions.>

Luck, thought Commander Lancaster. <Prepare to fire torpedoes, nuclear payloads, maximum yield damage with armour-piercing warheads. Let's do the bastards some damage, they won't be expecting us and their special fields to allow our weaponry to pass through do not appear to be engaged.>

<Strikepod in three seconds .... engaging catchment fields .... now! .... strikepod home and landed!>

<Fire torpedoes! Fire propulsors - get us out of here!> Commander Lancaster ordered.

The Third Imperium warships raced after the Vindicatus frigate which had suddenly appeared within their territory. They had never even suspected it had been there, scans failing to detect its presence. The first they knew of its existence was when the strikepod launch disappeared, and the torpedoes smashed at high velocity into their armour.

Without their special fields engaged to prevent weapons damage, whatever those fields or technology was, the nuclear torpedoes did considerable damage. They penetrated deeply into the starships, detonating within the skins. The first successful strike against the Third Imperium warships was achieved here in the Pathonis System.

Just over a minute later, sensor flares fired and the *Odyssey* frigate, beginning to receive long-range fire but deflecting it perfectly off its energy shields, jumped into hyper-space. It warped away, a big white flash hiding its exact heading.

The mission had been a success, and providing they evaded pursuit, they would get their intelligence back to Mercenary Lord Gavain.

*

The Hath System was within what had been the Helvanna Dominion, now the Helvanna Province of the Third Imperium or Third Empire. Relatively important within the overall structure of the Helvanna Province, it was on the coreward borders and doubtless about to become even more significant as a staging area for forces to travel corewards.

With a weak sun, it was not the best place to recharge jump initiation capacitors. It did have a well-sized commercial space station, and a number of private, luxurious space-based stationary residences. The rich lived in space here, but the vast majority of the large population lived down on the planets and moons, in appalling conditions more commonly seen out in the Boundary and Frontier, in situations that even in modern times were not viewed as acceptable for many of the lower classes.

The primary export from Hath was plenty of bodies for the House military, bioartificing and genetic manipulation of a scale and sophistication not regularly seen, advanced research and technological industries and an immense manufacturing base. A number of commercial shipyards were based here. Despite this its military defences were not high, the system seen as expendable, and under-invested in by even the Helvanna Dominion, its former House rulers failing to take advantage of its economic advantages.

The Hath System had fallen under the secretive shroud of the Third Empire. About two days ago the advance forces of the Third Empire had jumped in, supplementing the Helvanna house military ships already in-system. The Third Empire was not strong in this region of space, although that was not commonly known. They had sent what ships they could, but with their technology and the superior advantage that conferred, in an allied and pacified system it was of no real concern.

The squadron consisted of three S-class strikecruisers, a V-class battlecruiser, two of the brand new X-class destroyer-transporters, and the jewel in the crown, a Z-class juggernaut. The destroyer-transporters with an escort of either one or two strikecruisers went on a pre-planned circuit of the system, dropping forces down towards the inhabited planetary objects, whilst the commercial space station and the richer higher-class space residences were emptied by the Helvanna house forces. The system was put under a communications black-out, and the Z-class juggernaut and V-class battlecruiser took up as central a position as they could to cover all potential approaches into the system. No hostile intervention was truly expected, it was just standard operating procedure.

So when the incoming and unannounced jump signatures were detected, they automatically assumed hostile intervention and began to react.

Admiral Lucas De Graaf was watching the enemy ships within the Hath System with great interest, his dreadnought running on silent. The plan was Gavain's and his, he was proud to say, with the Mercenary Lord taking on his suggestions. To attempt an assault on the so-far undefeated Third Imperials was ambitious.

<Jump signatures detected,> said his scanners operator. Even running on silent, incoming jump signatures were easy to recognise.

<Red alert,> Lucas De Graaf said, <hold running silent until the trap is sprung.>

It was an unusual tactic, but the Vindicator Mercenary Corporation was going for superiority in numbers, combined with secrecy and surprise. They had inserted their squadrons of ships into the Hath System four days ago, under the very noses of the local Hath military forces. The Hath System had been chosen because it was so badly defended, and because of its position on the edge of Helvanna Province territory. Their escape route was clear and easy; the difficulty was going to be what surprises the Third Imperium threw at them, and the capabilities of their ships.

They had to strike hard and fast for a number of reasons, one of which was that they could not relay warning of their attack on the system. Another was the unknown abilities of their targets.

<They are moving towards the target area,> said his scanners officer.

<Begin forward movement,> said Admiral De Graaf, <full slow, prepare for the signal.>

The ships jumping in were their own, of course, and so the location of the 'unexpected' terminus point was already known to the vast number of ships that De Graaf had under his command. They were incommunicado, running silent, but all knew the positions they had to be in. De Graaf not only relied heavily upon their training, he knew he could trust in his officers to carry out their parts of the plan admirably.

De Graaf examined carefully what the enemy were doing. That was just one of the unknowns in this assault mission.

The Z-class juggernaut, vast, immense and terrifying, was called the *Zeus's Wrath*. It was slower than the battlecruiser next to it, but the V-class *Violent Storm* was keeping pace. They would reach long-range firing distance by the time the enemy ships had jumped in. They were already engaging their weaponry systems, raising shields, and readying the initiation of their special advanced anti-weaponry fields.

The destroyer-transporters were reacting with their strikecruisers, holding their separate formations too, but they were too far out. They were nowhere near full speed; the theatre commander aboard the juggernaut had sent the order for a slow advance of these elements, suspecting this may be a distraction. The X-class and S-class ships-of-the-line would come in as reserves, to support the heavier ships. The Helvanna house military were scrambling, and some would even reach the danger zone before the Third Empire ships, but they were viewed as expendable by the theatre commander.

The hyper-pulse communications generator within the Hath System was preparing to send warning that they were under attack, all the Third Empire and Helvanna starships were just reacting and perhaps no more than ten seconds into their reaction, when the first surprise was revealed.

The two interdictors the VMC had in-system activated their interdiction fields, preventing the Third Empire starships from jumping. The move was completely unexpected by the Imperials. The interdictors simultaneously fired their long-range weaponry, torpedoes streaking out even as they gave away the interdictors positions.

<Signal is given,> said the scanners operator. <Interdictors *Kinslayer* and *Kingdom* have engaged interdiction fields and have launched torpedoes and long-range weaponry, both targets.>

Admiral De Graaf, <Open fire, let's go hot, people.>

Apparently empty space opened up, with a blizzard of heavy-weapons fire. The majority of it was simply torpedoes, but some ships were now close enough to release partial broadsides of long- and medium-range weaponry.

The special shielding the Third Empire battlecruiser and the juggernaut used ceased to work; they had not fully engaged, still powering up, but suddenly they were failing. As explosions blossomed all over the hulls of the two warships, tremendous damage being meted out in this first fusillade, the two warships already began to suffer. The weaponry simply failed to pass through their physical forms as if they were not there, the torpedoes, missiles, and turbolaser fire biting deep into their superstructures.

<All ships firing, Commander-In-Chief,> said Captain Erica Georgia. <Fire, fire, fire,> she gave the order repeatedly.

Lord Gavain observed the damage his First Fleet had meted out in the first few seconds of the engagement. Although the *Vindicator* was not part of any of the fleets, he had wanted to be here, to see the outcome of the plan.

The damage they had done was phenomenal, to both ships, and this was at long range.

<All ships,> he said across the datasphere, as it kicked into action, connecting all the fleet together. <Advance, target both Red One and Red Two,> he named the enemy juggernaut and the battlecruiser, <Their new technology which makes them invulnerable to being hit is not working for some reason. Strikepods to launch from leading elements immediately.>

<Forty-eight seconds until reinforcements arrive,> said his scanners officer.

The entire First Fleet of the Vindicatus Mercenary Corporation was revealed in the system. They were not in their squadron formations, instead reorganised roughly into several different tiers of squads depending on their classifications and role in the pre-planned stealth attack.

The enemy juggernaut and the battlecruiser began firing on the interdictors, but they were already taking heavy fire. The *Vindicator* and the dreadnought *Thor's Hammer* were in the lead, along with all the other battlecruisers, Captain McDonnagh's *Carnivorous,* the *Cathedral,* the *Remembrance,* Vice-Admiral Kenzie Viederhauns *Revenging Angel,* the *Rebellious,* Rear-Admiral Saifa Al-Malli's *Vengeance* and the *Violator.* This was a heavy amount of firepower, all moving into medium range with their targets. Broadsides were opening up, heavier banks of weaponry firing on the enemy targets.

Strikepods launched in massive clouds from the heavy warships, streaking past the fighters and bombers that were already passing the dreadnought and the battlecruisers. The interdictors continued to take heavy fire, as the long-range weaponry from the star-carriers *Quintessential, Queen of Egypt* and *Quiet of the Void* pummelled the targets. There was another interdictor amongst them, the *Knifeman,* already firing up its interdiction field as the ships advanced.

Further out and coming from a different angle were the destroyers, the *Paralysis, Patriot, Undefeatable, Ubermacht* and *Unperturbed.* The volume of long-range fire they were unleashing was enough to raze a continent in the space of minutes, and they were directing it all onto the targets.

The strikepods struck home, the enemy ships special fields which made them invulnerable to weaponry somehow not working. Even as the strikepods struck like so many ticks, covering the hulls of the target ships, delivering three thousand marines onto their targets in seconds, the fighters and bombers were streaking through, swarming the enemy juggernaut and battlecruiser.

The leading dreadnought and battlecruisers of the VMC began to break, dispersing to present harder targets, as the strikecruisers using their superior speed reached medium firing range. They were coming from all directions, closing in on multiple vectors. The L-class *Linebacker, Loneliness,* and *Liberator* were joined by the S-class *Solace, Snake-Eyes, Slaughter, Serpent, Sanguine,* and *Sidewinder.* Heavier than old fashioned lightcruisers, but quicker and lighter armoured than the heavy battlecruisers, they were mere seconds away from launching their thousands of marines onto the targets as well.

Field Marshal Ulrik Andryukhin actually laughed across the datasphere as he used his rotary cannon to blast through the enemy Marines running down the corridor towards his squad. Sergeant Naomi Calaman joined her weaponry fire to his, and they deluged the enemy upgraded marines with rapid heavy-weapons fire.

Amazingly all that happened was that they went down, one or two of them not to get up again, but the rest of the enemy squad was getting back to their feet already. With a roar Ulrik Andryukhin sped forwards, an energised sword in his hand, cutting and slashing through the upgraded armour of the enemy in seconds.

<I want some of this armour, Naomi,> he said on their private comm-line.

<I knew you were going to say that, sir.>

<You developing a sense of humour, Sergeant? Sounds like you were taking the piss there.>

<Me, sir? Never, sir.>

An enemy Marine bearing the symbol of the Third Empire on his chest plate had his own sword up and firing, and with a blast of sparks the two blades met each other. <Fuck off!> roared Andryukhin, actually punching the Marine in the face with the barrel of his rotary cannon. The entire corridor flashed with the light and the resultant blood-spray as the enemy's head exploded painted the section.

<Ulrik to Jamie,> he said, <Jamie, we're taking the juggernaut now, but expect heavy casualties. The defenders have upgraded Praetorian Guard armour, and weaponry. We're going to suffer.>

<How much time to take the ships?> asked Lord Gavain.

<I'd add another two minutes to the target,> said Andryukhin.

<That cuts it close, we have to jump out then.>

<Sorry, but that's the truth, Jamie.>

<Do your best, Rik. Reinforcements are due in five seconds, we can have more Marines to you in twenty-five seconds. Gavain out.>

Real-space opened up with bright flashes of light, and the VMC reinforcements jumped into the Hath System. Admiral Danae Markos was in the lead, with the second dreadnought, the *Terminator*. Massive and overwhelming, it dwarfed the seven battlecruisers it had jumped into the system with.

Immediately, even as their shields were rising, the heavy warships began to change heading, advancing to close in on the beleaguered Third Empire ships-of-the-line. The heavier ships from the Second Fleet had joined the fray.

*

<We will reach the terminus point in three .... two .... one ..... exit!> the helmsman announced.

Admiral Silus Adare stood up from his flag chair, the anticipation hitting him hard. They had been waiting for Lord Gavain to cross into Helvanna Province, his message to taunt him appearing not to work. Then they had received the emergency distress call from the Hath System, with the initial images showing the system under attack. From the number of ships Gavain had deployed, it was a full-scale invasion.

<Show me visuals,> he ordered, <I want to see him.>

<The rest of the fleet has translated, Admiral,> said Captain Zehra Sahin. They had been waiting in considerable numbers near a stargate, ready to jump to any one of the potential targets that Gavain could hit.

<Sorry, Admiral,> said the scanners officer nervously, <there doesn't appear to be any enemy ships in-system.>

<What?> Adare's anger flared, and every member of bridge crew felt it strike them across the datasphere. <Explain. Where are they?>

There was a short wait as the scanners officers and communications officers frantically attempted to find out what had happened to Gavain's ships, but as Adare waited, he began to guess what had happened. He could see some Imperial warships, and the Helvanna house ships, but two ships-of-the-line were conspicuous by their absence.

<Confirmed, Admiral,> said the comms officer quietly, <Lord Gavain and the Vindicatus Mercenary Corporation hit in heavy numbers, boarded a juggernaut and a battlecruiser, and then jumped out-system. The entire attack took five minutes, we just missed it.>

<The bastard's done it again,> said Adare, shaking his head. All of a sudden, he smiled, the last reaction anyone was expecting. He sat back down in his chair. <Round one to you, Jamie Gavain.>

Chapter XIII

Lady Principal Sophia was keeping herself under control with every ounce of her ability. She was an accomplished diplomat and politician, with a long and successful business history behind her. She was richer than some of the people in this Council chamber on Leviticus, money made in her own right without her family's assistance.

Where her husband Lord Micalek Zupanic had sat, the woman she strongly suspected of killing him was instead in residence. Lady Wyn Zupanic, returned from the dead. With a severe and evil look, Lady Wyn had been feared through this region of space, her intelligence and spy network cast far afield. She had a reputation for cruelty and efficiency that even out-ranked that of The Spider.

Now, Lady Wyn was back in command of House Zupanic. No-one in this room believed the story that Micalek had been murdered by the man blamed for it, but there was also no-one in this room who wanted to question the version of events. Even perhaps Lady Sophia herself. Lady Wyn was now Lady Minister Wyn, of the Ministry of Transformation and Integration.

They were almost at the end of the lengthy Council session, Lord Brin Claes droning on about a new initiative to reach out to the Houses around them. They were interested in bringing in new Houses to the Union, and it was a subject all of them had strong opinions on, but Claes had a way of turning even the most exciting subject into a tedious lecture. Lady Principal Sophia was almost relieved when a servant came up to her raised seat, passing her a scrolling data-pad.

"Lord Minister Brin Claes," she said, "if one may interrupt for a moment?"

"Ah, of course, Lady Principal," said Lord Brin, inclining his head slightly. He sat down, not noticing the looks of relief on some of the other Lords and Ladies Ministers around him. Lord Jorrik Jorgensson sent a raised eyebrow coupled with a smirk to Lady Sophia, and despite herself she found it amusing, the intent of his glance at Lord Brin Claes being clear. There was something attractive about the Lord due to inherit the overall Head of Houseship for Jorgensson, but now was undoubtedly the wrong time for her to even think of anything along those lines. Her mind was firmly on the loss of her husband, whether he was a manipulative killer or not.

"One has just received a message from Lord Gavain. He was on a mission to assault and steal one of the advanced starships from the Third Empire, in the Helvanna Province –"

"Such a thing was not to be spoken about openly, even in this chamber," said Lady Wyn quickly. Despite the lack of trust, she had been informed of the mission. There was no way to avoid it. All the Lords and Ladies knew, in fact, they had voted to allow it in a closed session without record.

"- well it can now, Lady Wyn, do not interrupt," said Lady Principal Sophia, more sharply than she had intended. Her composure returned instantly, however. "Lord Gavain has sent word through hyper-pulse that the mission has been successful. They have stolen a juggernaut and, interestingly, a V-class battlecruiser from the Third Empire. They have returned to the Dark Heart Artificial System via the Web of Stargates, and will let us know what they find in short order. He assures us he has his best people on the work."

There was a round of applause from the assembled servants and aides, the shock and relief on their faces palpable. They had not known of the classified mission, of course.

"I presume he wants paying, then," said Lord Moafa Obamu sarcastically.

"Without doubt," said Lady Principal Sophia, with a small smile. "He is the Mercenary Lord, after all."

"Can we trust him to share all the information?" asked Lady Wyn.

"We can, perhaps, to an extent," said Lord Jorrik. "He is an honourable man, but he may retain some for his own use. Even if he does, it is more information on the enemy than we may have had."

"Who says they are our enemy?" asked Lady Wyn.

"The threat from the Third Emperor is real," said Lady Principal Sophia. "We have discussed this many times, since before you joined this Council Chamber. We know that the Third Emperor is moving this way, and we strongly suspect we are in his path of advance towards Mars."

"If that's his true target," said Lady Wyn, then she raised her hands, "although, I admit I am playing the Devil's advocate. The Third Emperor is most likely coming this way, our own strategists agree."

"Which is why we agreed to pay the Vindicatus Mercenary Corporation and the Vindicatus nation the money to find out," said Lord Obamu. "It was Imperial Crowns very well-spent, I think."

"We are not going to waste time discussing matters we already have," said Lady Principal Sophia. "However, Lord Brin, if one may continue on the very subject you were discussing? About nations wishing to join the Levitican Union?"

"Of course, Lady Principal, whatever you wish to say," said Lord Brin Claes, gesturing open-handedly. "You are the elected leader."

Elected leader, thought Lady Sophia. Real democracy with one-person, one-vote had been proven an outdated concept centuries ago, not being a form of government that could survive in space. The distances were too wide, and even before leaving Earth, mankind had found it did not truly work. There was a tendency for a democracy to become the preserve of a few. The populace preferred their leaders to be leaders. A number of different systems had been tried, the latest being the Imperial House system established by the True Emperor centuries ago. Some Houses allowed some alpha and beta class peoples to vote, but even then voting was restricted to members of the family within that House; it was more common for votes to be allowed on the Imperial Solar Administration Chancellors, or junior Administration servants, but even there it was typically achieved by Imperial appointment. Even that limited form of restricted democracy had not been an outstanding success, thought Sophia, with many systems and territories sticking to autocratic rule. Perhaps it was in mankind's nature to constantly rebel against forms of government. As a species we need unity, as individuals we resent it when the majority does not conform to our choice. Leaders rarely do everything that we want, so disappointment and dissatisfaction is inevitable.

"There is one nation that wishes to join us," said Lady Principal Sophia, "emulating membership of the Union in exactly the same way as House Jorgensson. They want to keep their independence in matters of military, justice and law, and monetary independence, and so are happy to join on the same terms as House Jorgensson, with one vote on the Council and without a Ministry. Although, they have offered to run a unified intelligence service for us, reporting into the Principal's Office. Those are the terms of their joining, and one is sure we will all agree as we agreed with House Jorgensson. In fact, this second-tier membership of the Union is what we are offering to the Houses around our lands."

"And who is this nation and this Lord?" asked Lord Jorrik Jorgensson, "or is the name of this person and this House somewhat obvious, considering?"

"Lord Gavain wishes to join the Vindicatus nation to the Levitican Union?" asked Lord Claes, incredulously.

"Yes," confirmed Lady Principal Sophia. "The second-tier membership suits him well. He can forge Vindicatus' own identity, but also joins the Union to gain our support. He needs it, too, despite the efforts of his own people. We can help him, as much as he can help us. May I remind you he has the best and biggest military in most of the Eastern Segment, with the largest number of Praetorian ships, and his own very effective intelligence network."

"The one thing we have never done is pass our intelligence networks over to centralised command," said Lady Wyn. "I would resist this element of the unification."

Of course you would, thought Lady Sophia, of course you would. "Which is why we will vote on it," said Lady Principal Sophia, "in two days time, on the next Council session. All one asks you all to remember is that we need Lord Gavain's help more than ever, both with his military, his tech and his intelligence operation, and the Unified Intelligence Network will report into me directly and as such be answerable to this Council. That is all, Lords and Ladies Ministers."

*

Juan Ramirez looked at the pint glass in front him. It was an old ancient Earth tradition, to serve beer in pints of glass. This retro bar deliberately tried to represent those old bars, although how accurate it was Juan could not say.

As he tried to focus on the glass of real alcohol, he found he did not care either.

"Wha' you saying, Ellen?" he slurred.

"You're drunk, Juan," she said, before giggling. "I wa - was only saying, that was one helluva battle in the Hath System."

"Sure it was!" shouted a Marine behind her. "You two from the *Vindicator,* the Lord Gavain's ship? Three cheers for Gavain! And the victory at Hath!"

The bar was mobbed with Marines and naval crew from the ships. Shore leave had been granted for all the ships that had taken part in the action, and many of them had headed for the capital city on Dark Heart Alpha. The burgeoning drinking and less acceptable districts of the city were full of the one third of all crew that were on shore leave, tens of thousands of military personnel swamping the area.

The cheers rocketed around the bar, and the terrified bar staff smiled as they accepted that this could get out of control easily. There were no drones serving in this bar, but real people. It provided jobs, ultimately, and it was a popular method of entertainment within the city amongst many of the colonists.

"James Gavain," said Juan, "By the Emperor, I mish him."

The member of bar-staff hanging around near them continued in her duties, but was paying attention without them realising.

"I am sure you do, but you need to be more careful," said Ellen Forrest. "Imagine if Admiral Andersson found out."

"Why, who elsh knows?" said Juan.

"That you're sleeping together? That you're in a relationship? What are you, anyway?"

"We have shpoken about a relashunship," said Juan, "He wants to wait, because of Admiral Andershon, but he says he lovesh me. I think it's as difficult for him as it is for me."

"Why? Have you never been in love before?"

"No," said Juan. "And neither has he."

"I keep forgetting you're not Praetorian-born, from the vats on Deimos," said Ellen Forrest. "It's not the Praetorian way to fall in love. We just don't. But more and more of us have been. Look at Field Marshal Andryukhin, rumour is he's moved on from the loss of Kavanagh and he's interested in Captain Georgia."

"Georgia? From our ship? The Captain?"

"The one and same, aye."

"Bloody hell, that's quiet," said Juan, ordering more beer from the waitress nearby, listening to their conversation. "So who else knows about me and James Gavain?"

"Virtually the whole ship," said Forrest. "I did warn you, Juan Ramirez. It was going to get around. You two make it far too obvious. You need to tell the Commander-In-Chief, and get him to sort it out with Andersson before he does hear. Then you're both fucked."

"I will," said Juan, "I will." And then he began to cry.

The waitress made an excuse, pretending she was ill so the duty manager allowed her to leave. It was a short ride back to her quarters. When she reached her apartment, she closed and locked both entrances, and went straight to a hidden compartment in her wall.

Sliding it aside, she reached the communications gear. Normally she used dead-drops, an old spy technique that was hard for modern technology to intercept or detect, but this information was so explosive she had to get it to her handlers. Lord Gavain and a lowly Midshipman, in love and having an affair behind the equally unspoken 'proper' relationship of no less than the Solar Administration Chancellor and Admiral Harley Andersson! It was just what they needed.

The Third Empire had given up on trying to get biomorphs into the system, although the agent was not to know about the insertion through the Interstellar Merchants Guild. She was a full human, a volunteer from one of the penetrated intelligence agencies within the Eastern Segment. Her handler was a full human. She did not know how big the spy network was here, but the information she had happened upon made it worthwhile. The only way to get spies onto Dark Heart was people with long background histories, Vindicatus technology was so advanced it would pick up biomorphs and even some of the more advanced implants used in the spying game.

So the full human took the risk of using her comms gear. Even if it was picked up, as the transmission eventually would, it would allow them to get the information off-planet before the sifting programmes of the planetary datacore mainframes identified it as covert intelligence. She would transmit her message, and then immediately move into a back-up cover and lie low for a long, long time.

In short order, the Third Empire would have the explosive propaganda they needed to rubbish the name of the 'hero' Mercenary Lord Gavain.

*

<Jason Bramhall, once again you have done an outstanding job, well done,> said Lord Gavain across the datasphere.

<Thank you, Jamie,> said Captain Bramhall.

<Gavain out.>

Signing out from the hyper-pulse communication, Gavain brought his attention back to the real world. He was stood on the primary observation deck of the Dark Heart Shipyard, inside the great curvature of the upper hull where it was possible due to the deck's slow rotation to see every part of the circular shipyards.

"Captain Bramhall has done well," said Gavain to the four people stood with him. "The new colony has been founded, in the triple star system, earlier this morning. The stargate linking it to the Web is already up, and a new HPCG station. I'm calling it the Bright Hope System, as it is our new hope. It's taken two of our colonyships, but it brings us closer to the Levitican Union."

"He's doing a fantastic job," Admiral De Graaf commented.

"Only three colonyships left though, then we're doing it the hard way," said Andryukhin. "Are you sure we aren't expanding too fast, Jamie?"

"The immigrants and refugees are still pouring in," said O'Connor. "And our own cloning and biovat facilities are increasing in size all the time. The population of Vindicatus is exploding."

Captain Georgia from the *Vindicator* was also present, the battlecruiser being one of the ships in dock for repair. "It's not my area, sirs, but surely with the Amerimax coming in from Praetor now we can continue growing rapidly?"

"We can indeed," said Lord Gavain, "and again, Praetor is largely thanks to Captain Bramhall. I am very impressed with the man. Excellent leadership, as well as command and strategic capability."

"Fucking reminds me of someone," joked Ulrik Andryukhin. Everyone present laughed.

"But to business," said Lord Gavain, as the ship in question rotated into view through the observational window strip. "How long until the *Zeus's Wrath* is fully repaired? I want that juggernaut in the field."

"Both ships will be fully repaired in a week, we have diverted a large number of crews to them both," said Admiral De Graaf. "The rest of the fleet will be fully repaired in two to three weeks. We are working round the clock, and the droid support is speeding things up. An amazing effort, all told. The Dark Heart Shipyards are large enough, and we have sent some ships to the Kavanagh Shipyards, diverting away from the construction efforts at both."

"We're building a large number of ships, civilian and military," said Gavain. "We were lucky to have no losses, in material if not our Marines. We need to divert to constructing only Praetorian ships now."

"We will," said De Graaf. "We're going to try and build our own juggernauts, but they will be months away from deployment."

"We are also putting their technology to good use, retrofitting to our own ships," said O'Connor. "It is happening now."

"My Marines are getting new equipment, its being mass produced now," said Andryukhin.

"Good," nodded Gavain. "And what of the capabilities of the captured ships, Lucas? And the intelligence we have gained, Jonathan?"

"The ships are phenomenal," said De Graaf. "They are built from an alloy we have never encountered before, but we can replicate it with our own mining activities and foundries. It makes the armour more effective, more resistance - and more conductive for their secret weapon. The 'phasing field' is what they call it, using technology based on that used to translate a ship into hyper-space. What the phasing field does is push the ship partly into hyper-space, which gives it that translucent, eerie, ghostly appearance. The power demands are high so it cannot be sustained indefinitely, and of course it falls afoul of interdiction fields."

"We were very lucky then that we were engaging interdictors to prevent them from jumping," said Gavain.

"Very lucky indeed, Jamie," De Graaf continued. "The phasing field takes five to ten seconds to initiate, which is very fast. Couple that with their heavier hulls and armour, improved weaponry systems in terms of turbolasers and torpedoes, and they are formidable already. The V-class battlecruiser was upgraded. The juggernaut itself is something else entirely."

De Graaf explained about the capabilities of the juggernaut. It was massive, capable of engaging several dreadnoughts without worry, where one dreadnought could engage three to four Praetorian battlecruisers. It was another, entire step up in warship design, unprecedented in its concept. De Graaf explained that it was designated a Z-class, and also ran through the information they had taken on the other classes of ships-of-the-line, W-class, X-class and Y-class.

"The enemy of the Third Imperium seem to be using these newly designed warships, and modified S-class, T-class, U-class and V-class ships, which are the generation directly before these."

"So they do have Praetorian origin then?" asked Gavain.

"Yes - and no," said O'Connor. "They are Praetorian next-generation, yes. No, in that they were not built by Praetorian techs. We have not located the homeworld or homeworlds of this Third Empire and the Shadow Emperor, but we know they were built and designed beyond the Frontier. This technology has in some instances been in design for nearly two decades."

"That long?" asked Andryukhin. "How? Did the False Emperor have it?"

"No," said O'Connor. "We have managed to get that from the datacores. The False Emperor did not even know of the existence of the Shadow Council, the people we thought controlled just the Faceless assassins. Their organisation is much bigger and wider than we ever suspected. The Shadow Emperor is the person who they raised as their 'Master of the First Circle', and they call their different operational branches 'Circles'."

O'Connor went on to explain a lot about the organisation of the Shadow Council, and this Third Imperium. "Their ultimate target is Mars," he confirmed, "that much is in the datacore. It is referenced in numerous motivational speeches given by the Shadow Emperor. They also have numerous references to something called 'the Railway', a big project, but we can't determine what that is. All we know is that the Third Imperium still has a large number of reserve forces waiting beyond the Frontier. We are only seeing the tip of their forces."

"By the True Emperor," swore Gavain, as he reviewed the suspected figures through the datasphere.

"We are fucked," commented Field Marshal Andryukhin, who then laughed at Captain Georgia's reaction.

"They won't all be aiming at us, but the Shadow Emperor intends to drive a wedge down from the Frontier directly to Mars. The Levitican Union lies in the way. We know that members of his lesser Circles have manipulated the houses and politics to their advantage, some of them like Helvanna turning 'loyal' as part of stage-managed plots stretching back years. The Levitican Union lies on the path, and the Shadow Emperor wants the Dark Heart System back. He hates you, Jamie."

"With damn good reason," joked Ulrik, getting a small amount of polite laughter.

"What have we got from the captured Interstellar Merchant Guild spy?" asked Gavain. "The biomorph who was inserted with the IMG delegation?"

"The rot in the IMG goes higher than we thought," said O'Connor gravely. "We know Jared Towers is one of the Circle of the Shadow Council, but it transpires that the Deputy Head of the IMG is also a Legate in this Circle. The IMG are penetrated by the Shadow Council, again, they have been for decades. The Shadow Council had been worming their way through Imperial structure since before Dissolution, well before."

"Why?" asked Gavain.

"In preparation for the fall of the Empire," said Andryukhin, who had reviewed this bit of the information with interest. "They knew the False Emperor was going to lead the colonised galaxy to destruction, so they planned well in advance. The Shadow Council was originally set up by the True Emperor, apparently, to serve as a back-up in case he should ever fall. That was their mission, and when the False Emperor took over, the Shadow Council prepared. Even better is the truth of who the Shadow Emperor is."

"Who is he?" asked Gavain.

"The Shadow Emperor is a clone of the First, True Emperor," said O'Connor quietly.

"No," said Gavain, "surely not?"

"A direct clone, just like the False Emperor was apparently," said O'Connor.

"We have the evidence?"

"We have all the evidence. He is a clone."

"This is explosive," said Gavain.

"It would tear a lot of the Shadow Empire's support away," said Andryukhin. "He claims to be the grandson of the True Emperor, as the False Emperor claimed to be the son. Let's hope the mental instability doesn't hold true either, but sadly, I think it probably does."

"We have this clone origin confirmed from where?" asked Gavain.

"The Hath operation, the biomorph spy, and the operation out in the Boundary," said O'Connor. "We have more than enough evidence to back it up."

"What will you do about the Interstellar Merchants Guild?" asked De Graaf. "The Deputy Head of the IMG being a senior member of the Shadow Empire is galaxy-rocking, almost as much as the Shadow Emperor being a clone. It knocks the impartiality of the IMG away, puts them under the same suspicion as all the rest of the old Imperial organisations and structures."

"I will inform the Head," said Gavain simply, "and then we will arrest all the biomorphs in the delegation here. We will keep that secret, and let the Head deal with the Deputy Head, but as for the Shadow Emperor being a clone - well, I shall think on it, but it seems one of the best ways of knocking his support."

"Have you seen the reports from Commander Lancaster and Captain Alansen, from the Pathonis System?" asked Andryukhin.

"I have been otherwise engaged," said Gavain. "We have been accepted into the Levitican Union, I have been dealing with that."

"That's fantastic news," said O'Connor.

"You are running their intelligence services," said Lord Gavain, directly.

"I - I am?"

"Yes, we'll talk on it later. What of the report from Pathonis?" asked Gavain.

"We have full recordings of what is happening there," said Ulrik Andryukhin, "and it is just as bad as the deathcamps we found in Compact territory, if not worse." He explained in great detail, even using holographic images that Alansen and Lancaster had recorded.

"The Shadow Emperor's insanity knows no bounds," said Lord Gavain quietly. "To use hybrids is an abomination. Human brains and thought processes sliced into alien life-forms is amoral. As for forcing people into collective borg minds - it is horrific, and not what we stand for here. Although I suspect some will find that less abhorrent."

"No-one will like the hybrid story," said O'Connor.

"That is being released as well," said Gavain grimly.

"We are giving this information to the other nations?" said O'Connor. "How much of it, if we are? We need to earn our billions of Imperial Crowns."

"All of them on the list," said Gavain without hesitation, "excluding some of the detail on the juggernaut. We want the construction kept to us, so we can build our own, but let me see the detail you want to send first. We will earn our money, keep the Vindicatus nation solvent."

"And the detail of the strange construction that Commander Lancaster saw them building in space around Pathonis?" asked O'Connor.

"Yes," said Gavain, "I suspect it has a link to this strange Railway project, but unfortunately we have no guarantee either way, and we did not see it completed. The images on that, as well, can be released."

"Of course, the Shadow Empire does have something they might want to release to the colonised galaxy on us as well," said O'Connor, slowly.

"What?" asked Gavain, frowning. He did not miss that everyone was looking at each other.

"Well, you, particularly, Jamie," said O'Connor, looking extremely uncomfortable.

"What is it?" asked Gavain. He was met with silence. "Someone explain."

They all looked at one another again, but surprisingly it was Captain Erica Georgia who finally spoke. "Lord - Jamie," she said, "we all know on ship that you have been engaged in relations with Midshipman Juan Ramirez."

Gavain looked shocked, his usual impassive facade slipping away in a heartbeat. For his older friends, it was extremely surprising to see, and just confirmed what they suspected.

"Unfortunately it has been becoming greater and greater knowledge," said Admiral O'Connor. "Rumours are spreading."

General Ulrik Andryukhin put his arm around Captain Erica Georgia. "I have been seeing Erica, Jamie. We keep it quiet, because it is personal to us ... and of course, people might think it is too soon after my relationship with Jules Kavanagh. But no-one cares about me and Erica. They will care about you and Juan, particularly as you are widely seen to be with Admiral Harley Andersson."

"I am - it is good you have moved on," said Lord Gavain, with something less than tact, as he looked at Ulrik. "I had no idea. But my relationship with Juan is between me and him, and nothing to do with anyone or anything else."

"Sadly that is not true, Jamie," said Lucas De Graaf gently.

"What do you mean, Lucas?"

"You are known to be seeing Harley."

"But I am not."

"He thinks differently, as does the media and many thousands, if not millions of people in Vindicatus."

"So?" Gavain felt exposed. This was his life, not theirs. He was also later to admit that he felt guilt. "What is this to do with anything?"

"Unfortunately we have recorded word going out through the HPCG network, describing your relationship with Juan Ramirez. It references Andersson. We suspect it has gone to the Third Empire, and if that is the case, the Shadow Emperor will use it against you."

"How?"

"Are you really so frikking blind, Jamie?" asked Ulrik. "It will cause doubt amongst the people here in this nation if you are revealed to be less than honourable in your personal life, especially on top of the untrue propaganda they have been putting out about you manipulating politics in the Segment."

"Less than honourable?" asked Gavain, his temper rising.

"It is how it will be painted," said Lucas, "quite beyond the fact that Harley Andersson will be greatly hurt, you bigger problem is that the two of you are the biggest names in Vindicatus. A disagreement, true or not, between you will cause problems."

"We are Praetorians, Jamie," said Ulrik. "Such relationship matters were not bred into us. They were bred out of us. But we have learnt despite that, and I think from the look on your face whatever you felt for Harley is gone, if it was ever there. But Juan has affected you."

"We have been carefully monitoring him, as a security risk," said O'Connor quietly.

"You have been doing what?" asked Jamie Gavain, fury making his voice go cold.

"We saw the potential," said O'Connor apologetically. "I am sorry, Jamie, but it is out there. There was a spy, a human spy whom we cannot protect against and we knew would slip through our net, who overheard discussion in a bar. There is a recording of Juan Ramirez talking about your relationship. It has been sent out-system, we did not catch it in time. The Shadow Emperor will receive it, and use it to cause doubt on your name and reputation."

Gavain forced himself to be calm. "How long do I have until it is in the media?"

"Not long. Hours, maybe days. It is the most logical thing for them to do as they have been conducting a propaganda campaign against you."

"Then I must go public first, limit the damage," said Gavain thoughtfully.

"We thought that the best idea," said Ulrik, looking at Erica. It was obvious they had discussed this before.

"And you must talk to Harley first," said Lucas.

"Why?" asked Lord Gavain.

"Jamie!" Ulrik virtually howled. "I do wonder about you, sometimes. I swear when they made you out of the molecular soup, the bioartificers forgot some important gene. Harley is not only a very good friend of yours, and a lover - hopefully a former one if you have that fucking decency - but he supported you all the way, from the Dissolution, to setting up the Vindicator Mercenary Corporation, and again in the Vindicatus nation. You owe him as much as you owe any of us. He also feels differently towards you than you do to him, out of common decency you must -"

"Ulrik, you go too far," said Jamie Gavain, sharply. His eyes had gone violent, and his fists were clenched. It was a release of emotion the icy man almost never showed.

"Let us call an end to this," said Lucas De Graaf quickly. "Jamie, one of us will come see you shortly. Can we be excused, please?"

"Yes, you all are," said Lord Gavain, and with uncharacteristic angriness, stormed, "Get out of my sight. Every last Emperor-cursed one of you."

Shortly he was left alone, hands pressed against the metaglass window, looking out at the rotating shipyards beyond.

Chapter XIV

<Midshipman Juan Ramirez?> said Captain Erica Georgia. It was night shift, and Juan Ramirez had returned to the ship, pulling a double-shift to cover for another officer's shore leave.

<Yes, Captain?>

<Lord Gavain wants to see you in his ready room. Report.>

<Yes, Captain.>

A replacement took his station as he stood, and walked across the bridge to the ready room. He felt the eyes of the crew on him, and knew what they were thinking. He actually reddened as the doors opened, then slid shut behind him as he entered.

"Juan," said James Gavain. He was not sat behind his desk, but instead stood, a drink in his hands. It looked like synthetic alcohol, and there was a glass for him.

"Jamie?" asked Juan, stepping forwards somewhat nervously. "I thought we were keeping this secret?"

"The secret is out, Juan," said James Gavain. "As I found out, some hours ago. We don't have much time, and we have to make a decision, you and I."

"What decision is that?"

"A decision on what we want to do, before I speak to Harley Andersson and tell him about us, and before our relationship goes public. This is either the beginning or the end, Juan. We need to talk."

Lord James Gavain sat in the Friederich-class lander, as it shuttled him down to the Heart Palace. It was entering the atmosphere, but he sat in one of the empty passenger cabins. He wore his military uniform, not his robes of House. House Gavain was making the speech, but it was the Commander-In-Chief of a strong military who was addressing the Houses of the colonised galaxy.

The message was only going to certain leaders and Houses. It would be heavily encoded, and sent in secret. He had chosen the people carefully, but he knew it had to be done now. The threat from the Third Empire was too great.

The drone with the inbuilt holo-camera recording his voice as he spoke.

"With the message, I am including a list of who I am having it sent to. I hope I find you well, and in a receptive mood," said Lord Gavain. "By now you will have received the intelligence I have sent you, as well as seeing some of the public news broadcasts I have released on the Shadow Emperor and this Third Empire of His. You may even have seen some news about me personally, but that may follow this message. Ignore that, the public propaganda is there to wage the media war against the Third Imperium.

"I am more concerned in private with real war. You will have seen the intelligence and reviewed it by now. The Empire is strong, more technologically advanced than we suspected, and more far-reaching in its ambitions. They head for Mars, and will take all in their way, and in addition, after that, this Shadow Emperor then wants to take the rest of the colonised galaxy. The time to stop him, to plan to stop him, is now. We do not have much time. We cannot allow him to reach Mars. He is already approaching the Mid-Sectors, and we are running out of opportunity to draw a line and stop him.

"I propose an alliance, between all of us. I speak as a representative of the Vindicatus nation, not the Leviticus Union, as you may well have heard that I am now allied to the Union. I have a plan, and this is it, laid before you, also under cover of this message. I appeal for co-operation between all our nations, that we work together to draw a line where we do not allow the Third Empire to cross.

"The first part of the plan is a challenge, to draw the Shadow Empire in and deal them a blow. They will respond, and we will fight and win. We can win, despite their superior technology. Consider the plan, consider my idea, and please, contact me back to let me know.

"In relation to the plan, I am asking all of you only to release it to certain people in your nations. Where I know some of your advisors are working for the Shadow Empire, I have told you and identified them. What you do with that information is up to you. But I suggest you follow the evidence I have given you, or the suspicions we have. We cannot allow this plan to leak. I have approached you, because I believe you to be anti-Imperium.

"This is the new Revolutionary Council, born again. We will face the Shadow Council, and we will win. I can only give you three days to respond, because then I must call the hyper-pulse meeting where we discuss the overall plan in much greater detail, and we submit the numbers on what we can provide to the resistance effort.

"With the Will of the One True Emperor, Lord Gavain out."

Harley Andersson looked up as Lord James Gavain entered his grand, resplendent, private office in Heart Palace.

"Jamie?" he said. "What are you doing here? I wasn't expecting you on-planet?"

"No," said Lord James Gavain. "You were not."

"What in the name of the True Emperor is wrong, James. I can see it in your face."

James Gavain came forward. He was in his military uniform, and he sat before Harley at his desk.

"Harley, we need to talk," said James, "I am deeply, deeply, deeply sorry. We do not have much time, I am about to go public with something. I am doing it for some of the wrong reasons, but, part of me is glad that the deceit is over as well."

Andersson looked down at his desk, and then looked up. His eyes were pinched. "I think I know what this is, Jamie."

"Do you? Are you sure?" asked James.

"I'm not sure," said Harley, "but you are here to tell me our relationship is over. To you of course, it never really was one."

"That is part of it, yes," said James quietly.

"Is there someone else?"

James took a heavy, deep breath, and began to explain.

It was night-time on Dark Heart Alpha, and Admiral and Solar Administration Chancellor Harley Andersson sat in his office on his own. There was a very large, real and unsynthesised alcohol drink by his side. Ice clinked in the glass as he drank from it, pulling a heavy draw.

The news was on repeat, the local Vindicatus news, the Levitican Union news - the two of which would shortly be the same broadcast, most likely - and the StarCom News Media.

The stories were overlapping. One was a heavy piece, describing the horrors of the Third Empire to the colonised galaxy. It was intended to drive people away from support of them, to make them think about what they were really walking into blind; ironically, in the shadows.

Even more ironically, another news piece was coming from two angles. One was from the Shadow Emperor's offices, announcing James Gavain as an immoral cheat, a personal attack on the Mercenary Lord. Another was from James Gavain himself, admitting a relationship with Juan Ramirez, naming him as his partner, and with a cut-piece from Harley himself, stating that he was fully in support of the relationship as he and Gavain were not partners.

War by news, he thought. It was a centuries old tactic, if not millennia old. The human race advanced in some ways, but never grew up in others. The tactics stayed the same, even if the methods changed.

The important thing was that it would not harm the Vindicatus nation and the millions of people that now resided here. He believed in the nation, even if he found it difficult to believe in Lord James Gavain right at this point in time.

He had assured James that there would be no change in their personal friendship, or their military and governmental dealings. He did ask for some space, however. James agreed, and for once Harley saw a glimmer that James Gavain was beginning to understand about relationships of the heart. Perhaps a bit too late for Harley, but the man was young, he kept forgetting. He had come far, and he was a genius in many ways, but inexperienced in others.

Harley sighed heavily, and finally let slip the tears that he had hidden for so long. There were not many; he had always known, deep down.

*

The Shadow Emperor sat on his throne within the *Emperor of Shadows* armed noble barge, the rest of the Shadow Council in front of him. As ever some were there in actuality, others were there via continuously streaming hyper-pulse message.

"What has been the effect of the release of the truth about Lord Gavain?" asked the Shadow Emperor.

"The information has played badly in some areas of his own nation, and the Levitican Union," said Legate Jared Towers, "and further afield many treat it as another part of the soap opera that is Gavain and Vindicatus. Ultimately, I am sorry to report it will not have the effect we hoped considering his own fast response and pre-emptive news broadcast on the subject."

"I suspect that they detected our humanist agent's message," said the Sixth Legate. "They had forewarning, it can be the only reason they pre-empted us."

"Long term it will cause doubt on Gavain's reputation, and that is what we want," said Jared Towers.

"We know he has also sent messages out to a number of nations which we currently register as anti-Third Empire or neutral," said the Sixth Legate. "We have not detected what the content is yet, although we are focusing efforts upon discovering its import. We can only assume it is anti-Imperium though."

"Naturally," said the Shadow Emperor, with scorn in his voice. "Make it a priority."

"We know they have significant intelligence on us, and of course captured two of our ships," said the Third Legate Jared Towers, with a glance at the Second Legate.

"That was inexcusable," said the Shadow Emperor, eyes narrowing. "How much can they know?"

"More than they have released," said the Fourth Legate. "They could potentially have much information on us and our activities, even you, Shadow Emperor. They will not know of the location of our base of operations for the decades gone by, although they will know the region. They may not have images of the Railway. The images released of the subjugation of a system have been identified as Pathonis, and we lost those ships too as they escaped."

"This is a failure of grand proportions," said the Shadow Emperor calmly. He was in good mood today, more balanced than normal. "We must accelerate the plan. Lord Gavain is endangering it, especially with his - very correct - public statement that we are heading for Mars. Where are we militarily?"

The Second Legate took the floor. "We are crossing into the Mid-Sectors, using the pathway opened up to us by the work of the political, intelligence and covert ops Circles. We are about to hit the moment of stretch, where we need to be concerned with protecting territory we have already taken, using House forces loyal to us and taken by us. We are about to become more reliant on them.

"Regardless, the Railway is still being constructed, so our fresh reserve forces in waiting can strike through. We are not taking heavy damage thanks to our technology. We are perhaps three weeks away from pushing into the edges of the Benedict Democracy, and the Calamarite Confederacy. Once we reach that area, the Mitsubasha nation will declare in our favour and cut their weapons support to both nations. They are weakened by our manipulation through Mitsubasha."

"Accelerate the plan," ordered the Shadow Emperor. "We must jump ahead, stretch into the Confederacy. I do not trust this Lord Gavain, he will be preparing a surprise for us."

"We can jump ahead, but we will increase the risk of failure," said the Second Legate. "We will leave a vast stretch of space with weakened protection and not fully subjugated."

"It must be done. Construct the Railway quicker, jump ahead. We will hurt the Confederacy, and damage the Benedict Democracy. Both are big, big nations, and the plan calls for the Democracy to be shorn in half and the Calamarite's to be damaged. Just do it, by my order," said the Shadow Emperor.

"By your command, Emperor," they all intoned.

"We will be in the Democracy and the Confederacy in three days," said the Second Legate, although it was obvious from her face and her comments that she thought this to be a mistake.

*

Lord Gavain sat within one of the operations rooms on the *Vindicator* battlecruiser, feeling a small amount of nervousness. The day and time had arrived, and he was sending out the hyper-pulse callsigns through the communications generators, to all the Houses and nations he wanted in this meeting.

It was only seconds that he had to wait until they began to hail, but in those seconds, he could not help but be anxious. His mind wandered, but he kept his eyes away from Admiral Andersson at his side. His presence in this operations room was to send a message; Admiral Lucas De Graaf was present as he was the Admiral-of-the-Fleets, and Field Marshal Ulrik Andryukhin was here as leader of the Marines, the human-borg Combined Army and the Droid Army.

In less than two and a half Imperial Standard weeks his fleets would be assembled, repaired, and ready to jump out to war again. It was that war he wanted to discuss today.

<First call coming in, Lord Gavain, it's from Earth,> said Captain Georgia.

<Put them through as they arrive, Captain,> said Gavain on the datasphere.

The operations room was arranged with a circular set-up in its rectangular dimensions, to allow the images of the various leaders and their advisors to circle round as they came into the audience.

Lord Gavain waited, and then nodded as the images of President Giovanna Pereyra and her Commander-In-Chief Jaiden Ryan appeared.

"Lord Gavain," she said, "we are the only two present –"

"As I warned," Gavain interrupted, "no-one else in this conference call knows who I gave clearance to, so, do not give away the information. As I said, you will not know who is in this call unless you give me clearance via the signal to show your presence."

Many light-years and solar systems away, President Pereyra took the rebuke from someone who she viewed as her inferior in terms of noble birth with a political and polite smile, also recognising it as good advice. She should have known better.

She glanced at Commander-In-Chief Ryan. It felt strange not to have Director Chbihi and even Vice-President Schneider present, but the intelligence from Gavain had a big question mark over Schneider which matched Pereyra's concerns, and Chbihi's organisation was holed with Third Imperium spies. The evidence there was quite good and hard, although incomplete.

The way the call was set up, she and Ryan could speak privately, or chose to speak to the group, or just to Gavain with a selection of a holographic touch-button.

Ryan looked at her, and shrugged.

First Lord Al-Zuhairi felt the connection, seeing the image of Gavain and the image of two shadowy people appear in front of him. He knew his own holographic representation would be just as shrouded to protect his identity. He saw the logic in the protection, and also knew he did not need it. It was good to see, through their open access to the system of the hyper-pulse communication, that Gavain had kept his word. First Lord Al-Zuhairi had expected nothing less.

"Lord Gavain," he said, "we await your words."

He looked at Chief Amab Al-Zuhairi, and his Chief Commander Omar Al-Saadi, then settled back to await the start of the galaxy-spanning conference.

Lady Principal Sophia smiled openly at Gavain as the holographic images appeared in the room she was using with the Levitican Union capital city.

"Lord Gavain," she said, "The Levitican Union is here."

She was alone, not even some members of her Council being permitted access, restricted by Lord Gavain. He had specifically denied Lady Wyn, because of her known connections to the old Rosicrux conspiracy.

The Arch-Chancellor Lucija Korhonen of the Korhonen nation was a borg, and famed for her iciness. It was the exact same reputation that James Gavain had in fact. She had also been one of the leading members of the Revolutionary Council that had disposed of the False Emperor. This sort of cloak-and-dagger meeting set her mind back to that period of time, the early days of the Revolutionary Council. She strongly suspected some of the members of the call would be the same.

The galaxy changed, but some things were constant, and whilst some players changed others stayed the same.

"Lord Gavain," she said, "we await your call."

"The great Gavain," her abrasive wife and leader of the nation's army and fleets said with scorn in her voice. Grand Marshal Anaes Korhonen was just as feared as the Arch-Chancellor Lucija Korhonen.

The Star Lord Carlos Cervantes, leader of the Cervantian nation, looked every inch the hard ruler he was. His nation had eaten through the Houses nearby under his leadership, and waged a long series of protracted wars with both Korhonen and Hausenhof. His brother Commandant-General Alvarez Cervantes led the armed forces, and had almost as much power as Carlos did. Simeon Cervantes, a treacherous snake trusted by very few people, was involved with the intelligence and exceptionally corrupt secret police alongside his sister.

"We are here, Mercenary Lord," said Star Lord Carlos Cervantes.

The Lady Katrina Van Hausenhof, new leader of the Hausenhof nation, sat serenely in her throne. By her side, as always, was her husband the Warlord Maximilian Van Hausenhof. He had killed his brother to place his sister and wife upon the throne of the Van Hausenhof House in Imperial times, and together they had forged the mighty Hausenhof nation.

"Gavain," said Lady Katrina Van Hausenhof, "an honour to speak with the man who has done us so much."

"Well met, Gavain," said Warlord Maximilian.

The Archon Jacques Devereux was in charge of the nation of Amiens, and he had attended alone. He was in many ways always alone. None of his Lord Generals or Lord Admirals were present, not even Lord Admiral D'Souza, whom Gavain had actually requested. He would decide if he would pass this information onto them.

"Lord Gavain," he nodded his head simply.

Paul Fallhouse, Marshal of the Armies and Vice-President of the nation of the Republic of Varrental, smiled despite everything at the image of Lord Gavain. He noted that there were many people here already, and he glanced at his mother. She was ailing, and weak, near death despite modern medicine, but the Lady and current President of Varrantal had wanted to be present to listen.

It saddened him greatly, but shortly he knew he would be inheriting the mantle of President of Republic of Varrental, assuming he won the six-way House vote, which was looking likely. The original four Houses had grown to six, not including those taken by force. "Lord Gavain," he said simply, "we are here and waiting."

The Chairman Bortan Ruci of the Calamarite Confederacy was in his full regalia, ostentatious and powerful in his main throne room. All the spectator seats were empty, his various advisors and the people of his confederacy of House Lords absent by request. By his side sat the leader of his armies and navies, Lord Commander Alia Xhepa, and his Director of the Intelligence Services, Degan Roshu.

The House of Xhepa and the House of Roshu were two of the most powerful, along with the House of Ruci, although there were many others in the Confederacy. It consisted entirely of smaller Houses, some no more than two or three systems big, all joined together in the name of unity. The politics was accordingly labyrinthine and devilish.

"As you requested, Lord Gavain," said the Chairman respectfully.

"Thank you all for attending," said Lord James Gavain, "it is appreciated that you have conformed to my requests in terms of secrecy. As I said, everyone's presence here in this conference will be hidden, until such time as it is necessary for us to reveal who you are. I will warn you now, once you see identities you may decide not to proceed with this endeavour, but I stress, the time has come for us to put aside our differences. Let us deal with the Third Empire and this Shadow Emperor, and then if necessary those of you at odds with one another can go back to your disagreements.

"The fact you are here tells me already that you recognise the so-called Third Imperium as the biggest threat we all face. What I will do is outline the proposed plan in slightly more detail, you can ask questions but some of the answers will only be revealed in detailed planning when you have committed yourselves to the operation - and the war that is coming."

He could see all the figures before him, and knew that the person who was speaking was President Pereyra, although the others would have no idea of her identity.

"Lord Gavain, you appeal to our better natures and our desire for survival in the face of this onslaught from the Shadows, but ultimately even though you offer to lead the combined forces that we commit, you still want payment for it. Why appeal to our natures and instinct for survival, when surely this affects your survival too? Why should you be paid by this group, when the rest of us - presumably - are not."

"Well, I am the Mercenary Lord," said James Gavain, "and you all know that military operations and their command and control is still the primary export of my nation. Yes, my nation's survival is at stake, both in the short-term in terms of finance, as well as the long-term from the Shadow Empire. But, you can all trust me, I hope, or you would not be here, and such a diverse coalition will need that trust in its leadership. Also, like some in attendance here, we are not on the pathway of invasion for the Third Imperium as they progress to Mars, but we will eventually be targeted. The Shadow Emperor wants the entire colonised galaxy in time, it is just for now his immediate objective is every system from the Frontier to Mars that stands in his way."

"Trusting you is an assertion open for debate," said the Chairman of the Calamarite Confederacy.

"But not one for this convivium," said Lord Gavain. "Allow me to outline my suggested plan in high level detail, the risks concerned and the objectives, and then we will decide if we will continue. If you agree, we will all be revealed to one another."

"This is exactly how the Revolutionary Council was formed," said First Lord Al-Zuhairi, grimly, one of the first founding members of that rebellion against the False Emperor.

"Which is why we know it can work," said Gavain, "but, we do not have much time. An hour ago, the Empire moved ahead in their invasion plans we think, beyond our projections, hitting the Benedict Democracy and the Calamarite Confederacy. For the plan to succeed, we need to decide today if we can proceed with the coalition, decide on the forces individually we can submit, and then begin committing them to the chosen theatre of operations."

"Where is the area where you want us to make our stand against the Third Empire?" asked Lady Principal Sophia.

"That will be revealed after you all commit," said Lord Gavain, "just for reasons of operational security, but it is in the Eastern Segment somewhere. It was the location, who I knew amongst your governments and houses, and the time limitations placed on us that defined who was invited to this meeting. As well as intelligence on allegiances to the Shadows."

"Which is why we could not invite some members of our Houses to this conference," said Archon Devereux.

"Yes," said Gavain, "I have told you who your traitors are, both known and suspected, what you do with the information is up to you. But allow me to explain the plan in slightly more detail first, then you can all decide what you want to do ..... But once you are committed, you are committed."

"We all understand the terms," said First Lord Al-Zuhairi, who was doubtless wondering why he was involved if the plan was to make the stand in the Eastern Segment. He was far too distant to get forces into that region of space in time. "Just precede, Gavain."

Lord Gavain sat quietly in the operations room, face impassive, not moving a muscle. Lucas De Graaf was pacing by the observation window, the blast shutters having been temporarily opened whilst they were in their long, drawn-out recess. His open anxiety was distracting. Andryukhin was sat down, evidently playing some kind of game on the datasphere from the movements of his hands, whilst Admiral Andersson sat near Gavain, equally stone-faced, an entirely different form of tension around him.

Abruptly, Andryukhin stopped playing his game and slapped his hands on the table. "Lucas!" he snapped.

"What, Rik?"

"Stop that, will you? It's fucking aggravating."

There was a long pause, and then Admiral De Graaf said with a straight face, "In that case, I'll carry on doing it."

Andersson smiled slightly, then when Andryukhin guffawed he too began to laugh. Even Gavain smiled, in itself something of a rarity nowadays.

"This waiting is torturing me," Andryukhin commented.

"Not much longer," said Andersson, checking his internal chronometer, "there's only another five minutes or so until we re-start the conference."

"Will there be anyone in it?" asked De Graaf. "How many have signalled attendance, Jamie?"

"None, apart from the Levitican Union," said Lord Gavain quietly.

"We knew they were going to," said Andryukhin, "Especially as we're about to become a part of the Union."

"The plan will only work if most of them say 'yes'," said Lord Gavain, neutrally. "We need a certain number in order to proceed, or we will be too weak against the Third Empire."

"Depending on how much military resource those that say 'yes' put in," pointed out Admiral Andersson. The other two in the room could tell from the way he spoke he still found it hard to address Jamie in private, but at least in public there was no sign of the difficulties between them. They were both too professional for that. How much Jamie knew of Harley's pain was another question, and Lucas and Ulrik were not going to ask either of them.

"Good point," said Gavain.

He was looking at the holographic display in front of him. The leaders called to the conference had been given a recess, in order to decide if they wanted to proceed. If they did not, they did not even have to signal a negative, they simply did not re-join when the hyper-pulse conference started again. Those who did want to re-join, had to signal a positive to Gavain prior to the conference commencement. On commencement of the conference, when they re-joined, the obscuring protective screens would be lifted and they would all find out who else had shared the conference with them, and who they were now allied to.

They would then receive the fuller details of the plan Gavain had outlined, with locations and positions, and would have a number of hours to submit how much military resource they could contribute, and when they would enter the staging areas Gavain was to give them.

So far, only the Levitican Union had affirmed.

What a coalition, thought Jamie Gavain, very careful to keep the thought to himself. Us and the Levitican Union, out of all of them. There was no way his plan could succeed with just their forces. In particular, he needed several nations to say 'yes' as they formed elements of the plan!

All of a sudden, the holographic display in front of him shone a different colour as one of the nations signalled they would join the coalition. It was quickly joined by another, nano-seconds later.

"Who was that?" asked De Graaf, mentally commanding the blast shutters to close as he turned away from the observation window.

Andersson, sat next to Gavain, leaned over. "The StarCom Federation, and the OutWorlds Alliance."

"They've been talking together, for them to both signal an affirmative together," said Admiral De Graaf.

"They both guessed they would both be in it," said Andryukhin, "not a hard guess, by any means."

"Without doubt," said Admiral Andersson. "It is good though. They obviously put more trust in us - and each other - than we thought. President Pereyra will commit a huge number of forces, as much as she can spare with the Suularitsaar League to defend against. Al-Zuhairi now understands why want him according to the plan outline, but must have been talking to –" Andersson broke off as another light came on the holographic panel floating in front of Lord Gavain.

"The Calamarite Confederacy," Lord Gavain said, "they are in the coalition."

"That's not a surprise," said Andryukhin, "O'Connor posted on the datasphere classified briefings, the Third Imperium is biting hard into the edge of their territory. They are taking heavy losses, already pulling back."

"We needed this conference yesterday really," said Lord Gavain, "before the Third Imperium struck the Confederacy. They could have saved themselves much of their losses today."

"The Benedict Democracy is coming off worse and we're only hours into the invasion of that part of space," snorted Andryukhin, "and Mitsubasha has declared itself part of the Third Imperium. It is proof that Mitsubasha was stoking the divisions between the two deliberately, in supplying them weaponry, vehicles, and ships. With Mitsubasha taken without a fight, the general forces of the Shadow Emperor have a heavy re-supply base in the Mid-Sectors."

There was what seemed like a long pause, and then Korhonen signalled that they would join.

"OutWorlds Alliance, and StarCom," said Andersson, "with Lucija Korhonen, they helped form the Revolutionary Council that took arms against the False Emperor."

"What about House Cervantes –" De Graaf began.

Andryukhin laughed. "They've just joined, Cervantia are in. All we need now is Hausenhof."

The next to send word that they wanted to be a part of the coalition was Amiens, and the Republic of Varrental. Even though they were antagonistic, they must have been discussing their participation with each other, guessing that they had both been invited. Gavain did not find it surprising; even after Dissolution, the politics of the real Red Imperium remained. Hausenhof signalled that they were joining slightly afterwards.

"They're all in," said Andryukhin with wonder, then laughing and slapping Gavain on the back. "You did it Jamie, they're all in."

"And it's time to reveal who we all are," said Gavain, smiling properly, even though he knew that many of them would have guessed.

"It just shows how much of a threat we all see the Third Imperium and the Shadow Emperor to be," commented Andersson, grimly.

Gavain just nodded, as the pulse-message conference began. He had his coalition, and a multi-national force had to be formed together for him to command.

Chapter XV

Commander Joanne Lancaster exhaled heavily. To risk her life and that of her crew was all part of the job, but the orders she had just reviewed in the privacy of her ready room was sheer insanity considering the powerful abilities of the Third Empire. They had come from Lord Gavain himself, with an additional note from Captain Bramhall offering her advice on how best to achieve it. She wished Captain Bramhall was here now.

She stood up, leaving her ready room and stepping onto the bridge.

<Captain on the bridge,> her second-in-command said, <You have the bridge, Commander Lancaster.>

<Thank you, command accepted,> said Commander Lancaster formally, continuing her passage across the small centre of operations and seating herself in the vacated command chair.

<All hands, this is Commander Lancaster. We have received new orders from Dark Heart. Much is happening back in the Eastern Segment in our absence, and Lord Gavain thanks us for our bravery in providing information that has been instrumental to future developments. He can say no more than that, but our contribution is more important than we can know.

<Our orders are that we are to discover the purpose, operating capabilities, and function of the Railway system. We do not know what it is, but Dark Heart thinks it may be linked to the construction we saw above Pathonis V. Our orders are simple - link up with the rest of the Vindicatus forces sent here to this section of space, and assault a system with a completed construction such as this. Our primary objective is to obtain this information. That is all, Commander Lancaster out.>

<Bloody hell,> said her second-in-command on their private channel, <Is this another suicide mission or what, Joanne?>

<We're supposed to be going home,> she said quietly through their private mental link, <Obviously not.>

<We only have corvettes and a number of frigates out here,> said her second-in-command, <that's not enough to assault a system with one of these strange constructed facilities within it. Especially now that they're all going to be on alert for us after completing the first ever successful mission against them.>

<Captain Bramhall says a sneak attack with a quick, well-aimed strike on a command centre,> said Lancaster, <with plenty of searching beforehand for a lightly defended system, and corvettes running silent to get close with the frigates for covering fire. I can't disagree, it's the only

way.> She shook her head, and then used the open channel, <Helm, navigations, set course for these rendezvous co-ordinates.>

<Aye, sir,> came the simultaneous response.

Let's go and get killed, thought Commander Lancaster.

*

Gavain stood in one of the towers of the Heart Palace, looking out at the simulated night-time of the planet Dark Heart. Without a real sun to warm or illuminate the planet, it was all achieved through powerful mechanics, science and technology that a primitive alien life form would have assumed to be the work of a god.

There was a harsh wind tonight, the carefully controlled climate centres having to allow it to preserve the eco-system and the dynamics of the rogue planet. In the distance, Gavain could see the well-lit tubes of the space-lift system, heading up in great columns like that god's fingers towards platforms connected to corridors, which crossed space to the other four planets in the Artificial System and linked all three rogue planets and two artificial planets together. Looking up into the night sky, you could see Dark Heart Beta and Dark Heart Delta, Gamma and Epsilon hidden from view by the visible planetary bulks and the dark, overcast clouds.

The city was lit and functioning, busy even now. Just looking at the cityscape of the megapolis made Gavain realise how much his nation had changed in such a short period of time. He was the Lord of billions of people now, primarily refugees from the wars afflicting most of the galaxy.

He was about to go to war once again to protect them all.

Leading the war of resistance would also allow him to earn enough money to keep them all safely in the black for a long period of time, especially with the amounts that he was charging the various members of the coalition. They resisted it in many instances, but he was seen as the best and most neutral person to do it. He was also just about the only leader getting the intelligence they needed which had made this resistance possible. That was a strong bargaining position indeed; he truly was the Mercenary Lord.

Juan Ramirez came up behind him. "The military and the government are assembled in the Cabinet Office and ready, Jamie."

"I'm coming, then," said James Gavain, nodding to show he had heard. "Give me a moment longer, please, Juan."

"Yeah, sure, Jamie," said Juan. There was a long pause, and then he said, "this is a great thing you're doing."

"It's just as risky as the rebellion against the False Emperor, if not more so," said Gavain. "At least then, we thought the False Emperor was just mad. In this case, we know the Shadow Emperor is, but we also know he is the genetic clone of the True Emperor. If I release that information, as many will see that as vindication that he is the rightful ruler as those that see it as making him a false copy. Now that information is out of my control, the other nations in the coalition have it."

"Then it is out of your control," said Juan simply. "I was vatborn, but my birth-house matron always said 'accept the things you cannot change, and change the things you can't accept'. We can't accept the Shadow Emperor, we can't accept who or what he is, so let's go and change it - because we can. Victory is possible, despite the odds. You can do this, Jamie, this part of the galaxy is with you."

Lord Gavain looked down, and then turned round. "Thank you, Juan. Walk with me to the Cabinet Office, it's time to go."

Lord Gavain stood on the podium, which had been rotated around so he faced the full semi-circular table of his government ministers, senior administrators, and his military officers, and had his back to the empty auditorium. The more junior administrators and military officers would be cascaded the briefing from these senior staffers, with some of the more sensitive elements removed.

He looked at his senior government officials, many of whom also held military ranks either in the Praetorian or House Guard elements of his armed forces. He had a new Ambassadorial Service Administrator, and the new Solar Administration Chancellors for the two newly colonised systems, those of the Praetor System and the Bright Hope System. His military had grown even more with the influx of House Guard starships, two entirely new fleets having been formed, and some of his support fleets swelling. His House Army was looking incredibly strong.

"Ladies, Gentlemen, and Androgynous," he said formally, "the Coalition of the Resistance has been formed."

Applause and cheering broke out amongst the assembled people, and looking at them as he waited for it to calm down, Lord Gavain himself felt a moment of reality strike him again. He had come so far, and had so much responsibility.

"I will speak of the Coalition in a moment, but first I want to look at what we in Vindicatus have achieved. We come from separate and disparate backgrounds - some of us are Praetorian Guard of both True and False Emperor allegiance; some of us are Erdogan, Aalborg Alliance, Van Der Meer and more from all over the Eastern Segment and even beyond. We are a free-thinking nation, with borg and human living in harmony. We have built a nation from under a million people, rising to nearly three billion in little more than a year. Projections are that we will hit ten billion by the end of this Imperial Standard year. We will hit fifty billion the year after, and two hundred and twenty billion if projections are correct for the year after that; a considerable future to fight for. We have built an infrastructure, we have colonised two more Systems and expanded. We have achieved logistically something very real and very amazing, and it is tough for some of us, and there will be mistakes we make. We must all be very proud of what we have achieved, and what we can achieve.

"But with all that comes responsibility. We must protect what we have built, we must protect the billions of people we now serve, and I lead as Lord. That is part of the reason Vindicatus has joined the Levitican Union. We are close to the Union, both in terms of our own history working together since the fall and Dissolution of the Red Imperium of Mars, but also personally with some of the Union's Lords and Ladies.

"That is also the reason the Coalition of the Resistance has been formed. Across the galaxy, trillions if not quadrillions of each of the Coalitions members face indoctrination into the Shadow consciousness. We face an unimaginable threat in the form of the Shadow Emperor and his Third Empire, and his desire to create a new Red Imperium. Already, they are approaching the Eastern Segment, and when they do, they are more than half-way to Mars. We will stop them, people, we will stop them.

"Besides us, the Coalition consists of the OutWorlds Alliance, the Calamarite Confederacy, the StarCom Federation, the Levitican Union, Amiens, the Republic of Varrental, Korhonen, Hausenhof, and Cervantia. We will make our stand at a place I will reveal shortly, but remember, this is a fantastic alliance of diverse nations and people, not seen since the Revolutionary Council. I will have operational command of the forces that each of these nations commits to the resistance, those forces that they have chosen to commit - and believe me, some are committing more than others. But I have not forgotten the need to protect my own people, and my own systems.

"In terms of numbers, we have eight fleets, of mixed Praetorian, House Human, House Borg, and Droid naval, marine and army personnel. That translates into sixty-six Praetorian Guard ships-of-the-line and warships, sixty-one support craft of Praetorian design, one hundred and thirty-four House ships-of-the-line and warships, and forty House support craft. A considerable navy and army, people, but it is now my responsibility after discussion with various advisors as to how to divide it to both protect our systems and commit enough to the Coalition of Resistance to allow this to be a success. I ask you all to remember that if the Coalition is not successful, the Third Empire will become so strong that eventually we will lose our nation to them, when they invade Dark Heart as part of their quest to conquer the galaxy.

"So; to the resistance effort I am committing all of the First Fleet and Second Fleet, all of our Praetorian Ships, and the Third Support Fleet. The Fourth Support Fleet is on extended operations against the Shadow

Empire, or will remain at home. The Fifth Fleet will be split, with the elements committed to the Coalition consisting of our Praetorian Marines, the droids and House elements remaining to protect our home systems. Sixth Home Fleet, Seventh House Fleet and Eighth House Fleet will also remain to protect our systems.

"In short, I am committing primarily only Praetorians to the Coalition. Please do not take this as an insult, or a sign of any preference. It is purely that the Praetorians stand the most chance against the enemy, and the greatest threat to the home systems whilst those Praetorians are gone is from the Zhou-Zheng Compact - the ships I am leaving here in Vindicatus are more than enough to face down the Compact and surprise them. I am protecting our people the best way I can, whilst ensuring our obligations to the Coalition are fulfilled.

"When it comes to the Coalition, we are being paid handsomely for my leadership of the Coalition. It appears I am the only person all of them trust, despite the propaganda issued by the Shadow Emperor. He has failed in that regard. I have not just paid attention to the war effort against the Shadows, but I have also thought of what to do if we win. The territory the Coalition takes will become an issue, and unlike many leaders in the past, I have thought about what we will do if we win. How we will rebuild the area - because believe me, the war we are about to wage will devastate system after system after system in a very wide region. I believe deaths amongst the civilians converted to the Shadow Empires collective consciousness, will be very high, and we have a duty to try and release them from this indoctrination, where we can. I suspect it will be impossible - it is the nature of what we are doing that we have to face the fact we will as a Coalition potentially be operating to levels of genocidal war in some ways of looking at it. Civilian deaths on the scale we are contemplating is a horrible consideration, and something which makes me lose sleep at night, but we are all agreed. The Shadow Emperor has corrupted these people, and whilst we will try to save them, we cannot guarantee that his brainwashing can be undone. I only hope history judges the Coalition, and me, kindly should we win - or lose."

Gavain stopped, taking a sip of the water in front of him to refresh his mouth. He felt what he was saying, and he could see the people before him were hanging on his every word. "That part of the speech will be broadcast to the nation," he said quietly, "after we have begun our war effort and the enemy know we have stood against them. This next part will not. Observe the plan."

A holographic map of the galaxy sprung into being behind him.

"The Calamarite Confederacy is putting up a resistance to the Shadow Emperor's invasion, but they will preserve as much of their forces as they can. The OutWorlds Alliance is frantically rebuilding from their losses, using their military manufacturing power-base. It is a fact that the Shadow Emperor's forces are becoming more and more stretched, although we have only estimates of numbers, and we do not know what his reserves are. As we make our stand in the Eastern Segment, once the Shadow Emperor's forces are committed, we shall choke his supply lines in two places, out on the Frontier by the OutWorlds Alliance, and in the middle regions where the Confederacy is best-placed to counter-invade. We think he has reserve forces out beyond the Frontier, and the Railway will somehow deliver them quickly across the stars to Mars, but once we make our stand those reserve forces may be used against us. We do not know, it is conjecture, although we are trying to find out. We will also attempt to locate the Shadow Emperor's homeland out beyond colonised space, and strike there, to smash his own manufacturing and replenishment support.

"That is the role of the OutWorlds Alliance and the Calamarite Confederacy, not the rest of us in the Coalition. We will be making our stand here."

The map refocused, zooming in on a particular part of the Eastern Segment. The assembled crowd began to speak and mutter as they saw the region of space Gavain had selected and obtained agreement from the other nations for, with graphics depicting staging areas for the forces and their targets.

"As you can see, we are drawing a line within Third Empire territory, and striking there. Logistically, all the members of the coalition can be assembled at the staging areas within three to four weeks, using stargates and in some cases our Web of Deepspace Stations. We want to strike at Third Empire territory to make a point - one, to send the message that the Third Empire can be stopped to the rest of the colonised galaxy, and two, to draw them in and make the Emperor commit his reserve forces earlier than he planned.

"The StarCom Federation is committing more than I hoped for, four full fleets of Praetorian-grade warships, and two fleets of House, not forgetting the support fleet elements. Cervantia, Hausenhof, Korhonen are submitting much smaller forces, but the Levitican Union is committing a vast number of their military. They are in the immediate firing line, so better for them to fight in enemy territory than at home. The Republic of Varrental and Amiens are submitting sizeable fleets.

"Operation Assemble is therefore completed with all of us in our staging areas. Note that I am not mixing forces; we all operate out of nation-specific staging areas, and enter nation-specific theatres of war. It would be too risky to mix military forces. Elements of StarCom Federation and our own Second Fleet will remain in the reserve staging areas back here in the Levitican Union and at two of our Deepspace Stations for Operation Jacknife, where we all jump into the enemy territory. Levitican

Union forces will not strike at all, even as reserve, although if things go seriously wrong we can commit them if necessary – but if that happens, I do not hold much hope for us winning long-term. We hammer the Shadow Empire, take their territory, and hold it. Then I taunt the Shadow Emperor."

There was laughter at this point.

"Once we hold the territory assuming we are victorious, we begin dealing with the planets within that territory under Operation Freedom. We invade on a surface level, and try to secure them – but it is doubtful how well we will be able to reverse the indoctrination that the Shadows have placed upon the civilians. We cannot afford to have our backs unguarded, so we will eliminate all populations if necessary."

He paused, waiting to see how they responded. There were some grim looks, particularly from the Erdogans. He wondered if this decision would cost him politically at home, but he knew there was realistically no other choice.

"Support forces will scout beyond the systems to provide us with detailed intelligence on enemy forces, to a level we will not have before we launch. I am not risking early scouting giving away the targets of Operation Jacknife. When the enemy arrive to strike back against us, I want Operation Freedom completed. We use that time to build up a wall of defences, strengthening every system we have taken in the Jacknife Defence Line. Yes, we are ruining an area of space on a level that is reminiscent of the Gulf of Medusa and the Droid Wars. There is no other alternative however. War is destructive, never constructive, whatever politicians may have said in the past.

"Then we wait for the Shadow Empire. Operation Diamondcut begins with their proper counter-strike to ours, with our Second Fleet, StarCom reserves, and the Levitican Union forces now able to be committed fully. Operation Diamondcut also involves the Confederacy and the Alliance striking at their support lines in the form of this Railway - and their home bases, should we be able to find them in time.

"The risks are considerable. We know their land armies are formidable, these hybrids being an unknown quantity. We can use our interdiction fields to disrupt the special shielding that makes them immaterial and prevents our weapons from hitting, something they will not be expecting at all, and we are working on special viruses to attack them with thanks to the capture of the juggernaut and battlecruiser. We don't know what the Railway is, and we don't know their true strength, although we have projections. We don't know what technology they have in reserve to use against us.

"You've seen the plan now. Success is not guaranteed, but it is our best hope to secure our future. Questions, please."

Lord Gavan inhaled deeply, and took another sip of water as they began to comment and ask questions.

*

Star Marshal Ngu of the Zhou-Zheng Compact still limped. The humanist Compact nation was extremely anti-borg, not allowing even mechanical repairs to body damage. His punishment for failing to resist the Vindicatus Mercenary Corporation's counter-strike during their invasion and eventual subjugation of the now defunct Erdogan nation had not cost him his head as he had supposed, particularly as he had proposed using the mercenaries in the first place, but his punishment had been a flogging so severe he had been hospitalised for several months.

He had had a replacement skin graft, but he was sure that Chancellor Zhou Mao had paid for it to be done improperly. He was in pain every day of his life now as a result of the punishment the Primarch and Primarchess had inflicted upon him, and the graft had caused more problems than it should have done. His right leg had to be regrown, and that did not seem to connect to his brain the way it should.

He limped into the Solar Throne-Room, the large audience chamber where the Primarch and Primarchess of the Zhou-Zheng Compact resided when they were on the home planet of Qiangdongnantus, in the Yunnani System, capital of the combined Zhou-Zheng Compact. The Grand Hall was typically the favoured celebratory audience chamber where the Primarch and Primarchess held various events and had their primary thrones, but the Solar Throne-Room had historical uses dating back centuries and even to a different House, now long-extinct.

It was large, with ranked and tiered seats all along its length for what they called the Compact Senate, where the System Senators sat, but in truth they had little power to influence the national politics of the Compact. Primarch Zhou and Primarchess Zheng ruled jointly with iron fists, and only the deceptive and manipulative Chancellor Mao Zhou perhaps had anything approaching influence upon them thanks to his position. Once, Star Marshal Ngu had that influence, but he was drastically out-of-favour.

He limped as quickly as he could down the long and wide aisle of the Solar Throne-Room, finally coming to the dais where the two thrones were kept. Chancellor Mao Zhou was present, as were the Primarch and Primarchess. The Senate had been in consultation, and had finished just minutes ago. The Throne-Room was eerie with such quiet and calm within it, the Senate meetings usually loud and unproductive. The decisions were made by the Primarch and the Primarchess.

A herald shouted, "All kneel for the Primarch and the Primarchess!"

All the guards, Star Marshal Ngu, and even the Chancellor went down to one knee and bent their heads. After a long, drawn-out moment the herald gave permission to rise, presumably at a nod from one or both of the leaders of the Compact.

Star Marshal Ngu stood, looking at his hated enemy the Chancellor Zhou Mao as he did so. The man had resumed his usual posture, hands folded and concealed inside the long-sleeved robes he customarily wore. He then quickly averted his gaze to the Primarch Zhou and the Primarchess Zheng, lest he be viewed as disrespectful to them.

The Primarch Zhou was old, and it showed on his face, whereas the Primarchess Zheng was young, beautiful and radiant. It was known that when Primarch Zhou Ze died, Primarchess Zheng Il-Sou would inherit sole leadership of the Compact, but there were already strong stirrings and rumours suggesting that Chancellor Mao Zhou should represent the House of Zhou and marry the young Primarchess. Ngu had already resolved that should that happen, despite his loyalty to both houses, he would take his own life. Chancellor Mao Zhou would otherwise do it for him.

"Star Marshal Ngu Soo Su, you have been summoned here for good reason," said Primarch Zhou slowly, his voice cracking. The man was not well. "Chancellor Mao Zhou has come into some interesting information."

"Chancellor Mao Zhou, explain to the Star Marshal," the beautiful and graceful Primarchess Zheng commanded.

"Getting spies into the Vindicatus territory is difficult," said the Chancellor, "but we have been building them up slowly. Earlier today the intelligence community of the Compact received word that there has been significant movement of Vindicatus Praetorian and House forces."

A holoprojector activated, showing figures and graphics, with cut-away visuals also displayed, showing numerous starships jumping out of a solar system, and a graphical display with numbers of suspected fleet assets.

"The House ships of Lord Gavain, many of which are ex-Erdogan, have been disappearing over a period of time out of the Dark Heart System. We do not know where, although there is a possibility they have been going to systems Gavain has colonised - but this is just hearsay and rumour, unsubstantiated as we have never received confirmation of these supposed colonies. Suddenly, yesterday, there was a vast movement, as numerous House ships disappeared, leaving only their Home Fleet. Additionally, all their Praetorian Guard ships jumped using the Dark Heart Stargate.

"We believe they are in the process of assaulting a major target; we know that Gavain has been speaking to numerous nations, and although no contracts have been posted on the Interstellar Merchant Guilds Mercenary Bonding Office, we suspect that he is engaged against the Third Empire in some way. Previously when his Praetorian fleets have disappeared in this way, we have learnt subsequently they have been engaged in some form of large action.

"We now therefore have an opportunity. We can take their Deepspace Stations, following the element of the Web that leads back to Dark Heart, and assault this system. We must strike back at the mercenaries for their betrayal of us, and their continuing support of the Erdogan terrorists. Star Marshal Ngu, what do you say?"

Star Marshal Ngu thought quickly, knowing his life could depend on the answer. Did he think such an assault wise? He thought definitely not, especially as they were about to engage in another House War. Could it succeed? He doubted Gavain was stupid enough to leave his system so wide open to attack as it appeared to be. Ngu was careful how he phrased his answer.

"Primarch Zhou and Primarchess Zheng, I will as always do as you command. If you want me to invade the Dark Heart Artificial System, then I will do so to the best of my ability. I counsel against it, however. Such an assault will be very costly and affect our upcoming House War without doubt, and I still advise that we should prepare to resist the Third Empire. We will not face them for many months, even a year, but eventually they will try to conquer the galaxy and we will become a target. Invading Dark Heart is not advisable at this time, no matter how wide it appears to be. Chancellor Zhou Mao, what do you favour?"

Chancellor Zhou Mao looked unhappy at being asked such a precise question for just a flash of a moment, but then his racial inscrutability returned. He looked at the Primarch and Primarchess. Star Marshal Ngu was betting that he had already discussed this with the leaders, and determined their thinking beforehand.

"I believe this is our opportunity, and we should strike, as soon as possible," he said.

"Then, it will be on your head should it fail," said Star Marshal Ngu quickly, "as I advise against it."

The Primarch and Primarchess actually exchanged a glance, which in itself was highly unusual. "Star Marshal Ngu, I am perturbed at your reluctance," said Primarchess Zheng, "we would have thought you saw the opportunity here."

"I see the opportunity," said Ngu, "But I also see how it could go wrong. The system is well-defended, and we do not have the information on those defences. It may be more lightly defended, but it will take at least two or maybe three full fleets for us to attack, and assuming heavy damage, the House War will not be feasible. With the greatest of respect, it is the House War, or this invasion of Dark Heart I fear."

Primarch Zhou wasted no time. "We want vengeance," he said. "Star Marshal Ngu, we hear your words against. As the leader of our army and navy, we have no doubt you will make your best attempt. But should you fail -" and here Chancellor Zhou Mao had his second drop of the mask, "- then we recognise it is not your fault as you counselled against it. Chancellor Mao Zhou is pushing for this, so he will bear the responsibility."

Star Marshal Ngu bowed. "I will do my best, Primarch and Primarchess."

"We know you will," said the Primarchess Zheng. "Handle the strategy with Chancellor Mao's supervision. If this fails, Chancellor Mao, on your head be it."

*

The Shadow Emperor was in a furious mood. None of his advisors had dared to come near him, and had run from his temper.

His noble barge had moved into the Benedict Democracy. Both the Democracy and the Confederacy were extremely heavily armed, thanks to their ongoing war promoted and supplied by the Mitsubasha nation, which had declared for him and become the Mitsubasha Province. The Democracy was taking the brunt of this phase of the invasion, and all was going to plan. The Confederacy, after initially resisting heavily, had been committing less of their forces, presumably after realising they were not in the main pathway of the invasion. They were still losing territory, but were ceding it. The Shadow Emperor's advisors thought that they were cutting their losses as best they could.

That was about the only good news he had. The spy network they had throughout the Eastern Segment was collapsing, as the various Houses and nations targeted the people his Legates of the Sixth and Fourth Circle had in place. He knew who to blame for that, there could only be one culprit, one person who had either obtained the information or penetrated his network enough to steal it. That was Lord Gavain.

He was going blind all across the Eastern Segment, the Inner Core Segment, the March of Hope and even more regions of space. Without the information on the enemy movements, the latter stages of the plan to re-take Mars could be endangered.

Further, the League of Suularitsaar was prevaricating. He had demanded that they launch a full-scale invasion on the Federation, ahead of schedule. They were seemingly reluctant to do so, and Jared Towers of the Third Circle advised that he thought their support there was beginning to loosen.

Much of the Shadow Emperor's support was dwindling. The indoctrination and subjugation of the conquered populaces recorded by Gavain had been released to media sources all over the colonised galaxy, and it was turning his support away in droves. Mitsubasha Province was resisting heavily, with unexpected rioting breaking out in what was supposed to be a safe area, drawing more of his troops away from the spearhead of the advancing front line. Further afield throughout the colonised galaxy, he was losing support in much the same fashion.

Even worse, Gavain had released the fact that the Shadow Emperor was a clone of the True Emperor, and not the grandson. At first, the Shadow Emperor had been apoplectic at what he saw as an outrageous lie. A few Houses actually swung in his favour, those predominantly True Emperor aligned historically and heavily clone-based, but they were few in comparison to those who reacted extremely badly to the lies.

Then he had questioned his own Shadow Council on the lie, and it was then that he had found out it was not a lie.

All his life, ever since being a child, he had been brought up to think he was the son of the False Emperor, removed from the Imperial establishment for his own safety and in case the False Emperor ever fell. It transpired that the Shadow Council he counted as his advisors were actually aware of the truth, that he was not the son of the False Emperor and was instead a clone of the True Emperor, and they had kept that truth from him.

The Shadow Emperor's identity was in tatters, his own impression of who he was and what he was doing rocked to the core.

He felt betrayed by his own Shadow Council. They had told him falteringly, with nervousness, reluctantly, but they could not deny it. He had demanded to be told the truth, and so it was revealed to him. The Mercenary Lord was not lying after all.

The Shadow Emperor had dismissed the Shadow Council, telling them all he would consider their fate. He had a sneaking suspicion that he was not the leader he thought he was, that in fact he was little more than a figurehead, and the Shadow Council was in true control of the Third Empire. They did what he said, but only because they needed him to unite the galaxy. Once he had formed the Third Imperium of Mars, how long would it be until they quietly disposed of him?

His paranoia had gone supernova, matching his anger. He did not trust his own Shadow Council. He was not who he thought he was, they had lied to him.

As his anger developed and he descended deeper and deeper into raw insanity, he resolved that he would not let them take his Empire from him. He would take the colonised galaxy, and slowly remove the Shadow Council one by one.

First Mars, and then them, he decided.

*

Da Wei Sao So Ani was third-in-command of the Zhou-Zheng battlecruiser *ZZCS Fucanglong,* reporting into the Shao Xiao, who in turn reported into the Captain of the warship, the Zhong Xiao. Since the conquering of the Erdogan nation, she had be re-assigned to this ship, in partial disgrace as she had once been liaison to the Vindicator Mercenary Corporation when they had been under contract to the Compact before turning traitor. Sao So Ani was much more than just the third-in-command though.

She was also a traitor, an Erdoganite sympathiser.

The ultra-humanist nation of the Zhou-Zheng Compact abhorred all types of cyborgs, and she was a cyborg. She feared for her life almost every day, worrying about discovery, but when the Compact had been formed and the pogroms against borgs began, she was protected only by her home district's lack of sufficient record keeping. She had turned traitor, seeing other Compact borgs like her being rounded up into the deathcamps, and she had begun to feed information to the Erdogan nation. The Erdogan nation existed no more, but they continued to resist in a fierce rebellion that the Zhou-Zheng Compact labelled terrorism. She did her utmost to help it succeed.

As the briefing by Zhong Xiao Chien finished, she realised she had just been given a tremendous opportunity to seriously hurt the Zhou-Zheng Compact.

"You may speak freely," said Zhong Xiao Chien.

There was a pause, and then the Shao Xiao said, "Are we really strong enough to invade Dark Heart, in your opinion, sir?"

"Yes," said Chien, "if the intelligence is correct. We may not have another opportunity to do so."

"When do we have to jump to the staging area?" asked Da Wei Sao.

"Immediately," said Chien, "we will recall all the crew on shore-leave, and jump as soon as they are aboard. We must obtain our position as soon as possible. We invade through the Web of Deepspace Stations as soon as there is confirmation that the Vindicatus forces are committed elsewhere."

The discussion continued for a while, before the Zhong Xiao dismissed them. The Shao Xiao returned directly to the bridge as he was on watch, and the Da Wei carefully and with practiced ease casually returned to her own quarters.

As she entered her quarters, she went to a holo-lith that was displaying a picture of her supposed family. Her cover story was that she was a human, conceived in a vat and brought up in a vat-house to unknown donors. The 'family' consisted of her nineteen other vat-siblings.

She waved her hand through the holo-lith, her fingers playing an imaginary tune as she did so. It triggered the secret access code, and the picture disappeared. It was replaced with a blank recording screen, which she sat in front of.

"Begin," she commanded, and the base of the holographic projector turned red to show it was recording her message.

"For the attention of Hornet," she said, using the codename of Feldmarshall Horatio Grant, currently under the protection of and serving the Vindicatus nation. "This is Little Snake. The following is confirmed, primary source information, direct from orders given by Star Marshal Ngu. It has been briefed by my superior officers, and military build-up is commencing. The target is the Dark Heart System of the Vindicatus nation."

Da Wei Sao outlined as much as she could, and then also downloaded a datastream from her own secret recording implants for background evidence and information. She was providing staging areas and rendezvous points.

"Little Snake, out," she said, ending the recording. She then manipulated the holoprojector to condense the message, and used her private quarters proper Compact-issued communications equipment to record a message replying to an 'old friend' she regularly communicated with. Often their messages were innocent, but sometimes they had just a little bit of extra condensed information in the header buffer, which was her passing on her intelligence to her Erdogan resistance handler.

This would be her only opportunity, as once they were in the staging area they would not be allowed to communicate for obvious reasons. At least she could warn the Vindicatus nation and her Erdogan masters what was about to happen.

Chapter XVI

<Lord Gavain, we have an incoming jump signature.>

<Amber alert, Captain Georgia.>

<Aye, sir.>

Lord Gavain stood, leaving the ready room and his desk to head onto the bridge, the doors cycling open and shut before and behind him rapidly.

<Commander-In-Chief on the bridge,> said Captain Georgia.

<You have the bridge, Captain,> replied Gavain, striding across the *Vindicator*'s bridge to the flag chair, seating himself comfortably in the repulsor-seat. <Report.>

<Incoming jump signature detected, a small squadron, six to eight ships. Translation time will be thirty-seven seconds and counting.>

<Admiral De Graaf is signalling First Fleet to amber alert,> said the communications officer.

<All hands, stand ready,> Captain Georgia ordered.

Lord Gavain pulled up a scanner sweep of the surrounding area. They were in an uninhabited system, out in a region of space which belonged to a very minor and small noble House. All of First Fleet was here in secret; it had been decided that none of the Houses where the staging areas were located would be informed of the massive fleets assembling in their uncolonised territory. All the staging areas were away from major trade routes, and so apart from the odd travelling ship, should be free from detection.

It was the only way to assure their mission was kept top-secret. Not enough information was held about some of these minor Houses to know whether they were allied with the Third Empire or not, and Gavain did not want the Coalition's build-up to leak. They were going to use aggressive force if they had to maintain that secrecy, he had written it into the rules of engagement for Operation Assemble so all the fleets would be working within the same operational parameters.

<We were expecting the Federation ships eight hours ago,> said Captain Georgia, <there seems to be too many for this to be a civilian enterprise, unless it's a convoy we're not aware of.>

<I hope it is the Federation, and not a local House military exercise,> said Gavain.

The seconds counted down. Lord Gavain watched the scanners display calmly. The system was virtually dead, the star so weak that inhabitation was virtually impossible. The planetary bodies did not assist possible colonisation. Mankind had colonised starker systems, but for whatever reason this one had never been deemed worthy. XW-1010, nominally a part of the small and insignificant House Narrough, had only gained significance because it was a perfect staging area for the Coalition of Resistance.

<Ships translating .... translation achieved,> said the scanners officer, Lieutenant Agrawal. <Ident pending.>

<A few seconds for the IFF signatures to kick in if they are friendly,> said Lord Gavain to Captain Georgia, needlessly. She was as aware as he was, and he realised that he was perhaps more tense than normal. This was the biggest undertaking he had ever conceived and led.

<Praetorian Guard ships, StarCom Federation markings,> said Lieutenant Agrawal. <Identity Friend or Foe broadcasts starting ..... they are the ships we were expecting, positive contact.>

<Incoming communications hail,> said Lieutenant Forrest. <Admiral Heinrich Haas, of the *SFSS Tartarus* hailing .... and Admiral Tomas Scanlon, of the *SFSS Tides of War*.>

<Accept the hail,> commanded Lord Gavain. The thought flashed through his mind that the last time he had met these names, it had been within the Levitican Union during the Levitican War against the StarCom Federation.

This was not a standard squadron; the two T-Class dreadnoughts according to the intelligence files belong to the 3rd Fleet and the 12th Fleet of the StarCom Federation. Admiral Haas had taken command of the 12th Fleet, formed after the StarCom Federation invasions of the Core and Mid-Sectors, and Scanlon had become an Admiral taking his former command of the 3rd Fleet after Gavain had destroyed or captured much of one of their squadrons.

The other ships consisted of a ferry-ship, which even now was beginning to deploy its cargo of intrastellar craft – there were several large constructoships moving out of its belly and hull bays. The remaining ships were battlecruisers and a star-carrier, from the two fleets of each of the Admirals if O'Connor's intelligence was accurate.

Two holographic images appeared before Gavain, one of the infamous Heinrich Haas, and another of Tomas Scanlon. Haas was a well-respected name since before the Dissolution and in the times of the Red Imperium, Scanlon another that was recognised and feared. They were amongst the best.

<Lord Gavain,> said Admiral Haas, <Well met.>

<Hail in the name of the True Emperor,> said Lord Gavain by way of reply. <I was not expecting both of you.>

Haas did not react. <We both wanted to be present to tell you that our forward elements are moving into the staging areas now,> said Haas, <although admittedly with different hours of delay. There is a data download informing you of the StarCom known positions and status.>

Lord Gavain read the data as it downloaded, being cleansed and scrubbed by the virus checkers before even being allowed into the quarantine zone of the mainframe. <Slightly behind schedule,> he said, <but not by much. I expect such logistical problems.>

<It happens,> said Admiral Scanlon.

<Has StarCom decided on the overall leader for your considerable contribution to the Coalition?> asked Gavain.

<I am the commander of the StarCom contingent, as you put it,> said Admiral Haas, <The chain of command will be from the StarCom Fleets to myself, and then me to you.>

<Acceptable,> said Lord Gavain. <Admiral Haas .... it is an honour, despite the different sides we have found ourselves on in the past.>

Haas merely raised an eyebrow. <Indeed, Lord Gavain. You have a fantastic reputation. Let's hope you live up to it.>

Admiral Scanlon interrupted, obviously tiring of the adversarial nature of his commanding officer. <Lord Gavain, StarCom has committed nine fleets of ships-of-the-line, six of which are Praetorian Guard, three are House-design, and there are no less than four additional support fleets. Our fleet-sizes are considerably bigger than most, with the possible exception of Amiens, as you can see from our Tables of Organisation.>

<It is a fantastic contribution, I have already sent my thanks to President Pereyra and Commander-In-Chief Ryan,> said Lord Gavain. He had been surprised at the strength of StarCom's commitment, and it had caused some heavy debate in the Levitican Union, at having such a heavy StarCom presence in the Eastern Segment. How they had reconciled this contribution with the need to defend against the League of Suularitsaar Gavain did not know, it was weakening their home military forces considerably.

He had also noted in the Tables of Organisation that two of the fleets had designations that O'Connor had not discovered previously; it appeared that StarCom's rebuilding of its navy and fleet was far in advance of what the rest of the galaxy suspected.

<Elements of our support fleets are moving into all the staging areas, with armed escorts,> said Admiral Haas. <It will take three to four days from arrival to construct the Stargates and space-based HPCG stations that you want in each.>

<It is vital,> said Gavain, <With the stargates we launch into our initial theatres for Operation Jacknife, and the HPCG stations allow us to maintain communications in the run-up to launch.> The stargates would link to the Web of Deepspace Stations he had around the Gulf of Medusa, allowing the transfer of starships even faster than would normally be possible. Stargates threw their starships further than ship jump capacitors could manage. The enemy would be totally surprised, if all went to plan.

Even more importantly, if they succeeded in the invasion, and held the territory they took against Empire reprisals, Gavain intended to create the Jacknife Defence Line, which would always be manned and beyond which the Third Empire would not be allowed to advance. Every nation would continue to have a part in the holding of the Defence Line, but that was far in the future, and there was a war to win first.

<We understand,> said Admiral Scanlon softly.

<Are your own forces in position, Lord Gavain?> asked Admiral Haas. <Here, and at your Deepspace Station?>

<Yes,> said Lord Gavain. <The Levitican Union forces are assembling in House Zupanic and House Marchenko territory at the stargates there, and once we stage out under Operation Jacknife they will be ready to jump into the staging areas if required.>

<It is genius, Lord Gavain,> said Scanlon.

<The Federation did much the same during the Expansion Wars,> said Admiral Haas. Then he relented somewhat. <Although admittedly we did not do it well, and Lord Gavain cut our stargate routes. I note your plan allows for the Levitican Union forces to protect the supply lines if needed. You have paid attention to every little detail of this. Well done, Gavain.>

<Thank you, Admiral Haas.>

<We'll jump out, and leave the ferry-ship and the constructoships under your protection,> said Haas. <The remaining HPCG stations and stargates will be built in the line of the staging areas, all nine of them.>

<Thank you,> Lord Gavain said again, <Operation Jacknife relies on surprise, heavy concentrations of force, and timing. We could not be doing this without StarCom's help, not just in your forces but in your expertise. Gavain out.>

Captain Georgia, who had been listening, said on their private channel, <That wasn't strictly true Jamie. We could have built the space assets with enough time, we have their technology.>

<But they don't know that,> said Gavain, standing and heading back to the ready room he had taken over, <I'm not sharing everything with our allies in the Coalition, as doubtless they are not with us.>

Gavain stood in one of the operations rooms, which had been converted to operate as the central war-room for him to command the vast armies and navies assembling under his command.

The holo-map before him had up-to-date information. Since the HPCG space station and stargate had been built in XW-1010, construction finishing yesterday, the staging areas were slowly linking up.

The Levitican Union and the Web were acting as a conduit for the more distant fleets to arrive in their staging areas, and so far secrecy had been maintained. There were only two reported instances where their build-up had been detected, in both cases lone civilian ships, and both had been detained.

The holo-map showed him the locations of the staging areas, with graphical flags to show where his Coalition forces were in terms of build-up. Deepspace Fourteen was the location for his own Second Fleet, and the military cargo-freighters of Third Support Fleet. XW-1010 was relatively close in astronomical terms to Deepspace Fourteen, and the newly-built stargate in XW-1010 now created a link to the Deepspace Station. XW-110 held First Fleet, and the armies of the rest of Third Support Fleet and the vast forces of Fifth Fleet.

XW-1010's stargate could also be reached by the stargate in Zupanic territory, where three fleets of mixed House and some Praetorian ships belonging to the Levitican Union were assembling. Another five fleets were assembling in House Marchenko territory at two different stargates, ready to link into other staging areas where the stargates were still being built. These were the second-stage reserves, and Gavain wanted to keep them in place and out of Operation Jacknife if he could manage it.

So, following them in a line from the Gulf of Medusa out parallel to Levitican Union territory was one staging area for Vindicatus nation forces. Above and below and further to the galactic east-east-north were two more staging areas for StarCom Federation Armed Forces. Then came a third and fourth staging area in zigzagging lines, for the remaining StarCom Federation forces, going from uninhabited systems. One fleet of StarCom ships was also being kept in reserve at a Marchenkan stargate.

Roughly from there the staging areas extended out, in a two dimensional line stretching in the order of Cervantia, Amiens, Korhonen, Republic of Varrental, and then Hausenhof. The division was not accidental, he did not want possibly antagonistic forces jumping even remotely into adjacent systems where old rivalries and recent bitterness could cause problems. The forces were still assembling, but he had a vast array of warship fleets and army units under his command.

In an entirely different region of space, Calamarite Confederacy and again in another the OutWorlds Alliance were building their forces for the strike after Operation Jacknife, building much more slowly to be ready for Gavain's word to launch.

He still felt some of the anxiety, but the plan he had imagined was beginning to happen in reality. Everyone was keeping their word so far. He was prepared for the unexpected, plans of battle and war never went as expected, but it was beginning to happen.

Their target systems were already highlighted on the map. They would cut into a significant portion of enemy territory, actually jumping beyond the edge to a quarter of the way in. Then they would move backwards, clearing out the enemy behind them, which the stargates had jumped them past.

Another two weeks, and they would all be ready for him to give the word to jump into the Helvanna Province.

*

Da Wei Sao Su Ani was at the tactical weaponry station, which was her position as third-in-command, in charge of the weaponry in all of the battlecruiser's firing batteries. The Zhong Xiao sat in his command chair, face the characteristic Zhou-Zheng Compact mask as demanded by their culture.

"Zhong Xiao to all hands," he suddenly said, using a holographic console over his chair to select the ship-wide hail system. "The fleet is now fully assembled at the staging area. We are outside Zhou-Zheng Compact space, close to the Gulf of Medusa, but you are not permitted to know any more than that. We await the signal to jump, to strike at the first Deepspace Station of the hated Vindicatus nation and its arch-nemesis of a ruler, the Mercenary Lord James Gavain. When the word comes, be prepared to give your life for the Primarch and the Primarchess. We now wait until that time. Zhong Xiao Chien, out."

The bridge crew did not speak out of turn under any circumstances, personal conversations not being allowed, but it was possible to see in the set of shoulders and the clenching of jaws the tension that existed amongst the operational crew. It could be in the next minute, or the next month, that the word came to jump and begin the invasion of Vindicatus.

With all her daily duties completed and no actual ship movement or even potential threats in the area, Da Wei Sao had little else to do, so she flicked onto the operational plans that she as third-in-command had permission to access. She sincerely wished that she had had a chance to transmit them to her Erdogan handler and get them to the Vindicatus nation, but part of the reason they were not released to even senior officers was to prevent the possibility of leaks. Spies like her could not always be detected, but they could be detained.

She did not even know if her message had been received, as there was no return reply from her handler required for her own safety, contact to be limited wherever possible.

She reviewed their situation. They were in an uninhabited system, actually within the Gulf of Medusa, not on the edge of it as Zhong Xiao Chien had deliberately misled the crew. The staging of five whole fleets of Zhou-Zheng Compact warships and military transporters was complete, they were fully assembled and waiting for the order to jump.

The Zhou-Zheng Compact relied on droids for its land army, not human beings. It was ironic in some ways; the Vindicatus nation of Dark Heart had once been a gigantic military base established by the Droid Intelligentia, those who had brought the human race almost to its knees during the Droid Wars. Droids without complete self-sufficient artificial intelligence would be returning to take it from the borgs, full humans and droids that now held it for the Lord Gavain.

It was a sizeable force, a significant proportion of the Zhou-Zheng Compact armed forces. Even with preparation, and the rumoured considerable defences of the Dark Heart Artificial System, the Vindicatus would be hard-pressed to defend against it if their Praetorian Guard grade ships had really left Dark Heart as Compact intelligence suggested. The Dark Heart System was a fortress, but this was an armada.

She wondered not for the first time if she could sabotage the fleet in some way, but her role was as a spy, not as a saboteur. If the Compact succeeded, she was much more valuable in her position under cover as an Erdogan and borgite sympathiser than as a failed traitor to the Compact.

It might take some time, but eventually, the order to commence the invasion would begin. They would jump to the first Deepspace Station, and take it with superior numbers. Then they would jump along the Web to the next Deepspace Station, and take that. Then they would use its stargate to complete the journey into the Dark Heart Artificial System, emerging in full force, in direct emulation of the tactics Lord Gavain had used to steal the system from the Rosicrux and the Shadows.

The Compact fleets were ready, and the staging area was set.

It was nerve-wracking, but all she could do was wait and see what happened.

*

Commander Joanne Lancaster frowned, feeling the weight of the responsibility upon her. It was not a good position to be in, having to lead a group of her comrades on a mission that she personally felt was doomed to failure. Her hand rested on a sculpture of a book raised up on a waist-height pedestal, the book to represent the ancient story of the Odyssey, the legend that her frigate the *SS Odyssey* was named after.

Jacked into the datasphere, she was warned that a person waited outside her ready room door to enter. She turned, stepping forwards and reaching for the water on her desk, desperate to hide her melancholic and despairing mood.

<Enter,> she gave the permission over the datasphere. The doors cycled open.

Marine Captain Alicia Alansen entered, dressed in casual fatigues and not her dress uniform or the power-armour of the Praetorian Guard Marines. They were all heroes for the intelligence they had gained on the Shadow Empire, apparently providing Lord Gavain with exactly what he needed, and the biomorph Alicia Alansen was more of a hero than most. Her actions on Pathonis V had been nothing short of legendary, and belonged in the hall of Vindicatus fame along with Field Marshal Ulrik Andryukhin, Brigadier Vantanik and Major Adeoye amongst other famous and accomplished Marines.

"Is all ready, Commander?" Captain Alansen asked.

"Yes," said Commander Lancaster, "I think so. We are all assembled here, and we have identified the target system. We are in our staging area; all I need do is give the detailed orders and we jump, and begin the mission in the target system."

"Which system are we targeting?" asked Captain Alansen.

"The conquered Stanchion System," she said, "once belonging to a small and minor House. The Third Empire took it two months ago, and our sources state that it is on the Railway, whatever that is. If the installation we saw being constructed above Pathonis was part of the Railway, then we should find a completed facility here at Stanchion."

"As good a choice as any," said Alansen, obviously having accessed the tactical information they had on the system in an eye-blink through her advanced biomorphic implants. "The former defences of the House that once ruled this system are weak, although it is a fair assumption that the Third Imperials have reinforced them considerably. It will still be extremely difficult."

"Which is why we jump in, approach by running silent, corvettes launch the initial strikepods from close distance and we get the mainframe downloaded quickly. We don't have to disrupt the Railway, the mainframe datacore download is all we need. We get it, and jump out quick."

"The mission objectives are as important as they are clear," said Captain Alansen. "Dying in performance of the mission will make it fail. Lord Gavain needs the information to be successful in his endeavour to defend against the Shadow Emperor."

"So, we will do our best," said Commander Lancaster.

The Captain Alansen seemed to cock her head to one side, a learned human gesture Commander Lancaster assumed. The inhuman cybernetic biomorphs aped human behaviour to make non-biomorphs feel more relaxed in their presence. "You are worried," said Captain Alansen, more as a statement. "Do not be. Lord Gavain would not be entrusting you with this if he did not have faith in you."

"He says I will be a Captain and you will be a Major after all this is done," said Lancaster gloomily, "We are commanding enough people on a dangerous mission. But it is not the rank I want. I want to be not throwing my life away on such a high-risk mission. We should be at home - and I never thought I would call Dark Heart that - fighting to defend it with the rest of our people."

"Well, all I can suggest is ....." Alansen paused, and then said quite sharply, "Pull yourself together, Praetorian."

Commander Lancaster looked shocked. "Captain?"

"You are now in operational command of the frigates *Odyssey, Obliterate,* and *Brilliance,* and the corvettes *Adventurous, Aggressive, Arduous, Armageddon, Avaricious, Armoured,* and *Avenger*. I am in command of their Marine forces, four hundred and eighty five Biomorphic Marines at full-strength. We face heavy odds, but we will and must succeed, as millions of lives of our Vindicatus comrades depend upon it, not including the civilians of our nation, and the lives of the people beyond Vindicatus in the colonised galaxy. We can and we will succeed in this, Commander Lancaster."

Captain Alansen leaned forwards, her jet black biomorph eyes frightening. "Have faith in yourself, sir," she said softly, "for failure is not an option."

*

Lord Gavain stood in the operations room aboard the *VSS Vindicator,* converted into the campaign war-room for the duration of the war of defence he had planned. He was the man leading the Coalition of the Resistance, and he would do his utmost to see it be successful. The overall objective had to be achieved, or the galaxy would eventually suffer.

The outcome was indeterminate, but he bore the responsibility well. To his crew and staff he appeared no different, he was the Lord who had brought them into the nation he had created. To his allies in the Coalition he appeared confident, capable and ready. To his friends, his closest friends, he knew he seemed apprehensive.

He was the type who would not let that apprehension stop him from making a decision, right or wrong. Sometimes the absence of a decision was more harmful than the wrong one.

Lucas De Graaf had openly admitted to Gavain that he had initially found the prospect of commanding First Fleet daunting, and he admired Jamie Gavain for leading the resistance like this. It was a massive undertaking, fraught with risk and numerous complications due to the different parties forming it. Lucas could not imagine it.

James Gavain's reply had been; "It is all experience. One day, you will be ready."

"Today is your day, I think, Jamie," had been Lucas's reply.

Today Lord James Gavain rested both hands gently on the holographic display console before him, completely immersed in the datasphere. His bodily functions were reduced, his implants regulating his physical form, to allow his mind invasive access and control of the systems-wide datasphere that they had created.

It was a complicated battle-net, one designed with multiple internal firewalls and safety buffers, with compartmentalisation built into it to prevent the loss of one ship, squadron or fleet imperilling the entire net. There were localised dataspheres as well, at fleet level, squadron level, ship level, and even functional unit level, all of them independent redundancies and back-ups should calamity befall them.

Lord Gavain's war-room was connected up to the secret net of continuously streaming hyper-pulse communications generators they had erected. Before him stood holographic representations of each of the national commanders, and their immediate sub-ordinates in charge of individual fleets where those nations had provided multiple fleets for the war.

There had been more engagements with civilian craft and in two instances military craft, and discovery by one of the local, small Houses was certainly a given any day now. It would no longer really be a problem - they were about to launch their pre-emptive strike into the Third Imperium.

All ships were in place, all fleets were ready to launch into the Helvanna Province.

Gavain quietly surveyed the people before him. Admiral Haas led the StarCom Federation, High General Luke Towers represented the Levitican Union, and Admiral D'Souza led the Amiens fleets, all people that Gavain either knew well or had dealt with in the past.

Of the others he either had extensive intelligence files thanks to O'Connor, or he knew through reputation. The Cervantian fleets were being led by Commandant-General Alvarez Cervantes, the Grand Marshal Anaes Korhonen was present for her military contribution, Marshal Paul Fallhouse led the Republic of Varrental armies and navies, and the ferocious Warlord Maximilian Van Hausenhof was present for his.

The Calamarite Confederacy and the OutWorlds Alliance had their representatives too, in Lord Commander Alia Xhepa and Chief Commander Omar Al-Saadi. They did not have a part to play in Operation Jacknife, but the later stages of the overall war-plan would only work with their participation, so they had every right to be here.

They were all formidable characters, and in competition with each other. Most had warred against each other at some point, either in Red Imperium times, or during this Age of Secession, post-Dissolution. The senior people being present was a direct result of posturing, a show of force to their often-times enemies. Perhaps that was the reason why Gavain had received a better than hoped for contribution to the Coalition from each of the contributory nations; it was born of a desire by each nation to outdo the other.

Ultimately, this was their best hope to stop the Shadow Empire, and if it failed there could be others, but none would be as effective or as safe strategically as this. For most of them, it was better to fight away from your land than in it.

"Ladies and gentlemen," said Lord Gavain, "we all have our targets, and we all know the plans. The stargates are ready, and we all know the requirements of Operation Jacknife. Each of you has operational theatre command; as soon as you can, re-establish links with me here so I can co-ordinate the overall war. Achieve your initial objectives, Emperor-willing. And by that, I do not mean the Shadow Emperor, as I doubt he will be pleased with our work today."

There was some laughter at that, others remaining stony faced depending on their characters and personality.

"All fleets, the time has come ...." Gavain paused, watching the large digital chronometer count towards zero, "the war against the Third Imperium starts now. Good luck, people .....

"..... All fleet commanders, jump!"

Chapter XVII

Real-space was ripped open as the warships of House Hausenhof's Fleet Ravage, Fleet Salamander and Fleet Destructor jumped into the Krieglach System. The Warlord Maximilian Van Hausenhof was in the specially designed command seat aboard his captured Praetorian dreadnought, the *HSS Taker of Souls,* and his eyes lit up with ferocious delight as the data began to feed into his command displays.

"Let slip the dogs of war," he whispered as the data flowed through, his unaugmented human eyes taking it all in with practiced ease. The Krieglach System was on the far galactic east-east-east of the Helvanna Province, a triple star system which had very heavy house defences dating back to times before the Red Imperium. It was a tough system to take, which was why Hausenhof had jumped in with three fleets, one to each sun and planetary system.

He could see that the enemy were focused in one of the planetary systems, opposite Fleet Ravage, although the defences in all three were powering up. Frigates and corvettes were already powering away from the main fleets, to scan the far-reaches of each of the planetary systems within Krieglach for any nasty surprises.

They had jumped in on the outer reaches, to give them time to power up shields and be at full combative ability. He had salvaged and refugee Praetorian ships, and high-grade House ships, some of the best available. The enemy were not hiding, forming up from their scattered formations into fleet formation. They were making no attempt to jump, relying in their technology and supposed superiority.

Maximilian Van Hausenhof grinned. Every fleet had interdictors within it, and the enemy would find their immaterialisation technology would not work. It was going to be a slaughter.

Marshal Paul Fallhouse was stood in the tactical area of the bridge of his warship, so he could read the tactical data as it came in. The dreadnought *RoVSS Varrental Hammer* was brand new, House-designed but with a hybrid of Praetorian technology salvaged from the Dissolution.

"We have arrived in the Alternmarkt System," his ship's captain said, "the fleet has fully translated."

"Inform me as soon as the hyper-pulse link is set up," said Marshal Fallhouse. The network of HPCG stations set up by Gavain would fire continuously streaming hyper-pulse communications towards the target system some ten to twenty seconds after arrival, to link the entire battlefront up and allow the commanders of nations access to the battlenet

Gavain had created. It would also allow them to contact their reinforcements, and commanders in other theatres.

The Alternmarkt System was relatively small, a single-sun system, but it was formerly significant to the Helvanna Province because of its manufacturing ability and military shipyards. There were no Third Imperium ships here, but there were plenty of the old Helvanna House ships present.

Marshal Fallhouse determined that his existing fleet could handle the defences here, the enemy were under-represented according to their pre-battle estimates. He ordered scouts out just to be sure there were none hiding, as that was always a possibility.

"Hyper-pulse link established," said his comms officer. "Attempting to raise Commandant Tanner now."

"Inform Beta Fleet to hold position, they are not required at this time," he said. "Advance to targets, all squadrons, split fleet formation. Engage enemy ships. I want Beta Fleet to be ready to jump in case we have any surprises."

"Aye, sir, message being sent now. I have Commandant Tanner."

A holographic image of Commandant Tanner appeared before Marshal Fallhouse. The Republic of Varrental had two systems to assault, and Commandant Tanner was leading the other theatre invasion. Fallhouse had decided on the same method of attack for the Bad Ischl System as for the Alternmakt System, with Delta Fleet jumping in first, and then Epsilon Fleet in reserve to jump in once the enemy were located and engaged. Zeta Fleet was a support fleet, and would come in once the system was secure.

"We have a heavy enemy presence, Marshal," said Commandant Tanner. "Some Upgraded Third Imperial warships, less than a squadron, but more Helvanna House ships than pre-estimated. I'm sending you the figures now."

Marshal Fallhouse read the figures. "Difficult," he said, "it looks like you have the enemy ships we are missing here in Alternmakt. But stick to the plan. Draw them in, and then launch Epsilon Fleet. I will warn the Leftenant-Commandant of Epsilon Fleet to be ready. Good hunting, Commandant."

In the Landquart System, Grand Marshal Anaes Korhonen breathed a sigh of relief. The hyper-pulse communications had kicked in, and she had been able to obtain full information reports from the two systems the Korhonen contingent had been assigned to attack.

The enemy were vastly under-represented, their estimations on the defences they would meet were out. Korhonen had sent four fleets into the Landquart and Chur Systems, with a fifth fleet in reserve, and two support fleets ready to jump in if they won. The enemy were just not there in the numbers they expected.

Anaes Korhonen was playing it carefully though. She was aware that as they jumped in, the enemy could all go to running silent, and take them by surprise. It was not standard modus operandii for the Third Empire and their Helvanna Province lackeys, but she knew in war to expect the unexpected.

In many ways, the initial invasion was not going to be the difficult part, she knew. They had little intelligence on the Third Imperium and the former Helvanna Dominion forces that was current, and they were striking deep into the Province. It would be the Third Imperium response that would be heavy and disastrous, that was why Gavain had insisted on reserve after reserve after reserve to be ready.

"We have heavy incoming fire!" shouted the tactical officer, "the enemy are turning to present broadsides."

"Fleet X is to present broadsides, give the order," said Admiral D'Souza calmly.

"Order given, Admiral!"

Admiral D'Souza was awestruck. They had jumped into the single-star solar system of Fleurier, Fleet X being nearly triple the size of normal post-Imperial fleets. In ship numbers they had provided slightly less of a contribution than the Republic of Varrental. Fleet XI was a support fleet, and ready to jump in on command. Admiral D'Souza had already warned them to stay where they were, the situation here in Fleurier was too hot.

"Torpedoes incoming, torpedoes incoming –" the ship rocked violently, and the echo of a nuclear explosion rang throughout the battlecruiser, "-damage decks five through eight, that was close, decompression in process. Damage control teams, respond and report!"

The Fleurier System was important to the Helvanna Province, large with over twenty habitable planets and heavily invested in. Yet despite that, it had little military presence historically, surrounded by numerous other high-military systems. The Third Imperium had changed that, for some reason.

The Helvanna Province had a vast number of house ships presence, virtually a full fleet by their standards, and additionally there were another sixteen Upgraded Third Imperium Praetorian ships, primarily consisting of their new W-class, X-class, Y-class, and Z-class warships.

Worse, those Upgraded ships had been running silent, and had pounced as the Amiens Fleet X translated in. Damage had been high in the first few seconds, and Admiral D'Souza had already sustained seven losses in the first minute and a half of the engagement. At least he had shields up and weaponry batteries firing now, and their interdictors were working, so the Third Imperium ships were discovering to their cost that their usual ghostly, immaterial protection no longer functioned.

"Signal Lord Gavain," said Admiral D'Souza, making the decision. "We need assistance, resistance is heavier than expected, our losses are mounting too quickly."

Commandant-General Alvarez Cervantes felt the recovered Praetorian battlecruiser he used as his flagship tremble slightly as it began to take heavy fire from the space station. The shields deflected most of the weaponry fire coming in, but no shield was ever perfect, and some of the heavy blaze of fire was making it through.

"Pull fourth and fifth squadrons up," he heard his Fleet Commandant say, "target the space station, we need to reduce its shields in the next two minutes before we start taking serious damage."

Alvarez Cervantes was content to leave the operation in this system to the Fleet Commandant, as he concentrated on the three theatres and overall command of the Cervantian forces. He had brought five fleets to the Coalition, four main fleets and one support fleet, so although in naval terms they were strong in relation to ground forces they were weak in comparison to the other nations. It was deliberate. He did not fancy their chances against the armies of the Third Imperium, being confident in his navy. His own prejudice as a naval officer had some bearing on that.

The pre-estimates of the enemy they would face were roughly accurate, in that they were not facing the level of resistance the Coalition was expecting elsewhere on the vast battle-front. Of course it was early, the name of the game was to take the systems quickly, and then await Third Imperium reprisals, and that could not be predicted.

Three of his naval fleets had jumped in to the Turlock, Monterey and Fremont Systems. Turlock and Fremont were lightly defended as expected, but heavy resistance had been expected in this one, the Monterey System. It was a binary solar system, with one of the planetary systems given over to heavy military research and considerable House manufacturing capabilities. His strongest fleet had jumped in here, only to discover that it was not as heavily defended as they thought. It had been conquered by the expanding Helvanna Dominion nearly three years ago, and the damage they had meted out in that conquering had been considerable.

All in all, his forces were getting off lightly so far he considered. He sincerely hoped that his usual enemies-now-allies in Korhonen and Hausenhof were having a rougher time of it. Although they were all linked in on the vast segment-spanning battlenet Gavain had constructed, for operational security systems the information flowed one way. The national commanders only knew what was happening in the systems they were assaulting, not in the other nations, in case there were security breaches.

<We do not require assistance, Lord Gavain, I am calling up one of my reserve fleets,> said Admiral Haas. <Haas out.>

Admiral Haas respected Lord Gavain considerably, but he did not like the man. They had been on opposite sides during the rebellion against the False Emperor, and again during the Levitican War. He did not trust the man's motives at all, but he saw the logic in striking against the Third Empire here rather than in StarCom Federation territory. He just also saw the considerable self-interest Gavain had in picking the Helvanna Province as the place for the Coalition's stand against the Shadow Emperor. It helped protect the Levitican Union and his own Vindicatus nation.

But Haas was a soldier, and he obeyed his President and Commander-In-Chief. And he loathed the Shadow Emperor and what he was more than he did the Mercenary Lord.

Admiral-of-the-Fleets Haas reviewed the data for all his StarCom Federation Armed Forces fleets. They were striking into the territory conquered by the Helvanna Dominion as they aggressively expanded post-Dissolution, which included some of the former Aalborg Alliance systems. As expected, in two of the systems they were facing heavy enemy resistance.

One of the nine StarCom fleets was in the Levitican Union, in the deeply placed second line of reserves, ready to jump by stargate to Gavain's first reserve line, and then on to any system in which they were needed. All four of the support fleets were being held back in that first reserve line as well.

For Haas's theatres of operations, he had further divided his eight remaining fleets, keeping three in reserve, whilst five main ships-of-the-line fleets jumped into their five target systems. They were striking the lightly defended Concord System, the heavy fortress system of the Pandrup System, the Bjerringbro System, the Rakkestad System, and the once-capital of House Lindholm of the Frederickstad System. The heaviest resistance was occurring in Frederickstad and Pandrup, and Haas authorised two fleets to jump in support.

Haas was in Frederickstad, and the resistance here was surprisingly heavy. It was densely populated, and The Third Imperium had still being trying to subjugate it, converting the populace into their hive consciousness. The former Aalborg Alliance members trapped here had been fighting back. Small ships were rising from the planetary surfaces, hassling the Third Imperium and House Helvanna ships present as they tried to react to the StarCom presence.

The Third Imperium was suffering, reliant on their advanced technology and their House Helvanna comrades, and the StarCom forces were matching them eight to one in some systems. Even the Z-class juggernauts were struggling with those odds, stripped of their immaterialisation defensive fields by the numerous interdictors Haas was fielding.

He grinned, despite himself. The enemy were going to fall.

Admiral-of-the-Fleets Lucas De Graaf said, <Rear-Admiral Al-Malli, bring 5th Rearguard Squadron to these co-ordinates,> and quickly flashed them onto the tactical map. Saifa Al-Malli, a senior commander and former captain of the *Vindicator* flagship of Gavain, responded in the affirmative.

They were invading the Hardangervidda System, a single solar system which was important because of its stargate, as well as being on the far galactic western edge of the Helvanna Province. The stargate would be used to link up to the Deepspace Stations in the Web, and allow a second line of reinforcements into the battlefront if required. De Graaf had to admire Gavain's genius.

There was heavier resistance here than estimated, partly because a squadron of Third Imperium Upgraded warships had been in obvious transit through, but Lucas De Graaf's First Fleet was more than capable of dealing with them. He had decided not to ask Gavain for reinforcements, as none were required. First Fleet was hitting in force, with overwhelming numbers.

The entire battleplan relied on overwhelming numbers, it was part of the genius of it all. It was a surprise attack on a wide battlefront, cutting the Helvanna Province into two.

There was an enemy juggernaut in the system, and no doubt they were wondering what they were facing. The interdictors were preventing their immaterialisation fields from working, and in addition they were facing the captured *Zeus's Wrath* juggernaut, now flying Vindicatus colours. Watching the two behemoths face off against each other was a first for the galaxy, and was going to become the stuff of legend, De Graaf was sure. His own T-class *Thor's Hammer* dreadnought was in support, and the Third Imperium and Helvanna forces were crumbling rapidly.

<Signal Lord Gavain,> said Lucas De Graaf. They were three minutes into the assault. <Inform him that we are predicting capture of the Hardangervidda theatre in seven to eight minutes.>

Lord Gavain registered the message from Admiral De Graaf, and despite his deep concentration and usual stony face, a small smile flickered at the pride he knew De Graaf would be feeling in reporting the impending fall of the Hardangervidda System. Gavain himself was proud of De Graaf, the man had developed so much from what he had once been, as an alcoholic Commander assigned against his will to the *Vindicator* battlecruiser by the Praetorian Guard.

The Vindicatus nation was about to gain some more ships, as De Graaf had numerous marine forces in boarding actions. In fact, the same was true in numerous systems, where the ex-Praetorian starships were able to use their strikepods to hit the Third Imperium ships. The rules of engagement said that where a national fleet was successful in taking an enemy ship in a boarding action, that ship became part of that nation's assets. It was indirectly leading to numerous boarding actions, no surprise to Gavain, and part of the reason he had for permitting that action. It would strengthen what would become the Jacknife Defence Line.

Reviewing the strategic battle-map of the entire Helvanna Province, the small House nations and the upper edge of the Levitican Union, the Province was coloured in red. Where the Coalition was fighting, in a line which literally divided the entire Helvanna territory into two roughly along its middle, the line flashed in alternate red then green colours. It was greener where the Coalition was succeeding.

Gavain was deeply relieved and pleased to see much more green than red already.

<A good start,> said Field Marshal Ulrik Andryukhin. He too was in the operations room aboard the *Vindicator*, having realised the value of being in a central command position rather than leading at the front as he usually did. He had responsibility for all of the Coalition's ground forces. Gavain would not take direct control of that, respecting Ulrik Andryukhin's abilities as being in advance of his own in that respect. <Frederickstad, Fleurier, Bad Ischl and Krieglach are tough zones, they will take longer than we thought.>

<Fleurier in the Amiens theatre is a worry,> said Gavain, <we're taking heavy damage, but I have reserves on their way. All else is within acceptable parameters.>

<We are nearing the point where the ground forces elements of the support fleets are to jump in,> commented Field Marshal Andryukhin.

<Take direct control, now,> Lord Gavain ordered. <Launch them as you see fit, Ulrik.>

Andryukhin actually laughed. <Thank you, Jamie, I'm looking forward to this fucker of a slaughter.>

It was going to be brutal, Gavain knew, the slaughter equally likely to be of their ground forces than of the enemy's. Whilst he was hitting with heavy naval superiority in the fifteen solar systems across the Helvanna Province, the ground forces would face partly or fully converted populations that would resist heavily. He was expecting some planets which just could not be conquered, where the entire population would have to be killed. He had authorised the use of viral agents and nuclear weaponry in such circumstances. Billions of innocents would die today, just along the Operation Jacknife line. The battles on the planets may even last weeks, if not into months. It would be hard.

The line of fifteen systems would become the Jacknife Defence Line, a line of systems they would hold at all costs against Third Imperium reprisals, and the eventual heavy response of the Shadow Emperor. The support fleets had ferry-ships with numerous fabricator and constructoships, and every system would be reinforced with static defences at a fantastic rate, even as the battles on the planetary surfaces raged.

Once the Jacknife Defence Line was secure and initial reprisals had been dealt with, naval ships would then move further galactically south within Helvanna territory, back towards the rear. Gavain would wait at least a day for all the ships in the Helvanna territory to be thrown at them in the Defence Line, and then they would begin the process of clearing the southern reaches of the territory.

His stomach turned as he thought of what he was about to order upon the galactic north of the Helvanna Province. However, it had been agreed with the Coalition, some of whom had been very angry to discover that he had lied to them about his military capabilities earlier in the year. Lady Principal Sophia Towers had been very vociferous privately in her condemnation of his duplicity, and what she described as a horrific power no man should ever have.

Nevertheless, there was no other option. He could not allow the Third Imperium to have solar systems anywhere near the Jacknife Defence Line, and the population would already be converted to the Third Imperium hive mind.

<Vice-Admiral O'Connor,> he sent the message.

<Yes, Lord Gavain?> came the reply from Jonathan O'Connor.

<The central system of Monterey is almost ready for your arrival. Jump now, in the time it takes to translate it should be largely pacified, at least navally.>

<Yes, Lord Gavain.>

<Assume position and wait for my command to launch,> said Lord Gavain.

*

<We are taking heavy fire, forward and starboard mid and upper shields down,> said the tactical officer, <damage being sustained, six decompressions. Nuclear damage and radiation spreading past defensive bulkheads.>

<Damage control teams to withdraw,> Zehra Sahin ordered, <close bulkheads further back, decompress the entire section. The people there are lost.>

<Aye, sir.>

On a private channel, Captain Sahin said to Admiral-of-the-Fleets Adare, <Silus, this is unbelievable. We're on a juggernaut, and we're losing.>

<Agreed,> said Silus, <The odds are not in our favour.>

As word of the massive invasion by a multi-national force consisted of untold fleet numbers had spread quickly throughout the Helvanna Province, Admiral Silus Adare had ordered his squadron to prepare to jump. Together with the squadron of General Helvanna, now Tribune Helvanna of the Third Empire, they had jumped into the Frederickstad System.

They had translated in hot, on the edges but near the reported fighting zones. They had come under heavy fire, but Adare had ordered his ships to engage their immaterialisation fields as soon as power was restored after the jump.

Only to find that they did not work.

The StarCom Federation starships had interdictor support, with interdiction fields engaged. As Adare's upgraded and advanced warships had moved in, their immaterialisation fields powered by warp technology had hit the inhibition fields of the interdictors, and had failed spectacularly. The warships, phasing in and out of hyper-space, had been stuck firmly in realspace. Without shields raised they had sustained heavy damage from the greater number of Praetorian-grade Federation warships.

Even when shields had been raised, the damage had been done. They were facing a new fleet of warships under Admiral Haas, Silus Adare's old commander when he had served the StarCom Federation. Haas's ship had been identified through the tactical analysis computers.

Adare had ordered the use of their advanced virus weaponry, trying to break into the individual Federation warship's dataspheres, and their overall battle-net. It failed, the enemy displaying a defence. It was impossible - how could they have defence against the advanced Shadow viruses?

Even the power of his *ISS Zero Tolerance* juggernaut was suffering, the Federation present in simply too great a force for their weaponry to change the direction of the battle. Adare could already see that the forces resident in Frederickstad were falling.

<Communications, signal the Tribune Helvanna,> Adare ordered. <All ships, disengage and prepare for jump to these co-ordinates,> he named a system further out and away from the reported battle-zones of the invasion.

Adare was in meltdown. He detected the hand of Lord Gavain in this, he just knew it in his bones. The Helvanna Province was falling already, cut in two under a massive invasion force from numerous nations Gavain had connections to. His own military forces, consisting of the upgraded and advanced warships and the House Helvanna warships were failing, either being destroyed, captured, or scattered.

"Tribune Helvanna here, Admiral," said the former General Helvanna.

"We are losing, Tribune," said Admiral Adare, "the odds are stacked against us. We must jump out, to this system. Frederickstad is lost."

Helvanna hesitated, lips thin, and then said, "I concur. Let's withdraw, and jump. If we can escape the interdiction fields. Helvanna out."

<Captain Sahin, withdraw and prepare for jump,> Admiral Adare ordered. <Connect me through to the HPCG station.>

<Connection established.>

<This is to all Helvanna Province forces in the fifteen systems along the enemy lines. This is Admiral-of-the-Fleets Adare. I am ordering an immediate withdrawal, to the galactic north. The enemy is simply too strong for us to resist. All ships, disengage and withdraw. Await further communications once you have reached safe systems. Orders effective immediately. Adare out.>

Withdrawing to the galactic north made sense. It brought them closer to possible reinforcements. What he had seen of the invasion force made him realise that the Third Imperium forces in the Helvanna Province were vastly outnumbered, and their technological superiority had obviously been countered. It could only be Lord Gavain behind it all. Adare wondered if he was directing the invasion.

Silus Adare relaxed then into his flag chair, but he noted Captain Sahin did not dare say a word to him. He was absolutely fuming. He wondered how he was going to explain this to the Shadow Emperor, and the Second Legate.

Execution was in the offing for the second time this year, and Adare began to wonder how he could save his own life.

*

<We have translation into the Monterey System, Vice-Admiral,> said his captain. <All systems at normal in one minute forty seconds.>

<Good job,> said Vice-Admiral O'Connor, <System status, scanners? Hail the theatre commander.>

O'Connor remained in his flag chair, awaiting the incoming communication from the theatre commander, Commandant-General Alvarez Cervantes of House Cervantes. As he did, scanners reported that the system had already been subjugated navally. The Cervantians were in the process of boarding and taking a number of Helvanna House ships, and even an Upgraded Praetorian V-class battlecruiser in service to the Third Empire.

There were also incoming jump signatures, but O'Connor prevented his captain from over-reacting. The system-wide datasphere being used by the Cervantian contingent of the Coalition, as well as the galactic battle-net maintained by Lord Gavain, informed him that the incoming warp traces were the support fleets ordered in by Field Marshal Andryukhin. The land invasion of the Monterey System was about to commence.

"Commandant-General Alvarez Cervantes here, identify yourself," was the immediate response on the comms channel.

"Vice-Admiral Jonathan O'Connor, of the *VSS Archnemesis*. The codename you need is - Armageddon."

"Ah, Lord Gavain's secret," said the Commandant-General.

"What is the status of the system, theatre commander?" O'Connor asked.

"We have secured it, and are just finishing the naval boarding actions. Your Field Marshal Andryukhin is sending in the ground forces. We will wait the proscribed eighteen hours for Third Empire reprisals, then we shall be launching out towards our second and third system targets, in the galactic south. All according to plan. Cervantia does as it promises."

"Well done, Commandant-General."

"How goes it in the other theatres?" Cervantes asked.

"Operational security, you know I can't share that."

The Commandant-General merely smiled. There was something unpleasant about the man, which communicated itself even across a holographic link. "No harm in asking," he said. "I have to ask, though - what is that thing you are aboard and sailing in my theatre?"

Vice-Admiral O'Connor hesitated, but knew he was allowed by the rules of engagement to say. The truth would be out soon enough, and Commandant-General Cervantes would soon know, as he would see it in operation shortly.

"It is a missile-cruiser, newly designed by the Dark Heart Shipyard. We have designated it AA-Class; originally it was going to be W-class, but the Third Empire beat us to it."

"And what is its purpose?"

O'Connor told him.

There was little reaction apart from a narrowing of the eyes from Commandant-General Cervantes. "I see. All of us in the Coalition know this is part of the plan, and so we are complicit in the atrocity you are about to commit, Vice-Admiral. All I can say, is that the name of Lord Gavain will be tarnished by this, and it will be interesting to see how history judges him. Saviour of mankind, or its arch-enemy. Even the two previous Emperors did not go this far. It is on a level with the Shadow Emperor's forced indoctrination of the conquered populaces, maybe worse, for at least he just raped their minds, not burnt their bodies."

"If he was not turning them into mindless slaves, we would not being doing this," replied O'Connor.

"Does it sit well with you, Vice-Admiral?"

O'Connor hesitated again. "No," he said, "the killing of billions of people never would, or could."

"I am seen as a monster by some," said the Commandant-General, "but even I am glad to hear you say that. May your soul find peace with itself after this, Vice-Admiral O'Connor. Cervantes, out."

<All system power restored and the ship is at full operation, Vice-Admiral,> said his captain.

<Are we in position?> O'Connor asked.

<Aye, sir.>

<Then sound black alert, launch is imminent,> said O'Connor. <All hands to prepare for launch.>

The AA-Class *VSS Archnemesis* missile-cruiser was of an entirely new design, and its Praetorian ancestry was there in some of its naval architecture. It had moved to a clear area of space, where it had open lines of fire in all the directions it needed.

It had the typical bulbous fore of the Praetorian Guard design, and two jump nacelles to either side, like wings. These jump nacelles were able to retract and were not fixed, and as the ship prepared to fire, the nacelles moved back deeply into the hull.

Numerous ports began to open all along the missile-cruiser's hull, revealing deep, cavernous launch tubes.

<All tubes open,> said one of the special weapons officers.

<Tears of the Moon warheads entering arming cycles, complete in five seconds.>

<All one hundred and sixty-eight missile engines have reached launch status, repeat, launch status reached.>

<Locking in jump points to each missile, confirming missile end-targets ...... navigational paths confirmed.>

<Recall and self-destruct mechanisms locked out, as per orders.>

<Arming cycles complete.>

<All missile coolant systems green.>

<Launch patterns loaded, waves of nine and ten per launch wave programmed.>

<Single launch command accepted, coded to Vice-Admiral O'Connor's security clearance.>

<InterStellar Hyper-space Missiles ready for launch, all systems go.>

And then, the bridge fell silent.

O'Connor made a last check of the missiles, his heart racing. He was all too aware that each missile carried a Tears of the Moon warhead. Each missile was locked onto a planet somewhere in the galactic north of the Jackson Defence Line, within the territory of the Helvanna Province.

It was too dangerous to allow the corrupted hive minds of the people of the Helvanna territory to be used against the invasion force. The Shadow Emperor could direct them to attack in droves, overwhelming the ground forces of the Defence Line in short order. It was doubtful that the indoctrination procedures could even be reversed, they were so deep into the human mind. The technology was too advanced.

Gavain had determined that they could not take the risk, and so had told the Coalition that he had the capability to launch Tears of the Moon Weapons of Planetary Destruction against the systems in the north of the Helvanna Province. In the south, they would try to conquer and undo the damage to the people, but in the north, they did not have that luxury. They had to eliminate the vast threat posed by the people, slaved to the will of the Shadow Emperor.

The Coalition had been divided on it, angry at Gavain for possessing the technology he had promised he had destroyed when he took Dark Heart. Eventually though, they had concurred, and saw the logic in his plan.

It was ironic, reflected Vice-Admiral O'Connor. Earlier this year, they were going to execute the reviled Silus Adare for launching one Tears of the Moon warhead and destroying Alwathbah in the Levitican Union. Now, in the Helvanna Province, Gavain was going to launch ninety-eight of the weapons.

Whether you were a war criminal or not, really depended on whether your side won the war, O'Connor reflected. It had always been the way.

<Incoming pulse channel message from Lord Gavain,> said the communications officer.

<O'Connor here, Jamie,> said O'Connor.

<Vice-Admiral, is Armageddon ready?> said Lord Gavain.

<We are on black alert, and ready to launch,> said Vice-Admiral O'Connor.

<Then,> said Lord Gavain, pausing before he continued, <Let history show that I gave the order to fire. Launch the missiles, Vice-Admiral. Gavain out.>

Vice-Admiral O'Connor jacked directly into the protected and isolated mainframe that controlled the missile launch sequence. He programmed in the command code, and then simply said aloud, his voice shaking slightly, "Armageddon."

In waves of nine or ten missiles, the InterStellar Hyper-space Missiles rocketed out of their launch tubes. Massive creations, as big as some corvettes, the missiles set off on separate pre-programmed destinations. With their auto-destruct programmes disabled, there was no chance of recall or interruption.

They sped off to a safe distance and then engaged their warp fields, jump initiation capacitors firing for about a minute before jump. Some of them would only jump once, some would have several jumps before hitting their target systems, but the unmanned ballistic missiles were fast and virtually unstoppable.

With searing flashes of lights, one after another, the missiles began to jump, ready to deliver their deathly cargoes to their targets.

*

<We have an incoming jump signature, Admiral,> said Captain Sahin.

<What?> asked Admiral Adare. <The enemy have followed us from Frederickstad?>

<No, the angle of approach is wrong,> said Captain Zehra Sahin. <And the jump signature is too small, it is corvette sized roughly.>

<A spy coming in?> suggested Admiral Adare. It could not be a civilian ship, civil shipping was still virtually locked down since the subjugation of the Helvanna people had begun.

<It has a small translation profile due to its size, we will know in fifteen seconds when it translates,> said Captain Sahin.

Admiral Adare stood up, suddenly suspicious. There was something not right about this.

They had jumped into a system in the galactic north, a fair distance away from the Frederickstad System. He was desperately trying to repair their battlenet, so he could command the disparate forces all across the Helvanna Province as they withdrew and retreated from the invasion.

The invasion force had cut a major hole in their communications networks, and whilst it was possible to still communicate with forces south of the invasion line, he had them all pulling north. He wanted to consolidate, determine how many ships had survived, and then plan a massed counter-attack on a weak point of the enemy invasion line. It would take time to plan, but within ten hours he hoped to be jumping back into the fray.

It would help to have something to report to the Second Legate and the Shadow Emperor, that he was striking back. It might stay his execution. He had already spoken with Sahin and Lamans, and if the order came for him to be executed for this failure, they would jump with their juggernaut away from Helvanna Province space.

<Translation,> said the navigations officer and scanners officer at the same time.

<Identify it,> ordered Adare.

<Target is an InterStellar Hyper-space Missile!>

Adare's eyes actually widened. An ISHM could mean only one thing. It was either a planetbuster or a starkiller, and either would not be good. How far was Gavain going to go?

<Put the system on red alert,> he said, <Prepare to jump if the sun is the target.>

<It is zeroing in on the fourth planet,> said Captain Sahin.

<Can we intercept?>

<No. Planetary defences firing, but no joy.>

<We have three more jump signatures, matching profiles!> said the scanners officer.

<That's every populated planet in the system,> said Sahin quietly on their private channel.

<I think Gavain has gone mad,> said Adare. <How dare he castigate me for Alwathbah, if he is capable of doing this. I actually admire the bastard.>

<The ISHM has penetrated atmosphere, detonation in two seconds.>

<Show me,> ordered Adare.

The holographic screen flicked to an enhanced image of the first target planet. He saw the flash as the missile detonated, and for a short while nothing happened. Then the atmosphere began to glow reddy-orange. It was catching fire, burning away with ferocious speed. Within seconds, the fire had spread across the length of the planet, moving out in a fast circle as the atmosphere was turning into a burning sheet of flame.

Within a minute, the planet would be dead.

The scanners flicked to the other planets, showing the same happening as the incoming missiles evaded all the defensive fire with their super-fast, enhanced main drive engines and shields. There was a space lift on one of the planets, leading to a commercial space station, and the atmosphere within the tube ignited, blowing all the way up to consume the space station before it could engage its safeties.

<We have reports coming in from other systems,> said Captain Sahin quietly.

<Relay them to me,> said Adare.

He began to receive the data. All across the northern territories of the Helvanna Province, his retreating forces were relaying the same information. The systems of the northern landholdings were under a heavy, wide attack of mass-destruction that was simply unprecedented. In some instances planetary defences were working, so some of the attempts were failing, but in many the missiles were unimpeded and simply broke through to deliver their deathly payloads.

Chapter XVIII

Lord Gavain was wearing his full red and black, expensive Lord's robes, and looked every inch the Mercenary Lord. He still refused to sit on a throne like the other House Lords, preferring a simple seat. The room he was in was nondescript, in reality a spare ops room on the *Vindicator*, but it specifically designed to prevent anyone detecting his location.

"To the people of the colonised galaxy," he said, his words being transmitted via pulse channel to media stations across the galaxy, "I am Lord Gavain, commander-in-chief of the Coalition of Resistance. The Coalition is a group of nations and houses, all joined together in secret to defend against the advancing wave of the Third Empire and the madness of the so-called Shadow Emperor.

"For obvious reasons I cannot confirm which nations are in the Coalition, but I am making this short address in order to give you all hope. Earlier yesterday, Imperial Standard time, we struck the first significant and successful blow in force against the Third Empire. Again, I hope you understand, but I cannot provide many details as we are currently in full military operation against the Shadows.

"What I can tell you is that we have successfully struck a vast number of Third Empire systems, somewhere in the Eastern Segment. We have struck on a broad front, which we now call the Jacknife Defence Line. We are holding it, and clearing the vermin that is the Third Empire from the surrounding region of space. The first of many successful blows has been struck against the Third Empire, and from this you should all take hope. We have demonstrated that the technology and military force of the Shadows *can* and *will* be stopped, that their inexorable and unprecedented advance *can* and *will* be halted. We have already done it.

"We are directly in the advancing path of the Shadow Emperor, and we send him this challenge. We are waiting for you, and you will not pass the Jacknife Defence Line."

The image of Lord Gavain rippled as the object flew through it, the holographic representation rocking and distorting like a water surface that had been disturbed. It slowly coalesced back into the form of Lord Gavain, but the image was stilled, and slowly faded from view as it was deactivated.

"Enough!" the Shadow Emperor roared. "I have seen more than enough!"

The assembled Shadow Council did not say a word. They were there either in real-life or in holographic form. They were becoming more and more concerned about the Shadow Emperor, his rages becoming more frequent and unpredictable. Some had already received direct threats from him, and the paranoia of the False Emperor and perhaps even the True Emperor was beginning to show within him.

Jared Towers, Legate of the Third Circle and the person with overall responsibility for setting up the political system for the conquered territory, watched the Shadow Emperor and the other Legates carefully. He had already heard rumours, and had been approached, by other Legates concerned with the clone Emperor's increasing mental instability.

He had not decided where his ultimate loyalty lay. The Shadow Emperor existed to unite the people, give the galaxy a figurehead to flock to before they were indoctrinated into the hive consciousness and essentially lost all self-will, becoming automatons, and slaves to the Emperor. His Tribunes, in charge of each Province, would form a part of the net controlling the slaves, and each individual system would have its own Prefect, who would also have some form of self-independence and be a hub for the collective consciousness in that system.

The indoctrination was virtually irreversible. Unlike the House Marchenko hive consciousness, and others that followed similar models, without direct connection to a controller, the slaves would cease to function. They would simply shut down, and die.

Jared did not fully agree with it, but that was his own personal thought. The madness of the Shadow Emperor had been firm on that, and the orders had been given and followed, the hive consciousness technology being upgraded, developed and tested nearly a decade ago.

It probably explained why Gavain had launched the Weapons of Planetary Destruction on the northern territories. He knew that the indoctrination of the hive consciousness could not be reversed. He probably feared their being used as human meat in a counter-invasion, and certainly that was one way in which the slaves could be used.

They had finally assembled to tell the Shadow Emperor what had happened together, each Legate feeling there was safety in numbers. The Shadow Emperor's fury had been as vehement as it was predictable.

"Shadow Council," said the Shadow Emperor, his tone low. "You have singularly failed to rid me of this Mercenary Lord Gavain, and now look at what your failure has allowed! He pokes fun at me, slaps me in the face!" The Shadow Emperor's tone went dangerous as he turned to the Legate of the Fourth Circle. "Who is in this Coalition of Resistance, Fourth Legate? Where have they struck, what is the situation now? It changes every minute that goes by!"

The Fourth Legate took the central stage, image jumping forwards. "The Coalition of Resistance is formed of the following nations," and he listed the ones they knew about and suspected. "We have the following information on their suspected military forces, but we know there will be reserves and more we have not encountered," and the information began to list above his right shoulder as he continued.

"They have struck in a line, this so-called Jacknife Defence Line, through the Helvanna Province. It stretches the entire length of the Province, directly in the path of our planned advance. The challenge is real. We have lost communications across the Province, with some reports of ISHMs strike in the galactic north, laying waste to a vast tranche of systems. To the south, we have isolated reports of more ships appearing.

"They have followed a 'scorched earth' policy to the north, laying waste to the systems. The intention is obvious, to prevent and limit our resources as we approach the Jacknife Defence Line. To the south, they are trying to pacify the region, to doubtless bolster their own defences. They cannot know that they will not be successful, that indoctrination is virtually irreversible. They will have another set of dying worlds on their hands."

"Evil," commented the Shadow Emperor, quietly. "My poor, poor people."

Jared found that hard to swallow, but did not visibly react. It was evil what they had done to the people in the first place, he thought.

"We will try and get vessels into the systems to spy, but our own forces under Admiral Adare are still in withdrawal and a state of shock," said the Second Legate, "Failure is not something we are accustomed to. Adare is doing an admirable job in the circumstances in pulling what is left of our forces back together."

"Yes, Adare," said the Shadow Emperor. "What is his excuse?"

"He offers none," said the Second Legate quickly, "and begs your forgiveness. He does point out that none of this was predicted - or to be fair to the Fourth Legate, predictable. The Mercenary Lord has displayed his famed strategic brilliance once again, catching us with standard Praetorian tactics of strength and surprise on an unprecedented scale."

If only he was on our side, thought Jared.

"Adare can be excused in this one instance," said the Shadow Emperor slowly, "but, Fifth Legate, if he fails again I will not even give the order. The Faceless are to remove him from command, permanently."

"Understood, Emperor," said the leader of the Faceless assassins.

"Have the Phantoms and the Foxes try to penetrate this Jackson Defence Line," said the Shadow Emperor, "but I am not hopeful considering how well Gavain defends his Vindicatus nation from our attempts to get in."

"Yes, Emperor," said the Legates of the Fourth and Sixth Circles.

"What are the projections for the future?" asked the Shadow Emperor, his suddenly calm face darkening again, "What is this accursed Gavain planning?"

"We suspect they will hold the Jacknife Defence Line, reinforcing it as we approach. It is where they intend to make their stand," said the Legate of the Fourth Circle. "It is there that he wants to draw us to battle, on his own terms."

"Then that is where we shall," said the Shadow Emperor.

"If there is any way to draw him out, that would be better -" began the Second Legate.

"Legate! We will not draw the man out! If he wants us to fight on his Defence Line, then that is where we will fight!" snapped the Shadow Emperor. "You know as well as I that he will not move, despite the provocation. I doubt even attacking his homeland would do it, do you? He has his eyes on something much bigger than Vindicatus, obviously. He wants to be me, he wants to be the next Emperor, doesn't he!"

"Poss - yes, Shadow Emperor," said the Second Legate.

Paranoia, thought Jared Towers. The Emperor had a point on the Defence Line though, they would not draw Gavain away from it. He cleared his throat, and said, "If Gavain will not move from the Defence Line, then we need to advance more quickly," he said. "We're not scheduled to reach Helvanna for another two months."

"Yes, Third Legate, I agree," said the Shadow Emperor. "Second Legate, draw up new plans. Shorten our front, and extend it quickly. Strike through the Benedict Democracy, get us to the Gulf of Medusa and running along it, heading for the Helvanna Province. Speed is now essential, not integrity of our conquered land."

"Yes, Emperor," said the Second Legate. "We do have an issue. Our forces are stretched thin, and this will put additional strain on the Railway. We do not have the forces available to hit the Helvanna Province and re-take it, without the Railway to pull our second stage armed forces in from beyond the Frontier. And those are reserved for the attempt to take Mars and fight StarCom."

"We are fighting them now," said the Shadow Emperor darkly. "Gavain sees we are heading for Mars, and so he puts up his fight here. He forces us to change our plans, to commit earlier than we intended to. So be it. Put the second invasion force into motion once the Railway to the northern territory of the Helvanna Province is established, I want them delivered into Helvanna and ready to strike in full, powerful, terrible force. And quicker than two months. It has to happen this month."

"We will be exposing ourselves on the approach to the Helvanna Province," the Second Legate warned.

"Do it!" screamed the Shadow Emperor. "I want this Coalition of Resistance smashed!"

Jared looked at the figures streaming into his mind. Even with the vast forces of the Coalition, which was based somewhat on guesswork and half-complete reports, the Third Empire had used a sizeable first-stage army and navy to advance through the colonised galaxy. It was thinning as they moved closer and closer to StarCom territory and the Core, but the intention was to take the borders of the Empire up to the Federation, and then use the Railway to shuttle the second-stage army down through their lands at unbelievable speed, crossing nearly half a galaxy in no time at all.

The second-stage forces would be enough to face this Coalition, providing their information was correct. And there was no guarantee of that.

The invasion of the colonised galaxy, virtually unchallenged, had just met the reality of war and of life. Nothing ever went as planned.

It would now become a race; advance as fast as possible towards the Defence Line ahead of schedule, before Gavain could pacify the planets and build his defensive fortifications.

*

<Admiral Delgado,> his communications specialist addressed him, <We have a firing solution request from the planetary surface, and the destroyers are not in a position to respond.>

Admiral Delgado broke off from what he was doing. He had been in command of the M-Class transporter *Monstrosity* for some time now under Lord Gavain, and was one of their more experienced officers. He was now in charge of the 5th Fleet, as well as the *Monstrosity* super-transporter.

<Tactical, do we have the capability?> asked Admiral Enrique Delgado, reading the details of the request from the Major on the surface. They were in the Hardangervidda System, leading the one-day old invasion of the planets. Out in the greater sphere of the solar system, constructoships brought in by the StarCom support fleets were already manuprinting and fabricating the defensive structures to harden the Jacknife Defence Line, whilst the battles raged on the colonised planets below them.

<Yes, sir,> came the response.

<Programme it in and fire when ready,> Admiral Delgado ordered.

Major Smythe, in his powerful four-tubed *Python* missile launcher, was panicking somewhat. The forward positions many kilometres away were being overrun by the enemy hybrid troops, and although his artillery battalion were providing as much supportive fire as they could, the enemy were just everywhere. This planet in Hardangervidda was turning into a world of death.

<The *Monstrosity* is responding, turbolaser and nuclear torpedo launch expected in five seconds,> said his communications Sergeant.

<Yes!> snapped Major Smythe. <Inform the battalion and the Lieutenant-Colonel. General warning on the battlenet, now.>

Sniper Sergeant Drapier heard the warning across the battlenet, and grinned. The support was heavily needed.

He focused his specially designed lasrifle onto another series of targets, painting them using his cybernetic implants within his mind, and then firing the trigger quickly several times, minutely adjusting the angle of the weapon. He watched ten of the enemy hybrids explode, their heads disappearing in puffs of cloudy, misty blood.

He was a long distance away from the battlefield, up on a mountain overlooking the capital city of the planet. They were still attempting to get in through the outskirts, the enemy hybrid troops focusing in on them in unceasing wave after wave. Even the local human populace were fighting against them, and the Marines were fighting at a ferocious rate. The battle had already lasted thirty hours on this planet, the attempt to get into the city ten of those hours, and it was not going well. The enemy land forces were simply too strong and too numerous.

The clouds above parted, and the turbolaser columns smashed down, striking like man-made lightning into the city blocks and the massed enemy.

Lieutenant-Colonel Zuo Li-Chan ordered his *Executioner* battlewalker to retreat and pull back, the glow from the powerful ship-borne turbolasers highlighting the darkening city as the planet's nightfall approached. He saw masses of the enemy hybrids, like some horror figures from a nasty nightmare, burning in the blasts.

<Turblolaser strikes confirmed,> he said, <Nuclear blasts imminent; regiment, all radiation shields raised.>

A series of affirmatives came back, even as the torpedoes streaked down and detonated. Mushroom clouds appeared above the city skyline, and the hybrid monsters roared and shrieked as the blasts caught them. Some fell, radiation sickness already hitting them. Hundreds of thousands if not millions of the slave-people had been incinerated in the multiple nuclear blasts, vast parts of the giant megapolis city being destroyed.

<We have a breach, all units, advance!> Lieutenant-Colonel Zuo ordered.

His *Executioner* battlewalker began to step forwards, firing weapons in all directions.

In the XW-1010 solar system, Field Marshal Ulrik Andryukhin read through the reports coming from the Hardangervidda System with growing unease and a sinking feeling.

Enemy resistance was higher than expected. Although they were not encountering many Upgraded Marines, there were vast amounts of the semi-alien hybrid soldiers on-planet. The populace were also fighting, running into their slaughter in such a way that Andryukhin was sure it was sapping the morale of his soldiers. It was not good for the soul to kill unarmed people, even if they were trying to kill you at the time. There were plenty of Helvanna House soldiers on-planet too, but they had largely been eliminated. It was the hybrid troops that were the toughest and the hardest to engage with.

It did not help that they were able to reproduce quickly, and were spawning more and more of themselves as every hour passed. They were present in such high numbers to start with, that the scans from space showed his forces were outnumbered nearly thirty to one.

He looked at the data read-outs, and reached his decision.

<Admiral Delgado,> he said, his communication going out through the inter-stellar battlenet. <This is Field Marshal Andryukhin. I am ordering all units to withdraw from the planets Schol, Kaan and Lukcso. Take the withdrawn troops and place them on the planet Tamen.>

<Yes, sir,> said Admiral Delgado, the confusion in his voice obvious. <What is the overall strategy? Are we retreating?>

<No,> said Field Marshal Andryukhin, heavily. <I am ordering heavy orbital bombardment from the destroyers. Every part of the planets is to be flattened. We need Tamen for the HPCG station and its manufacturing base, the other planets are disposable.>

<Understood, sir.>

Andryukhin had a heavy heart. This was sixth such time he had given such an order in the last two days.

*

Lady Principal Sophia Towers cleared her throat, and then sipped from the glass of water in front of her. She was at the head of the table for the Levitican Union, with Lord Minister Brin Claes as the Minister of Foreign Relations at her side. Lord Minister Vladmir Marchenko as Lord Minister for Military Defence was on her left hand side.

The conference had been called, Lord Gavain pleading with her to lead it. She was the only one he could trust, he said, and he would be busy with the demands of Operation Jacknife when it was needed.

She was still angry with him over the use of the Tears of the Moon on such a large scale, and had said as much, but she had agreed to it. She saw the sense in the conference, and the advantages to the Levitican Union.

Not for the first time, she began to wonder just how ambitious the Lord Gavain had become. He was turning into a very dangerous man, without question.

The holographic images had all appeared of the various minor House Lords and Ladies. They were in a special auditorium, where the assembled members of the conference could appear via continuous pulse channel to discuss what was happening out in the Helvanna Province.

She flicked her eyes across the people. There were no less than seven Houses here, whose lands had been violated as Gavain had built up his staging line of stargates and HPCG stations - something he was calling the Jacknife Support Line. It was like an old World War One trench system almost, with a reserve line for ships to move along and then forwards, propelled super-fast by specially built stargates. There was another House whose lands had been affected, that had refused to join the conference, instead demanding that the invasion in secret of their landholding be removed.

And there was the danger, Lady Principal Sophia thought. They had to prevent a hole in their Support Line appearing, so what else could a man with a vast interstellar army at his disposal do if one of the Houses whose territory they had unashamedly violated refused to co-operate. She had asked, and Gavain had merely asked if she could continue to try to establish a peaceful resolution to it, even offering reparations if necessary. If they were refused, he did not say what he would do.

There were also another eight small Houses present, whose landholdings consisted of anything from two or three systems apiece, to eleven or twelve systems. They were invited because they were between the Levitican Union and the Helvanna Province, and had a right to hear what Lady Principal Sophia had to say.

"One is glad, Lords and Ladies, that you are all present to hear what I have to say," she said. "We have much to discuss, one thinks.

"Firstly, one will take the step of explaining to you the main objectives of this conference. The first objective is to explain and apologise why the landholdings of some of you have been violated without your knowledge by the Coalition of Resistance, in preparing for the invasion of the Helvanna Province. It is of vital importance that the rear lines of the Coalition armed forces are protected, solid and secure as they fight against the tyranny that is the Third Empire.

"The second objective is to offer for you to join either the Coalition of Resistance ..... or, if you wish, to join the Levitican Union on similar terms as House Jorgensson and House Gavain. I will explain what the terms of both the Coalition, and the Levitican Union are. Either option is open to you. Do you all understand, and are you ready to discuss?"

She leaned back and waited for the questions to hit her.

*

Admiral Harley Andersson, the Solar High Chancellor for the Dark Heart System and of the entire Vindicatus nation, sipped from the fluted glass of cool, white wine. It had been imported, although 'rescued' may have been a more accurate term, by the refugees from the former Aalborg Alliance. It seemed fitting under the circumstances to be trying a glass.

He was sat in a suspensor-seat that was pre-Imperial era, in the Heart Palace. The cool artificial night air blew across him, and from his personal suite's placement in one of the towers he could look above into the fake sky and see some of the other planets of Dark Heart.

So many things to think about and remember, he thought. He was much older than James Gavain, remembering him as a young cadet still unfinished from the Praetorian Advanced School for Officers. He recalled the years of serving in different parts of the galaxy, the pride at watching Gavain proceed in his career, the onset of the revolution against the False Emperor. The end of the civil war had brought anything but the peace many had hoped. Andersson had always known it would be far from the end, but he had not expected life to be as complex and fast as it had been, as joyous and full of pain as it had become.

He sipped again, savouring the citrus taste, revelling in the soft tang after he had swallowed. He felt the sensations in his mouth and closed his eyes, relaxed in such a full way it was a complete rarity.

The message that intruded his peace across the datasphere was given the highest possible priority rating.

Feeling the irritation but far too professional to convey it, he accessed the header details. It was coming from the command and control centre, which sat like a brain at the centre of a nervous system, controlling all the military resources of the Vindicatus nation.

<Solar High Chancellor Andersson responding,> he said, opening the communications channel, and using his civilian rank without thinking. Sometimes he lost track of which role he was fulfilling, the dual military and civilian responsibilities he carried changing sometimes within the second.

<We have lost contact with Deepspace Eight, no warnings as yet. Admiral. They have failed to report in for three successive hyper-pulse transmissions.> All Deepspace Stations on the Web had to pulse confirmation of their security and integrity once every half-minute. An interruption could signify they had come under an interdiction field.

Andersson jerked fully awake, hand already reaching to his belt for the anti-alcohol dermajector. Deepspace Eight was the closest part of the Web near to Zhou-Zheng Compact space, and the best way for any Compact invasion force to begin the process of gaining access to the Dark Heart System. Add to that the increased probability of Compact aggression, according to the information from the Erdogan spies within the Compact, and this was a very serious situation.

<Sound full nation-wide alert, code red, inform we have a possible Scenario Orange under way,> Admiral Andersson commanded strongly. <I'm coming to the ComCen now.>

Da Wei Sao Su Ani read the battle reports coming through from the other ships in the advance fleet, standard status updates which just gave a top-level summary of damage inflicted.

It made grim reading, for the Compact. The *Fucanglong* had jumped into the area around Deepspace Eight with the rest of the fleet, the battleplan calling for the station to already be neutralised. It transpired that the fleet of Compact ships which had snuck up to the station, running silent, and tried a surprise assault with boarding parties had failed miserably.

They had been detected, tripping an unexpected droid mine field, and the station had shielded and armed itself. It had become a much tougher fortress, able to defend itself. It was only sheer fortune that their interdictorships had been close enough to the space station to prevent it from sending out its distress signals.

It took time to batter through the shields, and even more time to get boarding parties aboard. During this lengthy period of time, the Praetorian weaponry had already chewed through a number of Compact house ships, either striking them dead in the water or utterly annihilating them. More Compact fleets had begun to arrive, expecting to be able to pass through a captured station and jump onto the next target further in the Gulf of Medusa, only to find the station very much alive and firing back at them.

The station was simply overwhelmed, even Praetorian technology not able to withstand several Compact fleets massed against it, but Da Wei Sao hid her joy at the outcome. The plan allowed for a ten minute period of time to take the station, which considering who they were up against seemed far too short to Sao Su Ani, and it had taken nearly forty-eight minutes and more than four times the amount of starships to achieve. The Compact losses had been far beyond projections, and that was the cause for her joy.

The damage was considerable, and they had not even moved onto the second stage of their plan, which was to assault the second Deepspace Station further into the Web, Deepspace Three. Beyond that, they had to jump on to the Dark Heart System, where the real battle had to begin.

Zhong Xiao Chien stood by her side, and he swore in the old tongue. "If that is a sign of how strong they are," he shook his head.

"Zhong Xiao, private communications coming in from the Shang Jiang," the communications officer called out.

Zhong Xiao returned to his captain's chair, taking the call in private. The Shang Jiang was in charge of their fleet, one of the four fleets participating in the invasion. When he finished, he called for an announcement.

"All hands, this is your Zhong Xiao," said Chien, "the orders have been received. The battleplan has changed in view of the resistance encountered here at Deepspace Eight, and the likelihood and operating assumption is that the enemy are now aware of our approach. All four fleets are jumping on to Deepspace Three together, simultaneously. We all will jump through the stargate in three minutes time."

"Can a stargate handle that amount of ships at once?" asked the second in command. "Over a hundred starships in one jump is surely beyond safety limits for a stargate." Da Wei Sao agreed, but it would not be seemly within Compact culture to give any overt sign of challenge such as the second-in-command had done.

"Of course," said Zhong Xiao Chien confidently. "The Yi Ji Shang Jiang has spoken, we all obey."

Admiral Andersson frowned as he read the data reports coming through, streaming into his mind from the datasphere jacking.

Scenario Orange consisted of an analysis of likely attack by Compact forces, aiming for the Dark Heart System. The existence of Praetor and Bright Hope was still not known by the wider interstellar community, so most of the sub-scenarios within Scenario Orange ignored those systems. There were certain actions, such as ships pulling out of those systems and jumping back into Dark Heart, which had already happened.

Scenario Orange allowed for a typical trigger event, which had actually occurred; the fall of a Deepspace Station. There was only one close to Zhou-Zheng Compact space, and they had sure enough targeted it - if it was them, as that was still to be determined. There should have been enough time to get a message out at least to confirm an attack or the identity of an attacker, but perhaps an interdiction field had been used

All the Deepspace Stations had been reinforced and upgraded, partly as a response to the equally likely possibility of a Shadow or Third Empire strike. They expected it would cause a significant delay to the incoming force.

Scouts had been sent to Deepspace Three as a precaution, in the second line of stations with the stargates that would allow a jump into the Dark Heart system. There was no enemy presence detected there yet.

Andersson had given permission for Seventh Fleet to jump around Deepspace Three, although he was keeping Sixth and Eighth Fleets in the

Dark Heart System. It was a risk as they could translate as the enemy came in, but nothing happened. Now, Seventh Fleet had retreated to a safe distance, and the droid mines had all been activated in either terminus zone from the stargate at Deepspace Three. Any ship-of-the-line fleet coming in would face utter carnage waiting for them as they translated into realspace.

A message came in from Admiral Halvorssen, who was now in command of the Sixth Home Fleet. Admiral Grant had the Seventh Fleet, made primarily of Erdogan ships, waiting to exact vengeance if it was Compact ships that jumped into the space around Deepspace Three.

"Admiral Andersson?"

"Yes, Admiral Halvorssen?"

"What's taking them so long? We're waiting far too long for the enemy to come in."

"If it is Compact, they do not have Praetorian ships," said Andersson. "They will have been significantly delayed at Deepspace Eight. It has given us the time to get Admiral Grant's Seventh Fleet assembled and into position. Be patient."

"Admiral Andersson, Deepspace Three reports incoming stargate request, jump translation in progress. And it's large!"

"See?" said Admiral Andersson calmly. "All things come to those who wait."

"The enemy translation is going wrong, Admiral, we have a partial misjump in progress ...... they overloaded the stargate, the idiots!"

Horatio Grant, once Feldmarshall of the Erdogan Armed Forces and now commanding Admiral of the Seventh Fleet of the Vindicatus nation, watched in horror as his scanners officers reported of the impending mis-jump.

Even though it was likely to be Zhou-Zheng Compact warships, and the Compact had persecuted his own people, he was not so blind with rage and jealousy that he hated all of them. Some of them were decent human beings, some of them deserved to live, and to die as part of a massive mis-jump was not a nice way to go.

They were coming through the stargate, using a connection from the stargate at Deepspace Eight. The pathway from one stargate to the other had been overloaded, probably because the Compact had placed too many ships into the jump envelope, destabilising the particles that ripped realspace open into hyper-space. The pathway was destabilising as it neared the terminus, which was Deepspace Three, and when it burst back into realspace it would mis-jump completely, the opening into realspace failing.

To overload a stargate meant a vast number of ships. A stargate could transfer whole fleets in safety. They must have been desperate, trying to get to Dark Heart too quickly.

The scale of the impending disaster would depend on just how destabilised the jump had become, and how many ships were going to be involved in the misjump. Only a few could be affected, or it could be many, many more.

Grant had ordered all his House-design warships back to a safe distance, keeping them in running silent mode. They would remain hidden until the disaster was over. He had wanted to rescue the people aboard the Deepspace Station, who could be caught in the blast radius if it was strong enough, but there was no time to do it. Also, it might not be necessary, it all depended on the size and strength of the mis-jump.

They took interstellar travel so much for granted, and accidents were so rare, it was shocking when you knew you were about to witness something like this.

"Translation in three seconds, Admiral," his scanners officer said quietly.

The scene was of the deepspace station, hanging in the void of the Gulf of Medusa, in deep space with nothing around it. There were no ships visible, all running on silent, and all the defences were chameleonically fielded. It was just the space station, and deep, black darkness of the void.

The flash of light was phenomenally big, blinding even to shielded sensors. It was large because it heralded the arrival of four big fleets of ships, but then it flashed even wider, brighter and violently as the terminus point of the jump collapsed and the mis-firing of the jump began.

It was instantaneous, the hyper-space folding out incorrectly into realspace, physical objects trying to materialise into exactly the same part of reality as one another. The white light burnt red, orange, blacks and purples as the fires ignited and reality exploded violently.

Then the white light vanished, and all that was left was the detritus of the survivors and the awful wreckage of the carnage behind.

Light-years away, Admiral Andersson actually opened his mouth in shock as he looked at the pictures and tactical data being relayed from the Seventh Fleet warships. It had taken a while to establish a live hyper-pulse feed, as they had to wait for Admiral Grant to launch his counter-attack and for their own HPCG station in Dark Heart to make the connection.

Deepspace Station Three had been mostly destroyed, caught in the conflagration of the mis-jump. There was not much left to transmit hyper-pulse signals.

The mis-jump had taken out much of the defences around the station as well, although enough gun platforms and batteries remained to open fire on the dazed, malfunctioning and disordered Compact ships, or individual mines were still being activated and exploding. It was hard to judge, but Andersson's tacticians began to tell him that it looked like four fleets had jumped in simultaneously through the stargate, and that was what had caused the mis-jump.

Some of the ships were fused together, melded in impossible shapes and structures that belonged in some nightmarish horror story. Others had simply detonated, entire shipwide structural failure not even occurring, just never having been in this part of space. Some had suffered engine failure and exploded normally, others had ripped themselves apart in a multitude of different ways. Some had listed and collided with others. Others had been thrown into ships in front, behind, and to the side, crashing together.

There were still many that escaped unscathed, due to the sheer number that the Zhou-Zheng Compact had sent, but those were unshielded following the jump. Further, their human crews were in total shock over what had happened.

They were easy prey for the ships of Admiral Grant as they came in, zeroing in rapidly on the more dangerous targets. Torpedoes, laser fire, MACs and more began to pummel the void, and the burning blackness was strobed alight again.

"Prepare Sixth and Eighth Fleets for jump to those co-ordinates, fusion-tankers to be ready to follow once the warzone is secure," said Admiral Andersson. "We have a chance to end this quickly."

"Aye, sir, orders being given."

"And signal the enemy ships through the relay on Grant's dreadnought," said Andersson, "tell them I offer them the chance to unconditionally surrender, begin it on a constant relay."

Da Wei Sao Su Ani stood to attention as the Zhong Xiao got to his feet, itself in response to the turbolift doors opening.

"All hands, salute," Zhong Xiao Chien ordered, and they saluted.

The figures stomping through the turbolift doors were as immense as they were terrifying. They wore Praetorian Guard Marine armour, and they were imposing within it. Their weaponry was armed, rotary cannons cycling and chemo-flamers burning, laser-scopes and sensors scanning the room as they entered.

A figure began to detach from the rest, marching up to the Zhong Xiao.

Some of the Compact warships were still trying to fight on, but the Yi Ji Shang Jiang - who had amazingly survived the catastrophe - had finally given the order to surrender once the enemy fleet had appeared. They may have been using ordinary House ships, but they were fresh and the Compact ships that survived the jump were too damaged or unable to power up in time for defence. Some Zhong Xiao's had defied the orders and were fighting on, but most ships had surrendered in line with the Yi Ji's orders.

No less than twenty-one warships had surrendered to the enemy, which greatly outnumbered them, and were fresh and ready to fight.

The Marine stood in front of Chien, and said through a loudspeaker on his Y-visored helmet, "Captain, do you surrender formally in person to the Lord Gavain, and the Vindicatus nation?"

"We do," Zhong Xiao Chien bowed his head sharply, including at the waist, to show utmost humiliation and defeat.

Da Wei Sao felt relief. Her double-life as a spy was finally over.

Chapter XIX

Lord James Gavain stood in one of the observation lounges on the *Vindicator,* a respectful circle around him. It was a designated rest and relaxation area for the crew, but he noted that with his presence the entire area seemed a bit muted. He resolved to have another ten minutes or so as respite, before he headed back to the operations room where he was helping Ulrik Andryukin in conducting the Operation Freedom.

After a couple of more minutes staring peacefully at the stars, he was aware of someone encroaching on the bubble around him. His eyes flicked onto the man's faded reflection in the metaglass window, and recognised him.

"Jamie," the voice said as he drew level.

"Yes, Ulrik?" James responded.

"It's unusual for you to take time away from the war-room?"

"The crew need to see me," said Lord Gavain distantly, then relented and added, "and I needed the break. We are nearing the end of Operation Jacknife, I could afford the time away."

"Be careful not to do too much, you're using your full combat waking cycle, I have heard," said Ulrik. A Praetorian cyborg could use performance enhancing drugs and their inbuilt cybernetic implants to push themselves far beyond their normal sleep patterns - which in any case were vastly reduced on an unaugmented human beings sleep requirements - to stay awake, sharp and operational for nearly a full week at a time. It was dangerous to keep up continuously, however.

"There is so much to do," said Jamie distantly, again. "So much to be aware of."

"Yes," said Ulrik quietly, "and the decisions weigh heavy on you."

They were both silent then for a while, before James Gavain said, "I did not give the order to launch the Tears of the Moon easily. History will judge me harshly."

"You viewed it as necessary," was Ulrik's only comment. "And certainly, what we have seen in our land campaigns proves it. Their armies are too strong, these hybrid troops are stuff of nightmares. The populace turns against us where we have been able to liberate the planet, and where we cut the consciousness link, it's not like House Marchenko where they panicked - the converted population shut down and begin to die even as they go insane. There is great evil in this Third Empire."

"An evil I have matched with the mass use of the Tears of the Moon," commented Gavain.

There was another pause. "At least it weighs on your mind, Jamie," said Ulrik, "If it hadn't, I would be branding you the threat to the galaxy, and kill you myself."

Gavain looked at Ulrik then. "Thanks, friend."

"You're welcome," Ulrik laughed gently, but the man had meant it. "History will judge you badly, and you could sit on either side of it and say that perhaps it was wrong to use the weapons, perhaps it was right. Moral questions are not for us, we are soldiers."

"You are, I'm not," said Gavain, "I'm a soldier who is also now a responsible politician, and I made a soldier's choice."

"Let us not dwell on it," said Andryukhin.

"To the war-room," said Lord Gavain, turning and leading the way.

As they walked, leaving the observation room and entering the corridor outside, they switched to the datasphere as they could have the conversation without being overheard. In the corridors, too many people were close enough to hear.

<Have you seen the reports from Harley on the Zhou-Zheng Compact invasion?> asked Andryukhin.

<Yes,> said Gavain.

<What is your response going to be?>

<The Compact have declared war on us without the declaration,> said Gavain, <I'm authorising punishing strikes back in retaliation, at the same time assisting the Erdogan resistance. Their losses were so heavy, it severely affects the Compact military. I'm asking Harley to approach the Primarch and Primarchess directly, and demand reparations or we will invade their territory. It is an empty threat, we can do no such thing whilst we are engaged in the Coalition of Resistance operations here in Helvanna. I will use this as a chance to boost our treasury.>

<The Houses of Zhou and Zheng do not know it is an empty threat,> replied Andryukhin. <Most of our own people will not know that, it would be in your character to respond heavily.>

<No, they can't know that it is an empty threat, although they may suspect. After all, they thought we were distracted here in Helvanna, and they discovered we weren't. They have lost four fleets to their stupidity, thousands and thousands of trained military staff captured, another twenty-one starships salvaged and being repaired for us to use ..... whoever suggested this in their government will be losing his head. Their losses weaken them drastically.>

<It was such a stupid thing to do - why put all those starships through the stargate at the same time?> said Andryukhin.

<Their leadership panicked, their plan had not survived the first phase and overrun in terms of time, they had met heavier resistance than expected,> said Gavain. <Even without the misjump, we would have

surprised them, retreated to Dark Heart, and crushed them with our surprise defences there. They would have failed in the invasion attempt anyway, but our own losses would have been drastically higher. As it is, we've gained militarily.>

<The Erdogans are overjoyed,> said Andryukhin. <The ex-Erdogan populace are celebrating in the streets in Dark Heart, Praetor and Bright Hope, apparently.>

<Good,> nodded Gavain, <we need some ->

He broke off, as a priority communications signal had come through. <Gavain, yes?>

<Lord Gavain, we have a pulse-channel comms request coming in from Jacques Devereux, Archon of Amiens, coded for your eyes only.>

<I'll take it in the war-room, I'm on my way,> said Lord Gavain quickly.

He told Andryukhin.

<This is not going to be good,> said Ulrik, <I can feel it.>

<I agree,> said Gavain, darkly.

Lord Gavain entered the war-room, the rush of data flooding over him as he jacked fully into the battlenet. Field Marshal Andryukhin joined fully, and in some respects they were as one, linked together. As he proceeded to his control seat, he quickly reviewed the progress of Operation Freedom.

Operation Jacknife had concluded with victory in all theatres, although at some cost, particularly to the Amiens contingent who had suffered badly against the Third Imperium. That was partly why Gavain dreaded this upcoming conversation with the Archon of Amiens.

The Jacknife Defence Line was now established, with the predominately StarCom Federation-led support forces leading the vast logistical operation in manufacturing large quantities of gun platforms, missile batteries, mines, planetary guns and all other manner of surprises for the Third Imperium's answer to their challenge.

The multiple launching of the Tears of the Moon mass destructive weaponry had turned much of the northern Helvanna Province into a desolate wasteland of de-populated and ravaged solar systems. The media had finally got hold of it, and Gavain was facing a severe backlash in popularity, even in his own Vindicatus nation. The influx of refugees had stemmed considerably, as people galaxy-wide thought again about the Mercenary Lord.

But the destruction of so many colonised systems and the murder of billions of indoctrinated people had worked, completely breaking the back of the Third Imperium's presence here in the Eastern Segment. There had been numerous skirmishes amongst scouting parties and on the picket line that was the Jacknife Defence Line, with Third Imperial forces invariably coming off worse. They had not been able to mount an assault with their land forces, especially using indoctrinated civilian puppets as cannon fodder, and as Operation Freedom had unfortunately shown the Shadows were all too strong in that regard.

Operation Freedom was not going at all to plan. The planets within the fifteen systems within the Jacknife Defence Line had to be taken intact, for the purposes of helping to build the defence, and it had turned into a meat grinder for all the nations of the Coalition. Conventional Third Imperium military, if such a word could apply to the hybrid monsters they used, had all but been broken, but the people now fought against the Coalition armies where they had not been able to sever the links to their Shadow node-masters.

Where the links had been severed, the people were dying, not eating or looking after themselves, unable to function independently. No amount of medical intervention could undo the enforced slavery. Where the links had not been severed, the populace fought sometimes without weaponry, and it was a demoralising slaughter, with the occasional successful single or mass martyrdom attack.

Within the Jacknife Defence Line they had no option but to fight on the ground. Elsewhere in the galactic southern areas of 'conquered' Helvanna Province space, they did have an option. If they could not take a planet, they could withdraw, and blow it out of existence with the Tears of the Moon or with widespread orbital bombardments. Unfortunately that was happening more often than not - in space they were a match for the Third Imperium, on land due to the hybrids and the converted populace, they were not.

There were some success stories, planets that had been liberated of Imperial military governance without completely ruining them, but even there it was heartbreaking. The people, severed from their link to the Shadows, were dying.

Operation Freedom would be complete in another two to three weeks if projections were accurate, and then they would simply await a major Third Imperium reprisal whilst they fortified the Jacknife Defence Line up to the last minute. That reprisal would signify the start of Operation Diamondcut, the final attempt to stand up to the might of the Third Empire and the Shadow Emperor, a might they had yet to fully taste.

It terrified Lord Gavain at a deep level that they had not even seen the worst of the Third Empire's might and capabilities yet.

He sat in the control seat, and signalled the communications officer on the bridge, <Connect the pulse-channel,> he ordered.

Before him, an image of the Archon Jacques Devereux appeared.

"Lord Gavain," said the Archon Jacques Devereux. He was stoic and cold in most of his contacts and his public persona, and this was no exception.

"Archon Devereux, this is unexpected?" said Lord Gavain, cutting through any pleasantries.

"It is, for you," nodded Archon Devereux. "I will be brief. I am giving you one hour's notice of the nation of Amiens' intention to withdraw from the Coalition of Resistance, and vacate the Jacknife Defence Line and the entire Helvanna Province area of space."

Lord Gavain had suspected as much. Gavain was a straightforward person, as was Jacques Devereux, so the politicking and fake pleasantry he increasingly frequently found himself using was not needed here. "Archon, this puts us in a very difficult position. Why?" He suspected he already knew the answer, however.

"A number of reasons, Mercenary Lord," said the Archon, his tone dripping with derision at the title. "During Operation Jacknife, Amiens forces were suffering badly in the Fleurier System. Third Imperium defences and military presence was far heavier and higher than intelligence pre-estimates ever suggested. We requested assistance urgently, and you delayed. We lost significant assets before those reinforcements arrived. Some amongst my own advisors suggest this was deliberate."

"That is ludicrous," said Gavain, evenly. "The delay was for sound strategic reason, I had to ensure the situation in all theatres was known before committing reserves. Also, we do not want to reveal our full strength before Operation Diamondcut."

"The delay cost my military severely," said the Archon. "Many amongst my own think you have an arrangement with our enemy, the Republic of Varrental, who did not suffer nearly so badly."

"Do not bring your local political problems –"

"I must, for they have bearing," said the Archon.

"Are these advisors working with the Shadows?" asked Gavain, changing tack. "We know Amiens was heavily penetrated by the Shadow Emperor's spies and agencies, we know there will be more. Do you trust this advice?"

"We have acted on your information, and cut the Shadow Emperor's people out of my government and agencies where we could find them," said the Archon. "For that, I am thankful, Lord Gavain. But my advisors, some of whom I trust more than my family, have a point with how Operation Jacknife played against our interests."

"Do you believe I deliberately sacrificed Amiens personnel and forces?" asked Gavain.

There was a pause. "I will level and be honest," said the Archon. "No, I do not. But I also have my own political considerations, and the basic fact that our losses were so heavy, whatever survives this confrontation with the Third Imperium may not be enough to face the Republic of Varrental if hostilities between us resume again. We must withdraw before our losses become so high we cannot recover."

"You swore an oath to commit those forces to the end," said Lord Gavain.

"I am breaking it, Lord Gavain."

Gavain did not know what to say for a moment. "You put me in a difficult position," he said quietly, "I will have to re-arrange our defensive line to account for your missing forces. You do appreciate you jeopardise the defence against the Shadows here? Your name will forever be known as untrustworthy?"

"I will not be the only one to come out of this with a tarnished reputation, Gavain," said the Archon. "Yours is not surviving intact either, I think. The use of the Tears of the Moon on such a large scale is unprecedented. Your name will lie alongside the False Emperor's, and the True Emperor's, and many others for that. My own populace rail against it, public opinion has turned, as does your own I suspect. We only knew of what you planned when you revealed it to us after joining the Coalition, I have gone through with it, but I cannot in good conscience continue with it."

"You object now?"

"I do," said the Archon. "My soul cannot live with being a part of what you have done, Lord Gavain. You may see it as necessary, and so do I to an extent, but it is just as wrong. There must have been another way, although I do not know what it was. I was weak, I did not object strongly enough, and neither did the others. I must live with that. To fight evil with evil is never right."

"I -"

"No, Lord Gavain. This conversation is over. You have one hour from this very second until my ships begin to jump. Use it to plug the hole we will leave in your defence line. Au revoir."

The communication ended.

Gavain thought quickly. He would have to speak to the Republic of Varrental, as they might also want to withdraw if the Amiens fleets headed back to their territory. He would have to speak to all the Coalition members, prevent the fall-out from becoming worse. He would also have to move ships around, commit reserves he did not really want to commit. StarCom Federation was the most likely choice, as he did not want Levitican Union involvement to be revealed yet to the spies of the Shadow Emperor.

The Archon had painted a picture of moral objection, but it was equally as likely weakening over suffering heavy losses and wanting to preserve his military for future aggressions against the Republic of Varrental.

He was mortified to think later that he had only considered the Archon's moral objection as a possible truth, hours after the Amiens ships had jumped.

*

Admiral Silus Adare strode from the bridge of the *Zero Tolerance* juggernaut, leaving it in the command of Zehra Sahin. His nature was not one to worry about the current situation he found himself in, or to worry much about anything, but even he could feel the pressure at the moment. The Helvanna Province was virtually destroyed, and as the theatre commander the messages coming from the Shadow Emperor were not encouraging for him.

It was in his nature to look after himself, at the expense of all others. Zehra Sahin and Iyan Lamans were only at his side due to their continued usefulness and the fact that he personally needed their support from time to time. If it was ever in his interests to abandon them, he would without a thought.

He took a water from the moleculiser, and sat down at his desk in the ready room. He accessed on the datasphere, reading the latest bulletins and messages from the Helvanna Province and the wider Third Empire.

'Lord' Gavain's defence line was ingeniously placed. It took out some of what had been the strongest military systems in the Helvanna Province, but because of the distribution of stars also created an impassable barrier. His ships had also struck north of the defence line, eliminating stargates, so now the only way for the Shadow Emperor's forces to continue along their journey through the Eastern Segment to Mars was through one or more of the systems Gavain had taken. It was ingenious.

It was also inflammatory to the Shadow Emperor. He had demanded that the line be broken, but had finally relented as it was pointed out to him that there just was not enough resource in the Helvanna area to achieve the objective. The enemy were too strong, even for Third Imperium technology and resources.

There had been numerous engagements since the counter-invasion, but military actions for the moment were reduced to information gathering and harassment of the so-called Coalition. The destruction of much of the galactic north of Helvanna had severely hampered the resources for the military ships that had survived the onslaught of the Coalition.

Tribune Helvanna was not helping matters. She was expending her House military ships with stupidity, in an attempt to curry favour with the Shadow Emperor. It worked, but at terrible cost to her own people.

Adare could see that the approach of the spearhead of the main Shadow army and navy had increased. The Benedict Democracy was shattered, virtually eaten whole with the accelerated approach of the Shadow Emperor. The Calamarite Confederacy had ceased fighting virtually, realising after their initial losses that they were being ignored as the Shadow Emperor continued on towards Mars.

Even with the acceleration, it would take another four realtime weeks before the Shadow Emperor's front line hit the small enclave of Helvanna territory that remained intact. Then it would only be half a week on to the defence line, although Adare knew that the plan was not to advance further. The Railway would be brought up to this northern enclave of surviving territory, and then it would change the game. The Shadow Emperor would smash through the defence line the Coalition had created.

But Adare wondered at that.

Gavain was resourceful, and clever. He had demonstrated that with his galaxy changing gambit ripping the Helvanna Province apart. Their immaterialisation fields would not work, although there would not be enough interdictorships in the galaxy to protect against what was coming. Their viruses could not affect Coalition ships, although neither did they appear able to break through Shadow firewalls. There was no answer to the hybrids, as yet revealed.

Adare did not trust it. Gavain always thought ten steps ahead, and he would have more surprises in store. Personally, he knew who he thought was going to win this, even though the odds were stacked against Gavain, if only he knew it.

There was one order from the Shadow Emperor Adare knew he could complete easily; he was to attempt to bait Gavain, and draw him out. Adare doubted it would work, despite their history, but it also gave him an opportunity.

Adare accessed his personal data-store, and began to record a message.

<This is Admiral Silus Adare, Lord Gavain,> he smiled, stroking the black goatee beard gently, before removing his hand and clasping the half-empty glass of water. <My, my, what a mess of the galaxy you are making.

<I find it ironic that I was being tried for war crimes, particularly the one of using the Tears of the Moon and the destruction of Alwathbah. I look at what you have done, and do you know what? Suddenly I think that although you and I are different - you are more of a monster than I could ever be. War criminal? You think because you have the blessing of a small group of Eastern Segment and Core nations that you will be judged favourably by history? Being part of a large coalition does not make the

atrocity any less of an atrocity; the action you have taken will be judged as wrong by history, however right you think it was.

<Now, with the pleasantries out of the way and my point made, this is not the social call it has been so far. The Shadow Emperor has directed me to contact you. He urges you to surrender now, to pull the defence line apart and join him. He knows it unlikely, which is why he also wants me to challenge you.

<The Helvanna Province is now reduced to just eight systems in the galactic north. We have reinforced these, and we await you Gavain. We are withdrawing to this fortress area, and we challenge you to step beyond your defence line and come to us. The Shadow Emperor approaches, and when he arrives, you will die. He will strike rapidly through the northern wasteland you have created through your heresy, and rip your defence line apart. You know as well as I, it will be spring boarded from these eight systems. This is your only chance, Jamie my boy. Come and get me.>

Adare ceased recording. The aim was to try and tempt James Gavain into a strike against the eight northern systems that were untouched by the Tears of the Moon. It would not work, he knew, unless Gavain had already planned to do that. Gavain was not one to be tempted into stupid or foolhardy actions.

He did not forward the message to the communications officer for transmission however. Instead, he used his neural connection through the modem to delve deeper into his secret, reinforced section within the data-store. It was heavily passcoded and disguised, a little chamber of data that only he knew existed.

He began to record another message. Once done, he spliced it very carefully and cleverly into the original message to Gavain. With that done, he forwarded it to the communications officer, and ordered it to be transmitted.

Then he sat back, and smiled again. He wondered if it would work, or not.

*

The Stanchion System was small, a single-star system with an average sun. It had once belong to a small and minor noble House, swallowed months ago by the Third Imperium. Out in the Boundary, it was deep within conquered Third Imperium territory. It had a small population, and was distant from the local borders that were being policed by the ever-more thinning invasion force of the Third Empire.

The only thing which made the Stanchion System remarkable at all was the giant construction which had been fabricated and manuprinted, birthed by constructoships within a matter of days, shortly after the Shadows had arrived.

It was all peaceful within the system. Seven House warships, now fully converted to Third Empire loyalty, patrolled around the system. They stayed close to the construction, whatever it was, focusing on that rather than the designated jump points. It was obvious what they were there to protect.

Of far greater threat were the two upgraded S-class strikecruisers, in their Third Imperial livery. Fast but decently armoured, they could respond quickly to any threat. No threat was imagined or detected, but the fledgling Empire was taking no chances with its most important facet of the galactic invasion plan. The strikecruisers circled almost opposite each other around the gigantic construction, astronomically at a far distance but with advanced main drive engines mere minutes away in terms of response time.

There was no shipping allowed in or out of the system. It was on complete lockdown even now. Normally the lockdown was lifted after the system had been pacified, unless they were on the borders of the conquered territory, but not this one. It held one of the constructions, so nothing was allowed in or out.

All of a sudden, the peace was shattered as apparently empty space lit up with the firing of numerous strikepods. Simultaneously torpedoes streaked away, followed by turbolaser fire, slamming heavily into the construction at the same time as the strikepods hit. They bit into the hull, biting through it deeply and quickly, and then disgorged their contents.

Captain Alicia Alansen emerged out of the strikepod, the augmetics and her power armour quickly scanning the surrounding corridor they had dropped into from the attack vehicle.

She had two hundred and ten biomorphic Marines landed on the construction. The corvettes had approached as close as they dared, undetected with their slimmer profiles, and then launched all their marines. The frigates would hold in reserve, both to deflect incoming Imperial starships, and to launch a second wave of Marines when they knew the layout of the construction and had a better idea of targets.

<People, remember the objectives,> said Alansen, <get into the mainframe, download, and extract. We are not here to conquer the construction. We have only minutes. Get to it. Alansen out.>

Commander Lancaster aboard the frigate *Odyssey* felt the fear grab hold of her heart as her scanners officer reported that the strikecruisers were reacting. The House ships were also closing in, but the first strikecruiser would be in firing range within one minute ten seconds, the second in two minutes as it was on the far side of their attack.

Running silent she had no way to communicate with the other frigates. They would only reveal their position if Alansen called for reinforcements on the construction, or when the *Odyssey* fired.

<Paint the strikecruiser identified as Red One,> Commander Lancaster ordered as calmly as she could, <When it reaches this point -> she identified a place on the tactical map <-my order is to open fire.>

<We've hacked into the upper level of the datasphere,> one of Captain Alansen's lieutenants was reporting. <We have a layout of the station, transmitting to all units now.>

Alansen reviewed the data as her squad progressed quickly through the corridor. They were running blind, not knowing where they were going, searching for enemy to kill whilst they obtained the information she had finally received from her Lieutenant.

<Good work,> she said, looking at the layout of the station. Her initial reaction was that the station, for that was what it was, was constructed in a very alien-like way. These Third Imperials were something else altogether.

She handed out orders quickly, directing squads towards weaponry systems, a heavy contingent to the data-core, what looked like an engine room, and another towards the command centre. Her squad was closest to the engine room, about forty seconds away. It was quickest to burn through the decks beneath their feet, so they used a thermo-bomb.

It was placed and set within a second by her Corporal, and the squad moved back. It was on a remote detonation, and just as Alansen pressed the trigger, an enemy Marine squad appeared at the far end of the corridor and began to fire upon them. She lost two people in that initial fusillade, even as the thermo-bomb detonated with an explosive flash of fire.

The thermo-bomb glowed red hot, leaving a massive hole in the corridor deck plating, but it continued on downwards, burning through deck after deck.

Firing her rotary cannon, Alansen led the charge forwards, the enemy Marines moving out of the way of her squad's heavy weaponry fire into cover. The diversion was enough, and as she dropped down into the hole the thermo-bomb had left, she threw a hand clutching two grenades towards the far end of the corridor. All her surviving squad members did likewise, and they heard the detonations as they crashed into touch several decks below.

They had another two decks to go, and then they would be in the engine room. Another thermo-bomb was set for the final drop through the station.

The strikecruiser speeding towards the construction began to fire, joining its heavy weaponry batteries to that of the construction. One of the corvettes named the *Armoured*, still chameleonically fielded, had been found and was being torn apart. The strikecruiser launched a torpedo, and in seconds the corvette was blowing apart, even as they searched for the others which had scattered after launching their strikepods.

All of a sudden the shielded strikecruiser came under fire, as a frigate suddenly appeared in the depths of space to its starboard. Moments later, another began to fire from above, and another to lower starboard.

Torpedoes crashed against shields, turbolaser and Magnetic Acceleration Cannons fired. The strikecruiser reacted quickly, turning towards the greater threat it identified as the *Odyssey,* but already shields were beginning to weaken.

<Lancaster to Alansen, we have gone live,> Alansen heard as the battlenet went up, <We can launch strikepods in support.>

<Launch to these positions, Commander,> Alansen replied, <We are facing heavy resistance, upgraded Praetorian units only, and no hybrids as yet.> Alansen winced as she read the reports. One of the corvettes had already been, and the three frigates had engaged the first strikecruiser. The second was just cresting the station, and would be joining the fight in mere seconds. Navally they were outmatched.

<We need to be going in two minutes, Captain,> said Commander Lancaster. <We're launching landers for extraction now.> It was highly dangerous, the landers could be targeted easily by the strikecruisers. This mission was extremely hot.

<We're through, Cap,> her Corporal said.

<Engage!> ordered Alansen.

She followed her squad through into the engine room. She did not stop to wonder at its size, as they were already coming under fire, but it was fantastically large. The main power generator, with its secondary and tertiary slaves, were great constructions hanging by support struts in long tubular ring-like decks, scaffolded around their beating hearts. Numerous workstations lay at each level of the decking. The cavernous room extended for a long distance, workers scattering as Marines charged down towards their intrusion. The power generators throbbed out of time, leading to a continuous hum that ebbed and flowed, like music.

<There's too many, Captain!> her Corporal said.

<We have four more squads inbound within five seconds,> she said, <And strikepod reinforcements landing in two - squad, *hold*!>

<Red One's forward shields failing,> came the report. <Strikecruiser turning away to present port.>

<*Brilliance*, present starboard and full broadside on Red One,> Commander Lancaster ordered, with a snap. <*Obliterate*, forward-back manoeuvre, take out their forward batteries. Corvettes to harass, ignore Red Two.>

<Corvette *Avaricious* destroyed, no survivors,> came the report. <Instant destruction.>

Lancaster was beginning to lose what little faith she had in this mission. They had shut down some of the weapons batteries on the construction, but they had to stay close so they were taking heavy damage. The strikecruisers were ripping holes through her squadron, the *Odyssey* was dangerously close to losing its own shields on three planes of approach.

She had always felt this mission was doomed to failure.

<Alansen,> Lancaster roared, <Hurry!>

Captain Alansen ignored Lancaster, engaging her shoulder-mounted missile launcher and targeting a main trunk coupling on the secondary power generator, which was closest to their position. She fired a spread of high explosive warheads, the missiles streaking into the coupling. The coupling shattered, and whilst undoubtedly several decks or more would have just lost power, its immediate effect was to douse the enemy Marines near it with lethal bursts of raw, unrestrained charge.

They literally fried within their armour, melting into grotesque blobs and stains. Entire parts of the engine room began to shut down, several of the workstations losing power as they overloaded. Lightning crackled everywhere, until emergency shields kicked in and contained the catastrophic breach.

<We're in, Captain,> said her Corporal, <We're in.>

<Well done!> said Alansen. They were in one of the workstation decks, and her tech specialist had a physical jack into the mainframe port they had formed up around. <All units, we've breached the mainframe. Downloading and transmitting to the *Odyssey* now.>

<We have an incoming transmission, they've breached the mainframe,> said her data-tac officer.

<Finally!> said Lancaster. <Back-up transmissions to all the other squadron ships. Once download is complete and Marines are extracted, we scatter and withdraw, jumping at will. Corvettes to go without Marine extraction, frigates are to wait. Order is given.>

<Lancaster,> Alansen came through on a private channel, <I've ordered all other units to withdraw now, we're going to hold this breach in the engine room. If you have to leave us, then do so.>

<I'm not going without you, Alansen,> said Lancaster, <Just hurry. How long until download completion?>

<Forty seconds.>

Lancaster looked at the situation. It was not good. In forty seconds a lot could happen in naval engagements.

<Corvette *Armageddon* destroyed, no survivors,> came the report.

The strikecruiser identified as Red One was taking heavy fire on its unshielded bow, and with a catastrophic explosion, two nuclear-tipped torpedoes completely removed the forward bulkheads. The destruction actually rocked the ship, and had a chain reaction that overfed its shields, leading to more failures. The strikecruiser became naked, defenceless in terms of protection.

The frigates did not zero in, instead drawing closer towards the station. It confused the strikecruiser captains, who thought that they would automatically target the deshielded cruiser. They continued to batter all three frigates, which were hopelessly outmatched, beginning to exact heavy damage. The *Brilliance* and the *Odyssey* had already suffered major hull breaches, and were only a couple of minutes away from serious, irreparable damage.

<Download complete!> said the tech specialist.

<All units, mission accomplished!> roared Alansen, grinning inside her helmet like a madman. <Extract, extract, extract!>

The strikecruisers suddenly and unexpectedly switched targets. They ceased firing on the four surviving corvettes, which had suddenly disengaged and were speeding away, and even on the frigates. They were instead concentrating on the lander shuttles, which were pulling the biomorphic marines away from the construction.

The landers moved fast, but began to be ripped apart under the fusillade of fire.

<All surviving landers aboard,> came the report.

<Corvettes jumping.> With the corvettes gone, the mission had been accomplished, and the data from the mainframe had been taken.

<All frigates,> said Lancaster, <Disengage and jump out of the system.>

The frigates were scattering, and the strikecruisers were chasing. Although the frigates were faster, they would still be in range for long enough. The exit from the system of the corvettes had told the strikecruiser captains what the mission taskforce were about to do, and they were determined to prevent the frigates from escaping.

The *Obliterate* jumped, taking heavy fire even as it vanished in a flash of white light after the corvettes. The *Brilliance* began to jump, but a spread of torpedoes rocketed into its already-damaged rear engines, and the superstructure of the ship began to break apart even as it jumped. Its destruction was not confirmed, but large junks of hull did not disappear.

Lancaster swallowed, the image of a ship blowing apart as it jumped sure to live with her. Alansen was aboard the *Odyssey*, and the Marine losses had been heavy. Few landers had made it away from the station.

<Jumping,> said her navigations officer.

<We're safe,> said her second-in-command, relief flooding the voice. <Hyper-space achieved.>

Some hours later, Commander Lancaster ate the energy snack with relish as she reviewed the data. They had made a very short jump, only an hour and a half of transit time, before entering a much longer jump to another system. They were not necessarily in the clear yet, but she had ordered her squadron to jump to completely different systems. There was no guarantee all her ships would escape Third Imperium territory, but at least one would make it through. That was all that was needed to get the information out.

Alansen sat opposite her, in the ready room, also finishing her energy ration. It was specially designed for her system, to replenish her biomorphic body after combat. The version Lancaster ate was designed for her augmetics, and to counter the post-combat drug effects.

"Over four hundred of the four hundred and eighty five Marines lost," said Lancaster, "and hundreds more naval crew deaths, not to mention the wounded. I've lost four corvettes and a frigate, too. Lord Gavain will not be impressed."

The *Brilliance*, or part of it, had arrived at the immediate withdrawal jump point. It had exited hyper-space, breaking up as it translated. The *Obliterate's* captain, whose ship had been present, had sent Lancaster the visual recording of it. It broke the heart to watch.

"Lord Gavain will be impressed," said Alansen. "It was an impossible mission, and although our losses were heavy, we succeeded."

"We just have to get the data to him, now," said Lancaster. "If all goes to plan, one of our ships should be transmitting it within three real-time days."

"And what data," laughed Captain Alansen.

The data they had downloaded from the mainframe was unbelievable. Lancaster had reviewed it with growing disbelief. It was explosive in terms of import.

The constructions were part of the Railway. The Third Imperium or the Shadows, whatever you wanted to call them, had named the stations

Starterminals. The starterminals were the next generation in terms of stargate technology, and their function was never-seen before.

A starterminal operated like a stargate, in that it opened up realspace to allow starships to enter hyperspace and cross massive interstellar distances. However, where a stargate 'jumped' starships, only able to throw them a limited distance before they had to exit into realspace, starterminals operated differently. Providing they were all aligned and activated, a starship never had to exit hyperspace. They would merely continuously pass from starterminal to starterminal, crossing untold and unimaginable distances of space.

The Railway consisted of all these starterminals, being built in a line through conquered Imperial space towards Mars.

The overall plan was this. On reaching and breaching StarCom Federation territory, the Railway would be complete, with all the starterminals built. By this point, the Third Imperium army and navy, which had led the invasion, would be war-weary and exhausted at having crossed through the Frontier, Boundary, and Mid-Sectors to hit the Core. This was when the second wave of fresh and undamaged Third Imperial ships, which waited beyond the Frontier, would be thrown down the Railway to hammer through StarCom Federation forces and take Mars, literally rolling through the Core sector of space and over the Sol System.

Ordinarily to throw such a large number of ships through stargates would take the best part of three to five weeks in real-time. Even with stargates all correctly aligned, which they were not, ships had to exit each stargate jump, have several real-time minutes to readjust, and for the stargates to jump them again. Every so often the ships would have to exit the continuous jumping cycle and be checked for stress and damage, or there was the risk of hull failure.

With the starterminals, a gigantic corridor was opened throughout all of space, from one side of the colonised galaxy to the next. The vast fleets could simply transfer in the space of a couple of real-time minutes. Logistically, it was terrifying but also fantastic in terms of how it changed future naval warfare.

"The starterminals are amazing," said Commander Lancaster, "and that the Railway is the codename for this project to transmit the fleets onto the StarCom Federation doorstep ..... well, no-one had guessed or modelled it in the intelligence sims."

"This is dynamite," said Alansen. "We have exact numbers, designations, specifications, even personnel histories for the commanders of all of the Third Imperial fleets and their individual ships. That's those ships currently engaged in the phase to conquer towards the Core, and those that are waiting to jump down the Railway."

"Even better, we have the Shadow Emperor's orders that this second wave will be launched once the Railway reaches the Helvanna Province, to batter at the Coalition," said Lancaster. She laughed. "We didn't even know that Lord Gavain had taken Helvanna with the Coalition, we've been out of contact so long!"

"It was good to read," said Alansen, smiling widely. "We're fighting back. But the odds are heavy, we know that now we can see the numbers on the enemy."

"Yeah," agreed Lancaster, "and we know how the Third Imperium is structured. With eight 'Circles', each led by a Legate, with different functions. We had heard rumours of a Shadow Council being in charge of the Faceless even in the days of the Red Imperium of Mars, but we never suspected how big, large, or what its true function was. It is mind-blowing, some of this stuff."

"It is. But even better," said Alansen, "we now know where the enemy home planet is."

That had been one of the even more explosive revelations. The Railway led back deep into the Shadow Province, the name of the territory the Shadows had held in secret before even revealing their existence. Beyond the Frontier, in a quintuple-star system named the Creation System, lay a planet named simply Shadow.

On Shadow, there was the Temple of Shadow or the Shadow Temple, the palace of the Shadow Emperor and his hiding place for decades.

"Overall," said Joanne Lancaster, grinning widely, "With this information, we've earnt our pay, I'd say. Let's get it to Lord Gavain, and go home, finally."

Chapter XX

<Lord Gavain, the Coalition of Resistance have all connected through. Pulse-channels are open.>

<I am coming,> said Lord Gavain. He removed himself from the part of the datasphere that was enabling him to command the Coalition military, but took a quick moment before launching into the conference.

He was in the operations room, in the control throne which had virtually become his home in the last couple of months. He reached forward a hand, grasping the cup of real coffee, and took a heavy draught. He released some of the stimulants into his system, to force himself into a greater level of wakefulness.

He had much on his mind, beyond the massive operation in the Helvanna Province and the Jacknife Defence Line. There had been some riots in his own territory, the news of which was being suppressed. Not all of his populace approved of his actions with the Tears of the Moon, and there was even some emigration taking place. His popularity galaxy-wide had taken a heavy hit, with opinion polls divided. Some supported his actions, and saw him as a saviour, others saw him as the devil incarnate and just as bad as the Shadow Emperor.

What he had done would live with him the rest of his life. He had rarely felt guilt, but he felt his soul was forever tarnished now. He still believed there had been little other option, but billions of deaths lay on his conscience.

Juan Ramirez was telling him that he was having nightmares in his sleep. In many ways, Juan was giving Gavain a level of emotional support he had never felt he would ever need. After this was over, he would see Doctor Erin Presson in private, and have a psychological evaluation. He had confided in this to Andryukhin, De Graaf, and O'Connor, even Lady Sophia, as well as Juan, and they all agreed.

Apparently, he kept speaking of Silus Adare in his sleep. It was true that the message from Adare had torn into his heart. The man had been hated by Gavain for what he did to Alwathbah, and yet the message Adare had sent had an element of horrible truth to it.

On a practical note, the second message hidden within Adare's primary missive had even greater implications for Gavain.

<Jacking in,> he said to the communications officer, and a nanosecond later the conference data washed over him. His physical eyes closed, in his mind he entered a virtual conference room, where all the other leaders and military commanders of the Coalition forces sat.

<Lords and Ladies, commanders,> said Gavain by way of greeting, <Well met, in the name of the Emperor.>

"Which one?" said Admiral Andersson, here to represent the Vindicatus nation.

"It is probably best not to ask," said Lady Principal Sophia, which elicited a small bout of laughter from some of them.

In the imaginary representation of a conference room, Gavain had allowed for there to be a gap of two seats. It hammered home the treachery of the Amiens nation in reneging on their promises, the hovering name placards for Jacques Devereux and Lord Admiral D'Souza damning.

Nothing would be said today of Amiens pulling out, or the reaction of the Republic of Varrental. They had almost done the same, but Gavain had been able to hold them in with a promise he was sure he would one day come to regret.

Equally, nothing would be said of the new members of the Coalition, who were also present. They were some of the minor Houses, who had small systems between the captured southern territories of Helvanna and the Levitican Union. The contentious members were those who had joined the Levitican Union; some members of the Coalition claimed that Gavain had used his position to increase his ally, the Levitican Unions, strength. It was true that the Levitican Union had benefitted with additional members and territory as a result of this, but as Gavain pointed out, it just brought their border closer to the Helvanna Province, which was hardly desirable.

"Members of the Coalition, this is likely to be our last formal meeting before the Shadow Emperor launches his second wave of fresh troops at us," said Lord Gavain. "We know he will send them down the Railway to the northern Helvanna Province systems that remain, although we do not know where or when they will hit us on the Jacknife Defence Line, just that they will jump from the stargates there onto our defensive barricades."

"The intelligence your Commander Lancaster and Captain Alansen obtained two weeks ago could be battle-turning," said First Lord Al-Zuhairi. "Lord Gavain, I would like to give them an honorary OutWorlds Alliance medal for bravery, the Order of the Sun. If you permit it?"

"Thank you," said Lord Gavain, "They deserve the recognition, I permit it."

"It is important," said Admiral Haas of the StarCom Federation. "For the first time, we know the size of the enemy, and where their base of operations is. Why we never found this Shadow Province before, I cannot guess. We did have exploratorships heading out beyond the Frontier, in the days of the Red Imperium of Mars and the False Emperor."

"But the exploratorships in that section of space disappeared without trace, or returned with nothing," said President Pereyra, "and the Exploration and Colonisation Corps did not send nearly enough in comparison to other beyond-Frontier missions, probably influenced by the Shadow Council's Sixth or Third Circles. Their penetration of the Red Imperium of Mars in the decades leading up to the False Emperor's demise can only be guessed at."

"That the Shadow Council turned out to be real, and so powerful and organised, is history changing," said Arch-Chancellor Lucija Korhonen. "We never guessed. How many here used the services of the Faceless, I wonder, never knowing we were helping the Shadow Council penetrate Red Imperium society. They shaped us towards this time. They prepared for the False Emperor. It makes a mockery of the intentions of the Revolutionary Council, the rebellion, and the Dissolution of the Red Imperium."

"Well, we can stop it," said Primus Katrina Van Hausenhof.

"For once, we agree, Primus," said Star Lord Carlos Cervantes.

"Have you seen these figures on the enemy strength?" said Grand Marshal Anaes Korhonen. "They still outnumber us, nearly five to one. We build our defences and have our plans, but will they be enough? The Third Imperium and the Shadow Emperor are still statistically more likely to win, in all my simulations."

"We have all seen the official simulations," Lord Gavain interrupted sternly, "but we cannot allow for the effect of our engineered viruses, or how the enemy will react to our new interdiction surprise. We have ships with their immaterialisation technology as well, though we will most likely not be able to use it. We have upgraded many of our Praetorian Marines with their new, next-generation armour, nearly eighty percent of our Marine forces carry the upgrades. It levels the fight when it comes to boarding actions. Failure and defeat is far from guaranteed."

"Just likely with the odds stacked against us," said Grand Marshal Korhonen.

"We cannot simulate accurately," said Chairman Bortan Ruci of the Calamarite Confederacy, "and for those aspects of the plan that lie away from the Defence Line, success is more likely. The Shadows can only transmit their second division of fleets down the starterminal corridor of the Railway in waves, or we would see the same disaster that befell the Zhou-Zheng Compact when they tried a mass jump. Once those waves begin to hit the Jacknife Defence Line, we might do them some severe damage. I for one, look forward to taking my part in this war."

"It is that part of Operation Diamondcut that makes the simulations so difficult," said First Lord Al-Zuhairi. "How the enemy attack determines how successful we will be. Whatever happens, my fellow Lords and Ladies, we will hurt them. We cannot defeat them, take away their conquered territory, but we can hurt them so badly they have to stop. And then, the future is ours to make."

"We have other surprises too," said Gavain hesitantly, about to add something but then deciding against it. "We have theatre plans for each system in the Defence Line, back-ups in case they try to double-jump and bypass the Line, reinforcements they cannot know about, and more. I will also receive warning minutes before they are due to attack."

"How?" asked Admiral Heinrich Haas.

"I cannot say, to do so may jeopardise my forces," Gavain lied. He was a man of honour, and to lie deliberately in such a way was not his way. It was one more indication of how far he was slipping, he thought.

"Well, there is one thing for certain," said Warlord Maximilian Van Hausenhof. "We cannot allow them to land on the planets in the Jacknife Defence Line. We might be just about able to face them navally, and but in terms of troops and planetary army capabilities .... even without their indoctrinated populaces being thrown at us as cannon fodder, we cannot win."

"Agreed," said Lord Gavain, "a secondary objective is to prevent them from landing armies on the planets within the Jacknife Defence Line. Our naval forces are repaired, but Operation Freedom has been costly to our armies and troops. We are in no position to fight them on land."

"No plan survives contact with the enemy," said Commandant-General Alvarez Cervantes. "And their hybrid abominations are just too strong for us. Naval defence is our only hope, it has been proven to us."

"That is true," said Lord Gavain. "Operation Freedom is drawing to a close, but the cost on our ground forces has been high. We cannot fight the Third Imperium on land that is clear. Priority has been given to reinforcing marine contingents on starships, that is our best way forwards."

"How far away are we from facing the Shadow Emperor's retribution, and the start of Operation Diamondcut?" asked Lady Principal Sophia.

"Estimates are difficult, but it could be anything from seven Standard days, upwards," said Lord Gavain. A holo-map flashed into existence in the conference room. "The Shadow Emperor's first division of forces have bitten through the Benedict Democracy, which has now fallen apart almost completely, mostly swallowed whole by the Third Imperium. They have already begun to eat through the small Houses running up to the northern part of the Helvanna Province. Six days, and they will have crossed the space. After that, maybe a few more days to build the starterminals and complete the Railway, three at most, but more likely one day. I suspect the Shadow Emperor will not wait, and will launch immediately, although much depends on his advisors. Chief Commander Al-Saadi, Lord Commander Xhepa, move the OutWorlds and Calamarite fleets into their positions for Operation Diamondcut."

"As you command, Lord Gavain," said Chief Commander Al-Saadi with a bow, after a glance and receiving nod from First Lord Al-Zuhairi.

"It will be done," said Lord Commander Xhepa.

"So, seven days," said First Lord Al-Zuhairi, his deep Frontier accent barbaric and imposing. "Seven days, and we find out."

"All that remains," said Lord Gavain, "is to wish you all luck."

*

The Shadow Emperor was feeling a lot happier, and even had a sinister smile upon his face, something which made the rest of his Legates within the holographic pulse-channel conference discomforted. He was aware of that, and this merely added to his enjoyment of the situation.

The Shadow Council was almost in full attendance, the majority by holographic representation, there being a significant gap at the seat for the yellow-robed and coloured Seventh Legate.

"The Legate of the Seventh Circle," the Legate of the Sixth Circle was saying, "was as everybody in this room knows the Deputy Head of the Interstellar Merchants Guild. He was found dead earlier today, the cover story being an accident involving a multiple aircar collision."

"The cover story?" asked Third Legate Jared Towers.

"We have significant penetration of the IMG," said the Fourth Legate, of the Fox secret intelligence branch, glancing at the Sixth Legate. "I and the Legate of the Phantoms here directed the immediate investigation personally. The truth was not difficult to discover. The Head of the Interstellar Merchants Guild received information from Lord Gavain's agents that uncovered the Deputy Head, and he was removed on the orders of the Head."

The Shadow Emperor scowled at the mention of Lord Gavain. "The Mercenary Lord strikes again," he said softly. "The Seventh Legate will have to be replaced, his function as chief of my treasury is too valuable. Until a suitable replacement is found, Third Legate, you will take on the responsibility."

"Emperor, I thank you for the trust," said Jared quickly and smoothly.

It is not trust, it is a test, thought the Shadow Emperor. Be loyal to me. I trust none of you, your survival depends upon my mercy. Aloud, he said, "As ever, faithful Jared. Now, onto Lord Gavain and this debacle in Helvanna. Second Legate?"

"We are approaching the Helvanna Province, a mere five Standard days away now, my Emperor," said the Second Legate. She was there in person, the Shadow Emperor having moved his noble barge up to the front line. Her infamous and instantly recognisable face would no doubt cause major ructions within the colonised galaxy if her existence and identity were known. "We will have the Railway in place two days later. If your wish is still that we launch the reserve second fleets against this Jacknife Defence Line, we can do so at any point after that time."

"We will do so immediately," the Shadow Emperor said, "and you, Second Legate, will lead the invasion at its head."

The Second Legate nodded, accepting the imperial order without question. "As you command, Emperor."

"I do," said the Shadow Emperor. He wanted the Second Legate in at the forefront of the danger zone, and if she died, so be it. It was one less possible traitor to worry about. "How does the plan work?" he asked.

"We shuttle all of the second fleets down to the small part of the Helvanna Province that remains ours," said the Second Legate, "linking up with those elements of the first wave of spearhead fleets that are undamaged and ready to fight. I will jump them through the three stargates that we have built in the Dathosa System, hitting the Hardangervidda System with thirty-two ships, the Pandrup System with twenty-eight, and the Concord System with twenty-six.

"The real target is Hardangervidda and Pandrup, the first being where the Vindicatus ships have hit. Pandrup and Concord are StarCom Federation, but these are feints, at least initially. We have a second wave of twenty to twenty-five ships each that jump into Bad Ischl, Chur, and Frederickstad. We wait to see if they commit their reserves, but after a period of time regardless in the third wave we jump eighty-nine ships into the Fleurier System. This is a real target, we take it out hard and quick and we have penetrated the Jacknife Defence Line. A fourth wave of seventy-two ships jumps into Hardangervidda, and engages the Vindicatus ships whilst they are locked in battle with our initial jump. We expect the reserve StarCom Federation ships to jump into Hardangervidda and Pandrup, so another fifth wave of sixty-four ships jump into Pandrup. We funnel all remaining ships through Fleurier, which should by this point be taken, spreading out into the southern galactic territories and hitting their reserve lines of stargates. All these numbers are just ships-of-the-line, not including our supporting ships and dedicated army transporters. Our aim is to land ground forces during naval engagements; the length of time it has taken the Coalition to subdue the southern Helvanna Province systems tells us of their weakness against our hybrids and upgraded Praetorians."

"This plan crushes the Vindicatus ships, gives us access to their Web with the Hardangervidda Stargate," said Jared.

"Yes," said the Second Legate, "as we progress through the Jacknife Defence Line, we also move into the Web, and retake the Dark Heart System from Gavain."

"Excellent," said the Shadow Emperor.

"The choice of Fleurier was decided as we received intelligence from our operatives in Amiens that the Archon Devereux has removed himself from the Coalition. We suspect that this system will be weakened vastly in comparison to the others," said the Fourth Legate.

"We take the Jacknife Defence Line apart in three key places," said the Second Legate, "Hardangervidda, Pandrup and Fleurier. All the other systems are merely distractions, not our real targets. We move into their rear and gut them."

"I approve," said the Shadow Emperor. "Let it be done."

*

The Creation System consisted of five planetary systems, and was a veritable fortress in the way it had been strengthened and hardened with advanced defensive systems. Yet, every element of these defences were normally hidden, chameleonically shielded to hide their existence. Even though the Creation System lay far beyond the Frontier border of the colonised galaxy, secrecy had always been the watchword when it came to the masters of the system.

None of these chameleonic fields were in operation today. The system was laid bare, with every defensive and offensive asset in full view. In particular in one of the planetary systems, the first ever starterminal to be built lay resplendent in its reddy-orange colouring, an eagle with three black claw marks slashed through its body displayed proudly on its hulls.

Before the starterminal lay an even more disturbing sight. It was an armada the size of which had rarely been seen. They were ranked in fleets, the fleets arranged three abreast. The fleets stretched back for many astronomical units, and they were all lying pointing towards the starterminal.

The time for the second armada of ships to launch into the war had come.

The starterminal space station began to activate. Red warning lights began to revolve around its hull, as the station began to separate. Jump initiation capacitor vanes extended out from the spheroid shell, which was cracking open. The shell moved apart, the station dimensions widening as the starterminal went fully operational.

It took some time for the terminal to completely reach launch status, its entire design changing as it went into open position. In its dormant state it was a powerhouse, able to withstand heavy attack, but when it was open it was dangerously vulnerable.

The starterminal hit launch status, now transformed into a vast version of a stargate with a circular hole around its heavily armoured segments but on a much larger scale. It had a depth and length that stargates did not have, more a tunnel than the ring of a stargate.

The flashing red lights went into a solid red as the starterminal locked onto the next one in the line, a starterminal virtually on the Frontier.

All throughout the colonised galaxy, the starterminals were opening. They hit full extension, becoming operational, red flashing lights turning into constant red as one by one in the chain they linked into one another.

With a burst, the Railway went live, holes being ripped through realspace as they connected. A hyper-space tunnel the like of which had never been seen was created, crossing nearly half the colonised galaxy.

Hyper-Pulse Communications Generators opened small, miniature tunnels for vast distances to transmit messages. They would often link one to another, creating webs of small tunnels a nanometre wide insofar as dimensions applied to hyperspace, allowing almost instantaneous transmission of data.

The starterminals worked the same way, but on a much larger and never before seen scale.

The order was given, and the armada of fleets began to move forwards, towards the starterminal in Creation.

Before they were anywhere near the launch horizon, the starterminal ejected a small test probe. The droid probe floated out a short distance, before it was caught by the warp fields and pulled violently into the warp-tunnel.

It rocketed through the tunnel, crossing the vast distance of half a galaxy in mere minutes.

In the Dathosa System, months away by normal jump-travel, Silus Adare looked up at the starterminal as Captain Zehra Sahin said, <The probe is coming through.>

The Dathosa System had been changed in the time that the surviving Third Imperial ships had been sheltering here, awaiting the arrival of the main body of the navy. A mere day ago, the forward armada of the spearhead that was still strong and ready enough to fight had jumped in, so the system was already overcrowded.

There were three new stargates in the system, each one built specifically to launch the ships on towards the Jacknife Defence Line. Those ships in-system were already lined up, ready to jump through the stargates as soon as the signal was given.

Admiral Silus Adare felt his heart rate increase. Now was the time.

He watched the display as the test probe arrived, flashing into existence in realspace before the starterminal exit. It had crossed the vast distance in the space of ten or so realtime minutes, but it had been nearly half a year in transit time.

It detonated, so it was not in the way as the armada began to translate through the warp-tunnel. It was like the firing of a start gun.

The Dathosa System was too small to accommodate the vast armada that was about to jump into it sequentially from the Creation System. This meant that the ships already here, the remnants of the first armada that had crossed the galaxy and built the vast Railway, had to jump out and start the counter-counter-attack before the second armada arrived.

<The Second Legate is contacting us,> said Captain Sahin, <She is giving the go-order to all ships. Stargates are lighting up.>

<Fleet,> said Admiral Adare, <Head for Stargate Dathosa One. We are jumping to Hardangervidda. In five and a half minutes time, we start the next phase of this war. In the Emperor's name.>

He waited for them to coast in towards the stargate, and begin their jump.

James Gavain, he thought, I am coming to you. I hope you are ready.

The approach of the armada based in the Creation System was staggered and predetermined, but as the first four fleets entered the envelope of the launch horizon, they were caught by the powerful warp field and in the blink of an eye and a flash of white light, they were launched through the Railway.

*

Lord Gavain had ensured that he had received plenty of sleep before today. In the next couple of days, at any time, the Third Empire could begin their assault. Throughout the Jacknife Defence Line, and in other places in the colonised galaxy, all would be tense. Hundreds of warships, millions of soldiers and navvies, would be waiting for the word to come.

<Lord Gavain,> said Lieutenant Forrest, the communications officer on the *Vindicator*. <Incoming message for you, the code is unbreakable. It has your name in the header. Do you want me to forward on to you? We can't virus check it.>

<Forward it,> he said simply. If he was right, this was it.

The message was downloaded into his brain, and he opened the code. He knew he was risking his life right here and then. If he had been betrayed, if the code of the message contained a virus, it could kill him in seconds. He was basing his life on his judgement of the person who was sending it.

As the message unfurled in his mind like a rose budding, he felt the warm flood of relief as the normal broadcast played into his head. The message was not lethal, and instead contained what he hoped would be the salvation of the Coalition.

<All members of the Coalition,> Gavain suddenly announced, activating the emergency communications broadcast. His words were instantly transmitted through his web of HPCG stations to every single commander and senior officer in the Jacknife Defence Line. <This is Lord Gavain. I have received advance word that the Railway is in operation. Prepare for attack in the next couple of minutes. Red alert, and good luck.>

He then patched through to Lieutenant Forrest. <Comms, get me the Calamarite and the OutWorlds commanders.>

<Connecting, sir ..... hyper-pulse beams going out ...... connection made, you have them.>

In his mind's eye, an image of Chief Commander Omar Al-Saadi of the OutWorlds Alliance and Lord Commander Alia Xhepa of the Calamarite Confederacy appeared. They were each with their fleets, hidden in their launch positions. They had snuck into their staging areas in secret a few days ago, ready to jump when the word was given.

<Al-Saadi, Xhepa,> said Lord Gavain, <word has been received that the Railway is in full operation. The enemy are transferring ships through the warp-tunnel now. We are about to be hit on the Jacknife Defence Line in the next couple of minutes. You have the green light, launch your counter-strikes now.>

"By your command," said Lord Commander Xhepa.

"As you will it," said Chief Commander Al-Saadi.

<Battle is joined,> Lord Gavain said.

Chapter XXI

Silus Adare heard the general announcement that they were about to exit the jump, and stood. <All hands, prepare for battle,> he said across the local ship-wide datasphere. He was fully connected to the sensors, and they flashed white for a moment with overload as they exited the warp and plunged into real-space.

<Captain Sahin, take operational command of the ship,> he ordered, <Colonel Lamans, prepare your Marines.> In the short time it had taken to give the order, he was receiving scanner confirmations that his fleet had emerged unscathed from the jump, and the battlenet was up for his immediate command.

<All hands,> said Captain Sahin, <We are in the Hardangervidda System.>

Silus Adare had command of two Z-class juggernauts including his own, the monstrous behemoths that could take on entire systems. He also had three T-class dreadnoughts, eight V-class battlecruisers, ten S-class strikecruisers, four W-class star-carriers and five X-class destroyer-transporters. It was an amalgamation of different fleets, thirty-two ships that were a mix of Helvanna Province survivors and first armada spearhead ships.

Instantly, he realised that they had woefully underestimated the strength of the enemy defences and preparations. Gun platforms opened up, and droid mines began to explode along his unprotected ships' hulls, it being at least another thirty seconds until they could get shields up. Batteries were launching missiles and torpedoes in at them. The volume of fire was high. There was even a military starbase, firing at the utmost of long-range with heavy salvoes of torpedoes, one of seven that had appeared in the system. Seven was a ridiculously large number.

They had chosen an area out near the edge of Hardangervidda to jump into, to attract the enemy into the trap for when another wave of second armada ships-of-the-line entered the theatre. The enemy was waiting for them, a fleet fully shielded and firing at them with ferocity.

<Identification on those ships,> Adare said hungrily.

<Idents incoming,> said a scanners operator, <Painting them up on tac-map now, sir.>

As the information appeared, he grunted. <Admiral Lucas De Graaf,> he said, reading the intel report. <First Fleet of the Vindicatus nation. And they have a bloody Z-class juggernaut too. But no Lord Gavain.>

<We also have the Second Fleet out towards the centre of the system, under Admiral Danae Markos. We are outnumbered, two to one, although it will take their Second Fleet some seven minutes to enter the battle.>

<Twelve torpedoes incoming, trying to intercept ....>

<Star-carriers launching fighters!>

<Outnumbered for now,> said Adare. The Vindicatus Second Fleet was beginning to move in towards their position. The volume of fire his fleet was taking was immense, but they were strong enough to withstand it. <Hail De Graaf.> Adare sat back down in his flag-seat, and awaited confirmation.

<Comms opening .... they are accepting.>

Simultaneously as the comms confirmation was being given, Adare was giving orders to his fleet, Fleet Adare. He had his heavy ships moving forwards into the storm of fire lighting up the blackness of space, with fighter and bomber screens running out to take some of the damage. They were moving in a linear row formation, adjusting their position to face onto the oncoming three-pronged arrowhead formation of Admiral-of-the-Fleets De Graaf's First Fleet.

Lucas De Graaf appeared before Silus Adare, and he leaned forwards, smiling evilly. <Lucas,> he said, <I suggest you contact Lord Gavain, and tell him I want him here. Our final dance is due to begin.>

In the Pandrup System, Admiral Scanlon of the StarCom Federation had all his fleet on high alert. As the jump signatures appeared, he gave the order to change and come about, heading to the incoming danger zone. Estimates had the enemy at around twenty-five to thirty warships.

The vastly improved defences of the Pandrup System geared up, locating in on the incoming target zone. Operational orders warned that the enemy would come in vast numbers, and in waves, so the other StarCom Fleet present in the system remained further in, away from the terminus point of the incoming invaders.

<Admiral Scanlon, we have an interdictor generation platform in their jump zone,> his captain said.

<I know,> he laughed, <How fortunate. Activate it.>

The interdictor platforms had been designed by Lord Gavain's engineers. Based on an interdictor ship, they were lightly armoured, and had low manoeuvrability and were intra-stellar rather than interstellar. They were quick to produce, and had been produced in vast numbers. They were scattered throughout the Jacknife Defence Line. They were designed to counter the immaterialisation fields that made Third Imperium ships invulnerable to weapons fire.

But they also acted like any other interdiction generator, creating a gravity well. No interstellar ship could jump near a planet, because the gravity well would pull it in and destroy it, disrupting the jump. With the enemy fleet coming in virtually on top of one of their interdiction platforms, Scanlon had a golden opportunity to disrupt their invasion.

By activating it, as soon as they translated, some of the ships would be pulled in and try to materialise in the same place, causing a misjump. It would destroy the platform, but they were automated, powered by droids.

"Strike one for me," he said.

In the Concord System, Admiral Rembrand had overall command. It was lighter defended than it should have been, following the exit of the Amiens fleets. The StarCom contingent was now stretched thinner than it should have been, trying to cover the hole Amiens had left in the Fleurier System, but Gavain had promised quick reinforcements if necessary.

As the Third Imperial ships translated, the heavy defences of the Fleurier System opened up. Rembrand realised that she had little choice.

<Signal Gavain,> she said, <Inform him we have contact. We won't engage for several minutes due to their ingress point, but we will need reinforcements! Also ask permission to use the super-viruses, we need the edge!>

Unfortunately, the enemy had jumped into a section of Concord that had not been heavily fortified. It would take time for Rembrand to get her fleet into engagement, by which point the Third Empire would have their ships fully shielded. This was going to be a head-on scrap of epic proportions; whilst Rembrand had some Praetorian ships, most of the ships were House design. Hers was a mixed fleet. They were simply outclassed by the enemy.

The super-viruses Gavain had engineered and held in reserve were their only hope. And this was most likely just the first wave.

Lord Gavain heard the message being relayed by Lucas De Graaf, but even with his demonstrable capabilities to multi-task, for a short while he did not respond. He was busy with the incoming reports.

Hardangervidda had been hit by Silus Adare, but the situation there at the moment was definitely in their favour. Although Gavain knew it would not remain that way for long. They had a stroke of luck at Pandrup, which would severely hamper the incoming Third Empire fleet. Jumping in on top of a jump-destroying interdiction platform was just their bad luck and the misfortune of war.

In Concord, though, the strike was much more worrying. Outnumbered and outclassed, with their defences largely out of range, the odds were already against them.

<Prepare all reserve fleets to jump,> he ordered quietly. <Admiral Rembrand, use of the super-viruses is denied. Do not engage the enemy,

advance your fleet slowly and try to pull them into the range of our heavy defences.>

<Acknowledged, Lord Gavain,> said Admiral Rembrand, the frustration in her voice.

<I will have Levitican Union fleets jumping into your position once we have more commitment from the Shadows, I need to see where else they hit.>

Gavain then broke off, and said to Captain Erica Georgia on the bridge, <Erica, prepare the *Vindicator* for jump. We are to head through the XW-1010 Stargate to Hardangervidda.>

<Sir, is this wise? I would not question your orders, but to respond to Adare's challenge is ->

<- My order, Captain. Follow it.> As commander of the entire battlefront, Gavain had initially intended to remain in the rear to effectively monitor the Defence Line. He could do it on the front as much as in the rear, and the presence of Adare necessitated his entrance into the Hardangervidda theatre.

<Aye aye, sir.>

As he waited for the jump to commence, Gavain ordered for a communications pulse-channel to be sent to the target systems for the Calamarite and OutWorlds Alliance, telling them that battle had been joined.

In the Dathosa System, the first ships of the second armada exited the warp-tunnel. The stargates were already warming up, ready to launch the second wave on. There would be a short wait of a couple of minutes before more ships arrived, amongst them the flagship of the Second Legate, simply to ensure there were no catastrophic collisions with the number of ships transiting through.

Waiting and watching was another fleet, and in the centre of it sat the noble barge of the Shadow Emperor. He was here to watch his victory.

*

All was quiet in the Kandahoor System, once a part of the Benedict Democracy. The starterminal, fully open and operational with its constant red lights running to show that the warp-tunnel of the Railway was functioning, cast a glow throughout the system. A small number of strikecruisers circled it like piranhas, in defensive pattern, with captured and indoctrinated ex-Benedict House ships providing additional defence.

They began to react as the incoming jump signatures were detected. Warnings blared out amongst the Third Imperial ships as the size of the incoming attackers were estimated, and desperate communications went out for additional support to jump in-system.

The House ships had enough time to get within range of the starterminal, as the ships of the invaders translated. Thanks to the bravery of Commander Lancaster and her strike team, they knew the exact location of their target - the starterminal.

Alarm spread through the Third Empire ships as they realised a full fleet of Calamarite House ships had jumped in, virtually on top of the Railway.

Lord Commander Alia Xhepa laughed. It felt so good to be striking back against the Shadow Emperor.

"Incoming fire, Lord Commander," her captain said, "heavy incoming."

"We will withstand," she said confidently. "Isn't that thing beautiful?" she said, commenting on the alien-like design. "A shame we are about to destroy it."

"We have a pulse-channel comms coming in, from Lord Gavain," said her communications operator.

"Jump signatures incoming," her scanners operator said. "Estimate three to five ships."

"That will be the enemy calling in reinforcements, but we can handle even them," said the Lord Commander. "Play me Lord Gavain's comms."

She listened to the Lord Gavain's message, then announced to the crew, "Battle is joined on the Jacknife Defence Line. Even now, there are Third Empire ships running through this Railway of theirs. Let us take it out now, and really fuck them up. Xhepa out."

Their mission was to disrupt the Railway, as the enemy were flying through it. It would hurt their numbers, and cause untold and inestimable damage. It was a key tenet of Praetorian tactics to disrupt logistics lines, and that was what Gavain had charged them with doing.

Xhepa had relished this chance, but also knew that as they were destroying the starterminal, her massed fleets would be crossing back into Third Empire territory all along their border. They would try and retake the captured Confederacy space. Today was going to be a good day for her people.

"Eliminate the starterminal, and jump out," she repeated her orders to herself.

*

The Second Legate received the news that they had exited their jump into Dathosa from the Railway with her usual lack of reaction.

<Signal the Shadow Emperor, pay my respects,> she said. <Prepare to jump to Fleurier.>

As they moved forwards, to enter the launch zones for the stargates which were even now re-computing their target trajectories, she received data on how the campaign was progressing.

They were taking significant damage in Hardangervidda, Adare now having all his ships' shields up and beginning to mete some back out to Vindicatus forces. In Pandrup, there had been a disaster. Nearly a third of her ships had been destroyed by some unknown catastrophe which resembled a mis-jump. The battle there was already lost, but it was never intended to be anything more than a distraction anyway. In Concord they were in the advantage, although full engagement was yet to occur.

The second wave had already hit. They had jumped into Bad Ischl, Chur, and Frederickstad, engaging more of the enemy. To the Lord Gavain these would look like serious attacks, but in truth, the real attack had begun at Hardangervidda and Pandrup, and was about to change gear with her massive overwhelming jump into Fleurier.

Take Fleurier, and they would open up and flank into the rest of the Defence Line through their southern territories.

The Second Legate strongly suspected that the Shadow Emperor wanted her in the front lines to do away with her. The Shadow Emperor was becoming increasingly paranoid, and she wondered if she had not made a mistake. After all, it was largely down to her that the Shadow Emperor even existed.

<We have a problem!> her second-in-command suddenly shouted, his panic wide and heavy across the datasphere. <The Railway is under attack!>

<The Railway? How is that possible?>

<Calamarite Confederacy ships have appeared in Kandahoor, and are about to attack the starterminal. Their numbers are too large, we estimate they will be successful in two to three minutes!>

The Second Legate thought fast. This was not coincidence at all. She smelt the actions of Lord Gavain in this. They had never even suspected that the Calamarite Confederacy was a part of the Coalition, but in retrospect, their withdrawal during the invasion through the edges of their territory suddenly appeared to be a feint. Gavain had been plotting this all along.

<How many ships will be through the Railway at the point of destruction?> she asked.

<The fourth wave will be clear, but the fifth and sixth and some of the support fleets will still be in transit. It's impossible to tell how far along the tunnel they will be, and what effect the break of the Railway will have on the warp-tunnel. They could be destroyed, or simply thrown out.>

<But either way,> said the Second Legate, <Only the fourth wave will make it here.> She thought fast. The fourth wave was supposed to hit Pandrup in force. Much of their ground forces would not make it through, and their additional fleets. Gavain had removed their reserves.

<Inform the fleets in Concord, Bad Ischl, Chur and Frederickstad that they are to be ready to disengage and jump to new targets on my command,> she said. <Do not inform them that our logistics line is about to be interrupted. Taking Hardangervidda, Pandrup and Fleurier are our priorities. We still have the advantage.> She sighed to herself. <I will tell the Emperor, I doubt he will see it that way.>

*

The dreadnought belonging to Lord Commander Xhepa passed over the starterminal in Kandahoor, turning to present starboard flank. The broadside it roared down at the starterminal station was the final killing blow, and with a chain reaction, the extended and vulnerable station began to blow apart.

The Railway was disrupted, and jubilantly Lord Commander Xhepa ordered her forces to jump out. It was early yet, but the Calamarite part in this campaign had been done.

*

In the Fleurier System, Admiral Heinrich Haas felt his heart sink.

The StarCom Federation forces were strong, but were stretched thin. The golden rule about not mixing contingents had been broken in Fleurier, to ensure there was adequate coverage, and he now commanded not only his own sizeable fleet, but a smaller grouping of Republic of Varrental warships.

They were still outmatched though, as the pre-estimates of the enemy fleets jumping in estimated that there were between seventy and ninety warships incoming in three separate jump-points.

<Contact Lord Gavain now!> he demanded. <Reinforcements are urgently required!>

<Sir, I'm trying, but he has left the grid, the *Vindicator* is not answering. Apparently they jumped out of XW-1010 half a minute ago.>

<What? What is the fool doing!> roared Haas. <I knew he could not be trusted.> He regained control. <Then find me someone in command .... no, forget it. Call in my own reinforcements.> In the reserve line there were two StarCom Federation fleets. He was not going to forget this action by Lord Gavain. He gave the orders for them to jump into Fleurier, and sent a

message to Grand Marshal Anaes Korhonen and to Marshal Paul Fallhouse of the Republic of Varrental, asking for urgent assistance.

He also sent one to President Pereyra, stating that Lord Gavain had abandoned his position.

The Second Legate heard the announcement that they had exited the jump. They were coming under heavy fire already, the Fleurier System reinforced beyond all their wildest imaginings and pre-battle estimations. It had grown numerous military starbases, gun platforms, weapons batteries and droid mine fields.

Even as the enemy StarCom Fleet was identified as the top-secret new fleet under Admiral Haas, she gave an order to connect through to the hardcore Federation Admiral. The communication flowed through quickly, the link being made.

<Haas,> she said, allowing her image to be transmitted. <I give you this one chance to surrender. Or we will roll over you.>

<Never .....> Haas's voice trailed off. <Am I seeing things?>

<No,> said the Second Legate.

<You must be a clone, like the Shadow Emperor,> said Haas, his eyes narrowed, suspecting a ploy of deception.

<I am no clone, Heinrich,> she said, <I am Edrisa Constantin, former wife of the False Emperor, the Three-Month Empress.>

<He had you killed, executed for treachery.>

<He was right, I was a traitor,> said the Second Legate, and one-time Empress, <But reports of my death were very much exaggerated, just like those of Jared Towers. I led the group called the Shadow Council, I cloned the Shadow Emperor. Now, I ask you, abandon your President Pereyra and your Lord Gavain, and join the Empress you once swore to protect.>

*

"We have exit from the jump!" the announcement rang across Chief Commander Al-Saadi's bridge.

He felt a cold rush through his skin, his senses tingling. He actually stood, hands on the railings of his command section. The dreadnought of House Al-Zuhairi, flagship of the fleet, was amongst the first of the five waves of fleets he had jumping into this system.

They had lain in wait, and when they had received the go command Chief Commander Al-Saadi felt the joy. First Lord Al-Zuhairi would be in the third wave, insistent on joining the battle himself. This chance to strike at the heart of the enemy was too good to miss.

Sensor scans begin to immediately inform him of the enemy locations and strength. There seemed to be mainly support fleets here, waiting to enter the Railway on the first ever starterminal. There were significant defences, but they were not insurmountable. Even now, additional holes in the warp were opening up and InterStellar Hyperspace Missiles were exiting, heading for planets all over the solar system, launched at Al-Zuhairi's command. As they engaged navally, their Tears of the Moon warheads would be wrecking the enemy homeworlds.

Al-Zuhairi displayed no compunction about using such Weapons of Planetary Destruction. He did not have the same conscience as Lord Gavain was displaying, despite all his hard warrior's exterior. Life on the Frontier was brutal, and Al-Zuhairi was equally as brutal to survive it and lead a nation in it.

The OutWorlds Alliance fleets had journeyed deep beyond the Frontier to get here, to find the homeland of the Shadows.

The Jacknife Defence Line was the greatest trap in history. It was designed to pull the enemy in, commit them. With the Railway gone, they could not return fast enough. It was still important to stop the enemy in the Helvanna Province but it was here that the real fight, the real target of the campaign was to be struck.

Lord Gavain was a genius with balls of steel and a heart of pure titanium, in Al-Saadi's opinion. Who else would conceive of a plan using hundreds of warships as bait, knowing that they may well fail and be destroyed in the name of a greater good?

The OutWorlds Alliance warships were in the Creation System, at the other side of the galaxy in the homeworld of the Shadow Emperor, and they were going to utterly destroy it.

Chapter XXII

<The *Zero Tolerance* is coming about, presenting broadside to us!> said Lucas De Graaf's second-in-command.

<*Zeus's Wrath*, interpose yourself between us and the *Zero*,> Lucas De Graaf ordered.

The *Zeus's Wrath* moved relatively quickly, the helmsman of the *Thor's Hammer* diving the dreadnought down and to port to avoid the attempted broadside from the *Zero Tolerance*. Silus Adare was hailing them again, and De Graaf angrily shut it down. Four attempts in the last two minutes, the man was a menace. He was supposed to fight, not talk.

Vice-Admiral Kenzie Viederhaun was leading his *Revenging Angel* in fearlessly, upgraded armour and shields taking the incoming hits from both enemy juggernauts. The *Revenging Angel* was already suffering as much as the *Thor* was, but they were beginning to cause damage to the *Zero Tolerance*. It was coming under heavy fire from Captain Zane McDonnagh's *Carnivorous*, the *Cathedral* and the *Remembrance*, with the *Rebellious* just moving into position to support. The battlecruisers and De Graaf's dreadnought just about matched the juggernaut; without the captured *Zeus's Wrath* juggernaut in the fight, under the promoted Commodore Ffion Wybeck, this would be a very short engagement indeed.

<That unexplained jump signature has translated,> said his scanners officer, the joy in her voice, <It's the *Vindicator*! Lord Gavain is here!>

"Jamie?" said Lucas De Graaf. The Second Fleet was almost engaged, pulling in to strike against Admiral Adare's Third Empire fleet. <Hail Lord Gavain, why is he here?>

<The *Vindicator* has just jumped in-system,> said Captain Zehra Sahin on their private channel.

<Good,> said Adare, <Colonel Lamans, do your best. Hail Gavain now.>

Lord Gavain felt the rush as the battlenet reconnected, and he was once again in charge of the full intergalactic datasphere for the Jacknife Defence Line. He had not yet committed any reserves, and the danger of jumping whilst the enemy were still invading worried him but it had been a risk worth taking. Just a minute could change the shape of a naval battle, and being out for a two-and-a-half minute jump was highly risky.

He resisted the temptation to swear as he saw that Admiral Haas had already called up his reserves, committing them to the Fleurier System.

Admittedly the situation there was extremely dangerous, and the knowledge that they faced the one-time Empress of the Red Imperium was shaking to the core. The Shadows had no end of surprises for them it seemed, but it was another piece in the secret puzzle of Imperial history.

So far the only heavy invasion had been in Fleurier. The rest were spread out all across the Defence Line. Gavain found that puzzling; it made much more sense to concentrate forces.

That was when his scanners warned him that there was a large series of three jump signatures incoming to the Hardangervidda System. From the looks of it, sixty to eighty warships were jumping in on multiple vectors.

<This is Lord Gavain. Levitican Union forces, double-jump through the stargates to Hardangervidda and Fleurier,> he ordered. It was time to commit some of the reserves, those that Haas had not already commanded himself. <All other forces are to hold position.>

He reviewed a quick report stating that the Railway had been taken down, and that the Creation System was now under attack, before he demanded, <Lieutenant Forrest, hail Silus Adare.>

<Sir? I mean, yes, sir, hailing now ..... connection established.>

Adare appeared in Gavain's mind's eye.

<So, you finally appear, Jamie,> said Silus Adare tauntingly.

<I have,> said Lord Gavain. <Adare, you wanted to turn traitor to your friends in the Third Empire, and join my Vindicatus nation. I am here to prove I mean it. Transmit the Third Empire battleplans, and disable your fleet.>

<If I suddenly went back on my word,> said Silus Adare, <If I did not disable my fleet, you would be in a very weak position, I think.>

Fear drove a spike through Gavain's heart. Adare had warned him of the approach of the Third Imperial fleets, he had told him when the Railway had been operating. There had never been any of Gavain's scouts watching the Dathosa System, it had been Adare all along. But the man was not trustworthy, he had changed sides more than a chameleon changed its colours, and he was perfectly capable of going back on his word now.

<Adare .....> Gavain said warningly.

<Relax,> Silus Adare laughed. <Even now, Colonel Lamans is leading his Marines through my juggernaut, killing those crew loyal to the Shadow Emperor. Captain Sahin is transmitting the disablement codes to shut down the other ships in this fleet ..... now. And here are your battleplans, Lord Gavain. My new master.> He smirked at the word.

Gavain received the data, and with the sudden information, he knew what the enemy intended. It was also up to date, to the very second, telling him what the Third Empire were speaking about amongst themselves.

They intended to break through Fleurier into the southern systems, and to take Hardangervidda and Pandrup. The rest of it was all a feint.

Adare's fleet was shutting down, viruses spreading through their battlenet, launched by Adare himself. It was not the first time he had done this to his own people. He had done it once before, when he had been part of the StarCom Federation.

<Gavain to all commanders, receive this information on the enemy battleplans. All reserves, all reserves, commit now to Hardangervidda, Pandrup, and Fleurier. Admiral Haas, Fleurier is key, it is not to be lost. Defend it! Ignore the Empress! Fleets along the Jacknife Defence Line, prepare to split, reinforcements to the three target systems. The enemy battleplan is identified, we know where they are really hitting! All fleets, use of super-viruses is permitted!>

Gavain leaned back. <Adare, you may have just won this war for me.>

<It's not over yet, Jamie,> said Silus Adare. <You have to survive the onslaught coming into Hardangervidda. Shall we form up and fight side by side?>

*

The Railway fell apart with catastrophic consequences.

The warp tunnel crossing half the colonised galaxy collapsed. The feedback around the starterminal in the Benedict Province jumped to several over terminals, destroying them in the process, although the ones that were more distant survived.

For the ships inside the jump-tunnel, as it collapsed, their fate was equally as varied. The fifth fleet was utterly destroyed, some parts of wreckage turning up all over the Eastern Segment, thrown in all directions through hyper-space. In one instance a piece of hull even grazed through an atmosphere of a colonised planet, causing the populace to run for their asteroid shelters.

Some of the sixth fleet managed to survive, although they were never seen again. Those that survived the collapse emerged into deepspace, and without enough power and heavily damaged, their crews faced a long, slow death as their ships slowly lost the ability to support life. It was a cold way to die, in tombs far from civilisation, and they became the stuff of legend.

The support fleets following behind suffered some damage, some also dropping out into deepspace, but some managed to land in star systems, or exited at nearby starterminals. Others had just enough power to jump into friendly systems.

The Railway was broken, and in the process it had eaten into the power of the Third Empire.

*

Admiral Haas laughed as the message came through from Lord Gavain. "It appears I owe you an apology," he said to himself.

<Empress Constantin, my answer is – go to hell,> said Admiral Haas. He would never admit how close he had come to taking up her offer just then. He disconnected the comms before she could answer. <Data-Tac, release the super-viruses. Comms, signal the fleets, all data viruses to be released on the enemy. We have many more reinforcements coming in. Let us engage the enemy properly.>

*

First Lord Al-Zuhairi felt his dreadnought-size noble barge shake as it took a lucky pair of torpedo shots, but then in anger the rest of his squadron reduced the enemy ship into a burning hulk, completing its destruction.

"Al-Saadi," he hailed his Chief Commander, "we are in position above the enemy capital planet, Shadow. I am launching the Tears of the Moon warhead now."

"Understood, First Lord. The plan calls for us to retreat, and jump out-system."

"No," said First Lord Al-Zuhairi, shaking his head. "We are doing too well. Ignore Lord Gavain's orders, we are staying here and completely reducing these five planetary systems into nothingness. We are taking the capital of the Third Empire apart. They will not flaunt the power of the OutWorlds Alliance again."

*

The Shadow Emperor looked like death incarnate.

Encased within his grand imperial throne, his face was as inflexible and iron as the face-masks he had once worn as part of the Shadow Council, before the Third Empire had been born in fire and death. His hands gripped the arms of the throne in anger.

Jared Towers the Third Legate of his political caste stood before him, kneeling, head bowed in supplication. Jared was actually there, never far from the Shadow Emperor's side. He did not trust Jared Towers, but he trusted him more than most in his Council.

"The Ninth Legate and the Eighth have died in the ongoing destruction of the Creation System," said Jared Towers, his voice a whisper. "When the planet Shadow was bombed out of existence, they must have lost their lives."

"The Creation System, my home, lost forever," said the Shadow Emperor, his voice weak.

"It will take some more hours yet," said Jared Towers, "but we cannot stop the OutWorlds Alliance. They have hit it in too strong a number. We could send some of our border forces into their territory, to try and draw them away?"

"Do it," said the Shadow Emperor.

"I will inform the Second Legate Constantin," said Jared Towers, "by your will."

"The Railway is destroyed?"

"Yes," said Jared. "We have lost a significant proportion of the second armada. Enough of it survives, but we were already committed on the Jacknife Defence Line. The systems of Hardangervidda, Pandrup, and Fleurier are turning into bloody battle-zones, with hundreds of starships fighting apiece, but even if we are successful there we do not have the ground troops to take the planets. The reinforcements of the Coalition have surprised us, in terms of number of Federation starships and the amount the Levitican Union committed.

"My brother Luke Towers has appeared himself in the Hardangervidda System, fighting alongside Lord Gavain, who is also there. The treachery of Silus Adare has swung the battle, and the war. Our fleets are compromised. They have super-viruses that are eating through our defences, and Silus Adare himself had codes for access to all of the first armada ships and Helvanna Province contingents. The battling will take hours, and we may even win in Fleurier, but what then? We cannot proceed into the southern territories, as the ships from Pandrup and Hardangervidda will be able to meet us and stop us. We will be prolonging into weeks a war we cannot hope to win."

"What do you advice?" asked the Shadow Emperor.

"My Emperor," said Jared, swallowing deeply. "There can only be one step forward. We must think of the future. The only way to get to Mars is to sue for peace, to fall back, consolidate the territory we have taken and rebuild. We have vast manufacturing bases within our territory now, we need a number of years to recover from the loss of our birthing vats in the Creation System. We must do this. I am sorry, my Emperor, it is not what you want to hear, but ......" Jared fell silent.

The Shadow Emperor looked at Jared Towers with cold fierceness in his eyes. Jared could not look back at him, expecting to hear his death sentence screamed out.

"Prepare for a jump to the Hardangervidda System," said the Emperor quietly, surprising Jared Towers no end.

*

<Captain Georgia, there is a jump signature appearing, distant, on the edge of the system.>

<We've had Third Empire ships jumping in constantly, this is merely another,> said Georgia.

<It is on its own,> said Gavain, frowning, interrupting. <That in itself is unusual, they usually come in at least by the squadron.>

The fight in Hardangervidda was just reaching the half-hour point, and it had been brutal so far. It had become a classic multiple fleet action, the initial rush to deal as much damage to each other fading as the fleets withdrew, and then came back together again using various tactics and strategies to try and obtain an advantage.

Losses had been high on both sides, with many ships dead-in-the-water, and some outright destroyed. Admiral Adare's treachery had disabled his entire fleet utterly, so they were drifting, out of the fight, but there were more than enough of the Shadow ships to take their place. The fourth wave had hit, scant seconds before High General Luke Towers had brought the Levitican Union reinforcements and a half-fleet of Federation Praetorian ships in.

The heavy defences in Hardangervidda were playing their part, helping to tip the battle in the favour of the defensive forces. Nevertheless, this was going to become a long, protracted fight. The Shadows were not going to retreat, and were in large enough numbers that they could cause significant damage.

The *Vindicator* was already wounded, although not grievously. The dreadnought *Thor's Hammer* under De Graaf lay on its port, the *Zero Tolerance* fully in command of Silus Adare on its starboard, and together the three of them were ploughing through the vanguard squadron of one of the enemy fleets. The *Zeus's Wrath* and the vanguard squadron of Admiral Danae Markos's fleet were shortly behind them, adding long range fire as the mixed fleets began to make contact again after a brief five minute lull in the fighting.

<The ship has translated,> said the scanners officer. <It is of unknown design and origin. We have not seen anything like it.>

<Hail from Silus Adare.>

<Gavain here, speak Silus?>

<To save you the time, that ship is the Shadow Emperor's personal barge,> he said.

<No?> said Gavain, and then moments later the data that Adare had treacherously given them confirmed it. <So it is. The Shadow Emperor, here in person?>

<Lord Gavain!> said Lieutenant Forrest, <The Shadow Emperor Himself ..... he's hailing you.>

Gavain raised an eyebrow. <Put him through, then.>

An image appeared before the Shadow Emperor in his grand audience chamber. Third Legate Jared Towers stood by his side, impassive and supporting.

The Lord Gavain sat in an unremarkable military-design flag-chair, on a bridge that looked like every other Praetorian Guard bridge. The Shadow Emperor had expected more, somehow. The Lord was dressed grandly, in the expensive clothing and robes of crimson red and black that marked the colours of his nation – they were too similar to the reddy-orange and black of the Third Empire. Even the ostentation of the clothing did not make up for what the Shadow Emperor thought was a very understated man.

"Lord James Gavain," said the Shadow Emperor slowly, "I am the Third Emperor of Shadow. Few know my name, but it is Julius –"

"Constantin?" Lord Gavain finished. "If you are taking the House Constantin family name."

"Few knew that House Constantin formed the Imperial House of the Emperors," said the Shadow Emperor. "You do have good intelligence, it appears."

"War is about more than military assets," said Gavain, "it is fought not just on the battlefield, but in the hearts and minds of the people, with intelligence on the enemy, propaganda in the media, the willingness to go to any length. This is how I am beating you."

"That is far from determined yet," said the Shadow Emperor.

"The Railway lies in ruins, broken," said Lord Gavain. "The Creation System is being destroyed as we speak, if it is not already. We fight you here, and in Pandrup and in Fleurier, as you have abandoned your other system assaults. You may win in Fleurier, but it is not guaranteed, and anything can happen. Shadow Emperor, *you cannot win.*"

"And neither, Lord Gavain, can you."

"Can I not?"

"No. You may fight us to a stalemate here on the Jacknife Defence Line –"

"- which is all I wanted to do."

"Do not interrupt, child," said the Shadow Emperor calmly. "I am not used to it. We may come to a stalemate here, navally, but you cannot face my ground forces. It may take time, months even, but eventually I can have them here. My navies can rebuild and recover from their losses, and there is still more than enough here in Helvanna. In fact, my navies are still strong enough to make this fighting last weeks. Is that what you want?"

There was a pause whilst Gavain considered. "Are you about to make an offer?" he asked.

"Yes," said the Shadow Emperor. "I propose a truce. One between myself and you, Lord Gavain. It is not a peace treaty, not a promise that there will never be war, as I do intend to have Mars. You will not stop me there. But it can be a truce, a cease fire."

"We have hurt you enough to stop you," said Lord Gavain, "To my mind that means we have won. A truce is not what I want, I want a peace treaty, a promise that it ends here, today and now."

"You cannot have that," said the Shadow Emperor, shaking his head. "A truce, Lord Gavain. One you deserve for your efforts so far. A cessation of hostilities, for a period of, shall we say, three years?"

"Eight years," said Gavain quickly.

"No, too much can happen in just one year," said the Shadow Emperor. "Especially in these days and times. A truce for five years, then, with certain terms covering conditions in which it gets broken."

Gavain hesitated. "In principle, I agree then, subject to the rest of the Coalition's approval," he said. "Five years, and we agree the detail today. Not in person, though. I do not think either of us wants to step foot on the other's ship."

The Shadow Emperor laughed, and it was not a pleasant sound. "Neither of us are that suicidal. Very well, Lord Gavain, we have a truce. This war, is over."

When Lord Gavain communicated the news of the end of the Shadow War to the Coalition, many already knew as the fighting was stopping. The cheering and the jubilation was felt the galaxy over.

Chapter XXIII

The starbase had been built in the XW-1010 solar system, in House Narrough territory by a combination of StarCom Federation, Vindicatus and Levitican Union constructoships and technology. House Narrough was one of the small houses that, after initial indignation at having their territory pirated by the Coalition, had been grateful for the defence and had virtually jumped at the chance of joining the Union.

XW-1010 Starbase was a first of its kind, a military starbase that would be crewed and peopled by military units from three separate nations. It was not practical to have the entire Coalition crew it, but in the spirit of the newfound post-Dissolution alliance, it would be a multi-national armed base, the centre of the defence against the vast Third Empire.

Lord Gavain was being conveyed through its long corridors by a travellator droid, which eventually hummed as it came to a stop before the specially-built audience hall. Behind him were Admiral-of-the-Fleets Lucas De Graaf, the heavily injured Admiral Danae Markos, and Field Marshal Ulrik Andryukhin who for once had escaped a major engagement unscathed.

<Ready, people?> asked James Gavain. <They're all in there and assembled.>

<As we'll ever be, Hero,> said Ulrik mockingly.

Gavain snorted a little, looking out of the observation window of the corridor. Out there in space were assembled vast fleets, and it reminded him a little of the aftermath of the Battle for Mars which had begun all of this. The difference was that the fleets were mixed, House and Imperial Praetorian, with different colours and nationalities on their hulls.

Amongst them he spotted some of his new fleets. The losses he had taken in Hardangervidda had been considerable, but as many of those ships that could were being repaired. They had taken more salvage than could be dreamt, the Shadows not being able to recover all of their assets in the time period allotted. His shipyards in Blackheath and Dark Heart would be pumping out the new classes of starships, exact copies of the Third Empire ships and their own designs in a matter of weeks. They already had new orders from members of the Coalition.

<Are you alright, Jamie?> asked Lucas.

<Yes,> said Gavain, feeling a flash of irritation at the concern. They all knew how the months of preparation and war had stretched him, physically and psychologically, and that he fully intended to see Dr Presson on his return to the Dark Heart Artificial System. His closest friends could see the toll it had taken upon him. <Let's go in.>

And with that, he strode forwards, entering the audience hall as the immense bulkhead door cycled open.

The audience hall had numerous seats, which were occupied both by military commanders who were actually there, and holographic representations. Many more would view recordings of today's proceedings.

In the centre of the audience hall was a large circular table, around which sat the commanders of the various contingents and those of the politicians who could actually attend. Gavain gave a small nod to Lady Principal Sophia during the rapturous applause that greeted his entrance, as she had travelled up from Leviticus. Some like President Pereyra were too distant to attend, but their holographs were pristine and precise.

In many ways this was stage-managed, much of the detail already proposed and agreed, but it would be played out to those who had a right to see it and would only further cement the Coalition of Resistance.

As the applause and the cheering finally waned, an automated droid buzzed to appeal for silence. Gavain stood up in his position at the head of the circular conference, and began to speak.

"Lords and Ladies, commanders and politicians," he said, "a week ago, an event took place which will enter the history books. The Shadow Emperor, who rampaged through the colonised galaxy, irreversibly indoctrinating and enslaving untold trillions if not quadrillions of people, slaughtering just as many and striking fear throughout post-Imperial nations in this Age of Secession, was finally brought to a halt at the Jacknife Defence Line. The onslaught of a superior enemy was matched and defeated, with a mixture of amazing technological advances, feats of engineering on a scale rarely seen, intelligence gained bravely and at great personal cost, tremendous personal bravery of all our armed forces, and above all - the political will of the people in this room to work together, and make the Coalition succeed."

Applause broke out again, and after a short while Gavain appealed for silence once more through the announcement droid.

"No-one can be in any doubt that the Third Empire is still a strong and potent threat to be feared. Logistics and the failure of the Railway, coupled with the desire to progress too fast and too quickly, defeated the Shadow Emperor Constantin as much as anything else. It was the size of their success in conquering and rampaging through the colonised galaxy that helped us today. We can be under no illusion that the Third Empire, as it wrongly calls itself, is much larger and stronger than we of the Coalition are. Which is why, shortly, we shall discuss the ongoing future of the Coalition. First, however, we shall speak of the terms of the truce which we brokered on the battlefields of Hardangervidda."

He took a sip of water before continuing. "That you brokered, Lord Gavain," Lady Principal Sophia shouted out.

He smiled faintly at the laughter and smattering of applause, finding it all uncomfortable.

"The truce lasts for five years, after which date it expires. There is no guarantee that war will resume on expiry, but the Third Emperor has promised not to progress any further beyond the parallel of the Jacknife Defence Line towards Mars or deeper into the colonised galaxy. He will also not extend beyond the borders of the Third Empire, which now stretches from the Frontier, though the Boundary, and deep into the Mid-Sectors."

That had caused some contention with the OutWorlds Alliance and the Calamarite Confederacy, both of whom at the point of the truce declaration were trying to retake land and territory they had lost in the invasion. Gavain had appeased and delighted them with the next part of the truce. "As part of the Truce of Hardangervidda, the Third Emperor cedes back to the Calamarite Confederacy and the OutWorlds Alliance, as members of the Coalition, the landholdings he took. In terms of the populations he will remove them, as the indoctrination procedures they use to enslave the minds of the people are irreversible. There is no cure, unfortunately, and that is one of the great sadnesses of this entire affair. I did ask him to renounce the use of indoctrination and the hybrid armies, but he refused, and this point could not be won. That evil will forever remain a part of the legacy of the Third Empire, and a clear and present threat for today.

"In terms of the Jacknife Defence Line, they will draw their border on the eight systems that still remain of their so-called Helvanna Province. There will be a Demilitarised Zone, a no-man's land between the Helvanna Province and the Jacknife Defence Line which may not be crossed or entered, by civilian or military starship. It will be policed by droidships slaved to a joint datasphere to which both sides have access, to ensure impartiality and protection from smugglers and pirates attempting to cross illegally. Either side that sends military units into the region, will be breaking the integrity of the Demilitarised Zone and breaking the Truce.

"There will be no trade allowed, no crossing of civilians across the borders. All borders are closed. Even a minor military action, an armed scouting or a mistaken firing incident, will result in the expiry of the Truce. Build-ups along the borders are allowed, but we never, ever cross.

"Make no mistake, the Truce is designed for both sides to rebuild, and strengthen. An arms race is beginning. We are entering a Cold War, an old term where we do not fight, but prepare to fight. To that end, we must speak of the future of the Coalition."

Gavain took another sip of water. His throat was incredibly dry. "The Coalition must continue, its sole purpose to be to resist and prepare to defend against a renewed Third Empire invasion. The Jacknife Defence Line should be strengthened, as is right, but in the future remember that the Empire could strike in any way, in any direction. They do not have to go through the most direct route to get to Mars, still their stated aim and ultimate objective."

He paused. His own plans were to strengthen as much of the Gulf of Medusa as he could where it touched the Third Empire, but it was a wide border and would take much time. "I propose we build our own network of stargates and even starterminals, all along the border from Jacknife right up to the Frontier, to allow quick defence and transition of troops and ships. We can open the Coalition to any who want to join, particularly those on the galactic east-east, but it is designed purely to defend against the Third Empire. It is a mutual defence organisation with that stated aim - we will not be drawn into each others' local fights."

He looked at President Pereyra and the Federation contingent, and Vice-President Paul Fallhouse and his ailing mother, the President of the Republic of Varrental. The League of Suularitsaar had begun limited strikes into Federation territory, and war there was maybe only weeks away. Amiens, the traitors who pulled out of the Coalition, had waited until after the Truce was first declared and had then jumped into several Republic of Varrental Systems. Their war had begun again.

"It is going to be difficult. We all have our own mistrusts, our own concerns, and our own politics to deal with. I have no doubt they will cause us grief and make the future difficult. But the future of mankind depends on us holding together against the nemesis that is the Third Empire, with its enforced slavery and insane Emperor. I propose the vote now; do the members of the Coalition wish to continue to work together, in a new Coalition of Mutual Defence, to prepare for the day when we must face the Third Empire again."

The vote was held, and the Coalition of Mutual Defence was ratified.

*

In the corridors of the *Vindicatus*, Lord James Gavain walked down towards the mustering hall, from where he would be able to board a Friederich-class lander that would convey him down to the surface of Leviticus. By his side strode a person he never expected to be so close to his physical presence, but nothing post-Dissolution would surprise him in this galaxy any more.

Behind them both walked Captain Erica Georgia, openly arm in arm with Field Marshal Ulrik Andryukhin. It was probably to keep a check on the fierce-tempered leader of the ground forces and the military, the hatred in his eyes boring into the back of the man at James Gavain's side. Julia Kavanagh was dead, and despite his new relationship with Captain Georgia, Ulrik would never forgive Silus Adare for her death.

Jonathan O'Connor was also there, walking side by side with Major Adeoye, directly behind Captain Zehra Sahin and Colonel Iyan Lamans. Viktor Vantanik, the brigadier of the biomorphs, was there as additional security, but Gavain expected no problems. The treacherous Adare and his two closest fellow-traitors had nowhere left in the galaxy to run to.

"He does not like me," said Adare, not even looking back at Andryukhin.

"I do not share his hatred," said James, "I forgive the deaths of war, I am practical."

"Especially considering what you've done in this one," smirked Adare.

Despite himself Gavain wanted to strike Adare there and then, but refrained. "I never thought we would be here, like this," he said, as they entered the mustering hall.

"Neither did I," said Adare. "It feels strange to be on the same side, Lord Gavain, I will admit."

"It is a fact that without your turncoat actions, the losses in the Shadow War would have been far greater," said Gavain, "and for that we owe you. You as much as I saved the Coalition, to my thinking."

Adare laughed. He even looked untrustworthy, with his black hair, goatee beard and pointed eyebrows. "But no-one will credit me with it," he said. "You know, following your cold-hearted extermination of numerous solar systems in the northern Helvanna Province, it also seems unfair that I am still painted as the war-criminal."

Once again, the reminder of what he had done struck Gavain's heart like a knife, but he would be damned if he would show it in front of Silus Adare.

"Lady Principal Sophia is giving you a pardon," said Lord Gavain. "That is all the reward you will get. That, and I had to promise her that you will not set foot in her territory."

"Easily done," said Adare. They stopped before the boarding entrance to the lander. "So what will you do with me now, Jamie? You did state there would be a place for me in your Vindicatus nation, a home and a refuge for me and my people."

"Yes," said James. "I did. I will honour my word, Silus, even if I cannot fully trust you to honour yours."

"I am not trustworthy," said Adare, "But make it worth my while, and my loyalty is yours for that time being."

"There's rare honesty in that statement, at least," said Gavain darkly. "In truth, Adare, I may not trust you, but I do value your experience and your skills. I appeal to you to stay loyal to Vindicatus, and the Levitican Union, and in return I will do more than give you a home."

"Oh?" asked Silus Adare.

"Yes," Gavain nodded. "The Ninth Fleet and Tenth Fleets are being formed. I will give you command of one of them, and station you as the Vindicatus contribution to the Levitican Union's support of the Coalition. You will be under High General Luke Towers, which will cause you enough difficulty, as he will be commanding the Union's assets along Jacknife."

"You seem to trust me with much," said Adare, eyes narrowing.

"You will be watched," said Gavain, "Brigadier Vantanik here will never be far from your side, at least initially. And High General Luke Towers will also keep an eye on you. But you have command of one of my fleets. Your skill is too great to waste."

"Thank you, James Gavain," said Adare, "I never thought you would do that. I thought I would end up on a farm somewhere, or in the prison complex on Dark Heart Gamma." Then he laughed again.

"I keep my word. Do not let me regret it," said Lord Gavain, turning and entering the boarding tube to the lander. He had to go down to Leviticus, as his Vindicatus nation and House Gavain was now a full member of the Levitican Union. His presence was required, and had been absent for too long.

Much had changed in the Union in the last couple of months.

Lady Principal Sophia Towers watched as the new Council of the Levitican Union assembled. The Council Chamber had been restructured and rebuilt, widened and lengthened to accommodate all the extra people and heads of the various Houses.

She smiled at Lord Gavain, her friend and the architect of much of this. He had turned into one of the greatest friends House Towers and the Levitican Union had ever made, and personally one of her strongest supports. She was also aware from looking at him how much he had suffered personally with the launching of the Tears of the Moon, and knew they would speak later. She too had lost much of herself, as the presence of the hated Lady Wyn Zupanic in the room reminded her.

She cleared her mind of such thoughts, with the strength that made her such a brilliant leader. She banged the metal ball on its dais, calling the Council to order.

"Lords and Ladies, the new Council session of the revised Levitican Union is called to order. We welcome the return of James Gavain, House Lord of House Gavain of the Vindicatus nation, Commander-In-Chief of the Vindicatus Mercenary Corporation, a first knight of the Levitican Union, ward of House Towers, protector of the Blackheath System, a master of Tahrir ..... the victor of Jacknife and the Architect of the Truce of Hardangervidda."

Lord Gavain bore the welcome of the Council with his infamous impassive countenance. He stood, and gestured to the person at his side. "May I also present the Minister Jonathan O'Connor, House Gavain's contribution to the Levitican Union, to lead the Ministry of Intelligence and Information."

"Introduction accepted," said Lady Principal Sophia, banging the ball once more.

"With the formalities out of the way," she said, "we have a great many new introductions to make today. The Levitican Union has grown, my fellow Lords and Ladies. Let me show you."

A holographic map sprang into being in the centre of the room. The former borders of the Levitican Union were shown. "Our three-year history has been long and seen much change. At its inception, the Levitican Union consisted of House Towers, Obamu, Zupanic, Claes, Galetti, and Lapointe, the founding members. Last year, House Marchenko joined, and then more recently House Jorgensson, both of their own free will but also partly as a reaction to Third Empire interference, and a desire for freedom." As she spoke, the map changed, the Levitican Union colours widening into the blacker parts of the starmap.

"When Jorgensson joined, we created a second tier of membership, where full adherence to Union law and Charter was not required. Today, I am pleased to announce, that House Lord Oren Jorgensson has submitted a request for first tier membership, binding our Houses even more firmly together. That is our first discussion and vote of the day, ladies and gentlemen.

"Moving on, the Vindicatus nation under House Gavain joined, also on second tier membership. It is today that we also reveal that the Vindicatus nation has widened, with the first two systems colonised in an ongoing plan to widen the borders throughout the Gulf of Medusa. When Vindicatus had to defend itself against the Zhou-Zheng Compact, the Compact could not guess at how large the Vindicatus had grown. Today, our second discussion is how we respond to that attempted invasion, and how to respond to the continued persecution of the Erdogan nationals, and the deathcamps that even to this day the Compact keep in operation. A strong message needs to be sent to the Primarch and the Primarchess that an attack on one Levitican Union House, is an attack on all of us.

"A similar desire for protection and freedom, and a wish for belonging and unity, has led to this," Lady Principal Sophia continued. The holomap suddenly expanded rapidly, with numerous small Houses and territories suddenly appearing in Union colours, leading right up to the devastated southern Helvanna territories, marked 'Coalition'.

"Yes, the Union has expanded beyond our initial dreams of three years ago. We accept as both first tier and second tier members the following Houses to our galactic east; Houses Narrough, Evensor, Charlemagne, Keinharten, Diago, Sammeter, Lorenz, Hann, Fiescher and Le Fevre. Eleven new Houses, bringing a total of thirty-six new inhabited solar systems and a vast tract of space into the Levitican Union."

There was a long, prolonged bout of applause.

"Our third item on the agenda is to discuss integration in all spheres of all our ministries, and we expect this to take most of the day," said Lady Principal Sophia. "Remaining items if we have time, are to discuss the Union's military contribution to the Coalition, our proposed anti-hybrid bill, updated finances for the next year considering our new members and responsibilities, and a discussion on the new diplomatic plan for dealing with other members of the Coalition. We have an opportunity here to strengthen our position within the Eastern Segment, and to heal old wounds with the StarCom Federation following the Levitican War. We should look forward to peace, not to war, my Council."

That received the greatest round of applause of all.

Chapter XXIV

The shuttle lander had a significant force of starfighters surrounding its descent into the planetary atmosphere, which had fallen into a protective sphere around it as it left the *ISS Emperor of Shadows* noble barge. The Third Emperor was aboard, and he was not to be left unprotected under any circumstances.

The Third Shadow Emperor looked out of the observation windows of the military-class lander, as the planet surface rose up to meet them. The decision had been made, and he had chosen this system himself. It was large, but a single-star solar system, easily defensible and already being heavily fortified and reinforced in the manner that the Jacknife Defence Line had been. He was not so proud he could not learn.

The new planet, Mars Shadow, had been named partly after the planet Shadow that had been destroyed in the Creation System, and the planet he so desperately wanted in the Sol System. The uninhabited and newly colonised system was being named Constantin System, after his Imperial House. It was located at the upper reaches of the Mid-Sectors, near the Railway which was itself being rebuilt.

The Railway was being rebuilt down towards the Third Empire side of the Demilitarised Zone. It was being named the Helvanna Offensive Line, as it cut through some of the systems that remained of the Helvanna Province, but extended beyond to match the length of the Jacknife Defence Line and more.

He stared out at Mars Shadow as the single continent passed below them. It was very different from the dark world of Shadow, now dead and lifeless, but he wanted it that way. The time had come to surround himself with beauty, and this new paradise fitted his mood perfectly.

The great city of Juliusea was springing up, all golden walls, turrets, spires, and buildings. The golden city would be his new residence, whilst the Third Empire consolidated and became something new. One day, he would sit on his throne on Mars, but he was resigned to the fact that that day would not be today.

The lander brought him into his new home.

The Third Emperor Julius Constantin swept into his new throne room. It was cavernous and old-Earth cathedral-like, with murals depicting the onslaught of the Third Empire's invasion of the colonised galaxy. In a sign of hubris, there were many empty alcoves for the future stories of the Empire to be told.

The Shadow Emperor strode down the entranceway, up the dais steps and seated himself firmly in the Shadow Throne. Numerous soldiers, all belonging to his new First Circle Guardian elite, lined the entire room. He had sprung the existence of the First Circle Guardians upon his Shadow Council advisors, the revelation that in secret he had been forming his own protective elite a shock to them. The First Circle remained forever encased in their armour, and no doubt they were some form of hybrid, slaved to the mind of the Third Emperor.

He looked at the senior advisors who had survived the Shadow War.

His supposed mother, but in truth his creator, Edrisa Constantin the Second Legate of the armed forces wore her silver highlighted civilian robes of office, looking stern but as classically beautiful as ever. She concealed her emotions all too well, the Shadow Emperor thought, and perhaps of them all he trusted her least. She had turned on the False or Second Emperor, she could turn on him.

Jared Towers, the Third Legate of the political caste wore his white-lined robes, looking older than he had done up until recently. The stress of the Shadow War had told upon him, and now he had greater responsibilities than ever. Of all his advisors, the Shadow Emperor trusted him the most, which was not much.

The Legate of the Fourth Circle was the head of the secret investigations branch, the enormous division known as the Foxes, the people who were scattered into positions throughout the colonised galaxy. Some of them were already within the Coalition. He had proven his usefulness and his adeptness. He was the most duplicitous of them all, as calculating as the worried and stressed Jared but with the people in positions of power to do the most damage.

The Legate of the Fifth Circle, the Faceless assassin branch, wore her red with pride. The Faceless were still, despite their links to the Third Empire of Shadow, obtaining contracts from other parts of the colonised galaxy. She was still a favourite of the Shadow Emperor, and if he could but trust her, she would become his closest advisor. It all depended on how Jared behaved.

The Legate of the Sixth Circle, the Phantoms who performed all the covert operations that the specialists in the assassination circle did not, had his dark purple on prominent display. He was the one that the Shadow Emperor thought most likely to go, and he was already considering moving the Sixth Circle under the Fifth. The Sixth Legates days were numbered.

The rest were all dead. Their circles had fallen under Jared Towers, and that might also be why he was looking so stressed and tired. The more responsibility a man had, the more chance of failure.

"General Helvanna," said the Shadow Emperor slowly, "failed me. She is to be executed before the end of this Standard day, Fifth Legate. Increase the bounty on the head of Lord James Gavain, I will accept his death through any and all means possible, and instigate a new kill-order on the arch-traitor, Silus Adare."

"As you will it, Emperor," said the Faceless leader.

"We will not forget the end of my First Shadow War," said the Shadow Emperor, "even as we prepare for the Second."

"Do you intend to honour the truce, my Emperor?" asked Jared Towers.

"My word is my bond," said the Shadow Emperor. "It is not I who shall break it, although we shall be prepared for them to offer us the opportunity when they break theirs, which they will. The truce was necessary to recover from the Second Legate's *failure*," and he enjoyed her flinch at the stressed word. "It depends on how long it takes us to rebuild. I want the territory of my Third Empire, spanning nearly a third of the length of the colonised galaxy, to be reinforced and consolidated before we move on. I see now that we attempted to move too fast; we have lost the advantage of surprise, so we must build, and build quickly. You will all see it is done."

There was a chorus of assents.

"What of the Coalition?" asked Jared Towers. "What do you wish there?"

"This Coalition of the StarCom Federation, Levitican Union, Calamarite Confederacy, and OutWorlds Alliance – those four are my main enemy and my primary targets. Even the Republic of Varrental, Cervantia, Korhonen, and Hausenhof, all must suffer. They become liable for actions by the Faceless, the Fox and the Phantoms. Each of you, Legates, present your plans to me."

The three Legates chorused an affirmative.

"The one guarantee in this galaxy of mankind is that nothing can be predicted, not since the fall of the False Emperor," said the Shadow Emperor. "I made the promise not to invade Coalition space or cross the borders between us, but I said nothing of the rest of our borders. Second Legate, you shall begin plans for the Second Shadow War, the aim to be move us incrementally to our eastern flanks. We shall widen this corridor of territory we have taken, and work our way around the Jacknife Defence Line and this Coalition of Mutual Defence. We shall simply approach the Core from another direction."

"Certainly, Shadow Emperor," said Second Legate Edrisa. "What is my timescale?"

"That is determined by how quickly Jared can rebuild us," said the Shadow Emperor. "The loss of our heartland in the Shadow Province hurts us greatly. Once we are strong enough, you begin. Sort it with the Third Legate, and tell me of the timetable later. I will say yes or no. But one thing is for certain ......

"The Third Empire's vengeance has just begun."

*

Lady Principal Sophia held Benjamin Towers in her arms, as she looked up at the night sky. The underwater city of the Levitican Union Capital City had risen to poke its domes above the ocean, the above-surface climate forecasted to be tsunami-free for the next couple of Standard days.

Her baby son gurgled happily as she looked at the few stars and the much vaster region of blackness that held the Gulf of Medusa. Lord Gavain had widened the Gulf into the de-colonised regions of what had been the Helvanna Dominion, official cartographers all over the galaxy already re-drawing their starmaps. It was a terrible legacy, and one she knew that wore heavy on her friend's heart.

She sighed, deeply. Her own heart was not so care-free either.

The last three years had seen some terrible turmoil for her. The assassination of her father, Erik Towers, had hurt her deeply. There was the apparent love and treachery of Micalek Zupanic, and his death at the hands of his mother Lady Wyn, which she had yet to resolve. She still wondered to this day how deep his feelings for her had truly been, but in her heart of hearts, she wished it were true. She had to reconcile herself to the fact that she would never truly know.

She looked at Benjamin, in her arms. At least some good had come of the liaison with Micalek.

There had been some other joys, though. She had found her true mother, Elaine Towers, once known as Elaine Carrington. Both she and Luke Towers were overjoyed at the realisation. They had lost a father, and gained a mother.

It was typical Imperial politics, messing with the lives of the House families. It still survived in this Age of Secession, post-Dissolution.

The Levitican Union had bloomed under her leadership. It was financially stronger than ever, and had become a military powerhouse. It was now perhaps the largest nation in the Eastern Segment, and beaten only in size in the eastern part of the Mid-Sectors by the Calamarite Confederacy and the Third Empire.

Her friendship with Lord Gavain had helped shape the Union, what had been originally a business arrangement blossoming into something which had helped affect the future of this part of the colonised galaxy. That was a legacy to be proud of.

She kissed the forehead of Benjamin Towers, and put him to bed. As he lay in his suspensor-cot, the future of House Towers looked lovingly up at her.

A short distance away, the Fox member of the Fourth Circle looked at the display picture being sent back to him. It gave him a perfect view of Lady Sophia Towers' face, as she gazed down.

The Fox was relieved to see the plan was all working as it should. The Third Empire might be temporarily stymied, but this Fox member was bringing some vengeance back to the Fourth Circle. The true depths of the penetration of House Zupanic and House Towers, the unknowing utilisation of Micalek Zupanic and Lady Sophia Towers, could never even be guessed at by the counter-intelligence agencies of the Levitican Union. It was a long-term project which had already paid dividends, and in the future would only give an ever-increasing source of information.

The Fox had a perfect spy, with the perfect cover.

The Fox agent ate its rations, realising that the day's intelligence take was likely over as its vehicle of intelligence gathering was being put to sleep.

*

Lord Gavain left the bedroom in his personal quarters within the Heart Palace. He was not sleeping well, and he knew it was only partly that he disliked being in planetary environments, even an artificial one such as Dark Heart Alpha. The door closed silently on the sleeping form of Juan Ramirez, as he crossed into the main suite.

His mind was ticking over furiously, with far too much happening. He had been able to relax somewhat on the long transit to Leviticus, and again on the return to the Dark Heart Artificial System. After the months of tension, it was more than welcome.

On arrival at Dark Heart Alpha, Doctor Erin Presson had insisted that Gavain have a period of rest and relaxation, and he had refused. She had not been happy, but at least he had taken a small part of the first day to spend some time with Juan, in the canyons in the south of the planet near the big Planetary Engines that held the planet in a static position in space, revolving forever on an immovable axis.

The psychological counselling was helping. The depth of his feeling over the launching of the Tears of the Moon and the deaths of billions of people, even if technically they were already dead, surprised even him. The counselling would continue for some time, he knew. No action was without consequences, and for a Praetorian designed genetically to obey the often inhuman extermination orders of a mad Emperor, it was surprising maybe that he was in this position.

Andersson had provided some of the best advice, as ever he did. He pointed out that the process of breaking free of that genetic programming had begun when Gavain turned against the False Emperor. It had continued with his setting up of the Vindicator Mercenary Corporation, and then the Vindicatus nation. Even, Harley had said with a sad smile, his growing relationship with Juan Ramirez showed that a man programmed not to have emotional attachment could outgrow that genetic sequencing.

It was a dark secret that many Praetorian Guard ended up losing the ability to remain detached as they had matured, and the Deimos facility on the moon around Mars had held many whose programming had failed, before the Dissolution of the Red Imperium. Andersson argued that it proved they were human, that to fail and be weak were the flaws which made a person the person they were.

Lord Gavain was not sure. All he knew was that despite the propaganda of the Shadow Emperor, and what many of his detractors and even some of his own people within Vindicatus thought, he was not a monster. Launching the Tears of the Moon had been a hard decision, but it had been necessary.

To fight a monster that created human-alien hybrids and enslaved the minds of innocent civilians, with weaponry that could destroy those populations, planets and hybrids was in many ways fighting evil with evil. But there was no cure, no antidote to indoctrination, and so it had been necessary to prevent more falling to the slavery of the Third Empire.

It had been an age-old question, one that had haunted mankind throughout its history. They developed the technology of war, and used it, and then at a later date looked back and judged it wrong. Was it truly wrong and inhuman, or did it merely depend on which side of the line you sat? One side's inhuman and immoral weapon was another's excuse to invade, even if they had used them in the past. Where was the right in that?

Gavain shook his head, staring out at the fake stars. He did not have the answers. All he could do, he decided in his deep soul-searching, was to stay true to himself. He knew he wanted to create a world free from the worst ravages of the collapse of the colonised galaxy and the Red Imperium, and he would die to defend that world. He had called that world Vindicatus, and he would colonise more and more planets, and do anything to defend those planets and those people. The Gulf of Medusa would become his, and he would defend the innocent.

He would defend them whether those innocents agreed with his methods or not. If he had to sacrifice his own sanity and self-respect so that his people could live, and live free, then he would.

There would be a better future phoenixing into existence in his lands, and he would never stop fighting in the ashes of the Red Imperium to realise it, whatever it was that he faced.

And whatever it took, he would do, without limitation, whether it was judged right or wrong.

Liked The Book?

Age of Secession

I would love to have your reviews and feedback, if you would like to post this in the place where you bought the book. It all helps to spread the news about the Age of Secession.

Visit the website www.ageofsecession.com, for lots of new content and Age of Secession-related material. News, new releases, background to the series, and more being added all the time!

Roger Ruffles himself would love to hear from you, so either follow him on Twitter @RogerRuffles, or write to him at ageofsecession@gmail.com

If Facebook is more of your thing, there is also the Age of Secession page, at www.facebook.com/AgeOfSecession.

The Age of Secession Continues .....

CRYING MOON
Part I - Blood Money Trilogy

OUT NOW

The Tears of the Moon are weapons of destruction, capable of turning entire planets into tombs. A very dangerous man by the name of Mason Duboise knows of them, and as a former Imperial Intelligence and StarCom double agent, Mason is no stranger to duplicity. In the wrong social class, he has wept his own tears as he was forced to deny his son and his wife by the laws of the Red Empire of Mars.

He has a plan to steal the weapons, and sell them to the highest bidder, but life in the Age of Secession is never so straightforward. In the galactic south, a new threat is stirring, the xeno-religious extremists of the Suularitsaar. These extremist humanists dream of forming their own nation on hatred; a hatred not just of the augmented borg, but of even the more moderate unaugmented human.

To unite the family he has denied for so long, Mason Duboise will see billions cry as a result of what he plans. The Tears of the Moon will weep freely down the face of the colonised galaxy, even as Mason faces the assassin with no face to call his own.

Prepare for the Tears to flow.

Coming Soon to the Age of Secession .....

PAY DIRT: DISHONEST INTENTIONS

IN 2018

Life is tough for many in the Age of Secession, and for some it has become much tougher since the Emperors of House Constantin fell from grace.

Iain Briggs is a con-man, along with friends Dominic Gaiman and Marin Todor. They have moved from trick to trick, from planet to star system to intergalactic House since the Red Empire of Mars fell, each scam being bigger than the last.

The rise of the Vindicate Empire offers them their biggest and most dangerous opportunity yet, as this Fifth Empire looks to build landgates and starterminals across the colonised galaxy in every direction. It will revolutionise space travel, allowing trade to pass from one side of the colonised galaxy to another within a day, rather than in years.

Constructing a pathway across the stars, they will face the jealousies of leaders, the murderous intent of criminals, the hidden and dangerous motives of pirates, the wrath of the security forces of the nations they are working both for and against. This is the biggest job of all, and if any of them are to escape with their lives, they will have to succeed in a way they could not imagine when they started.

Most would see pay dirt as succeeding in one of the biggest construction jobs in mankind's history. They will see pay dirt as escaping with their lives, from an ever-deepening web of dishonest intentions.

Out Soon!

Go to facebook, twitter, or www.ageofsecession.com
for more details

Coming Later to the Age of Secession .....

In 2018/2019

Augmented Genocide

As the billions of Erdogan refugees make their home in the growing systems of the Mercenary Lord, back at home the Zhou-Zheng Compact have opened their deathcamps and are slowly exterminating their conquered people. There is not a single Erdogan family who has not suffered a loss, a relative dying in a work-camp.
This is the story of those who fought, against the Genocide of the Augmented.

The Lost Kindred

The Lost Kindred were abandoned.
It all began centuries before the Age of Secession started, but it will come to a head now. As the colonised galaxy turns upon itself, the Thirteen Kindred will return in greater force than ever before.
And the Kinsmen are angry that they were ever abandoned in the first place.

Adare's Legacy: Kingdom of Blood

It is to the Bandit Kingdoms of the Badlands that Caterina arrives with a child she did not want, but is now determined to protect whatever his origins. Abandoned by her former nation, all alone in a harsh and hostile galaxy, she finds she has to be as black-hearted as the pirates she now keeps company with.
She will stop at nothing to ensure that there is a legacy for the child of Silus Adare.
The Kingdom of Blood.

Collective Misdirection

It began with a virus, a simple line of quantum-locked code. It spread silently, the interconnected hive minds of the Nacrimosa Collective being a perfect breeding ground. Then one day, someone somewhere pressed a button, and an entire nation froze in terror as their minds shut down.
Who brought the Collective to its knees? The galaxy is being lied to, misdirected somehow, and what appears to be an opportunity for some might be more of a poisoned chalice than it first appears.
The Collective Misdirection must be exposed, before it is too late.